Ahead of his Time

by Adrian Cousins

Copyright © 2021 Adrian Cousins

All rights reserved. This book or any portion thereof may not be reproduced or used in any manner whatsoever without the express written permission of the author except for the use of brief quotations in a book review.

This book is a work of fiction. Names, characters, businesses, schools, places, locales, and incidents are either products of the author's imagination or used in a fictitious manner. Any resemblance to actual persons, living or dead, or actual events is purely coincidental.

www.adriancousins.co.uk

Part 1

1

3rd January 1977

Merlyn

Grace often pondered if her sullen demeanour could be attributed to the cold winter months. Not that she was one for prancing around Stonehenge on the summer solstice with daisies in her hair, but she always felt brighter at that time of year. Notwithstanding her loathing of the shite weather, Grace sensed a slight uptick in her mood today after returning to work following the way-too-long Christmas break. She'd spent that on her own as usual and, as she hated all festivities including the abysmal TV programmes on offer, it actually felt good to get back into the office.

However, tonight would definitely stick another dampener on her mood because her pathetic daughter would be around performing her usual begging routine.

She cringed at the thought of what new ridiculous scrape Jess might have got into and really couldn't understand how she could have produced such a disappointment.

Grace barged her way through the line of commuters who'd stupidly blocked the train station entrance as they waited for a taxi, all standing hunched up in their thick coats whilst stamping their feet.

"Excuse me! Excuse me!" she shouted at the idiots who eventually parted to make room.

"Oi, watch it!" a young lad called out as she nudged him out of the way.

Grace marched on. "Bugger off!" she muttered, as she stuck her nose in the air and strode purposefully across the car park.

Grace was thankful she only had that short walk home, and the decision to stay in her terraced house just half a mile from Fairfield Station had been a good one.

After her promotion to full-partner last October, she'd considered moving up to one of the large houses on the exclusive new development on Winchmore Drive. Unfortunately, the property with the large corner plot had already been snatched up, and she wasn't convinced the other houses were befitting her new lofty status. However, after procrastinating for a few weeks she lost out on all the properties, so had decided to give up on the idea. Anyway, she was comfortable, and with Merlyn as her only companion, there was no point moving.

Grace stepped into the dark hallway and snapped on the lights. She plucked up the pile of post, flung it on the console table and lobbed her keys on the top. Swanking from side to side, Merlyn sauntered through from the kitchen. He rubbed around her legs and arched his back whilst pointing his tail bolt upright.

"Evening puss-puss, I expect you're hungry."

Merlyn was the only reliable male she'd ever met, and she was quite contented to live her life with him as her only companion. The other partners at the firm were all male and often tried to treat her like one of the secretaries. However, she was a far more capable solicitor than her male counterparts – she knew it, and so did they – which made her so intimidating.

Her daughter, Jess, had moved out a couple of years ago, and now their relationship was strained even more than when she'd lived at home. Grace expected that tonight's visit would be short and painful as always. She fed Merlyn and positioned the kettle on the stove, planning to have a coffee whilst waiting for her errant daughter. After Jess had left, she could then enjoy her evening meal.

"Hi, Mum." Jess stood on the doorstep, wearing a long, filthy Afghan coat and that ruddy annoying smirk on her face.

Grace looked her up and down, turned her nose up, sneered and marched back to the kitchen. She assumed her wayward daughter would follow. Grace plucked her cheque book out of her handbag and opened the cover at the ready, hoping the request would fall below the two hundred pounds which she'd asked for last time.

Jess stomped in, following her mother after kicking the front door shut. "You not talking to me then?"

"Jess, how much this time?" Grace held her pen ready, poised over the cheque book. The sooner she could hand over the cheque and get her out of there, she could prepare her evening meal. There was no point in small talk – that was all done. Jess had decided on her life path, and that was that. Grace was no longer interested in whatever scrapes she'd landed in, and a cheque thrown at Jess every few months to keep her at bay suited her. She tucked a strand of blonde hair around her left ear, peered up at Jess and arched her eyebrow.

"Well, how much this time?"

Jess perched her bum on the kitchen table, scraped her long blonde hair back and adjusted her tie-dyed headband. "Mum, can we just talk?"

Grace narrowed her eyes, stared at her daughter, and huffed as she dropped the pen on her cheque book, now disappointed her idiotic daughter wanted to talk. Usually, this encounter was over in a few seconds, with a cheque handed over, and Jess would be off back to wherever she was squatting now.

"What do you want to talk about? It's all been said, hasn't it?"

"My father."

"No, Jess. That subject is closed. It closed twenty years ago when you were born, and I'm not talking about him now."

"Mum, I have a right to know who he is. I don't know anything about him, not even his name. I'm twenty-one this year, so I think it's about time I knew who he was." Jess stared at her mother's emotionless eyes, unable to guess what was going through her cold-hearted mind.

Grace sneered again as she stared at her disappointing daughter. "I'm not talking about him."

"You can't keep him from me; it's not fair. If you don't help, I'll find him anyway ... whether you like it or not." Jess stood and folded her arms. Merlyn sat staring up at her, licking his lips and yawning – she'd always hated cats.

"Well, good luck with that! He left the UK just after you were born. As I've repeatedly told you, he's not worth knowing. Anyway, why now? You haven't mentioned this for years."

Jess scowled at the cat, pulled out a chair and plonked herself down. "Can I have a coffee?"

Grace huffed again, relit the stove and fished a cup from the mug tree, now really annoyed the conversation was going to be far longer than she'd hoped. Jess had always been a real handful and, along with monumentally screwing up her education, she'd buggered off at the age of eighteen to live God knows where. Not that Grace gave a toss because she wasn't the maternal type. Jess had been a mistake with the one man she'd set up home with, and that was a long time in the past.

"I want to get to know him. You're not interested, so it would be good to have one parent who cares."

"How dare you. How dare you!" Grace spun around with her hands on her hips and glared at her daughter. "I'm the one who brought you up. I'm the one who's put up with all your antics over the years. I'm the one who works so hard to pay for your upbringing. And you, you stupid girl ... I'm the one who bails you out every few months because you can't take responsibility for yourself!" Grace felt her blood rising and was in a good mind to tell her pointless daughter to bugger off. It certainly wasn't her fault that Jess had turned out to be a useless no-hoper.

"Oh, come on! You never wanted me, and you brought me up because you had no choice. Don't pull the old, my-mother-cares routine. That won't wash with me—"

"No!" Grace leant across the table, cutting her daughter short, "You've no idea. You're away with the fairies! Take some responsibility, for God's sake, girl!"

"What like you did with me? You washed your hands of me as soon as you could. You're no mother ... you're a fucking robot!"

"Don't you use that kind of language. You're slipping into the gutter, girl."

Both women leant across the table, their knuckles now white as they pressed their balled fists onto the Formica top. Merlyn hopped up onto the table and stood between them. He swished his head from side to side as he observed the 'tennis match' and waited to see whose court the ball was now in.

Jess stood and huffed. "Oh, that fucking cat." Rummaging in her coat pocket, she fished out a scrunched-up packet of Camel.

"Don't smoke in here." Grace lifted Merlyn, cuddled him and nuzzled her chin in his soft grey fur.

With tears forming in her eyes, Jess lit her cigarette and blew the smoke into the air. She'd become so emotional over the last few weeks which was so unlike her as she had her mother's steel-like persona and now struggled to understand this new feeling. Jess firmly believed her mother loved that bloody cat more than her own daughter.

"Did you ever love him?"

"Who?"

"My father, of course. I'm not talking about the bloody cat! I'm well aware of how much you love that thing." Jess blew smoke at the cat that faced her, cuddled in her mother's arms. Merlyn didn't move, only slowly blinking as the smoke wafted around him.

Grace *had* loved him. Although they both were born in Fairfield, they hadn't met before attending St Andrew's University. The fact they both came from a small Hertfordshire town was the initial connection when they'd met in the student bar. She was in her first year, and he was completing his Masters – she quickly became besotted with him. The first year together had been bliss. They'd rented a small flat together and she'd never been happier. However, it went sour when he'd demanded a termination when she fell pregnant. They were too young, he'd said, and it would ruin their lives. Grace had wanted his child and the fairy-tale romance. After Jess was born the impasse between them eventually led to the relationship breaking down, and she was left holding the baby.

"No, I never loved him ... he was a waster," she lied.

Jess moved over to the window and flicked her ash in the sink.

"Oh, for Christ's sake, Jess! This isn't some squat ... use the ashtray."

Jess turned and looked at her mother as those annoying tears started to form again. She tried to blink them away and used her coat's dirty fur sleeve to wipe her eyes.

Grace set Merlyn down on the floor and plucked up her pen to write out a cheque. She hesitated on the amount as she pondered whether three hundred pounds would be enough to quickly persuade Jess to leave, as she was now tired of this conversation. Tearing off the cheque that she'd made out to Jessica Redmond for three hundred pounds, she turned and presented it to her.

Jess glanced at the cheque but didn't take it.

Grace waved the cheque. "Take it. It's what you came for."

"No. I want to know about my father. That's what I came for."

Grace folded the cheque and dropped it into the side pocket of Jess's coat. "Take it and go. There's nothing more to talk about."

"I'm pregnant." She turned from her mother and stubbed the cigarette out on the side of the sink.

"For Christ's sake, Jess. That's a sink! Use the bloody ashtray ... it's there on the windowsill."

"Did you hear what I said?"

"Yes. I suppose you'll want more money from me, assuming you're going to have this baby?"

"Is that all you can say? I wasn't expecting the delighted Grandmother reaction. But is that all you can come up with?"

"I'm not interested, and don't expect me to be. It's another stupid situation you've landed yourself in. I'll help you financially, but I don't want anything to do with it."

"Fucking hell! You really are a cold-hearted bitch!"

Merlyn hopped up on the counter and attempted to trapeze his way across the edge of the sink towards Jess. He presumably had no idea of the hatred she had for him.

"Don't you want to know who the father is?"

"Do you know?"

Jess shook her head in disbelief. Why she had expected anything else from her mother, God only knows.

"I'm not surprised you don't know." Grace folded her arms and looked down her nose at the disappointment that was her daughter.

"I do know!"

"Why did you shake your head when I asked if you knew, then?"

"I didn't! I shook my head at you and how uncaring you are!"

"Well, whoever he is, he'd better take some responsibility. That's assuming you're going to keep this bastard child?"

"Yes, of course, I am! I'll love this baby more than you ever loved me!" Jess placed her hand on her tummy. Although she was only a few months pregnant, she had that protective feeling for her unborn child. Now suspecting her tears were for the father, who she knew wouldn't be part of the child's early years.

"I want my birth certificate ... that's assuming my father's name is on it. Although being a poncy solicitor, you probably had his name erased from that by some legal decree at the same time you changed your bloody Christian name! He has a right to know he'll have a grandchild, you know!"

"He has no rights. No rights what ... so ... ever." Grace leant forward towards Jess. "He buggered off and left us! So, he's forfeited his right to know anything."

"If you didn't love him, why do you care? It doesn't matter, does it? You want nothing to do with him ... great ... fine, but don't stop me!"

"I did love him!"

Grace stood with her mouth gaping open, shocked at what she'd said. Then, stunned at her own outburst, she reached behind her to grab hold of a chair to steady herself before gingerly lowering to take a seat. She hadn't meant to say that, although it was the truth, because Jason was the only man she'd ever loved. All those years she'd stayed so strong, holding that lost love away from her heart – it was her way of coping.

"What's his name?"

"Jason ... Jason Apsley ... no middle name." Grace had changed Jess's surname when she was still a baby from Apsley to her surname – Redmond. She'd wanted to banish everything to do with Jason, including his name.

"Apsley, are you sure?" Jess sat at the table and narrowed her eyes at her mother.

"What do you mean, am I sure? Of course, I know who your bloody father is! More than you probably know who the father of that is!" she spat back, pointing at Jess's stomach.

15

Ignoring her mother's anger, she took a moment to think as that name was definitely familiar to her. "I've heard my boyfriend mention him. He lives on the Broxworth Estate."

"No, no, he emigrated to South Africa after you were born. The fact that some man has the same name must be a coincidence. I can assure you, Jason wouldn't live in that God-awful place. Good grief, girl ... don't tell me you're living up there now? For God's sake, you really have hit rock bottom."

Jess rummaged through her pockets again as she searched for her cigarettes. Grabbing the crushed soft pack of Camel, she fished out the last crumpled cigarette and straightened it before lighting up and flopping back into her chair. Her mother sat stroking the moronic cat that'd sprung onto her lap. The relationship with her mother had always been fraught, and she wondered if she could find her father, would that relationship be any better. Although he'd never wanted her in the first place, so maybe not.

Jess blew out the smoke to the ceiling, contemplating that she'd be raising this child on her own. Her mother wasn't interested, and her father, whoever he was, probably wouldn't be either. Although she loved her boyfriend, he wouldn't be there to support her unless there was a miracle. She felt the folded cheque in her pocket; at least if nothing else, her mother would keep supplying these, and she was going to need them. All she had to do was keep turning up from time to time, and her mother would produce a cheque just to get rid of her.

"I'm going now." Jess stepped over to the sink before stubbing out her half-smoked cigarette on its side, purposefully ignoring the ashtray on the windowsill. Jess knew how much that would annoy her mother, which felt good. She strode across the kitchen, stopping at the doorway to glance back at her mother, who continued to cuddle that ruddy cat with her nose nuzzled in his grey fur.

Grace didn't look up. Jess tutted before stomping through the hallway, leaving the front door ajar as she barrelled through.

2

16th January 1977

Cortina

Arm in arm, Sally and Brian enjoyed their early morning stroll up the High Street. The weak winter sun, low in the sky, glistened off the snow that had fallen heavily overnight. The pavement sported a beautiful white blanket, only punctuated by a smattering of footprints that appeared to weave chaotically ahead of them.

With all the shops closed, the street lay quiet. A paperboy on a bicycle passed them and pushed his way up the gentle hill leading to the main crossroads ahead. They watched the young lad negotiating the black slush as he rounded the solitary parked car, which must have been there all night as it sported a three-inch topper of snow. The windscreen had a clear patch on the passenger side where the thick sheet of snow had slipped and sagged down.

The traffic lights up ahead changed to green allowing a small white commercial Ford Transit van to trundle carefully down the road. The driver appeared to be gripping the steering wheel and staring bug-eyed out of the windscreen as the ruts of icy slush forced the wheels in a different trajectory to the driver's intended direction. He applied the brakes, causing the wheels to lock, resulting in Gregorio's Italian Bread van sliding gently into the parked car. The van came to a halt as the two vehicles gently nudged together.

The chrome wing mirror positioned at the end of the van's near-side wing, bent, toppled, snapped off and plopped into the slush. The slight jolting to the car resulted in a small avalanche that shook the snow from the side windows.

Brian dismissively shook his head. "I could see that coming. The roads must be treacherous this morning."

Sally stopped and pulled on Brian's arm. "There's been so many accidents since they put those traffic lights up last year. They were put in to make it safer, but it's worse now."

Joe slid back the driver's door and hopped out to inspect the damage. He rubbed his hands together, then beat his arms around his body. He'd foolishly left the bakery without his coat, so was just dressed in his blue and white striped apron on top of a roll-neck jumper that covered his bakers-whites. Joe assessed the stricken wing mirror as he continued to rub his hands together.

"You okay, mate?" Brian called across to him.

"Yeah, think so. Although the boss ain't going to be too chuffed about this," Joe replied. He'd retrieved the broken wing mirror and balanced it back on the front wing as if it would just click back on.

"Don't think you damaged the car as you only nudged it, mate."

"There's some yellow paint on my wing, so I think I've scratched it." Joe spun around as if looking for the owner. "No idea whose car it is. I'll have to leave a note on the windscreen."

Brian stepped onto the road and searched for where the car had been bumped. There was the slightest mark on the back wing and, after a quick visual inspection, he rubbed his gloved finger across the small white mark as if to erase it.

"It's a tiny scratch, mate. I wouldn't bother. Just get going, fella. Looks like it's been here all night with all that snow on it. I really wouldn't worry." Brian announced whilst he continually rubbed the scratch.

"Oh, Brian. Brian, look!" exclaimed Sally.

"What, love?"

"Brian, look," she repeated and pointed to the passenger window.

The two men gingerly padded their way around to where Sally was pointing at a man slumped in the passenger seat who appeared to be asleep.

"Oh, bloody hell, someone's sitting in there!" Brian pushed the chrome button on the door handle. The jolt caused by the opening of the car door instantly woke the young-looking man, who jumped in surprise.

"You okay, fella?" Brian asked, crouching down so he was at eye level with him.

The man yawned and stretched his arms, shaking his head.

"You been here all night, fella? You must be frozen." Brian felt his hand. "Yes, he's frozen alright. Colder than the dead."

"Where ... am I?" He glanced around his surroundings, a deep frown across his face, as his head shot side to side.

"You're sitting in your car. By the feel of you, I reckon you've been here all night. You're frozen, young fella. You'll catch your death out here."

The man stared at him and blinked a few times but didn't reply. Then his eyes darted left and right as if his brain was now on high alert.

Sally leant forward. "Are you okay? What you doing here?"

"Who are you? Where am I?" he spat back aggressively.

"You're parked up on Cockfosters High Street. I'm Brian. This is Sally." He thumbed in Sally's direction who crouched next to him.

"Joe," said the bread delivery driver from behind them.

"Who are you?"

"Martin. I'm Martin Bretton."

"Okay, Martin. I think you need to get yourself off home. As I said, you will catch your death out here. You look a little confused ... are you unwell?"

"Why is there snow? ... it's August ... why is there snow?" chanted Martin. He stared through the windscreen and appeared to be transfixed by something in the distance, remaining still, apart from the continued chant. "Why is there snow?"

Brian looked at Sally and shrugged. Joe reciprocated as they both glanced back at him.

"Is he drunk?" said Joe.

"Martin, it's January. You seem confused," added Sally.

"Where's Jason?" muttered Martin. He glanced at the driver's seat and laid his right hand on it as if checking for Jason.

"Is he the driver, young fella?"

Martin turned to face the three of them. "We had a crash. A crash with a white van."

"Hey, look, mate, I only nudged you. I haven't even marked your car, so I think a crash is a bit over the top, pal!" exclaimed Joe, as he leant forward.

Martin looked around himself as he tugged at his parka coat and rubbed his hand across the dashboard. He wobbled the gear stick, then stared back at Brian. "What car is this?"

Brian rocked back on his heels whilst holding the door frame, glanced at the car, and leant forward again. "It's a Cortina, MK3 Cortina. Does it belong to your friend Jason?"

"What ... What?" exclaimed Martin, as his eyes bulged.

"You got a number we can call someone for you? There's a phone box just up there," added Sally.

Brian turned to Sally and Joe. "He's not with it. I think he might need a doctor. Also, as he's so cold, he could well have hypothermia. Maybe that's why he's a bit strange, do you think? I mean, he said it's August!"

"Martin, what day is it today?" asked Sally.

Martin stared at them, then shifted his gaze to the snow-covered path. Eventually, he raised his head and looked back as they all awaited his reply. Now not confident of what he was about to say – but he knew he was right. "It's August the 12th. August 12th, 2019."

Sally looked at the others and arched her eyebrows as they all shrugged their shoulders. "Martin, it's Sunday the 16th of January 1977. I think we need to get you some help. You poor love, you're frozen."

Martin shot Sally a look, eyes bulging again. "What?"

"D'you know where you live?" she asked.

"What d'you mean, 1977?"

"Martin, love, I said d'you know where you live?"

"Four Ridgeway Avenue, Enfield," he stated, as he shook his head.

Brian, Sally and Joe stood and formed a circle as Brian shook the pins and needles from his left leg.

"He just needs to drive home; that's only about two miles away," said Joe.

"We can't call an ambulance as he doesn't appear to be physically hurt. I think he's just a bit confused," added Brian.

Sally leant into the car again. "D'you have the car keys, Martin? Oh, they're in the ignition, look." She pointed at the keys dangling from the steering column.

"Look, sorry, but I'll have to scoot. I need to get back to the bakery." Joe shivered and stamped his feet before waving the severed wing mirror. "I might have a bit of explaining to do."

"Yes, of course. Will you be able to move your van, or do you need a push?"

"No, you're okay, mate. I'll be fine." Joe gingerly made his way around the car, his boots sloshing in the slush as he carefully plodded his way back to his van.

"Martin, we think you should drive home now. Get yourself a hot drink and warmed up. You think you can do that?" asked Brian, whilst raising his eyebrows at Sally.

"Err ... yeah, think so," Martin replied, as he shifted his body into the driver's seat and swung his legs over the gear stick.

Brian grabbed the top of the car door. "Okay, Martin, hope you get warmed up." As he closed the door, a large sheet of the snow topper slid off the roof and flopped onto the pavement covering his goloshes.

Sally re-looped her arm in Brian's. "Well, what an odd man. Did you see that long scar on his face? It was a new scar, and the side of his head had been partially shaved. I reckon he's had some sort of brain operation."

"You're right, and what was all that about it being August 2019? Bloody strange if you ask me."

"I thought he was a bit creepy."

They stood and watched as a couple of cars passed the Cortina before it pulled out – no flashing indicator, kangarooing the first twenty feet – then stalled.

"He needs to pull the choke out; the engine will be cold," Brian muttered.

The car fired into life again, causing a punch of smoke to eject from the exhaust as it pulled off down the road.

"Come on, Brian, I'm cold now. Let's get home and get the fire on."

The Cortina turned left at the bottom of the High Street towards Enfield.

3

Brexit

Martin released his foot off the accelerator pedal and let the car coast to a stop as the front nearside wheel nudged the kerb. He sat and stared out the windscreen, shaking. Yes, he was cold and, once he'd worked out the car heater sliding controls, the heat helped, but he could still see his breath. Martin knew that although he was freezing, it wasn't causing the shaking. No, it was this morning's events that were the problem.

He peered down Ridgeway Avenue, where his home stood only thirty feet in front of him. However, to add to an already crazy morning, three people he didn't know excitedly scampered around whilst lobbing snowballs at each other in his front garden. The couple both appeared to be in their early thirties with a boy that Martin presumed to be about ten years old. The man, decked out in appropriate all-weather attire topped off with a woolly bobble hat, continually ducked behind an ancient-looking car that Martin didn't recognise – just like the one he was sitting in. The man expertly dodged the snowballs being pelted at him as he jumped back up laughing, waiting for the next onslaught.

This morning's events had shaken Martin, and now he truly doubted his own mind and sanity. The only answer was he'd lost the plot and gone completely mad. This was no dream; he was very much awake, alive and frightened.

Before he awoke to this madness, he was sitting in Jason's Beemer and looking at his phone as he scrolled through Facebook whilst on his way to work. It was 12th of August 2019 and, even though it was only just past eight o'clock in the morning, it was hot. Now, one hour later, he was sitting in a yellow MK3 Cortina. However, it was no longer hot; it was freezing cold as snow lay everywhere, and three strange people were in his front garden playing snowballs.

Martin scrubbed his hands over his face after he'd laid his glasses on the unfamiliar dashboard. His index finger discovered a strange indent near his left ear which ran all the way down his face. This was a line he'd never felt before – another odd thing. He flipped down the sun visor and studied himself. Yes, a red line *did* run down his face. A long scar travelled from under his chin all the way up into his hairline in front of his left ear, leaving a short stubbly patch of hair where the scar ended. At some point, it must have been shaved around the scarring and hadn't grown back. Repeatedly he ran his finger up and down the scar as if somehow that act would erase it. Martin was convinced it wasn't there an hour ago. No, definitely not.

Martin pulled at his clothes again. What was he wearing? These weren't his; they were really outdated. The sort of clothes he might have seen his father wearing in old polaroids before Martin was born. Although warm, and grateful for that, the green parka was definitely not his coat. Rummaging through the pockets, all were empty, no phone, wallet, not even fluff. Exiting the car, he hesitantly stepped forward, approaching the snowballing family.

"Excuse me, does Caroline Bretton live here?" Instantly dreading the obvious answer.

The woman turned to face Martin with a snowball in her gloved hand. Her arm was poised, ready to pelt it at the guy Martin presumed must be her husband.

"No. This is number four, sorry. Think you have the wrong house," she replied with her hand still in the air, holding her snowball. "John, do you know a Caroline Bretton on this street? I don't." She addressed the man who was peering over the roof of the snow-covered car in the driveway.

As he turned to face Martin, the boy achieved a direct hit to the side of John's head. The snow stuck to his hair in clumps, and the jubilant boy jumped up in a triumphant leap. "Yes, got you!" he exclaimed.

"Hang on, Peter, hang on." John put his hand in the air and turned back to Martin. "No, sorry, don't know anyone by that name. Sorry mate."

"How long have you lived here ... can I ask?" Martin grimaced, somewhat surprised that his voice sounded rather high-pitched and jumpy.

"Nearly six years. We know most of the people at this end of the street. Sorry old chap, never heard of this Caroline woman."

"Right. Okay, thanks," Martin huffed. Then, remaining rooted to the spot, he glanced at his house. The house, as far as he was concerned, he'd only left just over an hour ago on that hot August morning.

"Is everything all right?" the woman shouted across to him.

Martin glanced towards her and shoved his cold hands in his coat pockets, aware he was probably giving a competent performance that wouldn't look out of place in any zombie movie.

"Hey mate, you okay?" John called out, following up on his wife's question, which hadn't had a reply.

"Peter, come here, please." The woman gestured to the boy to come closer to her, presumably to put distance between the strange man and her son.

"Can you tell me the date today?" He didn't pose the question directly to one of the three, just an inquiry into the cold air.

"16th of January," replied John.

"And the year?" Martin asked, as he turned to look at John.

"1977." John turned and shot his wife a quizzical look.

"16th of January 1977," Martin slowly repeated as he shook his head.

"Yes, mate. Look, you sure you're okay?" John waved his hand behind him – a gesture to his wife and son to go indoors, which they did immediately.

Martin backed up a few steps whilst still shaking his head.

When back in the car, Martin glanced in the rear-view mirror at his house, which someone else now appeared to own. As he reached the bottom of Ridgeway Avenue, he headed north towards Fairfield.

Flashbacks had started, the first being the car crash that morning. Yes, he remembered it now. Jason had somehow driven straight into a white van. A bloke was shouting and trying to pull the car door open. His head hurt like hell as blood streamed down his face, which had been pushed into the airbag. Although that was it, he couldn't recall anything else.

The car tyres crunched the dirty rutted snow as he crawled his way along Welsfold Road in Eaton, a suburb of Fairfield. It was only a short walk to his old school, the City School, which he had fond memories of. Yes, he could remember details like that easily. However, trying to remember what happened after the crash this morning, no, he couldn't recall them. The snow had started to melt in the winter sun, leaving the roads and pavements covered in a mixture of white and grey slush. Three snowmen were dotted along the verges, all donning a carrot nose with striped scarves around their necks.

Martin parked twenty yards from his mother's house, killed the engine and sat for a moment. The drive here had added weight to what the couple at his home and the people in Cockfosters High Street had said this morning. There was no M25 on his journey. All the cars he saw were old, classic cars, like the one he was sitting in. With its retro bandwidth dial, the car radio played an interview with Roy Jenkins, the Home Secretary, about his decision to leave government and become the President of the European Commission – nothing was said about Brexit. This gave great sway to the ridiculous idea that he was in 1977. The crash in Jason's BMW wasn't an hour ago, but forty-two years two hundred and eight days in the future. Why he'd worked that out to the exact day he didn't know, but he had.

"Oh, come on, come on!" he blurted, slamming the palms of his hands on the steering wheel. No, this was just ridiculous, bloody ridiculous. Travelling through time wasn't possible. He sighed heavily, leant back and traced his finger up and down the scar on his face.

He didn't need to go and ask if Sarah Bretton lived at his mother's house, as that would have been a futile venture out into the cold. Whilst contemplating his next move, he spotted an elderly couple he didn't recognise as they strolled along walking a brown Labrador. They stopped at what he knew was his mother's house and tentatively trod up the drive. The elderly gent brushed the snow from the obedient dog's paws before unlocking the front door and disappearing inside. Question answered – his mother didn't live there.

The last two hours had seemingly drained his energy. Martin closed his eyes as a wave of exhaustion attempted to drag him back to sleep, causing the flashbacks to start again.

He could picture himself lying flat, presumably on a gurney, whilst a gaggle of frantically shouting people wheeled him down a corridor. He could recall the defused lights above appearing to shoot in and out of focus. He opened his eyes when nothing more came back to him.

Although Martin didn't know many people in Fairfield, he had when he attended the City School as his mother had before him. After attending university, he'd met his wife, Caroline, and they'd settled in Enfield. A sharp pain gripped his chest as he now feared he would never see his wife again. They'd had a few difficult years but had come out the other side stronger. Now they were so close, and she'd become his soulmate – yes, that old cliché, but she was. Raising his index finger, he wiped away a tear that had trickled from his right eye.

He did know Jason's ex-wife, Lisa Apsley, and probably too well, he thought. She lived a couple of miles away, so perhaps his next stop would be her house. Although, after this morning's events he doubted there was much hope of her actually living there and, if she did, he wondered what sort of reception he'd get. Pointless to attempt to find Jason because he had no idea where he was living since splitting up with Lisa.

As he expected, Homebrook Avenue was all wrong. Just like every other road in this weird and wacky world he seemed to have landed in. The house was there as he remembered it. However, on the driveway were two old-style cars which Martin believed wouldn't belong to Lisa.

He rang the doorbell of number twenty-two and stood back, waiting for a reply. After pushing the bell for a second time, a slim, attractive, thirty-something woman with long auburn hair and striking green eyes opened the door and offered a tight smile. Martin presumed she must be on her way out, or her house was freezing, as she stood at the door wearing a camel-coloured coat.

"Hello, can I help you?"

"Err ...does Lisa live here?" he mumbled. Clearly not – the answer was staring him in the face.

"No, sorry. This house belongs to Jason Apsley. I'm Jenny, his wife."

"Sorry, Jason who?"

"Apsley, this is the home of Mr and Mrs Apsley. Are you alright? You look a little peaky, if you don't mind me saying so."

"I know Jason. Is he in? I know him! We work together ... we work at Waddington's Steel," he blurted. Now feeling hopeful, the energy pumped back into him as if he'd just received an adrenaline shot.

"Oh, how odd. Very odd. Yes, he's in the garden. Could you hang on a moment, and I'll go and get him."

Now she was the one looking confused as she closed the door. Jason was here? Was it him? This was his old house, but who was the green-eyed woman? He wasn't married – he'd only just got divorced.

The door swung open, and there in front of Martin was his boss. Okay, with a beard and longer hair, but yes, this was him, Jason Twat Apsley. Well, that's what the staff called him behind his back – he wore that gormless look he often had – which many of the office staff would imitate when he wasn't looking.

"Oh, God, Jason, it's you! What's going on? The world's gone fucking mad. I thought I'd lost my fucking marbles, but thank God you're here. Who the fuck was that woman who answered the door, and where the fuck is Lisa? Anyway, what you doing here?"

"Martin, is that you?"

"Yes, of course it fucking well is. Who do you think I fucking am? It's me, Martin! Jason, what the fucking hell is going on? Where is everyone else? And why has every fucking nutter I've met today told me it's 19 fucking 77?"

"Oh, bollocks!"

4

Scotty, Beam Us Up.

"Jason, I don't understand what the hell is going on, and who the bloody hell is he?" Jenny stood in the kitchen doorway with her hands on her hips.

Martin had blurted out my previous life's history in the future 2019 as he stood on the doorstep whilst I sported my well-versed gormless expression. Jenny had stood in the hallway, copying me. Leaving Jenny transfixed, I'd ferried Martin into the lounge and shovelled him onto the sofa. I'd told him to sit quietly, and I would be back in a minute – delivered as if instructing one of my pupils. Fortunately, after his outburst he complied and was now nestled on our sofa, staring into space. I'd returned to the hallway gripping the lounge door handle as if barring the way through, thus protecting my family from some highly contaminated object shaped to look like one of my old work colleagues.

"Jen, I know this is a bit odd, but I used to work with Martin some years ago. I think he's a little confused, and I'm not sure what he's doing here. I'll sort it, don't worry."

'You're screwed, Apsley!'

That ever-so-annoying voice in my head taunted me. It had been waiting months for an opportunity, and now it had it. Escaped from its cranial cage, it now scurried around my brain causing havoc.

"Don't worry … what do you mean, don't worry! The bloke is a total nutter, and he's sitting in our lounge right now!" screamed Jenny. She rarely became animated, but now her kryptonite eyes burned green as her hands flailed everywhere, which almost simultaneously stopped as she

33

planted one on the wall and the other on the stair bannister. As far as she was concerned, I'd just let some nutter in the house and her worry was for the children.

"Look, can you sort the kids out? I'll deal with this. Please, Jen, let me deal with it."

"Jason, you better. I'm not happy that we've some weirdo in the house who thinks he's been teleported into this world like Captain Kirk from Star Trek! I can't *wait* to hear what he comes out with next! Probably 'Scotty, beam us up,' and we'll watch him disappear in front of our eyes! I can't believe you're not as shocked as I am. The bloke is completely barmy!"

"Okay, Jen, okay. Go and sort the kids out, and I'll see what I can do with him."

"Why don't you find it odd that this bloke turns up claiming he knows you and some ex-wife of yours from 2019? Christ, Jason, just get him out of our house!" Jen delivered her ultimatum and stormed past me, off to bathe the kids.

"Oh, bollocks," I muttered under my breath. This was the nightmare I'd hoped would never come true. But now it had, and I needed to think fast before this new wonderful life I'd carved out for myself started to unravel. I checked Jen had disappeared upstairs and stepped into the lounge, quietly closing the door.

"Look, mate, this isn't going to be easy for you. But we've a lot to talk about, and I can't do it here."

"What the hell is going on? And who the hell is that woman? More to the point, why does everyone I've met today reckon it's 1977? Jesus Christ, even the car radio in that yellow piece of shit was playing an interview from some politician from the fucking seventies!"

"Keep your bloody voice down. For Christ's sake, keep it down," I hissed, as I gestured my hands up and down, frantically trying to calm him. "Look, mate, I've somewhere you can stay tonight. Let's go there now and we can talk, as I can't talk here … alright?" I was just desperate to get him out of the house. Fortunately, one of the houses I'd purchased on the Bowthorpe Estate I hadn't rented out, so my quickly formulated plan was to squirrel him away in there until I could work out what the hell I was going to do.

"Right." Martin huffed. He looked exhausted. I remember that exact feeling five months ago when I'd made that journey back from 2019.

Shovelling Martin out the front door, I turned and bellowed up the stairs. "Jen, I'm just going to follow Martin home and make sure he's okay. I'll be about an hour or so." I hovered on the doorstep, waiting for her reply.

"Jen?"

"Okay!" she shouted down the stairs.

Clearly, she was really put out by what had happened, and I knew I had some tricky and difficult explaining to do when I returned home. So, I had to think fast; otherwise, everything was going to turn to shit.

"Right, mate. Follow me, and we'll talk when we get there. You're just going to have to trust me, and I know that's a real stretch at the moment. I was where you are now five months ago. I've done it, eaten the pie and got the t-shirt."

I trotted up to my new car, a Red Triumph Stag. I'd traded in the Cortina yesterday, and the Stag was my dream classic car. One of the perks of time-travel was purchasing an old classic car that was brand new and just off the production line. Martin trudged to the car he was driving and unlocked the door.

"Martin, wait, Martin," I called out and jogged towards him.

"What?" He replied sharply.

"Where the hell did you get this car from?" I glared at my yellow Cortina, which I'd sold only twenty-four hours ago to Coreys Mill Motors, a second-hand car dealership not far from the Bowthorpe estate.

"Well, hell, I don't bloody know! I just found myself in it this morning, didn't I? For Christ's sake, are you listening to me or what?" his aggressive reply flowed into a full-on rant. "That's just typical you, Jason. You don't listen, and you're never interested in anyone else but yourself. It's always been the bloody same with you. Do you know that no one, and I mean no one, on your team likes you? You should hear the talk behind your back in the office. Every day all of us moan about you. You're a right tosser with no people skills whatsoever!" He took a step closer and pointed in my face. "Yes, look shocked if you like. I bet you thought we were friends, drinks at Christmas and all that. Although Caroline likes Lisa, she thinks you are a right tosser and feels sorry for me that I have to work for you!"

I stepped back, nodding my head. Five months ago, his description of me was reasonably accurate – but I'd changed. Of course, he wouldn't know that because 12th of August 2019 was only a few hours ago in his world. I glanced up to the front bedroom window where Jen was standing glaring at us – understandably, she looked concerned. Although unable to hear our conversation, she could see the yellow Cortina. If she spotted the license plate when Martin drove off, that would be impossible to explain.

'You're screwed, Apsley!'

Sunday afternoon traffic was light; the journey across town was quick, and I was thankful for it. As he'd stood and bellowed at me before leaving my house, I'd noticed a scar all the way down the side of Martin's face. It wasn't there the last time I saw him on the 12th of August 2019, seconds before I ploughed the Beemer into the white van which killed me. Well, I think it did, and then transported me to 1976. I'd often wondered what happened to Martin in my passenger seat, and now I knew. But where the hell had he been for five months?

I thought about his rant. Yes, okay, I knew I was a bit of a dick back then but did all my staff hate me? Christmas 2017, I'd decided uncharacteristically to have a department Christmas night out and booked at a pretentious, over-priced brasserie. Sales had been way above budget that year, resulting in receiving a hefty bonus which had nicely swelled my pay packet. I intended to foot the bill for all twenty-five of my team as a gesture of thanks for delivering outstanding results and, of course, my bonus. At the time, I believed it was an inspired idea. Although I was miffed when Lisa said it was stupid because I wasn't particularly liked, and she suspected not many would turn up. This sparked another barney that bolted onto the previous festering arguments on the glide path to the end of our pointless marriage.

The long table was all decked out in festive cheer, bottles of wine liberally dotted about, and a champagne reception planned. Unfortunately, only three of my team turned up, and two of them were twenty minutes late. The young waitress standing with the tray of champagne flutes stood with a smirk on her face as it became apparent the vast majority of my guests had snubbed the evening – it was a total embarrassment. My team were probably all down the local pub laughing their heads off.

The young, clean-cut restaurant manager dressed in a sharp Savile Row suit conducted himself with great professionalism but still delighted in presenting me the bill for all twenty-five guests. He explained there's no allowance for reducing the bill for non-attending guests. It was in the small print apparently – which he calmly highlighted with a yellow marker pen on my bill – as I recalled accusing him of being a member of the Hitler Youth.

At the time I was furious and, every day for two weeks before the Christmas holidays, I proceeded to make their working lives a living hell. But they weren't ungrateful as I'd thought at the time. No, they just hated me, and looking back I winced at the memory. My team were right. Back then, I was a complete tosser.

I pulled up outside the partially furnished semi I'd purchased a couple of months ago. Something had told me not to rent it out, as I felt I might need it someday – that day had arrived. I checked my mirror as Martin pulled up close behind. I jumped out and hopped in the passenger seat of his car, the exact car I'd woken up in five months ago.

"Martin, you need to listen. I own these two houses. The one on the left, number eight, has some furniture, so you will be okay in there. The one on the right is a tenant of mine. He's a good friend, so he can support you as well. Do you understand?"

Martin nodded as he bowed his head and started picking his fingernails.

"Martin, do you understand?"

He shot his head up. "Oh yes, I fricking understand, of course I do! Everything's so normal ... what's not to understand? Bloody hell, Jason, do I understand? No, of course I don't bloody understand!" Verbal tirade delivered, he stared back down into his lap.

I leaned back in my seat and stared at the roof. Jesus, this was a disaster. I lowered my head and turned to face him.

"Martin, sorry mate, but this bit is hugely important. Look at me ... Martin ... look at me."

He slowly brought his head up and delivered that vacant, empty stare he'd developed.

"Don, who lives in number ten, knows nothing about where we've come from. Only one person knows, and I'll call him later as we're going to need his help. But for now, you say nothing. No one can know what we've gone through ... no one."

"What have we gone through, Jason? I'm so confused. I ... just, I just ..." Martin huffed and rubbed his hands up and down the side of his face. "This is nuts." He shook his head, dropping his eyes and resumed his lap-staring and fingernail-picking routine.

"Look, mate, we've both time-travelled from 2019 to now. Well, I arrived here the day we had the crash. I know that's ridiculous, but I've been living here for five months. It's very real, mate ... very real."

Martin whipped his head up and glared at me again, slowly shaking his head from side to side. "Fuck off, Jason."

"Martin, you need me! And I need you to hold your shit together. You can tell me to fuck off as much as you like, but the plain fact is you're going to have to believe me ... that's it. Right, we need to go into the house and put the fire on as it'll be freezing in there. First job though ... we need to say hello to Don, so no fuck-ups from you. You're an old friend who needs a place to stay for a while. That's your story, nice and simple. No more details ... you got it?"

"Oh, God. Okay. I must be dreaming. Christ, either that or I've gone nuts," he replied.

His comment made me smile as I hauled my way out of the car. I'd said those very same words over and over five months ago. Don answered the door immediately, as I guessed he would. His snooping skills were second to none, and he would have spotted us as soon as we pulled up.

"Evening, Don. You okay?"

"Yes, son. Who you got 'ere then?"

"Don, this is Martin, Martin, Don." I gestured my hands back and forth as a way of introduction. Don nodded whilst Martin remained motionless.

"Martin will be staying next door for a while. He's an old friend in a bit of a jam at the moment."

"You can say that again," Martin interjected. His hands shoved in his old parka coat and doing his new usual – staring at the floor.

I shot Martin a look, concerned that he'd forgotten my instruction to keep schtum. "As I was saying, he is in a bit of a jam. It's all on the Q.T. if you know what I mean?" I tapped the side of my nose to convey this was classified and metaphorically stamped *top secret*. "Can you keep an eye out and make sure he's okay? Just to give me a bit of time to get some stuff sorted."

"Of course, son, no problem." Don saluted and, for a brief second, he stood to attention. "Look, you coming in? It's a bit nippy on the doorstep."

We followed Don in through to the kitchen. Don shuffled his way there, wearing his tartan slippers which seemed never to be removed from the end of his feet.

"I need to borrow a bit of food from you ... just to get Martin through tonight, and then I'll set him up properly tomorrow. Will that be okay?"

"Yes, son, 'elp yourself. Sit yourself down, Martin, we don't stand on ceremony round 'ere. I'll stick the kettle on if you wanna drink?"

"Okay, we'll have a quick coffee, then we need to get on." I rummaged through the pantry and plucked out some essentials which would get Martin through the next day. Don and I chatted about football and my new car whilst Martin sipped his tea which he held like a tramp at a soup kitchen, all the time staring at the tabletop.

"Son, I see you sold your old car to this chap."

"Err … yes," I replied.

Martin just shook his head and tutted.

"Don, we'd better go. I'll be back in a few minutes when I've got Martin settled in."

I nudged Martin as he looked to be sitting in a trance. Lifting his head sideways, he peered at me with one eye. I gestured with my head, giving an instruction it was time to go.

"The fire will heat the place up in no time. Keep the lounge door open so the heat goes through the house. You know how to work a gas fire, don't you?" Martin plonked himself down on the new orange sofa, offering no reply.

"Right, mate, we need to talk. But I haven't got long as Jen will be wondering what's going on. When we had the crash, for some reason I was moved back to 1976. So tell me, what happened to you?"

"What the hell d'you mean you got moved back? You say it as if it's some normal everyday event. Either you or I've gone around the bloody bend. Can you hear yourself?"

"Martin, look around you. You've been here, what … six hours or so? This is January 16th 1977, and you're going to have to get your head around it … and quickly. I know that's tough. But I had to, and I did." He just stared and shook his head again. "Look out the fucking window. There's snow everywhere, and you don't get that in August, do you? I know this is tough to grasp, but you're going to have to come around to this, and bloody quickly I might suggest." I leant forward as if chastising one of my pupils at school, but hell, he was starting to annoy me.

Martin huffed again.

"Right, as I was saying, we had the crash. What happened to you?"

"No ... *you* had the crash! I just got a lift, and look what's happened."

I rolled my eyes, exasperated at him. "Okay, if you want to be picky ... I had the fucking crash. But what the hell happened to you? What can you remember?" I quelled my rising temper and moved away from the gas fire. The heat it was chucking out was melting the back of my legs, although I could still see my breath in the room.

Martin sunk his head in his hands, then started to mumble through his fingers. "I was knocked unconscious. I remember coming-to as I was being whizzed through the hospital corridor on a bed-type thing. All around me were doctors, nurses and paramedics ... whatever you call them."

"What then?"

"Then I woke up when that bloke pulled open the car door this morning."

"What bloke? I need to know who you've spoken to."

Martin huffed. "I was in that car." He pointed out of the window in the vague direction of the Cortina. "Some bloke opened the door and asked if I was alright. I've no idea what he was on about as he reckoned I'd been there all night. I mean, what was he on about? There was a woman with him and some other bloke, I think ... we only spoke for a minute or so." With his head still in his hands, he nudged his glasses up his forehead.

"Okay, who else?" I crouched down near him. As he lowered his hands, his glasses plopped back into position.

"I spoke to some bloke and his wife at my home. That's it until I knocked on your front door."

I stood up and moved to the window and yanked the curtains across. How on earth had he ended up in my old car? I'd have to zip up to Coreys Mill Motors and find out who they sold it to. However, what the hell I was going to say to Jen was my immediate problem. When I'd got Martin settled, I would ring George. I desperately hoped he'd have some pearls of wisdom to offer.

"Who's the woman and those kids at your old house?"

"Jenny, my wife. We've just adopted two children," realising as I said it that was going to be a lot for Martin to soak up.

"Your wife, your wife! Jesus, you reckon you've been here for five months, and you've already got married with a ready-made family. Bloody hell! And she knows nothing?"

"No, Martin, she knows nothing, and it must always stay that way. Do you understand?"

Martin sat back on the sofa but offered no reply.

"I'm guessing you're totally exhausted, so I suggest you get up to bed. I'll have to get going now, but I'll come back tomorrow." I waved the house key in his face and then placed it on the coffee table.

Martin nodded.

"Over the next twelve hours, you sleep, you talk to no one and you don't answer the front door … do you understand?"

Martin nodded. So far, he hadn't burst into tears. When I'd time-travelled, all I seemed to do was cry, but he looked to be coping far better than I had. Scooting back to Don's, I made an excuse about needing to make a private call and sat on the stairs dialling George's number.

I relayed the afternoon's events to George. He listened, only interjecting with a few *'ohs'* liberally scattered throughout the conversation. However, as I concluded my wild tale, I became quite concerned as he seemed very excited at the prospect of meeting another time-traveller. We agreed to meet at number eight tomorrow evening when I'd show him the second strangest thing he'd ever seen – Martin.

5

Ten years in the future ... 15th August 1987
Summer Ball

"What a bitch," he muttered to himself. Who the hell did she think she was? He'd brought her a slap-up meal, and then she reckoned she could leave the pub car park without him having his way. *Bitch*.

Trudging down Coldhams Lane with a cigarette stuck in his lip, he hadn't lit it yet, so now the filter had turned soggy. He'd just put one out, so wasn't quite ready to light another. God, she'd pissed him off. Alright, he thought, the Beehive Pub wasn't the best, and it wasn't exactly a restaurant. Besides, she was just a bit of scrag, so what did she expect? And bloody hell, *she'd* come on to him yesterday in the post office; all lipstick and hair, batting her eyelids and pouting like Madonna. She had *take me* written all over her face, and then she'd shoved him away – driven off – after a free meal whilst he got nothing.

She'd pay for this. Well, some bird would because no one refused him. No *one*. He removed the cigarette from his mouth and shoved it back into the packet. With midnight approaching, little traffic trundled up and down the usually busy road. Perhaps if his luck was in, some stupid cow would be tottering her way home on her own, and that lucky girl was going to get some. Well, he'd done it before and never got caught. He'd mastered the art. It was easy. Yes, he was going to take someone tonight.

He stepped into the cut-through lane entrance that led down to the City School playing fields. With only a few street lamps working, the lane had taken on a dark and menacing appearance. *Perfect.* At least half the street lamp covers appeared broken, probably where kids had pelted stones at the glass covers, which now hung as they swayed back and forth in the gentle breeze.

Yes, he thought, this was perfect.

He squeezed into the centre of the laurel hedge, thus concealing himself from sight. All he required was a bit of patience and see who came along – if she was young and hot – he'd take her. That post-office-bitch had got him worked up. Now he *needed* to have a release – yes, he'd go to bed satisfied tonight.

~

Sarah Moore slumped seething in the passenger seat of her boyfriend's car and, although she'd tried to calm herself after leaving the party, she knew she was going to explode. Never – never, had she been so pissed off with Scott.

"Stop the car," bellowed Sarah. She wasn't going to stay in the car with him a moment longer. *How could he have done this?* She was furious as the rage bubbled up – she wanted to scream.

"Don't be so dramatic! I'm not stopping the car. Just shut up, for Christ's sake. You've bloody well ruined the evening," Scott retorted.

"Don't, Scott. Don't you dare say that! You were the one with your hand on that trollop's knee, not me! It's not me who's bloody well ruined the evening. It's because your bloody brains are in your sodding trousers!"

"Oh, shut up, Sarah. You really are so stupid. For Christ's sake, woman, I was just comforting her! You talk as if I was shagging her on the table!" *Why were women always so dramatic?* Scott now wished he *had* shagged Paula. At least if he had, Sarah would actually have something to moan about.

"Scott, she wants you! She put that act on to get you to come on to her, and you fell for it. I bet you can't wait to shag her! In fact, drop me off now, and you can go back and screw her brains out because I don't care anymore! I just don't care!"

"Sarah, for Christ's sake. I don't want Paula. I touched her knee ... her fucking knee! I didn't have my hand up her bloody skirt, did I? This is ridiculous!"

"You might as well have." Jesus, what's the matter with men? *Why do they always think with their dicks?*

"I'm not talking about it anymore." Scott had had enough of this pointless conversation. Paula was nowhere near as hot as Sarah but well-screwable. Perhaps he should drop Sarah off and then get back to the party because Paula might still be there.

"Oh, you've decided, have you? The conversation is over because you've had enough. Scott says the conversation is over, and that's it, is it?" She leant across and screamed in his ear. "Well, I want to talk about it, tosser! You don't decide."

"Bloody hell, I'll have a crash! You've lost it, woman. Stop screaming."

"Stop the car and let me out. Let me out, Scott ... Now!"

Scott slammed on the brakes and veered to the side of the road. The car behind, which had been up his arse for the last mile, blasted its horn and swerved around him. He spotted the passenger giving him the finger out of the window.

"Fuck you too, mate!" Scott yelled. But it was too late to be heard – the car was long gone.

"Really immature! You're such a dick-head, Scott. Don't come around tomorrow as I don't want to see you." Sarah flung the door open and jumped out of the passenger seat. The car rocked as she slammed the door, surprising herself with the force she'd applied. He revved the engine and pulled away, screeching the tyres and snaking across the road as he disappeared into the night. Sarah stood halfway up Coldhams Lane, a couple of miles from home, wearing a short cocktail dress and regretting the four-inch heels.

Sarah glanced at her Gucci watch Scott had bought her two months ago for her birthday. They were just starting to go steady, and she'd thought it might be the real thing this time. But she was wrong, and she should've known dating a bloke from the office was never a good idea. She must have been stupid to think it could have ever worked because he had a reputation for being unable to keep it in his trousers. But Scott was a real hunk, and he'd charmed the knickers off her – literally.

Midnight. Christ, it would take ages to walk home.

Leaning backwards whilst hopping on the spot, she tugged off her stilettos. She'd have to walk barefoot as there was no way she could walk home in them after downing copious amounts of champagne cocktails. Not without the high probability of keeling over, and undoubtedly, resulting in a compound fracture. Oh, yes, that really would slap the icing on the cake of a shite evening.

Sarah prayed for a taxi to appear and was now regretting getting out of Scott's car. As it was a main road, she expected there would be many taxis at this time of night ferrying pissed-up revellers making their way back from town. Clutch bag in one hand, shoes in the other, Sarah marched home, seething and cursing all men.

Although it was a few minutes into Sunday morning, the air was warm with a refreshing light breeze. She thought the walk might clear her head, avoiding a hangover in the morning, so some good would come from the shite end to the evening.

This was the first proper event they'd attended as a couple, and she'd been looking forward to this year's office summer ball. Although it was more of a party in a large tent than a proper ball in a marquee. Scott had revealed his true self – wandering hands self – which had resulted in them arguing for most of the evening. Even though she'd told him to, Sarah was surprised Scott had driven off and left her at this time of night. Not that she'd now get back in his car. No way – it was a matter of principle. Anyway, a taxi would surely be along in a minute – she hoped.

Up ahead, she spotted the entrance to the cut-through lane leading down to the City School. It would take at least a mile off her walk home. Down the lane, through the school playing field and out onto Eaton estate. She knew this route well as she'd spent her school years there, leaving in the spring of '79 after the sixth form. However, she was never comfortable taking that route in the dark. No, she'd walk on, play it safe and pray for a taxi.

In the distance, she noticed headlights approaching. Had Scott come back for her? No, it had a light on top – oh good, she thought – a taxi. As the car drew closer, Sarah felt a wave of relief. However, its taxi-light wasn't illuminated, and now she couldn't remember if that meant it was for hire or it already had a fare. She stopped and waved her shoes in the air and then started jumping up and down to get the driver's attention. The taxi didn't slow and just careered on by. "Wanker," she muttered, before huffing and striding forward on her long walk home, now rueing the decision to get out of Scott's car.

~

He cupped the cigarette in his hand, ensuring the lit end couldn't be seen if anyone looked into the cut-through lane. Nestled in the laurel hedge a few feet into the lane, he was now bored. Although he'd only been there for five minutes, he knew he needed to be patient. He'd finish his cigarette, have another one, and then if no luck, he'd move on. He wasn't going to stand there all night and now suspected few idiotic women would be walking about at this time of night. Dropping the butt and stubbing it out under his trainer, he reached into the inside pocket of his leather jacket for his cigarettes. Peering through the hedge, he could see at least fifty yards down Coldhams Lane without sticking his head right out in clear view.

"Perfect, fucking perfect," he whispered. Some dumb pissed cow was marching barefoot up the road, swinging her high-heeled shoes. Nice, he thought. Slim, little tight dress, and very screwable. He breathed deeply to calm himself, his excitement building as the adrenalin rushed around his body. The anticipation was always better than the act. This was it, the glorious feeling of control and desire – he'd have what he wanted – he licked his lips.

~

Sarah stopped at the lane entrance and peered down what appeared to be a dark funnel, noting at least half the small street lamps were broken. She visualised the route, weighing up her options. It was only about a hundred yards to the gate, then on to the playing fields which she could sprint across, and then she'd be home. Decision time, long way home, or make a dash for it? She peered into the lane entrance again, placing her hand across the top of her eyes to block out the dim light from the streetlamp to her left. Could she see the end of the lane? Was anyone down there?

Out of the corner of her eye, she noticed sudden movement. Swivelling her head, she spotted Scott's car edging along the road – he'd come back. Turning to face the bright headlights, she stood with her chin up and the heels of her hands on her hips. Well, he *had* come back, but no way was she getting in the car. But a moment ago, she wished she hadn't got out of it. Hmmm, well, if he apologised, she might get back in – it would be sensible – but only if he apologised.

"Sarah, get in the car. Come on," Scott yelled, as he leant across the passenger seat. He nudged the car forward a few feet and was now level to where Sarah was standing. A few minutes up the road, a guilty feeling had made him complete a U-turn and return for her. Although Paula was well screwable, tonight's argument with Sarah had drained away any desire he had.

"Piss off, Scott. I don't need you," Sarah spat back at him. She was still fuming with him but unsure why she'd said that as she didn't relish the long walk home.

"Oh, Sarah, come on! I know you didn't mean what you said. I forgive you." He leant across the passenger seat with his hand outstretched as if offering her a lifeline.

Sarah glared through the open window. *Who the fuck did he think he was!* "Forgive *me*! You're joking, right? I've nothing to apologise for! You're the one who should apologise, not me. You're unbelievable! Piss off, you arrogant prick." She spun around and stuck her nose in the air, whacking her arm up and giving him the finger.

Scott threw himself back into his seat and shook his head. "Fuck her," he muttered. Ramming the car in first gear, he pulled away from the kerb. Glancing in the rear-view mirror he could see she'd turned around, watching him drive off. She stood with her shoes swinging on their straps twisted around her thumb, with her middle finger stuck in the air – he offered the same gesture back. When he glanced in the mirror again, she'd disappeared.

What a wanker! Apologise to him, no way! She peered down the lane again, then back up Coldhams Lane, chewed her lip and tried to decide which way to go. Sweet Jesus, if she stood here much longer, it would take all night to get home. It would be alright, *wouldn't it?* Anyway, by the time she got to the bottom of the lane it would only take a few minutes to cross the playing fields, and she could be tucked up in bed by half-past midnight. "Come on, get on with it," she muttered, huffed, and stepped into the lane, picking her way down on tiptoes. Although it was paved, all she needed now was dog poo between her toes.

"Good girl, good girl," he whispered and licked his lips. He placed the packet of cigarettes back in his pocket. He'd remained perfectly still for those few seconds when she was only six feet from him whilst she debated whether to take the lane route or not. Hidden in the thick laurel bush, he silently breathed in the sweet floral scent of her perfume. From what he could see through the leaves, she was stunning. He was lucky tonight. She wasn't some rough-looking dog from the estate, she was hot, and he was ready.

Releasing his breath when she was twenty feet ahead, he gently pushed away the laurel hedge branches. He had to be quiet as the next minute was critical to success. In another thirty yards she'd be close to the playing fields, and there he could get her on the soft grass. No one would hear. Perfect.

Sarah stopped short of the five-bar gate at the entrance to the school playing fields, turned and peered back up the cut-through. *Had she heard something? Was anyone there?* A shiver shot up her body and, although the night was warm, she'd developed goosebumps. Rubbing her arms, she peered back up the lane.

The few illuminated street lamps produced long, strangely-shaped shadows from the trees and hedges, which danced together across the narrow lane in the warm breeze. *Was one of those shadows a figure standing near the hedge? Shit, should she have come through here so late?* Sarah stopped still and stared at the silent shadow. All she could hear was the gentle breeze through the trees and the thumping of her heart. No, she couldn't see anyone, but she'd run now. In only a couple of minutes, she'd be out the other side of the fields and close to home – safe. Still standing on tiptoes, the arches of her feet had started to ache, so she turned and began to run.

He nudged himself gently into the laurel bush as she stopped and turned around. She wouldn't be able to see him, but she was spooked. He'd have to make his move soon – it was now – yes, now.

"Come on, Sarah, get a grip," she muttered, her shoes banging into her thighs as she picked up her pace. She moved her arm out away from her body, causing the stilettos to swing wildly on her thumb. At the end of the cut-through, she grabbed the gate latch and yanked it back, letting the gate swing open. Now she could see the school straight ahead and, without looking back, she bolted across the grass. She'd lost count of how many glasses of those champagne cocktails she'd swallowed tonight and now regretting it as her head started to thump. *Could she hear footsteps?* Just run, Christ's sake, run—

He sprinted through the gate onto the grass, which dulled the sound of his pounding footsteps. His prey was only ten feet away, running on tiptoes like a gazelle. Ten-feet, six-feet, four-feet. The adrenaline rush peaked as he leant forward – he knew he had her.

Sarah sprinted as fast as she could, without glancing back as she couldn't afford the time to do so. The sound of those footsteps was frighteningly close as they pounded on the grass behind her – as every second passed – the closer they came. Oh, Sarah, why did you come this way? Why did you get out of Scott's car – why? Tears started to blur her vision. Not again, please not again, her mind screamed as the sound of those footsteps thundered down inches behind her.

Reaching out, he whipped his arm around her neck, lifted her backwards, and threw her to the ground. He landed heavily on top, that very act thumping the breath out of her. The sexy, hot, blonde woman in the tight black dress fell silent. Pushing his hand on the side of her face, he forced her head into the grass.

"Make a sound, bitch, and you're dead."

She didn't move as her right eye swivelled around, trying to see him. He held his hand tight on her head and sat on her stomach, taking a moment to catch his breath. He had his prey. It was a secluded spot, and the air was warm. Perfect. He could have a play, take his time and savour the moment. He licked his lips.

"Please, please," she whimpered.

He loved this. She scrunched her eyes closed and shook. Her whole body now trembling – even better, he thought.

This wasn't the first time Sarah had suffered a sexual assault, and if they could be categorised, this was far worse than the last time all those years ago. Although her attacker had fled, Sarah wasn't sure how long she'd laid sobbing in the foetal position. Whilst he raped her, he'd held her head tightly to the ground. Sarah had managed to swivel her eye and look at him and, although dark, she'd recognised the face – a face she knew – a face she'd never forget.

6

17th January 1977
Boycie

"Have you reached a verdict upon which you all agree?" The court clerk stood erect, a confident boom to his voice as he addressed the foreman of the jury. The court was deathly quiet as everyone awaited the verdict. However, everyone knew it was a foregone conclusion as the jury had filed back into the packed court after only retiring for two hours. This was a discouraging sign for the defence counsel, who sat slumped on his bench, resigned to the inevitability of a lost case.

"Yes." came the reply from the foreman, a gentleman in his late sixties, wearing a green knitted cardigan with only the bottom leather button fastened. His checked-shirted belly pushed through the gap, giving the appearance he was at least eight months pregnant.

"How do you find the defendant on the charge of attempted murder, contrary to common law under the Criminal Law Act 1967, guilty or not guilty?" the clerk asked.

"Guilty," the foreman replied. Hands clasped behind his back and his chin in the air, now appearing pleased he'd conscientiously completed his civic duty.

The small gathering in the front row of the public gallery jumped for joy, cheering and hugging. Patrick Colney slouched in the dock, staring at the judge showing no emotion. His 'brief' had advised this was a likely verdict and had urged him to plead guilty, so he wasn't surprised. He wouldn't get long. He'd be out in eight, ten at worst, and his old man would protect him inside. Anyway, he had the 'Colney' name – no one messed with his family.

As he glanced up to the gallery, the cheering tossers calmed down. The family of Robert Moore, he presumed – the bloke he'd stabbed. His twin brother, Paul, stood staring at him. Patrick winked back and mouthed, "It will be okay. Look after Mum." He continued to stare up at the public gallery as two prison officers re-applied the handcuffs in preparation to transport him back to prison. His girlfriend didn't look at him as she sat with her head bowed below the railing, causing her mass of blonde hair to flop forward over her face.

Paul was seething. This was shaping up to be a really shit six months. His old man's sentence extended by three years for a charge of actual bodily harm to a prison officer, then his younger brother, David, had fallen to his death last September. Now his twin brother was going to be banged up as well. It took all his self-control, and he didn't have much, to not smash someone's face in.

The Moore family filed out of the public gallery, all except one averted their eyes from Paul. The teenage girl who'd caused all the problems to start with raised her chin defiantly and glared straight into Paul's eyes. Sarah Moore, that was her name. Someday, somehow, he'd deal with her. His now-dead younger brother, David, had enjoyed a fumble with her. Well, he'd do more than a fumble, and he imagined strangling the life out of the pompous little cow or pumping her full of heroin as he had Carol Hall. Paul smirked as he remembered squeezing the syringe into Carol's arm and watching her life drift away. Sarah Moore would get the same as no one got one-up on the Colneys.

Patrick's girlfriend stood and wiped her eyes on her coat's sleeve and then glanced at Paul. Although he was Patrick's identical twin, he was evil and she hated him. She loved Patrick, but his family were hell. His mother terrified her, and she wished Paul would die like his younger brother David had last year. She'd seen two men drop David off the roof of Belfast House but had kept that information to herself. As far as she was concerned they were heroes, and no way was she going to rat them out. The only disappointment was she wished Paul had dropped to his death along with David.

She knew Patrick was different, although no angel, because he'd stabbed that bloke, resulting in his appearance in court today. However, it was David's fault in the first place for being such a pervert. If David hadn't assaulted Sarah Moore, her father would never have bounded up to the Broxworth, and Patrick wouldn't have had to get involved.

Paul grinned at her. "I'll keep you warm at night while Patrick's away," he chuckled, before suggestively poking out his tongue whilst making a moaning sound.

"Piss off," she threw at him as she bolted for the exit door.

"Your loss, girlie." Shame though, as Patrick would be banged-up for a while and she was hot with a nice tight arse. Maybe he'd take her anyway, as there was nothing Patrick could do about it now. Paul stretched out his legs, propping them up on the seat in front as he raked through his pockets for his cigarettes.

Lighting up, he blew smoke out into the court even though some tosser had stuck a no-smoking sign up. Bollocks to that. He would have a smoke if he wanted. Apart from one bloke at the far end, the public gallery was now empty. Paul crossed his legs and studied him. He recognised him but just couldn't place where from or understand why he was still there. Paul decided to sit and wait and let the other bloke leave first as he wanted to see his face when he turned around.

~

I sat staring out over the emptying court. The drama was now over because the sentencing had been postponed for a week. Only a few court ushers were milling about, but Patrick's bloody twin brother was still sitting near the exit. He probably kicked the shit out of people daily, so he may well not remember the nose realignment job he gave me last September, but I didn't want to have to face him. I would just sit here for a few more minutes, and hopefully he'd have gone. Glancing at my watch, I had a few hours until meeting George. Martin had explicit instructions to stay in the house with the curtains closed. Christ, I hoped he hadn't done anything stupid today, like tell Don he's a time-traveller.

I needed to smooth things with Jenny after a particularly woeful performance when trying to explain what was going on after I returned from dropping Martin off last night. It was our first argument since we'd got married, and my claim that I'd worked with Martin in South Africa wasn't going to hold water for long. It had been relatively easy when I was the only time-traveller as I could manage myself, avoid cock-ups and control the lies. However, I now suspected Martin could prove to be a loose cannon that would blow ship-sinking-sized holes in my life.

Paul Colney was still there behind me, and I could feel his eyes burning holes in the back of my head. Bollocks. I'll just get up and go. Head down, I bolted for the exit.

"Apple, that's who you are! That pissing interfering school teacher. Why are you here?" Paul Colney faced me, eyes squinting, making it quite clear he had no intention of letting me pass.

"The name is Apsley, and I suggest you step aside. I want nothing to do with you." A confident reply, I thought, but I was shitting myself. If he knew that I'd been the one who persuaded Sarah Moore to spill the beans about David's abuse of her, and then I'd purposely let David fall to his death, he'd kill me or have me killed. Either way, I didn't fancy those scenarios. Paul seemed to weigh up his options. I guess he concluded a courtroom wasn't the best place for a confrontation so he stepped aside, allowing me to quickly make my exit.

God, I was knackered. I'd hardly slept a wink last night as I desperately tried to work out what I needed to do. Any sensible solution eluded me of how I could protect my life, this new wonderful life I now had. I think I eventually drifted off to sleep just as I conjured up the brilliant idea of burying Martin under the patio. However, I realised I'd borrowed that idea from *Brookside,* a soap I seemed to be fixated with as a teenager. I could even remember the characters and the storyline, which spookily involved a father abusing his stepdaughter called Beth. I'd heard that before! Anyway, a sodding good job I had today off as controlling a classroom of thirty kids was hard enough and nigh-on impossible with no sleep.

With a couple of hours to kill before getting over to Don's, I took a trip to Coreys Mill Motors. In front of the Portakabin sales office, in pole position, was a red Hillman Hunter. A *Deal-Of-The-Week* sign slapped across the window stated it was six-months-old, low mileage and a fiver short of six-hundred quid. I was giving it the once-over when the salesman approached.

"Af'noon, sir, lovely little motor this one. Only one lady owner who's had it from new. She only used it to nip up to the local shops, so it's practically as good as new. You fancy a test drive? I can grab the keys, and we can take it for a quick spin if you like?"

"No, thanks. Although I'm trying to persuade my wife to replace her Viva, which she seems overly attached to. This has four doors, and I see it has rear seatbelts fitted as well."

"Yeah, it's got all the modern features. Why the old girl had rear seatbelts fitted, hell knows," he chuckled. "But don't let that put you off ... it's a great car."

I shot him a disbelieving look. Was I hearing him correctly? I wanted the seatbelts, and this guy saw them as a negative.

A few weeks ago, I'd tried to buy child safety seats. Although in this era, they appeared not to be a safety feature that anyone believed were necessary. The sales assistant in Halfords, a small shop in the town centre, had looked at me strangely when I enquired if they stocked them. I recall him returning from the stock room with a wire child seat that could be strapped to a bicycle. When I pointed this out to him, he gestured around, and said – *"As you can see, this is a cycle shop, sir."* How the hell was I supposed to know that? In my day, I remembered Halfords sold car stuff as well. But the thought of Christopher rolling around the back seat and Beth in her Moses basket, both ready to be catapulted through the windscreen of Jenny's car, terrified me.

"Mr Apsley, talk of the devil and there you are." The sales manager had poked his head out of the Portakabin door.

"Hello, Mr Thacker. Good to see you again."

"You interested in the Hunter? Good cars, you know. I could look at doing you a deal ... shall we talk business?"

"Err ... maybe. You said, 'talk of the devil', were you talking about me?"

Mr Thacker had a quick look left and right and took a puff on his cigar. He raked his hand over his greying hair and nodded his head to beckon me inside.

"Mr Apsley, we had a strange thing happen, and I just can't put my finger on it. It's bizarre to the point that I'm considering I've lost my marbles!" He removed a blue-spotted handkerchief from his double-breasted suit pocket and dabbed his forehead, although it was bloody freezing in there.

"Oh, what's that then?" Thinking it couldn't be half as nuts as my time-travelling mate turning up in my old yellow Cortina.

"Your Cortina! We took it in on Saturday morning, then this morning it's disappeared – vanished as if in a puff of smoke! I was just going to ring the police to report it stolen, but there on my desk was the sales invoice with a roll of cash on top."

"Who sold it? Was it one of your salesmen?" Now bemused why he thought selling a car was odd for a second-hand car sales garage.

"This is the odd part. I sold it yesterday morning at seven-thirty. However …" he paused as if awaiting the drumroll. "… I didn't, did I? As we don't open Sundays," he said, waving the invoice in the air.

I reached out and took the invoice from his hand, and there it all was in neat fountain-pen handwriting. Sold by Charles Thacker, dated and time-stamped seven-thirty on January 16th 1977. The invoice displayed the buyer's details at the bottom. Purchased by Mr Martin Bretton, with his signature. A signature I knew very well. My mouth dropped open and my jaw sagged down as I stared gormlessly at the invoice.

"Do you see my point, Mr Apsley? I've gone barking mad ... mad! Barking mad." He flung his arms in the air. "And another thing, I priced the car up in my book on Saturday afternoon. I was going to let it go relatively cheaply as the new MK4 Cortina has just been released, but the cash left here is two grand! Look, it's on the invoice ... two grand! It's not worth half that!"

"Yes, this is very odd. I know it's a bit irregular, but could I borrow this invoice? I'll bring it back in a couple of days."

"Oh ... err, what for?" he questioned. Charles brought his hands back down out of the air and rammed his cigar back in his mouth again, puffing at it like Churchill.

"I just thought I'd do some checking on the buyer. Is that okay?"

"Yes, yes, to be honest it's put me in a bit of a spin today. I'll be glad to see the back of it."

"Thanks, Charles, appreciate that."

"What about the Hillman Hunter? Only one lady owner from new, so can we discuss a deal?" He returned the cigar to his mouth again and delivered a machine-gun laugh that sounded far too similar to Boycie.

I smiled at him and waved the invoice, "When I bring this back, we'll have a chat about it."

"Don't wait too long as that car will be snapped up soon."

I liked Charles, but he was a true second-hand car salesman, always half an eye on a deal.

7

Flux-Capacitor

Considering the complete madness of the past five months, the past twenty-four hours miraculous events should've been a walk in the park. However, discovering my old yellow Cortina was a time machine or some kind of portal that received time-travellers was a significant discovery and somewhat difficult to comprehend. Since September, my life had slotted into place. David Colney was dead, so no longer a threat to Beth and those five women he murdered in forty years' time. I'd settled into my perfect life with my new family and teaching career. But now I felt I'd been catapulted back five months and was being forced to start over.

Don confirmed Martin hadn't ventured out of the house all day and, as I stood on the doorstep banging on the door, I could see that the curtains hadn't been opened from where I'd drawn them last night. With no response from Martin, I rummaged through my pockets for the spare key and let myself in.

"Martin, it's me. Are you okay?"

No response.

Where was he? I completed a quick dash around, checking each room before vaulting up the stairs.

"Martin?"

Pushing open the bedroom door revealed him sat on the bed with his knees up around his chest, staring into space. "Martin, I was calling you ... Martin?"

He glanced around with that new hollow vacant look which he'd acquired. His glasses were on the bedside table, and his face had a few days of dark stubble, giving him a tramp-like appearance. I'd never seen it before, never clicked, but Martin reminded me of someone else. Although, at this point, I just couldn't think who.

The hair was different, and I was used to seeing Martin in clothes that fitted into the era of 2019, not his current attire that definitely belonged in the '70s. Hang on, I thought, Martin always smiled, but now with the few days' stubble and the solemn look without his glasses, he oddly looked like Paul Colney, as if he was his twin and not Patrick. A cold shiver slithered down my spine. Perhaps I was seeing things as I was tired, and this morning's events had sent my mind back to times I wished to forget.

"Martin, have you eaten?"

He shook his head, then looked down between his knees at the bed covers, wiped his eyes with the back of his hand and sniffed.

"Come on. I'll make you some dinner ... Martin, come on." I lobbed the green rucksack I was carrying onto the bedroom floor.

"I've brought you some clothes to get you through the next couple of days. I'm only a bit bigger than you, so it should all fit. There's a denim jacket, jeans, t-shirts and underwear in there. Oh yeah, I shoved a few toiletries in there as well."

Martin's head shot up. "Underwear ... your underwear!"

"It's clean! I could have brought you some of Jenny's knickers if you prefer! We'll get you sorted with clothes later this week, but it will have to do for now."

As we trod downstairs, I could see the figure of a man approaching the front door through the obscured glass. I pulled it open to let him in before George got a chance to knock.

"Evening, George."

"Hello, lad, well, this is exciting! Gotta say, I've been looking forward to this all day," he chuckled.

"Martin, go and sit at the kitchen table and I'll be with you in a moment," I said, grabbing his arm and gently shoving him in the right direction. He staggered on, still in his zombie-like state.

"George, this isn't a circus act! We're not the freak show next to the bearded-lady tent, you know!"

"No, sorry lad, you're right. Come on, let's have a chat with him."

As instructed, Martin sat at the kitchen table. With his head down, he'd stretched his hair back with both hands and held that position.

"Martin, this is George. He's my grandfather and knows everything about me. In fact, he's the only one who does."

George took a seat whilst I stuck the kettle on the stove and prepared to make Martin something to eat from what I'd purloined from Don's pantry.

"Hello, Martin. As Jason said, I'm George." He outstretched his arm, offering a handshake. Martin looked up but didn't take the offer.

"Is this madness true?" croaked Martin.

"Oh yes, lad, it is ... totally true," he chuckled. "It's taken me a while to get my head around it, but yes, lad, you *are* in 1977."

Martin sat upright, rolled his eyes and shook his head. "For fuck sake!"

George arched his eyebrow at me as I pulled out the car sales invoice from my jeans pocket and showed it to Martin, "Is that your signature?"

Martin peered at the document. "What the fuck! What ... I ... what's going on?"

I filled them both in on the day's events, having to bring Martin up to speed on previous events so he could keep up with the conversation. Although it was frustrating as he repeatedly threw in *'What the fuck,'* much to George's dismay at the language.

However, he shut up for a while when powering his way through the stack of cheese sandwiches I'd prepared. I guess he was starving after not eating all day.

He stopped mid-chew with a mouthful of cheese and bread mulching about in his mouth. "Can you both hear yourselves? You reckon that Cortina is a time machine ... it's not a fricking DeLorean! You'll be saying it's got a Flux-Capacitor next!"

George narrowed his eyes at Martin, "A what?"

"George, it's from a film in the mid '80s ... a kinda time travel film." Bloody hell, this was going to be a nightmare keeping these two on track.

"Look, what we know at the moment is both Martin and I time-travelled here and ended up in that same car. How it got from Coreys Mill Motors to Cockfosters High Street on Sunday morning, well, who knows. Also, how Martin ended up in it, we'll probably never know, as we never knew how I ended up in it last August. What we need to concern ourselves with are three things. Firstly ... can we get Martin back? Secondly ... if we can't, what do we do with him? As there doesn't appear to be another Martin Bretton in this world whose life he's about to take, that's going to make it tough. And thirdly... how do we keep him a secret from everyone?" I found myself pointing at Martin, who had his mouth open with mushed-up food sitting on his tongue – it wasn't a pleasant sight.

"Evening, gents ... who are we keeping a secret then?" Don closed the back door and shuffled in.

"Evening Don, come in." Jesus – now this got more complicated. I shot Martin a look, hoping he'd remembered the rules of what could be said in front of Don.

All four of us looked at each other, eyes darting back and forth – all with our secrets – with me holding all of them and Martin the unpinned hand grenade about to blow up.

Martin stood up, scraping the wooden chair across the linoleum floor. "I need a piss," he announced, padding off down the hallway.

Before anyone else spoke, the back door opened again—

"Daddy ... Daddy, look at the picture I've made at school today. It's our snowman!" Christopher bounced in, his blue school cap half-cocked, giving him the Benny Hill look as he waved his painting in my face. Jenny followed him in with Beth in her arms. Oh, for fuck sake, could this get any worse? Jen gave me a kiss and smiled at Don and George. None of us had uttered a word since Don arrived, and now we all stared at Jen.

"Hello, boys. Are you three having a secret meeting? Is this your den?" she giggled and then instantly frowned as she detected the tension in our faces. She must be wondering why we were in this house and not Don's.

"Daddy, look. Look at my picture." I picked Christopher up and studied the picture as he pointed to the snowman.

Christopher gave me a guided tour of his painting as he pointed to each part. "That's the snowman we made yesterday. That's me. That's you. And that's Mummy with

Beth. He'd painted us as stick-men; Jenny had blood-red hair, right down to her ankles, which was precisely where my blood had drained down to. This was a bloody nightmare.

"It's terrific! Well done, Chris. Very good indeed ... aren't you a clever boy."

"I knocked on your door, Don, but saw all the lights on in this house, so assumed you must be in here," Jenny said, as she turned and smiled at everyone again.

Her gorgeous smile evaporated as she noticed Martin plodding his way back into the kitchen, cleaning his glasses with a piece of toilet paper. She shot me an angry look, scrunched her face, and raised her eyebrows – oh poo – I was about to be sucked into a giant black hole.

Fortunately, George spoke, which offered me a glimmer of breathing space.

"Take the kids next door, and I'll sort Martin out."

"Come on, Chris, I've got some cakes next door, and you can show me your picture," said Don, as he took hold of Chris's hand after I'd lowered him to the floor.

Jenny was still glaring at me as we all stepped through the back door, leaving George and Martin on their own.

"Jason, why's that nutter in your rental house? What the hell is going on? I thought you were taking him home!" Jenny hissed.

"I brought him here as he has a few issues at home," I replied, trying to think on my feet as we crossed over the driveway into Don's kitchen.

"Well, you'd better explain *that* as well!" Jenny stood on the doorstep, glared at me and pointed at my old yellow Cortina. The black hole was sucking hard.

8

Quicker Than The Human Eye

Don enjoyed seeing the kids, but he could sense the tension between Jenny and me, and I guess he had a million questions he wouldn't mind machine-gunning my way as well. He was savvy enough to know now was not the time and expertly entertained Christopher with a set of dominoes he'd tipped onto the carpet.

The two of them built various structures which Christopher took great delight in knocking down whilst he had half an eye on the TV, showing the Hong Kong Phooey cartoon. The question was, who was he? The mild-mannered Janitor – could be! Well, yes, this was probably Jenny's question – who was I? Trouble is I didn't have a striped cat called Spot to get me out of this particular dilemma, and diving into a filing cabinet drawer wasn't going to turn me into a number one super guy – quicker than the human eye. I might have found it funny if I wasn't so consumed with the events of the past half hour.

Jenny played with Beth as she laid her on a blanket in the middle of the room, leaving me to try and work out my next move. Now I had Don wondering about Martin and Jenny seething about 'Martin the nutter' as she'd now described him twice. To a lesser extent, I was also concerned about what the hell George and Martin were talking about next door. I felt doomed and panicky and now convinced myself I could feel my chest tightening. Oh, bollocks, was I going to have a bloody heart attack? Well, if I was, it might be a way to escape this particular dilemma.

"I'll take Beth home and start tea. Can you bring Christopher with you?" Jenny called across to me, whilst I debated the state of my breathing.

"Jason, I said can you bring Christopher home?" She glared at me with those kryptonite eyes which seemed to bore deep into my skull.

"Yes, Jen. Sorry." I jumped up from the sofa and escorted her to the door as she turned and shot me an angry look.

"Don't be long. You and me need to have a chat when you get home."

I nodded and plodded back into the lounge.

Don arched his eyebrow and nodded to the kitchen. "Right, Chris, my boy, stack those dominoes in the box for me so you're ready to go home for your tea. I just want a quick word with your dad."

Don joined me in the kitchen, where I'd padded to and now stood leaning up against the sink.

I scrubbed my hands over my face. "For Christ's sake!" This was a nightmare, and I was struggling to see my way out of this one.

"Right, son. I'll help you get out of this mess you're in, but I need to know what mess it is. What I do know is looking at that chap next door tonight, he's the spitting image of Paul Colney. I didn't notice it yesterday as I didn't really look at him. So, my boy, what's going on ... who is he?"

I huffed and glanced at Don, not knowing where to start.

"Come on, son, talk to me. You know you can trust me." Don shuffled over to the cupboard beside me, pulled out a bottle of Whyte & Mackay whisky, then grabbed two glasses from the draining board. "Get this down you; this always does the trick."

I downed the whisky as instructed. "Look, Don, I've known Martin for years, many years, and I've never seen the resemblance to Paul Colney until tonight. Martin has always been clean-shaven with short hair. I've never seen him without his glasses until tonight, so I guess I've missed the likeness. However, you're right, he does look like him. Seeing Paul Colney at court today triggered the resemblance when I laid eyes on Martin tonight."

"Right, son, but that aside that's not what the issue is with Jenny, is it?" Don lifted his glass with his index finger pointing at me.

"'fraid not, Don. It's …" I shut my mouth, uncertain of what my following words could be.

"Well, son, what is it then?"

"Don you trust me … yes?"

Don nodded.

"I'm gonna need some time on this one. Can you just keep an eye on him next door for me and ensure he doesn't do anything stupid?"

"Like what."

"I don't know … just keep an eye out. I promise I'll tell you everything as soon as I can." I grimaced, praying Don wouldn't push it further regarding what might constitute stupid.

"Yes, son, of course. But don't suffer on your own here. You and your family are the most precious thing in the world to me. I don't want anything going wrong, and I'm worried about him and any connection he may have to Paul Colney. Because as sure as eggs are eggs, looking like he does, there must be a connection."

"Cheers, Don, thank you. I'll update you as soon as I can. Look, can you keep hold of Christopher for two minutes whilst I nip next door? Then I must get going."

"Yes, son, but don't keep that wife of yours waiting."

I nipped back to number eight, desperate to find out what had happened whilst I was with Don, all the time frantically trying to work out what the hell I'd say to Jenny when I got home. When I re-entered the kitchen, George was in full flow. Martin was standing by the sink gazing out the kitchen window, zombie-like, as he stared at his own reflection.

"So, as I said, lad, there must be a reason."

"A reason for what, George?" I asked, as I closed the back door.

George shook his head at me, then raised his eyebrows as he nodded in Martin's direction. "You're back then, lad. Jenny doesn't look too pleased ... is she alright?"

"No, George, she isn't. I have some difficult explaining to do when I get home."

"Oh, Christ, lad. Can I help in any way?"

"No, George. I'm just going to have to work this one out on my own. Although how I explain the Cortina being here ... I have no idea."

Martin turned and faced me, his hands shoved in his pockets. "George said you came back for a reason. So, I must have come back for a reason too. Do you think that's possible?"

I shot George a look, concerned with what he'd told Martin. George shook his head to confirm he hadn't divulged anything he shouldn't have.

"And he said you have taken the place of another Jason Apsley, who's disappeared. Is that right? Fricking hell, I can't believe I'm saying this."

"Yes, it is, and I don't know what happened to the other one. He was born in 1934, and yes, mate, I've taken his place. He would be the same age as me now if he existed. When I arrived, I just slotted into his life. Everyone seemed to know me and assumed I was this *other* Jason. We must be identical, but what the hell happened to him, well, God knows. It seems that you've come back as yourself as there doesn't seem to be another Martin Bretton in this world." I held up my hands. "Well, we don't know that, of course, but you showed up at my house, so I guess there isn't."

"There's my dad."

George and I shot each other a look and then stared at Martin.

Martin gawped at us both, eyes darting from one to the other. "What?" he questioned, raising his hands.

"Hang on, lad. Are you saying your father is called Martin Bretton as well?" George glanced at me again. We both knew what each other was thinking.

"Yeah, so what? It's just a coincidence, that's all. No real drama there."

George and I leant back in our chairs, George raised his eyebrows, and I shrugged back.

"Possible, I guess," I said to George, and he nodded back.

Martin grabbed the spare chair and slid into the seat. "What's going on? Why d'you two keep looking at each other?"

"Martin, do you have a middle name?" It wasn't unusual to call a son the same as a father, especially if it was a family name. However, the name Martin wasn't exactly a traditional name through the generations.

"Trevor."

"Right lad, and what's your father's middle name?"

"Trevor."

"Lad, you're telling me your parents named you after your father with *both* Christian names the same? Well, there's nothing as queer as folk as they say."

"That's a bit odd, mate, don't you think?" No, that was more than odd. George and I again glanced at each other, both raising our eyebrows, realising Martin had potentially returned and taken the place of his father, but hell – why?

"Well, yeah, I see what you mean. But it's just a coincidence, that's all. My parents didn't name me after my dad, as Mum hadn't met dad when I was born."

George and I swivelled our heads and gawped at Martin, both of us simultaneously exclaiming, "What?"

"I was three months old when Mum met my dad, well, my stepdad. As I said, it's just a coincidence that we both had the same Christian names. It's always been a talking point over the years on what a funny coincidence it actually was."

"Lad, where is your stepfather now, well not now, in 2019?"

"I'm afraid he died of cancer when I was twelve, three days after the millennium."

The back door swung open as George and I pondered this new information. I recalled what Martin had said yesterday about me and the fact that I was never interested in anyone else. Of course, back then, I wasn't. I never knew he lost his father at such a young age.

"Son, Jenny has phoned asking if you've left. I said you had, so you better get going, or she's really going to have your guts for garters."

"Christ, thanks, Don, I'm coming." My head was now pounding, and the thought of facing the Spanish Inquisition led by Jenny Apsley as the Grand Inquisitor didn't help.

"Go, lad, I'll sort Martin out. I'll call you at school tomorrow lunchtime with any update, but go now."

Taking Christopher into my arms as Don slung my coat around my shoulders, I scooted back to my car. Not only now getting ready for the grilling which awaited me at home, but also praying George could hold it together and keep everything under wraps with Martin and Don.

9

18th January 1977

Instagram

For the second consecutive night, I'd achieved hardly any sleep. When I arrived home last night, we'd fed the kids, then Jenny organised bath time whilst I busied myself in the kitchen. The atmosphere was treacle-thick, and neither Jenny nor I approached the massive *'elephant in the room'* until after I'd read Christopher his bedtime story. When we did, Beth had a screaming session which took Jenny an hour to get her back to sleep. It was gone nine when the *'elephant'* was discussed.

All I could muster up was Martin had purchased my old car on Sunday. Fortunately, I had the invoice in my pocket, and Jenny didn't question why the car was sold when the garage was closed or that Martin had paid a bloody fortune for it. She accepted Mr Thacker had achieved a quick sale, but I stumbled when she challenged me on why I had the invoice.

I injected an over-elaborate lie about Martin and girlfriend trouble to cover up the reason for staying in the rental house, and the Grand Inquisitor accepted this story. However, my well-versed ability to lie had left me high-and-dry as she scrutinised the version of events regarding my friendship with Martin. When specifically pushed on why he'd returned from South Africa, and when we both worked at some company called Waddington Steel, I sunk further into the cavernous hole I was digging for myself.

Jenny was not angry; it was far worse. I could see in her eyes she was losing trust as all my answers were vague, and now the last five months were unravelling at high speed. The only slow down to my life falling apart was when Beth awoke, hungry and screaming her head off, but that was just hitting the pause button. For the second consecutive night, we went to bed on an unresolved argument.

Although I loved my job as a teacher, today, I just wasn't in the mood for it. I desperately needed to get hold of George, although he'd said he would call me at lunchtime so I'd just have to wait, but Jesus, that was hours away. So, when moping into the school office, I decided I'd just have to get on with it. The efficient Miss Colman was already in the office, and as always, looking efficient.

"Morning, Mr Apsley, cold again, isn't it? I didn't like all that snow we had at the weekend. They forecast more tonight; did you hear?"

"Morning, Miss Colman," I mumbled, not really in the mood for talking as I rummaged through my pigeonhole, yawning my head off.

"Are we tired, Mr Apsley? That was a very big yawn," she said, as she passed me a hand-delivered letter. The envelope just bore mine and the school names but no address. I gathered up the letter with some other school paperwork, shovelled it all in my briefcase, and headed off to the staff room. I was going to need copious amounts of coffee to get through the day.

The morning lessons dragged. I set my students tasks that negated the need for much involvement from me, which was unfair to them, but hey, I was pooped and had nothing to offer them this morning. Whilst the class were reviewing an exercise just before lunch, I'd actually nodded off in my chair. As I slipped into a well-needed slumber, one of the students who sought some assistance with the exercise I'd set had come up to the front and nudged my shoulder. As I jolted awake, the inevitable happened as all thirty students fell about in hysterics. I was fully aware the incident would go around the school like wildfire. The only positive was this rather embarrassing episode couldn't be posted on Instagram. Teachers in forty-years time, I imagine, had a much tougher time.

I padded into the office just after noon.

"I'm expecting a call from The Fairfield Chronicle between now and one. Can you put it through to the staff room when it comes through, please?" I asked Miss Colman.

"Of course. Oh, Mr Apsley, is there a news item you're reporting?"

"What?" I shot Miss Colman a confused look.

"Fairfield Chronicle ... the call you said about?"

"Oh, I see. No, my good friend, George, is a Type-Setter there."

"Oh, how exciting, working for a newspaper! He'll get to see the stories before anyone else! Is there an exciting news item today?"

"Yeah, very exciting. Sorry ... I have no idea." It didn't take much for Miss Colman to get excited. She lived on her own, and I knew any snippet of gossip had her ears pricking up. I thought if she'd lived in my day, she would have loved all forms of social media, posting daily, and probably creating and updating her stories hourly.

"By the way, don't forget Mr Clark would like you to interview the two gentlemen this afternoon for the temporary caretaker role. The interviews are at one and two pm."

"Oh, bollocks," I mumbled. Fortunately, Miss Colman didn't hear me.

"I do hope Mr Trosh soon recovers from his operation. He's always so helpful, and the school just isn't the same without him."

"Yes, Clive is a lovely man. I think, Miss Colman, you carry a torch for our dependable caretaker." I swivelled and smirked at her, knowing full well I was right as she often conjured up jobs for Clive to complete in the school office just so she could have him close by.

"Mr Apsley! Really! I'll have you know that I'm a respectable lady, and Mr Trosh is a gentleman!"

"Quite." I moved over to her desk and had a quick glance left and right to check no one overheard us, which would have been impossible as we were the only two people in the office, but I seemed to have copied this manoeuvre from Miss Colman over the last few months. "Miss Colman, everyone knows you have a soft spot for Clive, and everyone also knows he would do anything for you. If I've learned anything over the last five months, if you get a second chance, you have to take it. I suggest you get yourself up Fairfield General later today and see how Clive is. I know he'll be over the moon to see you."

Miss Colman burned bright, the flush rising up her face akin to an unstoppable flow of red-hot lava. "Mr Apsley! I shall do no such thing!"

"Yes, you will. Even if I have to take you up there myself." I smiled as she shot her hand to her mouth. Her neck and face still burning bright, lighting up the room like a Belisha beacon.

Miss Colman coughed, shuffled some papers, then drummed her fingers on the table. "Well, perhaps I could go and say hello. That would be a nice thing to do, wouldn't it? Although, Mr Apsley, do you think it's appropriate for a single lady to visit a gentleman in the hospital?"

"Yes, I do. As I said, you'll make Clive's day."

"Really, do you think so?"

"I know so. Take this opportunity, Miss Colman. If you don't, I guarantee you'll regret it."

Miss Colman looked excited and had developed a glow, no longer caused by embarrassment but by the anticipation of seeing Clive. We all knew she held a candle for him, and we all knew that she was his siren. They just needed a nudge.

I left the office and trotted off to the staff room, hoping George would call soon with an update on last night's events. Flopping down on one of the armchairs, I lit a cigarette and closed my eyes, although quickly realising I was close to nodding off again. Yawning, I rummaged through my briefcase, searching for the CVs for the two interviews. When extracting the heap of paperwork, the envelope which Miss Colman had handed me this morning slipped out. Plucking it up, I reviewed the front again.

Jason Apsley

City of Fairfield School

Strictly Private and Confidential

The staff room phone rang. Colin Poole, who'd just entered the room, grabbed it as I jumped up from my chair. I strode towards him whilst tapping the unopened letter on my wrist.

"Jason, it's Miss Colman; she says she has a call for you."

"Thanks, Colin," I mumbled, as I took the receiver whilst staring at the envelope in my hand.

"Mr Apsley, I have a George from the Fairfield Chronicle on the line, putting you through now."

"Thank you."

"Hello."

"Hello, lad. Look, I haven't got long as there's a bit of a flap on here. They've changed the front page at the last minute, so we've got to work frantically to get ready for the print run. Anyway, don't panic; Martin is fine. I nipped in this morning with some food, so he can get through today. Can we meet after work at the pub so I can bring you up to speed? I can't talk now as I said there's a bit of a flap on here."

Whilst George was talking, I'd thumbed open the envelope and shaken out the single sheet of paper.

"Yes, George, that's—"

"Lad, you there?"

"What ... sorry. What did you say?"

"I said to meet at the pub tonight. You okay? You sound distracted? Lad?"

"Err ... yeah ... fine, George. See you then ..."

I plopped the receiver back in the cradle and stared at the letter. My hand had now started to shake, so I gripped the paper with both hands. My heart rate had increased and was now thumping in my chest as I wandered back to my chair. Dropping the letter on my heap of paperwork, I fumbled through my pockets for my cigarettes.

"You okay, Jason? You look a little peaky. Nothing wrong, I hope?" Colin called across from the end of the staff room as he smelt the milk bottle and the foil cap before plopping some in his tea.

With my arms gripping the wooden armrests, I perched on the end of the chair as cigarette smoke wafted up my face. Closing my left eye to avoid the smoke, I re-read the handwritten letter.

Hello Jason,

I'm sorry to approach you like this, but this is not an easy letter to write. My name is Jessica Redmond, and I believe you are my father. After over twenty years, I know this will come as a shock to receive this letter, but I would like to get to know you, although with a heavy heart I will accept if that's not what you want. I really want to meet you, and I will be in the Beehive Pub on Coldhams Lane at 6pm on the 18th and 19th if you feel you could come and meet me. I don't want anything from you, but just the need to meet you.

Sorry for my ramble, and desperately hope to see you soon.

Your daughter

Jess

"Jason, you sure you're okay?" Colin stood a few feet from me, stirring his cup of tea.

I glanced up and removed the cigarette from my mouth. "Sorry, Colin. Err ... yeah, I'm fine."

"Anything I can help with?" he offered, still scraping the spoon around his cup.

"No, but thank you." Sitting back in the chair, I wondered how it was possible that everything had turned to shit in such a short space of time.

Two days ago, my life was bloody perfect. Now Martin had landed in my old car; Jenny knew something was up; Don was fishing for information which I had no idea how I would sort that out, and Christ, now *other* Jason's daughter wanted to meet me – for fuck sake – what a nightmare. Could I just ignore the letter? Jess had written she'd accept if I didn't want to get to know her. If I didn't turn up, that would be that – or would it? Perhaps she might change her mind and then come to seek me out at school. Or worse, she'd discovered where I worked, so she might have fathomed out where I live. If she turned up there, oh Christ, the nightmare would get worse.

10

Olivetti

Both George and Jess wanted to meet me tonight, but weighing up the choices, I quickly concluded Jess would just have to wait until tomorrow. Coffee and cigarette finished, I nipped through to the office to pick up my first candidate for the stand-in caretaker job.

Roy was pushing me to take the Deputy Head position and was chucking jobs my way, presumably to get me in the swing of the role. However, I still wasn't sure I wanted the position and certainly didn't want to conduct these interviews today. Although I was experienced at interviewing in my previous life, so not a difficult task, but staying awake through them would be the tricky bit.

Miss Colman was busy folding letters and stuffing them in envelopes as I padded into the office. "Miss Colman, is my first interview here yet?"

She looked up, performed her signature quick check left and right, and beckoned me over, which were her usual actions before launching into some juicy gossip.

"Mr Apsley, not that I'm one to gossip, as you know." She leant in a little closer, glancing left to check Roy's office door was firmly closed.

"Yes." Not as friendly a greeting as I would usually give, but I wasn't in the mood today.

"Well, Roy has some detectives in his office at the moment along with Mr Foord from the Education Authority. Obviously, I don't know what it's about, but I've heard a little of the conversation—"

Roy's door swung open, and he poked his head around the door frame.

"Miss Colman, can you dig out those purchase records for the new Olivetti typewriters we acquired last year, please?" Still gripping the door frame, he glanced at me, then back at Miss Coleman.

He appeared to sport a ruddy complexion, which I now knew to be a sign he was under pressure.

"Bring them into my office as soon as you've found them, please." He swivelled his head back in my direction. "Jason, can you join me in my office?"

I glanced at Miss Colman, who arched her eyebrow at me as she busied herself rifling through a filing cabinet drawer. When entering Roy's office, I noticed three gentlemen who Miss Colman was presumably about to describe when in mid-flow of her gossiping. Two were seated, with one standing behind them, and they all swivelled around to look at me entering the room. Apart from the one standing, we were all of a similar age – early to mid-forties – the other probably ten years older and what hair he had left was grey and combed over to cover a blotchy scalp.

"Gentlemen, this is Mr Apsley. He's my acting Deputy Head."

Am I? News to me, I mused.

"I thought it would be appropriate to bring him into the conversation in case I'm not available should you need further assistance after today," blustered Roy, as he re-took his seat in his brown leather swivel chair.

I stood, feeling slightly concerned that another pile of shite was about to drop on my head as I gawped at the three men, now wondering what the hell was going on.

With a similar hairstyle to Roy, one of the gents sitting turned to me and flipped over the cover to his notebook. "First name, Mr Apsley please," he said, whilst repeatedly clicking the pen on and off as he looked up at me.

"Jason, no middle name." He made a note in his book, repeating what I said word for word, not that I believed he noted down anything other than the words Jason Apsley. He then slipped it into his jacket pocket and refolded the overcoat on his lap.

The other seated gent stood, leant across and offered his hand.

"Malcolm Foord, Hertfordshire Education Department. Good to meet you at last, Jason. Roy has been extremely complimentary regarding you, and we very much hope you take the Deputy position permanently. The position at one of our premier schools is—"

The detective who'd just taken my name coughed and interrupted. "Yes, thank you, but can we get back to the matter in hand, please?"

He glanced and nodded at the man standing who'd so far said nothing as he stood with his overcoat folded over his hands clasped in front of him. He turned slightly to face me.

"Mr Apsley, what I'm about to tell you is highly confidential, so we will need to rely on your cooperation and discretion." He stopped talking, presumably awaiting my confirmation which I supplied with a nod of my head. Now I was more than a little concerned, considering they'd asked for information about the school typewriters.

"I'm DI Roberts from Hertfordshire Police. My colleague here is DI Litchfield from West Yorkshire Police." Oh, bollocks, this wasn't good, but at least I was getting a heads up, I guessed.

"A letter was typed on an Olivetti typewriter, the exact same model that you have at this school, and sent last September to the West Yorkshire police, the Yorkshire Post and four national newspapers. It was an anonymous letter that claimed to know the assailant of two serious crimes. The envelope had a Fairfield post-mark, so you can see we are extremely keen to ascertain where this letter was typed and obviously who typed it."

Jesus – now I was blushing. The word *guilty* must have been radiating from me, almost expecting a flag to pop out of my ear with a *'guilty, it was me'* sign on it. All I could manage was to croak a timid "*Oh*" as a response. A knock on the door afforded me a few seconds to recover my composure. Miss Colman scooted into the office, clasping a manilla folder which she attempted to hand to Roy. DI Litchfield intercepted it, whisking it out of her hand and offering no response. Miss Colman hovered for a few seconds; I could tell she was gagging for information.

Roy nodded at her. "Thank you, Miss Colman." With that, she backed out of the room, leaving the door slightly ajar. Roy nodded to me, so I leant across and closed the door, thus spoiling Miss Colman's opportunity to earwig the conversation. I expected she would now have a glass slapped against the wall or be peering through the keyhole.

DI Litchfield had flipped open the file and now looked up at Roy, turned to me and back to Roy. "The school purchased twenty Olivetti typewriters in May 1976." He glanced back down at the invoice. "I'm assuming those twenty are still at the school?"

Roy and I looked at each other, he responded. "Yes, as far as I know. We've not had any reason to replace any of them as they are quite new."

DI Lichfield scratched the end of his nose, something he seemed to repeat every few seconds, then continued the conversation with Roy. "Who has access to the typewriters at the school?"

"All students taking the two-year Pitman secretarial training. We have three classes that regularly use them as part of their education."

"Who else would use them?"

"No one. The only other typewriter is in the school office, which Miss Colman, my secretary, uses. I'm certain that's a different model, and she's the only other person who requires the use of a typewriter."

"Please can you arrange for a list of names to be prepared of the students taking the Pitman course?"

"Yes, of course. I'll ask Miss Colman to pull that together today for you."

"Yes please, sir. I'll get an officer to collect it later this afternoon."

DI Roberts interjected. "As we discussed earlier, we'll return at four-thirty this afternoon with a forensic officer. We will need to look at each typewriter, so we'll collect the list then."

"I think that will do for now. Obviously, as stated, this is in the strictest confidence, and we'll return later as discussed." DI Litchfield stood and shook Roy's hand and turned to shake mine, his grey eyes boring into my head. I was convinced he could see into my brain and the big guilty sign that was waving at him from behind my eyes.

DI Roberts opened the door and stood waiting for his colleague as Miss Colman fell in. I guess she was leaning against the door as it was yanked open. She recovered herself by grabbing the bookcase, although her face was burning bright with embarrassment. A wisp of hair had escaped her perfectly formed bun and now hung over her left eye, which she blew out of the way only for it to drop back again.

"Oh ... Mr Apsley, hum ... err.... your interview is here waiting," she babbled and blushed even brighter as she grabbed the errant wisp of hair, trying to persuade it to return to its allotted position.

"Thank you, Miss Colman. Can you show these gentlemen out, please?" replied Roy, oblivious that his secretary had been clearly caught in the act of snooping.

The two detectives brushed past Miss Colman, although DI Litchfield turned back to look at Roy and then me. "Are any of the students in the secretarial classes male?"

"Good grief, no! Being a secretary is not a man's job. Why on earth would you suggest that?" Roy fired back. If ever I needed reminding that I was living forty-years in the past, Roy had just delivered it.

DI Litchfield smiled. Although Roy had asked the question, he looked at me. "Males tend to hit the keys harder, making a deeper indent on the paper," he replied, as I flushed bright-red ... again.

11

Magaluf

The two interviews were conducted as requested by Roy. However, the process in this era was very different from my previous interviewing experience in 2019. With no computers or internet, the applications consisted of a typed covering letter and the candidate's CV. Disappointingly, I couldn't trawl through Facebook to look up their profiles and see what misdemeanours they'd got up to in their social lives.

Back in my days as Sales Executive for Waddington Steel, that was always the part which I used to find the most entertaining. Having a candidate sitting across the desk looking all professional, when only a few minutes ago, I'd spotted a cringe-worthy picture of them when pissed in a nightclub or trying to set light to their farts as they bent double with a cigarette lighter between their legs.

I recalled interviewing Martin about eight years back; well … eight years back from 2019 and not 1977. He arrived well-turned out in a smart new suit, sitting ramrod straight, although slightly nervous. A few moments earlier, I'd trawled through his Facebook account which, unfortunately for him, had very low-security settings. I was able to access many of his holiday posts which showed Martin and a group of his mates during pissed-up nights in Magaluf.

One picture had caught my eye, showing whom I presumed was Martin performing a selfie with a girl who'd won the Miss Wet T-shirt competition. He had a bottle of beer in one hand, his other draped over her shoulder, and his tongue poked out at one very visible nipple straining against the wet t-shirt.

I remember having that picture in my mind as Martin recounted his hobbies were supporting community projects, reading, and occasionally socialising with friends. Unsurprisingly, he didn't mention drunken nights out and nipple-licking of equally drunk girls.

With the entertainment mounting, I was intrigued to hear more about his involvement in the local community. Very noble, I thought. Indeed, this would demonstrate there was a certain level of maturity, despite the nipple-licking event. Martin talked through how he often supported his local healthcare centre by providing transport for the elderly to attend appointments and collect and deliver prescriptions. Yes, very noble.

As he was from the generation who daily posted their life story on Facebook, and it appeared in his case to be hourly, I was surprised I could only see one Facebook entry about his community work. That entry I recalled was him moaning about having to fumigate his car after reluctantly agreeing to take his mother's neighbour up to the Health Centre, as the usual ride had let the old-boy down at the last minute. The picture he'd posted was of him with a plastic peg on his nose whilst wiping the car seat. The caption read, *'Aftermath of taking that piss-reeking old codger in my car. Never again!'*

Although at the time I was concerned about his moral compass, I did, however, offer the job to Martin. It was a junior role, and we all have to start somewhere, I thought. The other plus point, or actually less negative, was his dodgy Facebook entries were less offensive than most other candidates. The world had moved on in those eight years. Martin had matured, which wouldn't have been difficult based on the low point he was starting from. He'd married, become very competent at his job, and now had followed me back forty years into the past – all regular everyday events.

Now interviewing in 1977, there was no requirement for the candidate to provide identification for proof of right to work and no DBS checks. I could have been interviewing and potentially employing some nutter or a serial killer. This role's essential requirement consisted of two main threads. Firstly, would they look good in a brown smock-coat and secondly, could they use a screwdriver. Both candidates seemed more than competent in both categories. However, rather than offering the job to the second candidate who had some previous appropriate experience, I thought this could provide a temporary solution to what to do with Martin – assuming he was capable of using a screwdriver.

Both DIs returned with the forensic officer just after four pm, and Roy left them in my capable hands. However, after guiding them to the secretarial training suite, they closed the door on me, leaving me stranded in the corridor.

Last September, when I typed the letter about the Yorkshire Ripper, I'd harboured a niggling concern about the possible exposure as the author and the potential consequences that could entail. Earlier today, I'd realised my school-boy error of posting them locally, thus giving the letters the Fairfield postmark.

Over the past four months, there were no reported arrests for the two murders in West Yorkshire. I'd made the reasonable assumption my letter was treated as the work of some crank or would-be Mystic-Meg. Or perhaps some other charlatan horoscope nut who claimed to be able to predict the future, but hey, I would say that as I have the star sign of Aries. Why they were so interested in who typed it, I couldn't fathom, unless they believed it was the real killer who'd fabricated a wild story to deflect the murders from themselves and onto Peter Sutcliffe.

I was sure if they could link the letter to one of those typewriters, there was no way they could connect the letter to me as anyone could have used it. Four months on, my fingerprints would no longer be on the typewriter.

With the door closed on me, I wandered back to the staff room, reasonably confident that I had nothing to concern myself regarding this particular issue. However, then the obvious occurred to me and produced a cloak of doom that flattened my mood to a new low. The police were not lifting fingerprints, as they already had mine on the letter I sent. Oh, bollocks, I'd been such a pea-brain. I didn't think about fingerprints when I'd sent the letters. At the time, I was only concerned about the typewriter being traced. I'd not concerned myself with DNA being harvested from the licked stamps and envelopes, as in this era it hadn't been discovered. However, like a total numb-skull, I hadn't considered that the paper and envelope were smothered with my sweaty fingerprints. Now all they had to do was fingerprint everyone, and I would be caught.

Slipping ever further into a melancholy mindset, I considered what else could turn to shit today. As I chain-smoked through a packet of cigarettes, I half expected the forensic officer to be able to pinpoint me as the perpetrator just by flicking his powder and brush around. Yes, I was losing all sense of proportion.

The situation escalated a few minutes before five when the detectives had finished their work and presented me with a receipt for one of the typewriters they were seizing for further investigation. Roy was stunned, and we discussed for some time how one of our students could have typed a letter about some crime committed hundreds of miles away in Yorkshire. I tried to play down the situation, saying it was probably coincidence and just a school prank which had got out of hand. I was now regretting the decision to send the letter in the first place as it seemed to only have the effect of putting the school under suspicion and not leading to stopping the Yorkshire Ripper as intended.

With the trepidation of what George had to say at the pub tonight, and then the impending doom of a continued argument with Jenny later, I left school feeling quite depressed. Today really had turned to shite.

12

Corona

The Three Horse Shoes lounge bar was reasonably quiet, with only three other punters enjoying an early evening drink. It was one of the few times I'd ventured into the pub when Dawn and Dennis weren't perched on their designated bar stools. Ensconced on Dennis's stool and nursing my pint, I waited for George, trying to avoid thinking about the day's events. When George arrived a little after six, he wasn't alone as he'd brought Martin with him.

"Lad, I stopped by and picked up Martin. Thought it would be good to get him out of the house.

"Right … okay," I nonchalantly replied. "You'll have to drop him off though, as I can't be late tonight because Jenny is seriously on the warpath. The tanks are on the front lawn, so to speak."

"I am here, you know!" interjected Martin. He did look a little brighter today, although he still had that mopey look with his hands stuffed in the pockets of his green parka.

"Yeah, sorry, Martin," I offered with a wave of my hand as an apology.

"Lad, I presume it didn't go too well with Jenny last night, then? It was a bit tense in that kitchen when she walked in."

"Oh, George, it was a bloody disaster, and she's seen his car!" I pointed at Martin, who was now taking a butchers around the pub and the few other punters who were sitting at a table near the cigarette machine – he'd probably never seen one of those before.

"Ah, sorry to hear that, lad. You did sound a bit distracted when I called at lunchtime. I presume that's been playing on your mind all day."

Brian, the landlord, plonked George's pint on the bar. George turned to Martin, who appeared transfixed by the One-Armed-Bandit fruit machine as another punter slotted five-pence pieces into it and repeatedly yanked down the arm. He was starting to look like a right weirdo as he stared gormlessly, mesmerised by the wheels as they spun around.

"Martin, what you 'aving?" asked George, whilst Brian waited with an empty beer mug in hand in anticipation.

"Oh, err … bottle of Peroni, please," he offered back over his shoulder as his head moved rhythmically with the arm of the fruit machine.

"Sorry, sir, did you say a bottle of Pernod?" questioned Brian, who sported a baffled, bemused expression.

"Oh … what? No, no … I'll have a bottle of Corona then," Martin threw back but was still transfixed on the Bell-Fruit machine.

"I've got orange or cherryade. Which one? They've both passed their Fizzical," he chuckled.

I could see it would take a long time for Martin to fit in here. He looked confused as Brian held up the two bottles of fizzy drinks. I interjected to end this mayhem before Martin made an irreversible time-travel cock-up. "Brian, he'll have a pint of Skol." I shot Martin a look to shut his mouth as he turned and performed a fish-like impression.

"Oh, okay. Wish you'd make your mind up. It's a bottle of Pernod, then cherryade, now a pint of Skol," Brian muttered, as he put the two glass bottles of fizzy drink down and reached for a pint glass.

Drinks in hand and peeling Martin away from the one-armed-bandit's hypnotic motion, we gathered in George's favourite bay window seat.

"Right, lad, let's bring you up to speed. What I believe, talking to the lad 'ere last night," George nodded to Martin, who was in the process of necking the pint in one gulp – I guessed he needed it. "After your accident on 12th August 2019, you died, and Martin ended up in a coma or something like that, as he can't remember anything past the accident, only snippets of being in a hospital. Then, what I reckon is, he died on 16th January 2020 when he failed to recover from the coma."

I'd worked that much out myself. Martin said nothing as he repeatedly pushed the centre of his glasses back as he tipped his head forward and leaned in. George was obviously speaking in hushed tones, as the content of this conversation for any normal person was ridiculous.

"Yeah, I've got that. What else did you discuss?"

"Right, well. You time-travelled for a reason, and we both know what that was."

"What was that then?" Martin interjected.

"Not now," we both replied in unison, as we turned and looked at Martin. He squinted and pushed his glasses up his head again. This certainly wasn't the time to explain to Martin that I'd saved my best friend in 2019 from suffering child abuse, and she'd now become my adopted baby daughter.

"So, lad, I reckon the lad here has time-travelled for a reason too. All we have to work out is what that is. In the meantime, we need to work out what we do with him. As we said yesterday, he's not slotted into another Martin Bretton's life."

Although George and Martin had not come up with much during their conversation yesterday, there seemed to be nothing worse happening to add to my already disastrous day.

"You said your stepfather had exactly the same name but died in the year 2000. I think you need to tell us a bit of history about him, like where was he in 1977, i.e., now?"

"Mum and Dad met at the Mandela concert at Wembley in '88. I was only a baby, but Mum went to the concert with some friends, and she met my dad there. Apparently, Mum was separated from her friends, bumped into these two American guys and spent the whole concert with them. One of those guys became my stepdad."

"So, your stepfather was an American?"

"Who's Mandela?" George interjected.

"What? You're joking, right? Everyone knows who Mandela is!" blurted Martin.

"Hang on, hang on." I slid a pound note across the table. "George, can you get the drinks in. I don't want one, but Martin has necked his down already." George looked at me and nodded, knowing that I'd have to get Martin's head straight about living in a different world.

"Martin, look, I know this is all nuts, but you're living in a different time. Mandela was a political prisoner who'd not come to world attention in 1977. Peroni and Corona beer were not commonplace in pubs. You're going to have to work hard every day at this, as I still do five months after arriving here. Okay? Do you understand me?"

"Yeah, yeah, I know. I still can't get my bloody head around this and that I'm actually here."

"Well, mate, you are, and you'd better start getting used to it. My life is a billion times better than it was in 2019, I can tell you. Well, it was until Sunday."

"What ... when I arrived at your doorstep?"

"Yep, and now everything seems to be unravelling."

"I'm sorry about what I said to you on Sunday. You know ... about everyone hating you back there ... y'know ... at work and stuff." Martin looked away from me, breaking eye contact. I presumed he was feeling a little embarrassed, although he had no reason to be.

"Martin, don't be. You were absolutely right in what you said. Over the last few months I've changed, and the Jason you knew back then was a right tosser. What you said was true."

Martin raised his eyebrows, nodded and smiled for the first time in two days. "Yep, you were."

"Yeah, alright. You don't have to look so smug about it."

George re-joined us at the table with Martin's pint. I nodded that I'd put Martin straight on a few things.

"So, Martin, your stepdad was an American. When did he come to the UK?"

"Dad worked for BP and was seconded over to complete a two-year contract in the late '80s. That's when he met Mum and didn't go back. They married in 1990 when I was just two years old."

"Do you know where he was in the late '70s? Presumably, in college in the States, I guess?"

"No, he was fifteen years older than Mum, so he'd be in his early thirties. Probably about the age I am now. I don't know what he was doing then, although he would have been living in America at the time. I remember him saying that he never found the right *Gal,* as he put it; then the first time leaving the States and within his first week here, he met the woman of his dreams."

"Well, that seals it, lad. Your father is in America now."

"Fricking hell! My dad's there right now, isn't he? And we're the same age ... fuck me!"

"Mind your language. There's no need for that, d'you hear?"

"Sorry, George," I said.

"Not you lad ... 'im." George thumbed towards Martin.

"Yeah, I know, but I thought I would say it for him until he gets the hang of it." I grinned.

"Oh, I see. Well, I've only met two time-travellers, and they both have mouths like sewers."

Martin pointed at me and laughed. "You should've heard him at work! Every other word he uttered was either *Fuck,* or *Bollocks.* We all reckoned he'd got Tourettes!"

"Tour-what?"

"Forget it, George. Right, let's get back to it." Now checking my watch, concerned I really needed to get going soon. I had the grovel-to-Jenny path to crawl along tonight, so being super late was only going to add shards of broken glass to that already super-tricky path to squirm across.

"What about your mum? She'd presumably be of school age now. Is that in Enfield? That's where you come from, isn't it?" I questioned Martin as he proceeded to gulp down his second pint.

"No. I was born and raised here in Fairfield."

"Thought you said this lad worked for you? Didn't you know anything about your staff?"

Martin choked and snorted beer down his nose. "Ha!" He wiped his nose and table with the sleeves of his parka, both arms performing a synchronised movement to clear the mess he'd made. George screwed up his nose at the revolting sight whilst I just shook my head. Martin smirked at me as he continued to swirl the spat beer in a circular motion with his sleeve.

"George, back then, or future then, I … how shall I put it without you chastising me for my language … I was a—"

"A right tosser – that covers it," Martin blurted out and grinned.

I pointed at Martin. "Yup, that about covers it."

"Oh right, okay, lad. Carry on about your mother." George shot me a confused look. I shrugged, guessing I'd have to go into greater detail with him at some point about my not-so-wonderful previous life.

"As I said. I was born in Fairfield and went to school here. The same one as my mum did … the City School."

"You went to the City School, really? And your mum, when was she born?"

"1961. She'd be … err … sixteen now."

I glanced at George, both of us raising our eyebrows.

"Fricking hell, my mum is still at school!"

"Martin, what's your mother's name."

"Sarah Bretton."

I thought for a moment. Nope, I didn't know a Sarah Bretton. "No, that's presumably her married name. What's her maiden name?"

"Moore. She was Sarah Moore before she met Dad. I was originally called Moore and then took my stepfather's name when they married."

"Good, God! Really?"

"You know her, lad?"

"Yes, George, I know exactly who she is!" I'd seen her at school today and yesterday at court in the public gallery when Patrick Colney was found guilty of stabbing her father, whom I'd now discovered would become Martin's grandfather. The court case which I instigated by encouraging Sarah to speak out about David Colney – a very small world indeed – and she was Martin's mother.

Martin stared at me, eyes wide, as he shot a look at George and then back to me. "How would you know my mother?"

"I'm a teacher at Fairfield City School, and your mother is one of my students. This may scupper an idea I had today on how we could integrate you into this world. As I see it, the biggest problem we have is Martin doesn't exist, as he's landed with no history. He hasn't dropped in to take the place of his father; therefore, we have to create a history."

"What's your plan, lad?"

Martin had drifted from the conversation, sitting further back than George and I. The first few weeks of time-travel were tough, and I guess he was trying to get his head around the knowledge about his mother. George and I assumed our position leaning in close to whisper.

"There's a temporary position for a school caretaker. Clive, the caretaker, has gone in for an operation and needs six months of convalescence. I'm conducting the interviews, and I thought I could engineer it so that Martin gets the job. I reckon I can circumnavigate the paperwork, and also I'll be able to keep a close eye on him. If I can swing it, I thought we could buy some time as clearly he can't just mope about all day."

"That's a cracking idea, lad. I think you should do it."

"But what about his mother being a student?"

"Lad, you can't worry about that. She won't know him. Anyway, he'll be the school caretaker, so she won't give him another look."

"Do you think?"

"Yes, lad, I do. We have no choice, do we?"

"George, you're right … I don't think we do."

We had our strategy in place, which I planned to get to work on in the morning. We were still unclear why Martin was here in 1977. Maybe there was no reason, and he'd just followed me here. George ferried Martin back to my rental house as I headed home for my continued interrogation. I was concerned my other closest friend, Don, would need some answers soon, but my immediate problem was Jenny and the urgent need to repair the damage to haul my life back on track.

13

Walmart

Leaning against the door frame with my arms folded, I stood and watched Jenny kneeling on the lino floor, playing with the kids in the bath. Christopher's plastic U-boat submarine fizzed along in the bath, powered by a bicarbonate-soda tablet; a really innovative little gadget, I thought. Jenny had brought it from Woolworths as one of his Christmas presents. I felt slightly tearful, a feeling I hadn't experienced for many months, but life was unravelling, and now I feared this wonderful sight of my family was drifting. The more I reached out to save it, the further it drifted away. Jenny turned and smiled.

"You're late home, darling."

"Yes, sorry, took George for a pint."

Jenny turned back to Beth, who was nestled in her arms as she swished her back and forth up the bathtub.

"Shall I put them to bed for you?" Jenny didn't answer but carried on swishing Beth whilst Christopher laughed at his submarine, which zipped along, crashing into the end of the bath.

Although we'd only officially adopted them both for just over a week, the children had lived with us for over a month now. The transformation in Christopher was nothing short of miraculous in such a short space of time. No longer was he the little lad who winced every time you moved your hand. I suspected that had been an involuntary movement he made as he prepared for the inevitable slap or beating he was used to getting. Now he was a happy, carefree lad, accepting the love we gave him with his frightening past now evaporating. He was so young, and I hoped he never remembers his first five years.

I had to get this situation sorted and quickly. Not for me and my desire to keep my family, but for him. Christopher and Beth deserved a loving and stable life which Jenny and I would give them, but that was only going to continue if I could get myself out of this hole. Jenny still hadn't answered and ignored the atmosphere, almost tormenting me with her silence as I waited for the argument to restart for the third night in a row.

"Jenny, did you hear me? Shall I put the kids to bed?"

"Can you take Christopher and read him his story? I'll get Beth ready, and she'll go down after she's had her bottle."

"Okay." I knelt beside her and searched her eyes, desperately trying to figure out what was going on in that beautiful head of hers.

"We can talk afterwards, alright?"

"Okay." I nodded, as tears pricked at my eyes. I turned my head so she wouldn't notice.

After getting Christopher off to sleep, Jenny handed me Beth to settle into her cot. I cradled her as she yawned and stared up at me with those bright blue eyes.

"I'll start supper if you can settle her, please. She's been winded," Jenny threw back, as she purposefully bounded down the stairs.

I tucked Beth into her cot and gently smoothed her wispy white-blonde hair.

"Oh bollocks, Beth, I have truly cocked up again. Not really my fault this time, but everything is turning to shit. I could do with your usual advice or bollocking that you used to give me when I'd done something twattish, which we both know was quite often."

Beth looked up at me and smiled. Did she have memories of her previous life and recall the stupid scrapes I got into? No, she was probably filling her nappy. I will admit that I was thankful Jenny changed and washed the nappies. Although the '*new man*' I was, especially for this era, nappy changing just didn't appeal. I'd shown Jenny the new disposable ones that some chemists like Boots and Timothy-Whites were now selling. However, even though we were reasonably loaded, Jenny thought they were way too expensive.

"Look, Beth, what am I going to do? I can't explain Martin's arrival, and the longer he's here, your mum will question it more and more. God, I hate lying to her. Christ, also, what am I going to tell Don? He knows something is up, but telling them both Martin and I are time-travellers is not possible. Can you imagine how they would react if I told them you and I were best friends from the future and I'm not born until March this year? Jesus, Beth, this is a bloody nightmare. I thought dealing with that bastard who would've abused you was difficult enough, but this is on another level."

'*Told you on Sunday, Apsley ... you're screwed.*'

I ignored my mind talk. Of course, Beth offered no help and continued to smile up at me. I rested my head on the cot railing before standing up and scrubbing my hands over my face.

"Come on, Apsley ... think," I muttered, as I tried to suppress that ever-so annoying voice in my head which was now on a roll as it tormented me.

The floorboards on the landing creaked; I spun around. There Jenny stood, leaning against the door frame, tears in her eyes. We just stared at each other for what seemed an age. My jaw fell open whilst Jenny wiped her tears with the back of her hand.

I broke the silence. "How long have you been standing there?"

"Long enough." Jenny continued to glare at me, searching my eyes for answers.

"Right," I huffed. I guess she'd heard it all. Tuesday the 18th of January seemed to be pumping out disaster after disaster, and it just kept giving.

"Why were you saying those ridiculous things to Beth? Why, Jason?"

I moved towards her and reached out for her hand, but she snatched it away and moved back a step which caused the floorboards to creak again. I'd vowed to sort those floorboards out many times in the last few months and thirty-odd years in the future. Jenny had never moaned about it, although Lisa had on many occasions.

"Jason, I don't understand why you were saying those stupid things … you need to start talking."

"I was just … err … just telling Beth a bedtime story."

"No, you weren't! I heard you … I heard all of it. Jason, tell me the bloody truth!"

This was it. I'd reached the point of no return. Jenny wasn't going to accept some rubbish that I could conjure up in a few seconds. It may be time to come clean – whatever the consequences.

Taking a deep breath to give my brain one last second to come up with some believable shite before my mouth blurted out what presumably would be the most ridiculous story Jenny had ever heard – my brain failed to deliver.

'Screwed, mate!'

"Jen, I need to talk to you. But I will need George here with me to do that." God knows how, but I managed to appear calm, clear and concise.

"Jason, you're scaring me. What's going on? And why do you need George here? I'm your wife, and I don't understand what he's got to do with our relationship?"

I moved towards her and grabbed her shaking hands, pulling her closer to me. "I ask that you trust me. Trust me, Jen. Let me ring George. I'll get you a drink, then we'll talk ... but George must be here."

I left Jen sitting at the kitchen table with a substantially large glass of wine whilst I phoned George and prayed he could come immediately. Thankfully he recognised the gravity of the situation, threw Ivy an acceptable excuse and said he'd be over in ten minutes – ten very long minutes – which I used to power my way through two cigarettes on the doorstep before going back into the kitchen.

"Jen, George said he will be here in a few minutes. Before I say anything else, you know, really know in your heart that I love you? Also, I've *not* done anything that falls foul of our wedding vows."

"Lying?" She didn't look up but just repeated that word. "Lying?"

"Withholding some truth, yes ... but not strictly lying."

I plonked my bum in the chair next to her and took her hand. She didn't fight me but looked up with tears trickling down her face. We stayed motionless, not uttering a word until George arrived – I was devastated.

George didn't knock but burst into the kitchen and stood and stared at both of us crying as we held each other's hands. "Oh hell, I knew this day would come; just knew it," he blurted, as he hung his coat on the handle of the yellow Ewbank carpet sweeper propped up against the kitchen wall.

"Sit, George. I will get you a whisky." I released my hands from Jenny and nipped through to get the whisky bottle from the drink's cabinet in the lounge. When I returned, George had taken Jenny's hands in his.

"Right, lass. We've known each other for a few months, and I'd like to think we've grown quite close … would you agree?" Jen nodded and glanced at me as I placed a glass of whisky in front of George, then looked back at him.

"I hope you think of me a sensible normal kind of chap?" He raised his eyebrow, George Sutton style. It was a question that seemed to hang in the air, waiting for my wife to respond. I looked down at their hands, Jenny's tiny slim fingers dwarfed by George's huge fists.

"Yes, of course, George. You and Ivy are wonderful people. I don't think I've ever met such lovely people as you both. It's fair to say that Jason and I love you like parents … but George, what's going on?"

George swallowed the whisky in one slug and took hold of her hands again.

"Lass, I wanna tell you a true story." Which I thought sounded a bit like Max Bygraves, although there was nothing humorous about this situation.

"All I want you to do is listen to me. Then, when I've told you this totally true story, we can talk … is that a deal?" George asked, raising that eyebrow again.

Jenny shot me a look, her face screwed up in a mixture of confusion and anger, then stared back at George. She looked scared, and I hated it. I loved her, and this was killing me.

"Jenny lass, do we have a deal?"

"Yes … yes, George."

I stood leaning up against the sink, gripping the edge with such force my knuckles were white as George relayed the story of my time-travel adventure. To be fair, as George had all those months ago, Jenny listened without interrupting. With her hands clasped in his, she occasionally glanced up at me. Listening to the story George told was difficult to hear. Although I was living it, clearly to any sane, normal human being it was so bloody ridiculous, and it was a miracle he'd ever believed me. I now feared my marriage was over because this was going to be too much for Jenny. Well, it would be for any reasonable person, and I knew this would be too much for her to take in without thinking George and I had lost our marbles.

George concluded my tale and, for a few long minutes, we sat quietly staring at each other. I fidgeted with a dishcloth whilst George rattled the change in his pockets – Jenny just stared at me.

"Jen?" She didn't waver – just continued to stare – her emerald eyes had taken on a darker shade, and I now felt they were piercing my skull.

"You remember I bet a hundred pounds on that Grand Prix race last October, and you thought that was madness? Also, remember that little argument we had when I placed a bet on Jimmy Carter winning the American Presidential election even though all the political reporting suggested Ford would win?"

Jen just continued to glare at me, not blinking.

"Well, those bets weren't a risk; they were facts as I had the knowledge." Jenny huffed, then gulped down her wine before dismissively shaking her head.

I pushed on. She hadn't thrown us out – yet – so I carried on trying to inch her mind closer to accepting this madness. "You often comment I do and say silly things … you say you like that about me." I rambled on with whatever popped into my brain. I should have prepared this speech and practised it so I was ready to wheel it out when required. However, I never thought it would be needed, so I just carried on blurting out my random thoughts.

"You remember our first night here in this house when you said that Alan was going to see The Clash gig in Islington? I said I loved The Clash, and *London Calling* was an epic album. That album will be released in a couple of years, but to me, it was old punk before my time. It was just one of the million time-travel cock-ups I've made that you never really noticed. Do you remember?"

Jenny didn't move a muscle but turned up her nose as if George or I had relieved our bowels of unwanted gasses.

With no answer from Jen, I bashed on with my babbling. "You remember before Christmas when you were annoyed that Woollies had sold out of Space Hoppers, and I suggested Amazon might sell them? We then had this big debate about what Amazon was, and I said I'd bumped my head and was talking gibberish."

Still no movement from Jen, and George was now playing his second symphony via his loose change jingling in his pocket.

"Well, Amazon is the world's biggest online retailer. You can order what you want on your computer, and they deliver it the next day. You'll remember when you questioned why I purchased shares in McDonald's restaurants and an American supermarket called Walmart, and I said they were an investment for the kids' future. You said that no one had ever heard of them and I was wasting money. Those two businesses in thirty years' time are two of the biggest companies in the world. The kids will become multimillionaires."

"What about those pocket computer companies you mentioned, lad?"

"Apple and Microsoft? Yeah, their stock is not available at the moment. I'm not sure when, but it will only be a few years and I'll invest in them as well."

I pulled out a chair and took Jenny's hand in mine as if that act would somehow transfer my knowledge through our skin and she would believe me – I was becoming desperate. "Christ, Jen, I know how this sounds, but it's the truth. You'll see over time as everything I say is going to happen … will happen. It changes nothing about us … nothing."

Jenny pulled her hand back and turned to face George. "I'm so disappointed in you, George. I just don't know what you're playing at, but I had you down as a decent man … how wrong I was!"

"Jenny, lass—"

Jenny turned to me. She wasn't angry, but disappointment oozed from her. "I'm off to bed. I suggest *you* sleep on the sofa." She scraped her chair back and marched out of the kitchen.

I sprung up from my chair, causing it to flip back and crash to the floor, whilst George grabbed my wrist and pulled. I glared back at him as he shook his head.

"Sit, lad."

"Oh, for fuck sake! Can today get any worse?" I blurted, as I buried my head in my hands. On this occasion, which was extremely rare, he didn't chastise me for my vulgar language.

"Lad, she's going to need time. You have to understand that what we've just told her is hard to take. Remember when you first tried to tell me? I just laughed and thought you were a nutter. We can show her the truth over time … we can."

I nodded. Of course, George was right, but how long would it take, and would Jenny stick it out whilst I tried to convince her?

"Lad, remind me of some of the events of this year. I'm hoping you can think of some key ones that will happen soon. It will really help the lass understand this is all true."

"Jesus, George, it's hard to think ... this year is the Queen's Jubilee, but everyone knows that. I've written down about ten years' worth of Grand Prix results in case I forget them, but often I refer back and wonder if I've got some of them wrong."

"Well, lad, you've got them all right so far."

"Yes, I have, and I'm totally convinced I have this year's correct. It's an easy year to remember because Niki Lauda won the title after his crash last year. I predicted Scheckter winning in Argentina last Sunday and scooped over a grand. The manager at the bookies in the High Street has actually barred me. He said I couldn't enter his shop again as I'd cost him three and a half thousand pounds in four months. To be honest with you, winning bets at the bookies has become boring because I already know the result. It's not as if I even need the money, based on the number of diamonds I have stashed in *other* Jason's safety deposit box. There's no fun in it anymore. It's just a money-making process and, to be honest, it's a ball-ache going into the shop. It was so much easier when I was able to place the bets online."

"Online, what's that, lad?"

"Oh, yeah, sorry, George. You remember I said you can access things called websites on your pocket computer, it's through that."

"Ah yes, lad, that radio waves thing."

"Ha, yeah, kind of. Anyway, Reutemann wins next Sunday in the Brazilian Grand Prix, but that's no great shock. Anyone with an interest in motorsport could predict that, so that's not going to cut the mustard with Jen."

"Right lad, nothing you can think of in the next week or so?"

"No, George. It's not easy to recall news items from forty years in the past. Often when I hear a report on the radio I can then piece it together and remember what will happen next, but I would need the prompt first. It's not as easy as you might think. I mean, apart from the Titanic sinking the year you were born, do you know anything else that happened that year?"

George leant back on his chair and rubbed his chin. "No, lad, you're right. Come to think of it, I don't think I do."

I picked up the chair that was still upturned and stared out of the window – my reflection bouncing back at me. I raised my hands in the air and started a conversation with my reflection. "Jason, what are you going to do?" My reflection didn't answer and just played *Simple-Simon* with me.

"1977 ... hmmm ... 1977." My reflection offered nothing new. "I think Marc Bolan and Elvis Presley die this year, but not sure what month."

"Really, Presley ... he's not that old. Who's that Bolan chap."

"Think it's Presley's lifestyle. Heart attack, I think. Marc Bolan, he's a big pop star."

"Never heard of him."

"I guess you haven't," I chuckled. "We're getting nowhere, and we have to sort Martin out as well. Also, Don's going to be a problem as he's fishing for information."

"Lad, I will ensure Martin is okay this week. You worry about Jenny and try and think of an event which happens soon that will convince her." He stood and grabbed his coat. "Chin up, lad. She'll come around."

George left me with my reflection and a large whisky for company.

"I'll have one of those as well, please."

A reflection of Jenny had appeared in the window as I stood at the kitchen sink. I spun around.

"How long you been standing there?"

"Long enough."

14

19th January 1977
10CC

He spotted her going into the pub on his way to meet his contact. It was only a fleeting glance as he waited at the traffic lights at the top of Coldhams Lane. She must have walked from the car park, which backed onto the alley that led through to the Broxworth Estate. He watched as she hovered at the pub entrance, checking her makeup in a compact mirror. He wanted her, but he had to meet his contact and couldn't keep him waiting – frustrating.

He smoothed his hand over his hair, then plucked a cigarette from the packet lying on the passenger seat and pushed in the cigarette lighter. He wondered who she was meeting.

Nudging the volume up on the radio, *'The things we do for love,'* boomed from the speakers, a quality Sharp system he'd torn out of an old Renault 12 that some dickhead had left unlocked. However, some tosser had ripped off his car aerial and he now had a coat hanger stuck in its place – kids on the estate, he suspected. He'd put the word out for information on who'd done it – they'd pay for that.

A loud car horn brought him back from his lustful gaze as some wanker hooted him because the lights had turned green. She looked up at the traffic lights but not at him. "Fuck off, you wanker!" He gestured in the rear-view mirror, revved the engine and pulled away with a screech of tyres on the wet road. If he was quick and his contact was on time, he could be back here in an hour and then maybe he would wait near the pub until she came out. If she was on her own, he might fancy some tonight.

An hour later, he arrived back at the pub and parked at the rear of the car park, squeezing the car beside the corrugated fabricated garage. He'd reversed in so he had a clear sight of the side of the pub and down Brooks Road.

He'd give it half an hour and, if she came out, he'd take her. If not, it would have to be another night – but he was going to have her soon. Now back in the driver's seat, he waited after he'd peered through one of the pub's side windows to check she was still there. At first, he'd been unable to see her and was about to leave when he spotted her saunter back from the toilets and join a bloke at the far end of the lounge. The geezer had his back to him so he couldn't see who he was, but hopefully she'd leave alone.

Duncan and Julie, the landlord and landlady, were on their own at the bar. Julie was perched provocatively on a barstool on the punters' side of the bar. Her short skirt and stockings stirring memories in him of when he'd had her in the toilets last Saturday whilst her idiot husband stood chatting to a group of locals twenty feet away. In her late thirties, she was older than he liked them, but she had a thirst for sex that Duncan apparently couldn't satisfy, but he could – and had on many occasions. Gawping at Julie through the window, he considered forgetting the other one tonight. He could stroll in, have a pint and take Julie in the ladies toilets or DD toilets as that prick Duncan had renamed them.

Duncan was such a dick-head. He had his close-knit group of crony punter friends and thought he was *'The Man.'* Him and his twattish cronies all laughing when he'd changed the toilets signs from Gents and Ladies to SD and DD – *Shake dry and Drip dry.* "Well, Duncan, you prick, I've had your old lady many times in your DD toilets," he whispered, as he walked back to wait in his car.

He decided he wanted the other one tonight, but only if she was alone when she left so he could easily take her. If not, the backup plan – he would go back in later and take Julie. She was constantly gagging for it – she never let him down.

Half an hour passed and, with three cigarette butts flicked out of the car window, he decided to give up. It would have to be another night – but soon – he had to have her. Tonight, he'd have Julie as a consolation prize – she'd just have to do. At least she was always willing, and there was no fight or forcing himself, although that was the part he loved most. It was a pity she didn't struggle just a little bit rather than tugging her knickers aside and begging for it.

He inched his white Ford Capri's long bonnet from its hiding place but quickly applied the clutch and brake as he spotted her. She'd left on her own and was now bounding down Brooks Road towards the estate. She was going to go through the alley – perfect. He reversed up, exited the car and lit a cigarette.

He followed her as she carried on down Brooks Road. Her long blonde hair bounced as it flowed over the collar of her Afghan coat, which covered her tight arse lingering underneath. She swung her suede-tasselled handbag as if she didn't have a care in the world. However, in a few minutes, he was going to change that. It was cold, and snow was in the air, but that didn't matter as she was hot, and he was ready.

He'd started *taking* in the summer. His first was in that very same alley, and now his appetite for taking was growing. It was so much more satisfying taking it than some bird just offering it.

One last drag, he dropped the butt onto the wet pavement and followed her. Even though it was still early, not quite eight o'clock, the rush hour was over, and the street lay deserted. She would arrive at the alley entrance in less than a hundred yards, and she'd have to walk down it to get through to the Broxworth because there was no other way through.

He kept close to the bushes that overhung the terraced houses' garden walls which stretched down the road's left-hand side. He checked his balaclava in his coat pocket and felt the woollen fabric between his fingers. He'd slip it on as soon as she entered the alley, and she'd be all his to enjoy.

She didn't even stop to look, not even a glance. The silly girl just turned into the dark alley without a care in the world. Yes, this was fate tonight. Those traffic lights earlier were on red so he could see her going into the pub. It was meant to be, and now only a few seconds to go before he'd get what he wanted. The anticipation and excitement were a drug, an irresistible thirst that was building in him.

He reached the alleyway entrance, stopped, held his breath, and peered around the corner; there she was, only fifty yards ahead. Although pitch black, he could make out her movement as she marched through the alley in her knee-high white boots. He slipped on his balaclava but was disappointed he had his heavy boots on, so creeping up would be difficult. Keeping close to the wooden-panelled fence, he picked up his pace. He planned to grab her about halfway through, where the alley opened up behind the block of garages and was only visible from the allotments. Now slightly heady as his heart rate increased, a feeling which came just before he took them. The thrill was intoxicating.

~

Jess replayed the meeting with her father in her mind as she stepped into the alley. She was so chuffed her father had turned up tonight because, after sitting in the pub for over two hours on Tuesday, she'd feared he wouldn't show. Now she felt relieved and excited she had a 'Father'.

Although initially it had been slightly awkward as neither knew what to say, the conversation eventually started to flow. Jess replayed snippets of the conversation over and over, analysing the meeting. He looked younger than her mother and had a modern attitude that surprised her. Maybe that was due to him having a young wife and small children. Tonight was the first step in getting to know Jason, and she decided she liked him.

Now she had her own flat that provided some stability she could prepare for her child's birth, although it was grim and had been empty for five months after some druggy woman overdosed last year. The sadness of the child's father not being there for her was crushing, but she knew she'd just have to get on with it.

Her father had wanted to know so much about her mother, which was not a total surprise after twenty years of no contact. How they were ever together, God knows. Her mother dressed like an old granny with her stuck-up *'I'm better than you'* attitude. She wondered what had happened to make her so old before her time. Especially as her father, who was a similar age, acted and dressed so much younger. He'd even used the word *cool* a few times, which had made her smile.

The alley was devoid of street lamps, but she knew it like the back of her hand and could confidently negotiate her way around the metal dustbins positioned by the back gates of the old flats. Fifty-odd yards along the pathway, Jess jumped in surprise as a cat shot out in front of her. It meowed and then trotted back up the path into the darkness. Jess stopped and caught her breath as her hand shot to her stomach, performing that involuntary maternal act. She swivelled her head around to see it disappear. Jess hated cats, especially Merlyn.

Did she hear a scrape – was that a shoe scraping on the pavement? Jess stood still as she peered back up the alleyway. The light emanating from the flats was too dim and, although her eyes had adjusted, she couldn't see anything. Now her breathing became heavy as if she'd been running. The cat had disappeared, but Jess could still hear it meowing only a few feet away. All she could see were flakes of soft snow as they wisped down, the stillness of the air allowing the flakes to drop vertically to the pavement, laying on her coat sleeves and clinging to the fur cuffs. No, there was no one there, just that bloody cat meowing. Now feeling the cold, she turned and picked up her pace.

He stood utterly still, concerned she could see him or his breath when she'd turned around. He held it for a few seconds as the cat rubbed around his legs, meowing. He considered kicking the cat away but was concerned it would make too much noise, so he encouraged it to go by gently lifting his boot and nudging it. He could see her silhouette only twenty feet away. Her body form became clearer as the snow lay on her head and shoulders, which formed a white glow around her like the Ready Brek adverts. '*Central heating for kids,*' she was hot – it was now – *take* her.

Jess marched on, but there it was again, that scraping sound. Closer this time and too heavy for it to be that cat. She spun around again and gasped. Only a few feet away hovered a dark shadow, illuminated with the white snow that lay across his head and shoulders. Although unable to identify any facial features, a set of teeth appeared as he grinned and closed in towards her. Transfixed by fear, Jess seemed incapable of moving her feet which seemed welded to the pavement – *run Jess, run*—

Too late.

He grabbed her neck, spun her around, and kicked her legs away, causing her to thump down to the pavement.

"No, please, no – I'm pregnant, please, please, no!"

He thrust his palm on her head, squashing her cheek to the cold, snow-covered tarmac. She struggled, which he liked, but she was no match for his size and couldn't wriggle free. Tears clouded her vision as Jess realised no amount of floundering would be enough to move his bulk that now pinned her down.

The cat stepped over her head and looked up at him, but he ignored it and continued enjoying his prize.

15

A few hours earlier
Pony

I'd debated whether I would meet Jess tonight, but hey, could life get any worse? Besides, this wasn't Jess's fault. Although she was *other* Jason's daughter, as far as she was concerned, I was *other* Jason, so I felt duty-bound to meet her. George had omitted Jess's existence in the story, which he relayed to Jenny last night, and I was grateful for that.

Arriving early, I decided to wait before going in and watch to see who entered the pub. Not that I knew what Jess looked like, but I assumed not many twenty-year-old females would be entering a pub at six in the evening on a cold Wednesday in January. The winter had been fierce following the hot summer, and I'd seen more snow in the last month than in my lifetime. Maybe global warming hadn't taken effect yet. I certainly couldn't remember a winter like this one and, sitting here in my Triumph Stag, I missed the heated seats my crushed Beemer used to offer.

Two men, I guess in their mid-fifties, parked up a Dewhurst Butchers Mini-van. Still wearing their bloodstained aprons and white hats they jumped out and marched towards the pub entrance, presumably, grabbing a swift half before finishing up for the evening. They were the only punters to arrive for the next half an hour.

Nothing more had come to light regarding the confiscated typewriter. After last night's events – that problem, although huge – had sunk way down on the disastrous-issues-to-resolve list. After George had left last night, there was a slight improvement when Jenny reappeared at the kitchen door. Of course, she wasn't convinced of my story; I mean, what normal person would be? However, the fact she'd listened to George's and my conversation had helped.

Jenny had demanded to see my list of Grand Prix winners, which I duly showed her after retrieving it from its hiding place from the top of the Welsh-dresser. Jenny had a perfunctory flip through the pages, keeping my book to study again later. Although it would take weeks, it would help Jenny believe every time the race winner was as I'd predicted. Unfortunately, despite her slight thawing, Jenny still relegated me to sleep on the sofa, resulting in acquiring a rather painful, stiff neck due to a somewhat uncomfortable night.

A couple of minutes before six, a young, tall, slim woman with long blonde hair, wearing an old Afghan coat and white knee-high boots, stopped outside the pub entrance. I hadn't seen her approach, so I assumed she must have walked from the other direction.

She rummaged in her handbag and plucked out a compact, then checked her appearance in the mirror as she waved it around, inspecting her whole face. She glanced up as some tosser in a white Capri wheel spun through the traffic lights after being hooted by the driver behind. She then snapped the compact closed and marched towards the pub entrance. It was a reasonable assumption she was Jess – well, here we go, time to meet my daughter – no, *his* daughter.

Apart from the community centre, the Beehive Pub was the nearest drinking establishment to the Broxworth Estate, and I'd frequented it a few times in the past five months. It was a spit-and-sawdust type of establishment, and I'd wondered why Jess had chosen this place. Maybe she lived on the Broxworth? However, if the blonde woman was her, she was not someone I recognised, although I'd only seen her from a distance.

The pub appeared quiet, with only the two blood-stained butchers sitting at the bar, chatting to a woman I recognised as the landlady, perched on a barstool. Her low-cut, skin-tight top barely held onto her ample chest. She sat with her legs crossed, causing her short skirt to ride-up, revealing the top of her stockings. The two butchers appeared torn between gawping at her chest and thighs as their heads rotated between the two areas. The blonde, still wearing her coat and sipping an orange juice, waved at me from where she was seated at the end of the lounge bar. I headed her way, assuming she must be Jess or, if not, a working girl looking for business because the pub was well known for hosting that kind of transaction.

"Jess?"

"Yes, hello, are you Jason?" She offered her hand and lifted herself slightly out of her seat.

"Yes, hello," I smiled, unsure what else to come up with. Although I'd improved and was now much more engaging in social settings, this was awkward. Fortunately, after a slow start, Jess filled any awkward silences with her verbal diarrhoea.

It was clear from the conversation that her relationship with her mother wasn't a good one. However, she appeared keen to hear about how her mother and I'd met at university. Of course, I had no bloody idea, so I kept my answers vague.

Concerningly, I discovered that Jess and her mother had returned to Fairfield ten years ago, and Grace, as she now called herself, now lived in the old town. As we'd never met and not wishing to impersonate *other* Jason more than was necessary, I would need to try and avoid her. However, as I had no idea what she looked like, that would be tricky and added another issue to my disastrous-issues-to-resolve list, which was exponentially growing.

As I feared, Jess lived in a flat on the Broxworth Estate, and after extracting Don and Beth from there last year, I was concerned about having another connection to that God-awful place. Jess had attended the City School, like me and every other bugger I seemed to be meeting. She now worked part-time in a second-hand book store in the old town. Reading between the lines, I got the distinct impression she heavily relied on hand-outs from her mother, who'd carved out a successful career for herself, putting that first above Jess or building any other relationships after *other* Jason had left.

Jess didn't seem to blame *other* Jason for leaving her mother, and I detected she considered I was best away from her, stating she was impossible to get along with. Overall, I liked Jess. She was easy to talk to, with a relaxed attitude. However, I had this niggling thought that I knew or had seen her before, and more than once. I couldn't place where, so put it down to this strange situation that she was my daughter, but not, therefore it was my mind tricking me into thinking that she looked familiar.

We both didn't know what we wanted from our relationship. When I asked why she'd now made contact, Jess was at first cagey with her reply. I sensed she had a specific reason for unearthing me at this point, so I pushed her on it when she returned from the toilets. The Dewhurst butchers had gone leaving only the two of us and the landlady at the bar.

"I got you another orange juice."

"Thanks, Dad ... is it okay to call you that?" She flashed a cheeky smile, looking out of the corner of her eye as she lit her cigarette.

"Um ... err, well—"

Jess waved her hand which held the cigarette. Then, propping her chin up with the heel of her other hand, she balanced her elbow on her knee, which now jiggled up and down. She was either nervous or needed to revisit the toilets. "No, I'm only joking – it is an odd situation, though."

"Why now, Jess? You didn't really answer me when I asked earlier."

Jess continued jiggling her leg, blew a plume of smoke towards the ceiling and turned to look at me. "Because you're going to be a grandfather."

"Oh, wow! Well, congratulations ... you didn't mention a partner—"

"Odd word ... you mean a husband or boyfriend, I presume?"

"Yes."

"Well, yes, the father is unfortunately not going to be around. He will be in the future. We love each other, and he'll be there for the child when ... when he can."

"Does he work away?"

"Uh-huh, something like that." Jess dropped her eyes and wiped some imaginary dirt from her boots.

"I can help. You know, financially. I don't want to interfere, but I'm in a position to help."

"Maybe ... maybe ... but that's not why I wanted to meet you ... it was more about ... well, I thought you should know."

"Yes, I'm so glad you did. Look, I want to apologise for not being a father to you, causing you to grow up in a single-parent family. That was wrong, and I'm sorry." Well, it felt the right thing to say, and if *other* Jason sat here and not me, perhaps that's what he'd have said. I certainly wasn't pleased she'd made contact, though, as it was just piling on the problems I now faced. Although George and I knew she was not *my* daughter, as far as the rest of the world was concerned, she was.

Jess shrugged and stubbed her cigarette out. "Hey, it's no big deal. I'm cool with it."

"You really shouldn't smoke whilst you're pregnant. It'll harm the baby."

"Ha, didn't harm me. Mum used to smoke like a chimney. Anyway, that's all a conspiracy theory. Ciggies aren't that bad for you."

Clearly, I wasn't going to convince her, not in this era.

"Can we meet up again? Perhaps I could meet your wife and, you know, my half-brother and sister?"

"Jess ... it's complicated at the moment. I need to tread carefully when I tell my wife about this."

"Fuck, she doesn't know?" Jess plucked another cigarette out of her packet. "You really are a secretive one, aren't you?" Jess grinned, looking intrigued as she could see I was starting to squirm.

Shaking my head, I declined the offer of a cigarette as she lit hers and started her knee-jiggling routine.

"Jess, give me a few weeks, and then we can meet again. All I ask is for a little time. Have you told your mother we're meeting?" Concerned that this Grace Redmond would surface to cause more problems, which would be the tipping point in my ability to cope at the moment.

"No, she probably thinks you still live in South Africa."

"Okay. Can we keep it that way for now?"

"Yup. I've no need to tell her. If she asks if I've found you yet, I'll just lie."

"Jess, thank you. Look, I'm sorry, but I'm going to have to go now. Do you have a phone number I can contact you on?"

She shook her head, looking down at her boots again. "No, the flat hasn't got a phone."

"Right, well, give me your address. You can contact me at school."

I wasn't sure how to deliver an appropriate goodbye. I offered my hand to Jess, which she ignored, instead tightly hugging me, which wasn't what I'd expected. Although I'd just about cleared my affliction of OCD and rarely concerned myself about Ying-Yang, it seemed fate was playing a cruel game with me this week.

When Jess handed me a 'Pony' beermat, the slogan *'Pony the little drink with the big kick'*, with her address written across the middle, it gave me a slight shudder – Flat 120, Belfast House, Broxworth Estate – Carol Hall's old flat.

16

Mary Celeste

I'd lied to Jenny, and it was one of many that I'd spun out over the past five months. Earlier that day, I'd left a note on the kitchen table stating I had a teacher review meeting after school and would be back late. This covered the time with Jess, but I wondered what reception I'd receive as I was home later than planned. That's if I'd get any reception and would have to prepare to spend my second night on the sofa. Or perhaps worse, find my belongings left on the porch with the locks changed.

As I swung the Stag onto the drive, the lack of Jenny's car parked on the drive concerned me. There were no lights on in the house, and the curtains were open, affording it a ghostly vacant look. My home now reminding me of the haunted house at the fairground, which my grandparents took Stephen and me to every summer.

Jenny was always home when I returned from school, so where was she? I immediately thought she'd gone to her parents and, if she had, I prayed she'd said nothing about the previous night. I regarded her parents as friends, and I imagined the disappointment on their faces when Jenny told them she'd made a huge mistake by marrying an unstable nutter. Until I could convince Jenny I'd travelled from the future, I needed my story to be kept between us.

'No chance of that, Apsley, you don't listen! I keep telling you, you're screwed.'

That pesky voice in my head was probably right. Convince Jenny that Martin and I were time travellers. Ridiculous!

But then I considered the reason she wasn't home could be worse. Had she just left me, taken the kids and gone into hiding? Or even more disastrous than that and had a crash, causing the kids to be catapulted through the windscreen because that bloody car had no rear seatbelts? All that time protecting Beth, killing David Colney, and now she would be a dead child following a road accident. Was that a kind of poetic justice, as that was my route here to this world?

Traffic accidents were more common in this era. No one but I could see that, as it seemed normal to everyone because they didn't know any different. The limited or no in-car safety functions, lack of seat belts, and drunk driving totally acceptable – just a matter of whether you could get away with it rather than being socially unacceptable – all added up to frequent car crashes where death was not unusual.

I decided to drive past her parents' house and see if her car was there. At least if it was, I knew she was safe, although it would worry me what she was saying to John and Frances. The journey to her parents' home and back took less than fifteen minutes. Jenny's car was not on their drive, and I'd considered nipping up to Fairfield General to check if they'd been admitted after a car accident, but I decided I was now being dramatic.

Rubbing my hand across the top of the gas fire, I could tell it hadn't been on for hours – where was she? Returning to the kitchen, I grabbed the kettle and next to it was my note from this morning. Jenny had crossed through my words and added on the bottom, *'Will be back later. Get yourself something to eat.'*

No *love you*, or *darling*, written, but then what did I expect? The good news was she was coming back and, so far, it appeared she hadn't had a car accident. I considered ringing around her friends to check if she was there, but that was really unusual for her to go out at this time of night with the kids. It was early evening, and Jenny was a stickler for keeping to the kids' allotted bedtimes.

Laying open next to the note was my Grand Prix results book which Jenny had taken yesterday. The book listed the races with the winner and any podium places I could remember. Also, I'd added any notable incidents, such as significant crashes. I'd reviewed them many times and knew them to be correct. Time travel came with the ability to correct the past, but it also came with a heavy responsibility, something George and I had discussed repeatedly.

Before the police incident on Monday, I'd considered typing a letter to the British Grand Prix driver, Tom Pryce. He was one of the most talented drivers of the '70s and recognised as a potential world champion of the future. However, I knew in March this year, he would die on the Midrand track in the South African Grand Prix. There were two reasons that I never wrote that letter. Firstly, I expected it would be ignored as any sane person would, suspecting it was penned by some mystic with a Ouija board. Secondly, if, by some miracle, he did believe my prediction and decided not to race, the future would be altered. This would render my predictions going forward useless when he won future races, which he wasn't supposed to be in.

Plucking up my notebook and rubbing my hand over the page, I hoped it wasn't for the second reason. Allowing Tom Pryce to die so I could keep winning at the bookies was a terrible reason for hoping my predictions continued to come true. Next to my entry of the March Grand Prix, where I'd written, 'Tom Pryce dies', scribbled in pencil and not in my hand, was a series of question marks. Had Jenny read my book and put the question marks there? The shrill of the phone jolted me back to life. I snatched up the receiver of the push-button trim phone from the wall.

"Evening, son, been ringing you on and off for over an hour."

"Hello Don, sorry I've been at a meeting. You okay?"

"Yes, I'm alright." The phone line became muffled, although I could hear Don talking with his mouth away from the receiver, "Christopher, careful with your drink, please, Sonny-Jim."

"Did you say, Christopher? Don, hello ... hello ... Don, hello."

"Sorry, son. Your boy has got a plastic cup of squash, but he was struggling to hold it."

"Is Jenny with you? I was wondering where she was." At least I'd located her. Although Don was a big part of our lives, I was surprised she was there tonight. Christ, I hoped she wasn't talking about, well – you know what.

"No, that's why I've been calling you. Now look, I don't want to come between you two, and I know something strange is going on with this Martin chap. I'm sure you'll tell me when you can, but Jenny came around about an hour ago asking if I could mind Christopher for her and then went next door with the baby. She's been in there with that Martin chap for over an hour. Now, son, she's a grown woman, and I can't stop her, but something's wrong with that bloke. Sorry, son, I know you said he's a friend, but he's not right, and I don't like the thought of Jenny around there."

"Oh, bollocks! Don, I'm on my way."

My mind was reeling from what was being said between Jenny and Martin, knowing he was a loose cannon. Now I feared he was talking about me when we worked together and what a tosser I was. Then there was Lisa, oh bollocks, he would be talking about my ex-wife, and for sure, everything would be relayed with a negative spin on it.

Don had positioned himself by his front window as I arrived. He caught my eye and beckoned me over. I trotted up to Don's front door as he opened it and stepped out onto the porch, half pulling the door closed behind him.

"Son, listen, don't go in there all-guns-blazing. You need to keep a calm head. Whatever it is, you two have got to sort out, getting heated or angry ain't the answer."

"I know, Don. I know."

"Alright then, son. Off you go. Christopher is happy enough, so don't worry about him. Whatever you say and do next door, remember that lass of yours is special. Don't lose what you have, my boy."

Well, I would try. The events of the last fifty hours had turned my life to shite, but he was right because nothing mattered as much as keeping Jenny. I took a deep breath and rammed the spare door key into the lock. Stepping inside, I expected to hear talking, but no, the house was deathly quiet. Concerned what the next few minutes would bring, I nudged open the kitchen door, spotting plates and cups across the table which Martin had used and left. Presumably, he'd decided he wasn't going to wash up. "Well, mate, there's no dishwasher available now, so you'll have to get used to it," I muttered.

As they weren't in there, I glanced in the dining room and lounge and found what I didn't expect –nothing – the house was deathly quiet. There was only the upstairs to check, but I could see no good reason for them to be up there.

"Hello," I bellowed out to the house – nothing, not a peep – this was like the Mary Celeste.

Placing my boot on the bottom stair, I peered up and called again, but nothing. *No good reason,* I thought. If they were upstairs and quiet – why? Would they be in some lovers' embrace? I had history of this.

Before Lisa and I split up, I had this very same situation when standing on the bottom step and calling out hello, receiving no answer, although I knew Lisa was home. The house was not huge, and I knew she could hear me. At the top of the stairs was the family bathroom. As the door was ajar, I could see Lisa wasn't in there, but still no answer. As I moved up the stairs, that squeaky floorboard had given her away.

Through the stair spindles, I spotted a leg disappear into what is now Beth's bedroom. That naked leg was covered in hair with a snake tattoo above the ankle – a man's leg, not Lisa's. At the time, it was just a spare room with built-in sliding mirrored wardrobes and a double bed. Shocked, I'd frozen on the stairs. It wasn't rocket science; Lisa had another man in the house who was wandering around naked. I remember feeling I really didn't care. In fact, I might even say I was relieved, which is an odd reaction to discovering your wife has a lover in your bed, but I think it was the realisation that we both knew our marriage was over.

As I reached the top step, Lisa replied as she came bounding out of the bedroom in her dressing gown, flushed and sweating. Not being a total idiot, I took the opportunity to make her sweat a little more whilst deciding whether to punch the snake-tattoo man or leave for the pub.

"Lisa, I was calling you."

"Oh, hi, Jason. I've been in bed with a headache. Can you nip out and get some tablets? There aren't any in the bathroom cabinet?"

"Oh, really? I'm sorry to hear that, but I know we have some in the spare room."

"No, no ... we don't, we don't."

"Yes, Lisa, we do. I'll get them for you. I must say you look quite unwell and very hot and flushed."

Although I didn't care she'd been playing away, as we both knew our relationship had been over for some time, my male pride was dented. I was going to milk this moment and get the most out of watching Lisa in her state of panic. Lisa stood by the spare room door, I guess, trying to quickly think of a reason to prevent me from entering and discovering her naked lover. The squeaky floorboard was now playing its repetitive tune as Lisa nervously jiggled on the spot, but I was curious to know who it was, so I pushed my way past. The room appeared empty, but there was only one hiding place, and that would be difficult as those wardrobes were crammed with winter clothes and various boxes of tat. Glancing at Lisa, who squirmed as she stood with her hand planted across her mouth, I grinned ear to ear. I inched open the wardrobe.

"No, you're right. There's none in here. I'll nip out and get you some."

"Oh, God, thank you so much."

The relief on Lisa's face was as if she'd just received the all-clear from some deadly disease. Smiling at her, I laid my hand on her elbow, then turned back to look at the wardrobe. Lisa glared at the five-inch gap between the mirrored sliding door and the wall where some winter coat sleeves had sprung out, and I guess now praying that her nude lover was hidden deep inside behind the coats.

"But it would be good to check anyway. That head must be pounding ... or perhaps you've had a good pounding?"

The relief on her face evaporated as I leaned back and pushed the door open. It glided on its runners, stopping as it nudged the rubber stopper. Nestled between the coats was a pale, hairy male backside. I didn't stop to see the rest of him, as dented male pride had taken over. Instead, I left for the pub, where I proceeded to get hammered.

17

Eliza Doolittle

Why the hell I thought Jenny and Martin would be in a lovers' embrace, I have no idea. But I guess my mind was on over-drive with the concern of what the hell they were talking about, well, more to the point, what Martin was saying. I knew Martin was a *ladies' man* and always seemed to have a volley of women attracted to him, but I was disappointed with myself for thinking Jenny would be sucked in by his magnetism. So, as I checked the bedrooms, I gave myself a bollocking for entertaining those thoughts.

'She's better than that, Apsley. And you should remember how lucky you are, you tosser.'

I agreed with my mind talk as I peered in all the bedrooms. The upstairs proved to be as empty as the downstairs. However, as I glanced out of the back bedroom window, I spotted them standing on the patio, illuminated by the light from the kitchen window. Martin stood holding Beth wrapped in a blanket whilst Jenny powered her way through a cigarette, which was not a good sign as she'd given up as soon as we'd adopted Christopher and Beth.

Steeling myself for what was about to come, I opened the back door as they stepped back to the house. Martin and Jenny looked up in surprise to see me standing there. For a few seconds we all stood still and stared at each other in total silence.

Back in the kitchen, Beth became the prize in a game of pass-the-parcel. Martin handed Beth to Jenny, who in turn passed her to me, so she could remove her coat which she folded and plonked on the countertop. Martin stood in that old parka staring at the floor, which suggested he felt extremely uncomfortable.

"Can we all sit, please?" Jenny instructed, as she took her seat and folded her arms. She seemed very calm and controlled, which was the exact opposite to me and, I suspect, Martin. I shot Martin a concerned look, but all he offered was a raised eyebrow. Beth wriggled in my arms as I tried to settle her.

"Jenny—"

"No, Jason. Please let me say something first," she interrupted, as she held up the palm of her hand to me. "So, Martin and I have had a long chat. At the moment, I just don't know what to think. I have you and George telling me some ridiculous story which Martin here seems to be going along with. I can only conclude this is some elaborate ruse which the three of you have concocted, but for what reason I have no idea—"

"Jen—"

"No, sorry, Jason. Please don't interrupt me. Let me finish what I have to say. What I do believe is that you're a good, honest man."

"Yeah, right!" blurted Martin. Both Jenny and I swivelled our heads to look at him as he slouched in his seat, arms folded and shrugging his shoulders.

"As I was saying, you're a good man, so I can only conclude that there are two reasons for this story. Firstly, I'm wrong about you."

"No!" Although technically, she was correct. *Bollocks.*

"Let's face it, Jason. We met in August last year, so we haven't known each other long and I know nothing about you apart from what you've told me. There's no one in your past you've introduced me to, and your closest friends, George and Don, have only known you for the same amount of time. It would be reasonable for me to conclude that you're not who you say you are." Jenny stared at me, her vivid green eyes boring deep into my skull.

Beth settled as I gently bounced her on my arm as she laid her head on my shoulder. Martin sat there, leaning back on the chair legs, watching the show.

"What's the second reason?"

"The second reason you came up with this story is because it's true, which is frankly ridiculous. What the three of you have concocted is hugely elaborate, so I'm at a loss as to why you would go to all this trouble to come up with it."

"Jenny, we haven't concocted anything; it *is* true! I know how much of a stretch that is to believe, but it is. When we both time-travelled, only our bodies came. I just wish something would have come with us like our wallets or phones, which would show you we *have* come from the future. But hell, unfortunately, all we have is our bloody memories."

"I have a tattoo," Martin interjected, sporting a stupid grin.

"Well, that's great, Martin. Although I'm so pleased for you, what the fuck has that got to do with this conversation?" I raised my eyebrows at him as he grinned back, rocking his chair back and forth.

"Well, I think it might help, that's all. It's a tattoo of my wife's name with our wedding date on it." Martin jumped up and threw off his coat, then yanked up the sleeve of his jumper. "Look, I'll show you." And there it was, on the inside of his lower arm – *Caroline 27 May 2012.*

Jenny stared at it, then looked up at Martin and back at me. "You could've just had that done."

"Why would I have a tattoo like this if it was fake? Anyway, you can see that it's old. If it was new, it would be red and sore around the edges. You can see how hairy my arm is, and that would've taken weeks to grow back after I had it done."

"Jenny, he's right! Look, feel it. That tattoo isn't new."

As Martin sat down and laid his arm across the table in front of Jenny, she rubbed her index finger across it. Fortunately, Martin had dark hair and was covered like a gorilla.

He now looked rather pleased with himself as he turned and grinned at me. "Think I've proved it for you, mate."

Jenny stopped rubbing his arm and huffed. "Well, it's not proof. But I will admit it would be odd to have a tattoo if it wasn't true. Anyway, why would you have a tattoo like that? I thought men only had them if they were in the Navy?"

"Jen, tattoos are really popular with men *and* women in forty years, especially millennials. Tattoos are really sophisticated, and it's considered an art form."

"You don't have one! And what are millennials?"

"No, it was never my thing, and to be honest I just didn't fancy it. Millennials are those born around the '90s up to the millennium … the year 2000."

"And you said women have them as well? That's really odd."

"Caroline has two. One on her ankle of a champagne glass and a rose on her bum," Martin interjected.

Jenny screwed up her face as if a bad smell had just filled the room. "Well, I'm sorry, Martin, I don't think that sounds very nice." Martin appeared offended but chose not to answer back.

"Jen, it was different then. It was common for women to have tattoos ... different era."

"Common, you're right. I wouldn't be seen dead with a tattoo!"

"Anyway, look at his arm. With all that we've said, this has got to help convince you, hasn't it?"

Jenny chewed her lip and shook her head. "Jason, it's ridiculous. How could you time travel?"

"I have four of them, you know," Martin announced, as he stood up and rolled up his trouser leg to reveal another tattoo on his calf. The Manchester United Football Club badge with '*20 league titles Champions 2013*' inked below and again heavily covered in black hair.

I never thought that the act of Martin removing clothing would be such a wonderful moment. However, this second tattoo further supported our story, and this one, as did the first, also had a date on it.

Martin seemed excited now that he had an interested audience to view his body art, and I could see Jenny was intrigued. What I hadn't expected was to see the fourth tattoo just above his right ankle. There was no date on this one, as there wasn't on the stag head on his shoulder, but it was the most distinctive tattoo of the four and the only one I had previously seen. I realised there would be no need for him to drop his trousers and show me his backside if he was so inclined to do so, as I'd already seen it once before nestled in between mine and Lisa's winter coats. Lisa had clearly thought the act of Martin removing his clothing was wonderful as well.

Now knowing that Martin was one of my ex-wife's lovers was somewhat of a shock. However, I shoved that thought to the back of my mind, as the current dilemma was far more critical.

Jenny relayed the conversation she and Martin had had before I arrived, and it seemed that Martin had painted, as expected, a particularly poor account of my character. However, now learning that he was shagging my ex-wife a couple of years ago didn't exactly make him a candidate for GQ's man of the year. The positive note was Martin's account was identical at the points where it crossed over with the one George delivered the night before. Jenny played along, asking questions. Whether that meant she was softening to the idea we were time travellers, I wasn't sure, but it was a good sign – wasn't it?

"Tell me about your ex-wife. I want to know what she was like and why you split up?" I could see it hurt her to discover I was previously married.

"Nothing to tell, really. We married in 2006. Not sure why but we just did. I guess it was okay to start with, but we drifted and then she left me for another bloke." I looked at Martin, raised my eyebrows, and took great delight as he flushed and resembled a cooked lobster. "I think she had a few affairs whilst we were still married."

"Lisa talked to my Caroline all the time. Think she left you because you were a right tosser and a miserable one at that!" he batted back at me.

"Yes, okay, Martin, thank you for that. I think we've established I wasn't the nicest person back then. But to be frank, your input to the state of my marriage to Lisa is not required." And there was a double meaning to that now. "Anyway, I don't think your marriage to Caroline was so perfect, do you?"

"What d'you mean? Caroline and I are very happy. She used to tell me all the time that Lisa had been on the phone moaning about you and wished she could find someone else."

"Well, she did, didn't she, eh?" I pointed at him, now angry that he had the gall to be so high and mighty.

"You two, stop it, stop it!"

We both looked at Jen. She was right, and anyway, why did it matter Lisa and Martin had had a fling? Hell, I didn't care then, so why did it matter now?

"In your motor-racing book, you've written down that one of the drivers dies in March. Is that true?"

"You asking me that question, does that mean you believe me now?"

For a moment, Jenny stared at me, then closed her eyes as I could see the tears welling up, causing her long eyelashes to become moist. She leaned back in her chair and huffed.

"Jen?"

She opened her eyes which now had a watery film across them. "Oh, Jason, I don't know. I want to say yes, but I feel so stupid. My heart wants to believe, but my head is screaming at me that you're some strange man who I should leave now and have nothing more to do with."

"Jen, please don't say that … please." I wanted to leap across and put my arms around her, but I had Beth nestled on my shoulder. Anyway, I didn't think she would accept my hug at this precise point.

"Well, Jason, does that racing driver die? Assuming you're telling the truth for one crazy moment." She picked at a chip of her red nail varnish on her thumb and bit her bottom lip.

"Yes, Tom Pryce dies at the South African Grand Prix in March. It was a horrific accident that also killed one of the marshals."

Jenny leaned forward across the table and pointed a finger at me. "And you're going to let it happen? Why would you just let him die? If you know this, that's as good as murder!"

"What the hell could I do to stop it?"

"Well, you could phone the authorities or write to him. Do something for Christ's sake! You're telling me that two men will be killed, and you do nothing! What kind of man are you, for Christ's sake?" Bollocking delivered, she sat back, folding her arms.

"Jen, listen. I've thought about telling someone, but I've had this problem before, and I know no one will believe me. You don't believe me, so who the hell is going to believe it when I write a letter to Tom Pryce saying you're going to die in a few weeks? Think about it ... no one ... no one will believe that, will they?"

I stood and moved Beth to my other shoulder as my arm started developing pins and needles. Jenny sat with her arms tightly folded, sporting a deep frown across her face. I guess, contemplating what I'd said.

"Oh, for fuck sake. This is bloody nuts ... fricking nuts," Martin blurted, jumping up from his chair and striding off into the hall.

"Where you going?"

"For a piss!"

I walked over to the sink, turning and leaning against it as I stared at Jen. I needed her to believe me, almost wishing Tom Pryce died next week and not in March so she could see I was telling the truth. Although not proud of myself for wishing a man to die early.

"Yes, I do see that. If you said something about it, no one would believe you. But Jason, two men will die."

"Look, Jen, I had the same dilemma last September. George and I discussed it for weeks but never came up with a solution. There's a serial killer in the north of England, and he goes on to be one of the most infamous serial killers of all time. I can't remember how many women he killed, but the murders started last year and continued until the early '80s. George and I just couldn't figure out what to do. I know his name, but not when he kills. To be honest with you, I'm expecting, any day now, to hear that he's killed his third victim."

"What did you do?" her voice had slightly softened.

"I wrote a letter to the police and some newspapers. That may have been a mistake, as the police came to the school yesterday because they've traced the typewriter I used to write that letter. Now I'm concerned about what will happen if they can pin it on me."

Martin padded back into the kitchen and plopped back into his chair. "Pin what on you?"

"I typed a letter last year stating I knew it was Peter Sutcliffe who committed the murders in Yorkshire."

"Who?"

Jenny shot Martin a look. "Do you know who he is? Jason said he was the most notorious serial killer of all time. I'm a bit surprised if you haven't heard of him, or is this where your elaborate story starts to fall apart? Perhaps you two forgot to talk this one through!" The softness in her voice had instantly evaporated. Once again, she looked tearful, and I could sense her anger bubbling. Her head was again winning over her heart. "Well, Martin? Don't just sit there with that gormless expression. Have you heard of this Peter Sutcliffe?"

"Err ... nope. No idea what you're on about." He opened his hands and raised his eyebrows at me.

"Oh, for fuck sake, Martin! What d'you mean you never heard of him? The Yorkshire Ripper ... everyone's bloody-well heard of him!" Now he really was pissing me off.

"Oh, him. Yeah, yeah, of course, I've heard of him. But that was in the '60s or '70s, wasn't it?"

"For fuck sake, Martin, this is the bloody '70s!"

"Oh yeah. Ha, I forgot."

I shook my head in disbelief. Although he was only ten years my junior, he was just like all the other air-heads I used to work with. Far too many millennials had their bloody head stuck in social media rather than actually listening and debating real news. Christ, I even remember Kyle, the office junior at Waddington Steel, didn't even know who Winston Churchill was. When it came up in the office conversation, Kyle thought they were talking about a nodding dog and some insurance company.

"So, you *have* heard of this killer then?" I could feel she wanted him to know – her heart fighting her head for supremacy.

"Yeah, yeah. Some nut job went around killing women. I think they named him the Yorkshire Ripper, after Jack the Ripper. Anyway, what's this letter you're on about?"

I passed Beth back to Jenny and propped open the back door, seriously in need of a cigarette. With my lungs filled with smoke, I bashed on bringing them both up to speed with the events regarding my anonymous letter.

I relayed the story and what had happened on Tuesday at school when the police arrived and removed one of the typewriters. As I recounted my tale, I once again became increasingly concerned that my fingerprints had been lifted from the letters and pondered if they were mine or *other* Jason's. Did we have the same ones? I was reasonably clear if the police could identify the actual machine used, it would be impossible to identify the author without fingerprints. My other concern was what the police wanted with the author, as the killings seemed to have stopped or had he just taken a break. However, any day now, I expected there would be news of another gruesome murder.

One thing for sure was Martin would be absolutely no help, as he wasn't even sure which bloody decade the murders took place in. That all said, the top of my disastrous-nightmares-to-sort list was convincing Jenny who I really was. The pendulum was swinging wildly back and forth, and if the expression on her face was anything to go by, it suggested it wasn't currently in my favour.

"You may not have heard anything from your letter as they have arrested him and are now just tying up the loose ends. If he hasn't committed any more murders, perhaps your letter has stopped him?" Martin offered up.

"Oh, I don't know. It's too much to think about at the moment. The only thing that really matters is you, Jenny, and you trusting and believing me. I just don't care about anything else. It'll be a hell of a long time to wait until March 5th, when Tom Pryce dies, for you to see that *I am* a time-traveller."

"And me! Can I remind you the reason I'm here is because you can't drive properly. Having that crash, you caused my death!" Martin had taken up rocking back and forth on the back legs of his chair with his hands stuffed in his jeans pockets.

"Yes alright, Martin, and you! And yes, I'm sorry I killed you. But right now, I need Jenny to believe me as my whole life depends on it."

"Jason, I don't know. As I've said, it's too ridiculous, and I can't believe we're actually having this conversation.

Anyway, I think it's time to get Christopher home to bed now, and I can't talk about this anymore tonight. My head is thumping. It feels like a bomb has gone off between my ears."

Jenny stood and handed Beth back to me as she leant across to retrieve her coat. I grabbed her hand, but she pulled it away glaring at me. "Don't, Jason. Let's just get home and get the kids to bed."

Martin continued to rock back and forth on his chair, now sporting a stupid grin. "Yes! Yes ... I've got it!"

Jen and I stared at him, both wondering what the cause of his outburst was.

"What have you got apart from that stupid grin?"

"Proof old buddy ... Proof!"

"Martin, spit it out. I'm tired, my head hurts, and I want to get the kids home," Jen fired back, as she fastened the buttons on her coat.

"Back to the Future, my old friend. Back to the Future!"

"Martin, what the bollocks are you talking about?" I was becoming as frustrated with him as Jen appeared to be.

"Back to the future! Come on ... Marty knows when lightning strikes. The exact moment that stops the clock on the Town Hall ... well, we know when lightning strikes!"

"No, I don't. I've no idea when lightning strikes. Anyway, the Town Hall clock worked the last time I looked at it back in 2019."

"Not lightning ... a bomb!" Martin rocked forward on his chair. "We know when there's a bomb!" He jumped up from his chair, causing it to clatter to the floor as he thrust out his arms as if willing me to know what the hell he was talking about.

"Martin, are you playing bloody charades? For Christ's sake, what are you on about?"

"Oh, Jesus, man. Do I have to spell it out for you?"

"Yes!"

"19th January 1977, the Fairfield-Four! At eight-fifteen, a bomb rips through the Bell Pub in town … sixteen people killed and many injured. Bloody hell, man, you must remember all the stories when the four men were released from prison in the late '90s? Their conviction was quashed because of some technicality, and there was uproar in the town about it."

I passed Beth back to Jenny and slid down onto the nearest chair. "Christ, yes of course, but I'm astonished you know the date. I know all about it, but I would never have been able to guess the exact date. You weren't even born, and neither was I for that matter … how the hell do you know when it was?"

"Mum was at the Festival House on St. Stephens Street. She was into amateur dramatics when she was a teenager. That night she was there completing rehearsals as she played Eliza Doolittle in the play, My Fair Lady, and The Bell Pub is opposite. Mum kept all the newspaper clippings in a scrapbook. Apparently, my grandparents were in a right state until they found out she was okay."

"Jason … Jason, he said the 19th of January." Jenny blurted, the colour draining from her as she pointed at Martin. "What's the time now?"

I turned and looked at Jenny, then glanced at Martin. "Oh, bollocks!"

"What?" he said.

"Martin, today is the 19th of January." I looked at my watch. "It's five past eight ... that bomb goes off in ten minutes!"

"Well, that will prove it then!" He grinned, generally looking pretty delighted with himself.

"Martin, in ten minutes, sixteen people are going to be blown to smithereens!"

His jaw dropped, realising the enormity of the situation.

"Have we got the Yellow Pages in here," blurted Jenny.

"Fuck, no." I bolted out of my chair and ran through the open back door to Don's. I raced in, grabbed his Yellow Pages and ran back. Don shouted after me, but I didn't have time to explain, just calling over my shoulder that I'd be back in a moment. Slamming the heavy yellow book on the kitchen table, I thumbed through it as I ripped over the pages.

"Shouldn't we be calling 999?" suggested Martin, as Jenny and I pored over the book with my finger chasing down the page.

"No time," I yelled back.

"What you looking for?"

"Shut up!" Jenny and I yelled in unison. Jenny grabbed a pen from the kitchen worktop. Then, whilst juggling Beth, she made a fist of her hand and hovered next to me with the pen at the ready.

"21748," I yelled.

"217 ... what was the last bit?"

Martin was peering at the place where my finger had stopped, the telephone number and address for the Bell Pub. "Err ... that's not enough numbers. You're missing one. All numbers have six digits."

"Shut up!" We both shouted.

"48 – 21748."

"Got it." Jenny and I ran into the hall. I grabbed the receiver and dialled whilst Jenny held out her fist where she'd scribbled the number.

It started to ring. Jenny and I stared at each other, our eyes locked together, praying we had enough time. I placed my hand over the receiver as I waited for an answer. "Shit, they'll be able to trace the call. I can't do this."

"You've got to. We've no choice! If you're right, people are about to die!"

I grabbed Beth's shawl off Jen's shoulder and wrapped it around the phone's mouthpiece. The ringing just continued. I looked at my watch, eight-eleven. "Jesus, this thing goes off in four minutes. Come on, come on, pick up the damn phone."

After what felt like a lifetime, the call was answered.

"Bell Inn. Hang on, please."

"Hey, hello, hello," but all I could hear was the receiver had been placed down and the man who'd answered it shout, *"1:85, please."* The background noise was full of chat and laughter from what I suspected would be a busy pub.

A thunderous whoomph powered through to my ear, causing me to yank the receiver away from my head. Then there was nothing – no noise – no dialling tone – just some crackles of a disconnected line.

18

20th January 1977

The Deadwood Stage

Alex stopped and consulted his order book at the door of flat 120. Although he always knew what every one of his customers ordered each day, it was prudent to check new ones. Smiling to himself that he was correct, well, he always was as he prided himself on knowing his round. Placing the two milk bottles on the doorstep, one gold top and one silver top, Alex called out as he did at every door, '*Watch out, watch out, there's a Humphrey about.*'

Alex pushed his Unigate peaked cap back on his head – just like Reg Varney – before swinging his wire bottle holder and whistling *'The Deadwood Stage'* as he strode along the landing. He loved Doris Day. It was proper music, not that disco rubbish that continually clogged up the wireless airwaves.

Jess woke as she heard the bottles clatter down on the doorstep and that annoying whistling the milkman always seemed to be doing, the same tune every day. Her eyes felt heavy and sore. For a brief second, she wondered why, but it came rushing back into her head like a tsunami of terror, washing away all other thoughts. The flat felt cold. However, rather than turning the fire on, she pulled her coat tightly around her, desperate to sleep and never wake up. Fighting her thoughts, her stinging eyes released their tears, and she sobbed into the sofa cushions until exhaustion dragged her back to a fitful sleep.

~

Paul eased himself up in bed and reached behind to yank the pillow up behind his head. He grabbed his radio and cigarettes from the bedside cabinet, knocking the stack of Men-Only magazines that slid sideways and tumbled to the floor. Their glossy covers of glamorous naked models sprawling out, with this month's centrefold, Cassy, smiling back at him as she squashed her breasts together, her lips pouting.

"One day, gorgeous, it might be your lucky day." He felt a stirring below as he gazed at her picture and lit his cigarette. Still leching over the glossy photo of Cassy, he poked his tongue out and wiggled it at her as he yanked up the radio aerial, extending it to its full height. Paul thumbed the dial around to the pre-set medium-wave station of Radio 1.

Noel Edmonds was yakking on about his *School Report* slot, and then that knobby jingle 247 radio 1. *"The Drifters for Debbie in Lancashire, and You're more than a number in my little red book,"* announced Noel.

Paul blew the smoke to the ceiling and then leaned down to grab the magazine to get a closer look at Cassy. He turned the magazine to study the centrefold who, with her long blonde hair, reminded him of Patrick's bird. His outstretched arms caused a long blob of ash to drop to his chest, which Paul rubbed into the white cotton, resulting in a long black streak staining the top of his vest. He chuckled to himself; perhaps a trip up to see how that bitch was today. Now Patrick was doing time, and even though she'd told him to piss off in court on Monday, it was the brotherly thing to do.

~

Jess opened her eyes as the daylight eased its way into the room through the yellowed-smoke-stained net curtains. Now shivering, although she was unsure if that was because of the cold or the horrific event last night – perhaps both. With so little sleep and fighting the feeling of exhaustion that tried to pin her to the sofa, she struggled up and lit the gas fire.

There was no way she could report what happened. The police would never believe her. Anyway, they would take the attitude that she was a slag from the estate and probably deserved it. So, what was the point? She didn't know who'd attacked her, so reporting some big geezer wearing a balaclava with breath that stank of stale cigarettes, wouldn't be taken seriously. Also, that description could describe half the blokes living on the Broxworth Estate. No, she'd have to put it behind her and tell no one. Why had she gone through the alley at night? She knew two women were raped last year, so she berated herself for not being more careful.

~

After enjoying a few moments with the picture of Cassy, Paul threw on his clothes that were liberally scattered across the bedroom floor. He planned to attend to business first, a meet with Cal Gower to hand over a package, then some pleasure. Paul hated playing second-fiddle to the Gowers, but that was the order of things. He knew that bending to Cal Gower was a necessary evil to maintain his position and keep the Colney business thriving. No one worried Paul, apart from Cal and his family. He knew his place and the unthinkable consequences of trying to upset the order.

Paul closed the flat door behind him but stood still as he scanned the view in the square below. The Filth were everywhere, uniform and plain-clothes crisscrossing the square near the community centre. He spotted numerous police vehicles, Pandas and at least one Jam Butty. This wasn't good – this meant heavy shit was going down – he knew he'd have to act fast.

Glancing across to the flats of Shannon House, Paul could see Cal staring at him. He held the stare as Cal shook his head and drew his finger across his throat. Paul had been in the drug distribution scene long enough to know his place, and the contents of his jacket pocket would be enough to give him a stretch longer than the courts would slap on Patrick. Cal's actions were clear – if he fucked up now, he was a dead man.

"Fuck." Was this a raid?

Stepping back into the flat, he needed a moment to think. Ma had gone to the shops; pity he needed her help now. The Old-Bill would love nothing better than to catch him holding this lot. Paul held the brick-shaped package in his hand as his mind whirred around, weighing up his options. Patrick's bitch – that was it – if he could get across to Belfast House, he could stash it in her flat. If this was a raid, they couldn't pin it on him, and that silly bitch would go down. However, if they found the package, Cal would kill him. With no other choices in front of him and the need to act fast, Paul left the flat again. All he needed was a few minutes without being seen, and he would be in her flat.

Paul scooted around to the back of the flats, keeping close to the tree line and out of view. He stopped for a moment at the rear of Belfast House, looking at the very spot where his brother, David, had fallen to his death. It had destroyed Ma as David was her favourite of the four boys. For the last few months, he and Patrick had tried to find out what happened that day in September. No way David had just fallen off the roof, and they knew there was way more to it than what that pompous, stuck-up coroner had said.

Refocusing, he moved on to head up to Jess's flat. So far, he'd encountered no one, and The Filth seemed to be focused on Shannon House. Perhaps finally, they had the balls to deal with the Gowers, which would be a result, and he could then climb up the food chain with them removed. Paul Colney, head of the *firm* in Fairfield – he liked the sound of that.

~

Jess's heart leapt as her front door took a fist hammering. She peered around the kitchen door and stared at the obscured glass – the thumping continued.

"Open the fucking door, you bitch, or I'll kick it in."

Paul Colney, why was he at the door? She didn't want that evil bastard in her flat, especially today, but she knew he'd persist. She gingerly moved down the hall, still hugging her coat tightly around herself. "Piss off, Paul. Just piss off," she shouted through the door. Her voice was shaky and high-pitched, as her usual confidence had been left in that alley last night.

"Open this fucking door, bitch. I will, I'll kick it in," he repeated.

Knowing he would, Jess stepped forward and turned the Yale lock. The door flung open, causing the handle to bounce into the wall and nestle into the wall's pre-formed dent before Paul grabbed the frame and slammed it shut.

"What d'you want? I don't want you here," shouted Jess, as she stepped back a couple of paces to maintain the gap between them.

"Shut up, bitch. Make me a coffee and get out of the fucking way." He pushed past her and stepped into the bathroom before slamming the door and sliding the bolt across. Scanning the room, the only hiding places were in the toilet cistern or behind the bath panel. He knelt, took out his penknife and attacked the rusted screws along the bottom edge of the stained wooden board. Unfortunately, the thin blade bent in the screw head. "Fucking hell, come on."

Folding the blade away, he flipped out the longer blade. However, that appeared too fat to fit into the screw head. "Bastard."

"What are you doing in there?"

"Shut up, bitch." He slammed the knife into the lino, stood and repeatedly kicked the panel in fury until it splintered and cracked.

"What's going on!"

Ignoring her, he stood on the toilet seat, lifted the cistern top and gently placed the package on top of the ballcock. It would have to do until The Filth moved on. Paul yanked open the door and faced Jess, who was still standing where she was a few moments ago.

"Where's my coffee, bitch?" he spat at her.

"Get out, get out! What have you done in there?" Jess bellowed at him, her usual confidence now returning.

Paul grinned and stepped towards her. With his face inches from hers, he placed his hands on the sides of her head. "Look, girlie, there's no Patrick now to hide behind, so you'll have to be a good girl for me now." He roughly grabbed her chin, "You keep that pretty mouth shut, and you talk to no one about me. I ain't been 'ere today. You're going to keep something for me for a few hours, okay? Now get your bony arse in that kitchen and make my coffee."

Jess would normally stand her ground with Paul. Although he was a psycho, he never overstepped the mark because Patrick would have killed him – but he was right, now she had no protection. Her only option was to make his coffee and then get him out of her flat as soon as possible.

Paul loomed over her shoulder, her hands trembling as she spooned the coffee into a chipped mug. His breath stank of stale cigarettes as it wafted past her neck, and he rubbed his hand across her bottom. Immediately, with the mug in her hand, she swung around and whacked it into his face. Paul jolted back as he swatted the mug away, which flew across the kitchen and landed on the cooker, cracking as it bounced to the floor.

"Piss off!" she screamed.

Paul stepped closer to her and grabbed her forearms, grinning, with his mouth now only inches from her face.

Jess shuddered – the scene from the alley resurfaced – although it had never really sunk from her mind.

"Watch it, girlie." He pinned her arms to her side, stuck out his tongue and licked her lips – she wanted to throw up.

"Nothing you can do about it, and don't think you can go running to Patrick. He can't help you even if he believed you."

Jess shoved him away. "Piss off!"

Paul stepped back and laughed. "Now get another cup and make that coffee." He rubbed the front of his jeans. "Then, as a thank you, you can have some of this."

"Piss off. I wouldn't touch you! You should be in jail, not Patrick. Even better … dead like your pervert brother!"

Paul leapt at her, spinning her around and pinning her arms behind her back as he leaned towards her ear. "Don't you fucking talk about David, *bitch*."

"You should have been thrown off the flats with him!" She leant forward to get away from the stench of his breath. "Those blokes deserve a medal for ridding the world of that scum brother of yours, and you should be dead with him!"

Paul spun her around again so that she faced him. "What fucking blokes? What d'you know?"

"Nothing!" Jess stared at his wild eyes, realising she'd blurted out in anger and to the worst person possible.

"Yeah, you do, you bitch. Who told you? What do they know?"

"I said nothing! I don't know anything! Let go. You're hurting me."

Paul let go of her arms but grabbed her chin and squeezed, causing her lips to pucker. "I'll fucking kill you if you don't start talking."

Jess felt her knees starting to buckle. She thought of the baby inside her and what would happen if Paul became really violent. She knew this bastard was feeding off her fear, but her uncontrollable shaking wouldn't stop. "Get off me … I'm pregnant. Get off me," she managed to squeeze out through her squashed-up lips.

Paul didn't react to what she said and didn't seem surprised, as if he already knew – but he couldn't know – she'd only told her mother and Jason.

"You won't be pregnant for long if you don't start talking." He tightened his grip on her chin and placed his left hand around her throat. Jess knew this psycho would kill her without batting an eyelid. She had to get rid of him for the baby's sake.

"I saw it happen … I saw it! Please let go of me … please." Jess could feel her airways closing as he squeezed her neck. His eyes black and cold – devil eyes – he was going to crush the life out of her. She didn't have the strength to fight as tears rolled and now accepted the inevitable would happen.

"What—did—you—see?"

Jess felt her head go light as the lack of air scrambled her brain. He let go of her neck as she gasped for air. Before she could compose herself, he grabbed a handful of hair and yanked it hard.

"I killed the last slag that lived in this shit hole. Start talking. Otherwise, you're joining that bitch."

Jess knew he would, and it didn't surprise her that he'd killed before. She had to talk to save her baby. Anyway, she didn't know who'd thrown David to his death. Probably some other low-life like Paul, so what did it matter if she ratted them out.

"Okay ... okay! I'll tell you. Let me go ... I will tell you ... Please."

Paul refused to let go. "Fucking talk, bitch!" he screamed at her.

"I ... I was ... err ... I was walking ... err—"

"Talk!"

"I ... I was walking down Thetford Lane, across the fields behind the flats. I saw two men throw David off ... they threw him off.

"What men?" Paul's nose touched hers as his spit covered her face.

"I don't know ... I don't remember ... Please, I don't know. I think one of them drove off a few hours later in a yellow Cortina. He was too far away to see, but it looked like the bloke on top of the flats because he wore the same denim jacket." Jess's eyes watered as he held her hair tight. "Let me go ... let go, you bastard."

As Paul let go of her hair, Jess shoved him away and took a step back. She momentarily considered sticking her knee in his groin but lost her opportunity as he turned and smashed his boot into the cupboard next to the sink. The flimsy plywood door collapsed and splintered as his foot travelled through it, knocking bottles of cleaning fluid which cascaded and scattered as if he'd delivered a strike in ten-pin-bowling.

Jess's eyes were wide with terror as he stepped towards her. He smiled and stroked her hair.

"There, that wasn't so hard, was it?" He walked to the kitchen door, turned and faced her, "You ain't seen me today. Say nothing. You talk ... I'll kill you."

He grinned and blew her a kiss.

19

Lusardi

We'd only managed to catch a few hours of sleep, as we'd spent most of the night talking. So, as morning came, we were both understandably exhausted. After leaving Martin last night, we'd both driven into town. St. Stephens Street appeared cordoned off, with dozens of emergency vehicles scattered up and down the hill, their blue spinning lights piercing the low grey fog that hung in the air.

After settling the kids, we caught the news that Gordon Honeycombe presented on the ITN News at Ten. The breaking news item was a report that a bomb had ripped through a town centre pub in the Hertfordshire town of Fairfield. There were no details of casualties, but a call received by the BBC from a fringe Irish Republican terrorist group had claimed responsibility. It was reported the group claimed to have tried to deliver a warning call to the pub minutes before detonation but stated the line was engaged.

Jenny said the Bell Pub was run by the O'Briens, a well-known family with strong Loyalist links. This clearly suggested the reason for the pub being targeted. We agonised over the fact that we'd phoned the pub and, whilst on hold, had prevented the terrorists from delivering their warning. Before I'd time-travelled back, had that call got through? Although sixteen people had lost their lives the first time around, would there be more this time because my call blocked the warning call?

There were only two possible reasons Martin knew the precise moment that the bomb was going to explode. The obvious one was he was somehow involved in the bombing. This was the explanation that Jenny hung onto for most of the night. As tiredness took hold of us both by the early hours and her thankfully strong belief in me, she started to come around to the second ridiculous possibility that Martin and I were, in fact, time-travellers. I was fully aware that sleep deprivation was probably the cause for her softening, and by the end of the day, her head would have taken supremacy over her heart.

There was only one topic of conversation at school on Thursday, the bombing of the Bell Pub in town. The whole school seemed to have been placed in limbo, as every time a student, teacher, Trish or Roy opened their mouths, it was to discuss the bombing. Every break time, I found myself with my colleagues huddled around the staff-room radio listening to the updated news reports. By mid-afternoon, it became clear the timeline hadn't changed because sixteen people were confirmed dead – precisely the same number of fatalities the first time around.

I approached Roy regarding the temporary caretaker role, advising him of an old friend's suitability whom I could vouch for. An old friend was the best description I could muster up. In reality, Martin wasn't an old friend, but the bloke who used to take the piss out of me at work and screw my ex-wife. However, I needed to secure him employment, so telling Roy that Martin was some wanker who'd knobbed my ex-misses wouldn't have worked.

Securing a capable caretaker with the necessary skills to change a lightbulb and know which way to hold a screwdriver was way down Roy's list of essential tasks. So, after he replied, *"Yes, yes, fine, whatever, Jason,"* I knew I'd accomplished my mission. However, the thought of Martin at school with his sixteen-year-old mother as a pupil was bound to be a disaster. But hell, at this stage what choice did I have? For sure, he couldn't just sit in that house all day long.

With the school day completed, I zipped up to prepare Martin for his new role. Primarily to check he had everything he needed and talk through the plan so we were both on the same wavelength. That plan would consist of a created history which we would need to keep as simple as possible and memorise.

Parking up on the drive of number eight, I nipped in to see Don. He deserved some explanation of what was happening, albeit more lies. As always, Hawkeye-Nears had spotted my arrival. In fact, he probably spotted me before I even turned up – his snooping abilities were that good. He was there on the doorstep to welcome me and, of course, sporting his tartan slippers.

"Hello, son. Everything alright?"

"Yes, Don, just come to check up on you-know-who, but thought I'd come and see you first. I know you're entitled to some answers."

Don ushered me in through the porch. "Sit yourself down, and I'll get us a drink."

I plonked myself down on the sofa whilst Don shuffled off to the kitchen. Christ, I had to get some sleep tonight. I could feel my eyelids drooping and was starting to lose the ability to function.

Don padded his way back with two glasses and that bottle of whisky. Although I often refused drinking at this hour, I was too tired to argue.

"Right, son, get that down you." He passed me what looked like a triple shot.

Don sunk into the armchair next to the TV and, with a well-practised move, flipped up his legs onto his leatherette pouffe as he sipped his whisky. He stared at me across the top of his glasses but didn't speak.

"Don, I'm not sure where to start …"

During my five months living forty years in the past, I'd become creative and cute on my ability to lie, well, more to the point, withhold the truth. It was a necessary skill that I'd had to master. Five months in, there seemed to be no sign of a reverse time-travel procedure to take me back to 2019, nor did I want that to happen. So I had to be sharp and skilled at keeping my real identity under wraps. As I sat on Don's sofa, nursing a large whisky with drooping eyes, the problem was those skills were not sharp enough to perform as well as I needed them to.

"Son, take your time. As always, I'm all ears. But remember my boy, nothing you say will be a problem for me. You and your family are the most precious thing in my life. Whatever scrape you may be in, all I'll do is be here for you." Don raised his glass and then downed the contents, grimacing as it burned its way down his throat.

"Obviously, you've seen the news last night?"

"Of course, son. Bloody unbelievable. And here in Fairfield. Don't tell me that bloke you have holed up next door has anything to do with that!"

"Oh, no … nothing like that."

"Thank God for that. Although I said it didn't matter what scrape you were in, being involved in a bombing would be a bit of a stretch for me to understand." Don slopped another generous measure of whisky into his glass and waved the bottle at me. I shook my head, declining the offer.

"So, son, who is he next door? And why is your young lady concerned about him?"

"He used to work for me, and he's just turned up out of the blue. There's some things in my past that I wanted to keep under wraps, not only from Jenny but everyone …

nothing dodgy or criminal ... just stuff I want to move on from. Martin is part of that past." I took a sip of the whisky and set it down on the sideboard next to me, realising drinking when tired was not a good idea. "Jenny is pushing for information, which I understand, but as I said, I would rather keep it in the past. I know that's not possible with him here ... so I suppose I'll have to talk it through with her."

Don leant forward and flipped his legs off the pouffe. He held his glass up and pointed at me. "Son, you're going to have to talk to her. If you say it's nothing criminal, you've nothing to worry about. She loves you, and she'll take it in her stride. Don't underestimate that girl. She can cope with your past and move on far better than you think. You mark my words ... d'you hear?"

I nodded, trying to stay awake. "I do, Don ... I do."

"Good. Now I'm not nosing in, but can I help in any way?"

"For the moment, just keep an eye on Martin for me. I've got him a job as a caretaker up at the school to start putting his life together."

"Right, well, as your chief intelligence officer, I can inform you that he had two trips out today. He walked out at about ten this morning and returned about forty minutes later. He had a paper folded under his arm, so I assume he nipped up to the newsagents. Then he went out just after three o'clock in the car for about an hour and didn't come back with any shopping bags, so not sure where he'd been."

Like an adrenalin shot, this news instantly sparked me awake, now concerned that my newly acquired loose cannon was firing large time-travel-cannon-balls all over 1977 Fairfield town. "Right Don, thank you. I need to go and check up on him."

"Bring my Yellow Pages when you come back, can you son? You didn't say what you wanted them for."

I stopped at the doorway to the kitchen, grabbed the door frame and glanced back at Don. No plausible lie was entering my brain fast enough.

"Son, just bring them back, and tell me when you can ... alright?"

"I will, Dad ... I will."

"Good, I'm always here for you, my boy. Now off you go and do what you need to do."

I was so blessed to have Don as my honorary father. He and George were the rocks of my existence, and for sure, I knew how lucky I was to have them as part of my life. Although we'd only known each other for the short time I'd been living in this alternate world, the friendship and trust we'd built were priceless to me. For sure, Don would need answers, and soon. Scooting across to number eight and barrelling through the back door, my immediate concern was what Martin-cannon-ball-Bretton had been up to today.

I found him slumped at the kitchen table with his head in The Sun newspaper. His head shot up as I entered the kitchen and he quickly thumbed back to page three, spun the paper around, exclaiming, and I quote, *"Look at the tits on that!"*

I rolled my eyes as he waved a topless, almost full-page picture of a very young Linda Lusardi at me. "Christ's sake, Martin, is that all you're doing, lusting at nude pictures all day?"

"Well, nothing else to do ... can't even load up *'Pornhub'*. I can't believe there are no mobile phones and no internet. It's like living in medieval times. Do they still have public hangings in this era?"

"Oh, for Christ's sake, Martin, grow up! And I think you can live without *'Pornhub'*. Anyway, with your antics with Lisa, I'd have thought you've already had your fair share of gawping at women's tits!" I seemed to have raised my voice and pulled the conversation back to Lisa. I knew it wasn't that I cared they'd got it together, more the denting of my male pride.

Martin flushed and looked highly embarrassed as he folded the paper and plopped it on the table. The front page displayed the headline *Fear in Fairfield*, with a picture of St. Stephens Street full of emergency vehicles and debris strewn from the collapsed Bell Pub.

"Yeah, that's a bit embarrassing. Sorry about that." Well, it was an apology but not exactly an act of contrition.

"You're sorry ... is that it?" I flung my arms up in exasperation.

"How did you know it was me she was seeing?"

"Remember the day you hid in the wardrobe and revealed your arse?"

"Yeah. But as I said, how did you know it was me? And when did you know? You never said anything, and it was over a year ago. I can tell you if I caught anyone knobbing my Caroline, I'd have smashed his face in!"

"Oh, so no bloke can knob your wife, as you put it? But it's okay for you to knob anyone you like! Double standards, mate!"

Martin nodded and held up his hand.

"I didn't know it was you until yesterday when you showed me your snake tattoo. The very same tattoo on the leg of the bloke hiding in the wardrobe that day."

"Oh."

"Yes. Oh, indeed! How the hell did you and Lisa end up having a fling? It was common knowledge that we were finished, and I'll be honest it really doesn't matter now. Also, I was no saint during our marriage, but I can't understand how you two got together."

Martin shrugged.

I carried on. "I mean, she's about ten years older than you. Lisa was always fit, but your wife was stunning, and more importantly she's a really nice girl. I don't get it ... why would you cheat on her?"

Martin shrugged again.

I plucked up the back of a kitchen chair and slotted myself down in it. Fishing out my cigarettes, I lit up and dragged across a small blue china plate to use as an ashtray that still held the remnants of Martin's lunch.

"Why? It's like having fillet steak at home and nipping out for a Big Mac."

Martin shrugged again. "I did play away a bit. I know it's wrong, but women just seem to be attracted to me. They always give me the come on, and I can't help myself."

"Oh, right, well, lucky you! Mere mortals like me don't have that problem!"

"Well, you've done alright, mate. Your missus is stunning."

"Martin, it's not about how stunning a woman is or her cup size! It's about love. Christ, man, you need to grow up!"

Martin bowed his head, the dynamics of the conversation reminiscent of our time at Waddington Steel. Although he was good at his job, there were occasions in the early days when I'd have to give him a dressing-down regarding his behaviour. As a lad in his mid-twenties at the time, it was to be expected.

He looked up, appearing teary-eyed again. "I'm sorry, Jason. Lisa and I got together in the summer of 2018. There was a BBQ at your place, and you were your usual boring self and didn't join in as you wanted to watch the Wimbledon singles final. After a while, a few joined you, including Caroline. Lisa and I stayed out in the garden and just hit it off."

"You mean Lisa gave you the come-on?"

"Err ... yeah."

"Well, no need to get all teary-eyed. Apart from perhaps my dented pride, I really couldn't give a shit."

Martin sniffed and wiped his eyes on his sleeve. "Ha, I'm a bit teary as I'm never going to see Caroline again, am I?"

I huffed and blew out some smoke. "No, mate, I don't think so. I don't want to go back and, even if I did, I have no idea how that would work."

Martin nodded and looked down at the folded newspaper.

"So, you went out to get a paper today. Where did you get the money from?"

"Your missus. I asked her yesterday if I could have a bit of cash. She didn't mind and gave me a couple of quid. Ha, I thought, bloody hell, that's not going to go far. I felt like a street beggar who'd just been given a penny. I didn't say anything because that would have been rude. Of course, after visiting the newsagents, I realised that two quid can buy quite a lot. The Sun was only five pence, and I bought myself a couple of Cadbury's Rumba bars; unbelievably, they were only four pence each!"

"Right. Did you say anything strange in the shop?" I asked, concerned that he seemed incapable of understanding anything about this era. I mean, had he not heard of the concept of inflation?

"No, not really. Just said to the bloke can I have a scratch card as well, but he just looked at me blankly, so I didn't push it."

"Fuck sake, you're going to have to get a grip. Bloody lottery scratch cards didn't exist in the '70s!"

"Right, that's why he looked at me a bit odd."

"Did you go anywhere else?"

"Frig sake, Jason, you're not my dad. You're treating me like a ten-year-old!"

"Well, you're acting like one!"

Martin huffed and looked back down at the paper, grabbing it and flicking to the back page, which displayed a picture of Brian Clough with the headlines, *'Forest thrash Rovers – Clough says you don't want roast beef every night!'*

I glanced at the text that reported Brian Clough thought it was wrong to have so much football on television, like having a Sunday roast every day. Not sure what he would make of the football media coverage in 2019. I stubbed my cigarette out on the plate – not the best idea – but I knew there wasn't an ashtray in the house. Martin stared at the paper, although clearly not reading it.

"Martin, have you been anywhere else? I need to know."

Martin refolded the paper and tossed it across the table before looking up at me. "Went for a drive, didn't I … just a … just a look around." He shrugged his shoulders, frowned and looked out the kitchen window.

"Just a drive?"

"Yep," emphasising the 'p.'

"Nowhere in particular, then?"

"Nope," again, emphasising the 'p.'

"Did you stop anywhere or talk to anyone on your drive?"

"Nope."

This conversation was how I imagined a conversation would go with a stroppy teenager. As with any teenager being interrogated, his one-word answers were clearly covering the truth.

"Martin, I know we aren't exactly bestie buddies, but the only way forward is complete honesty between us."

Martin looked at me, huffed again and shrugged his shoulders. "Alright, I went up to the school and sat and watched as the kids came out. I wanted to see if I could spot Mum."

"Oh hell. Did you see her?"

"No, well, I don't think so. I don't really know what she looked like at sixteen. I've seen old photos, but that didn't help much."

"Martin, you know you can't talk to her, don't you?"

"Of course! I'm not going to say hello, Mum, am I!"

"You can't talk to her at all. You have to keep away from her … there can be no altering with her timeline."

"I may have to—"

"No! You don't," I quickly interrupted him.

Martin scraped his chair back, sighed as he stood up and walked to the window. "Jason, what the hell am I going to do here in this world? I want to go back. My life was in 2019 … I can't believe I'm actually saying it. It's ridiculous. Time travel, I mean, it's madness."

"I know you do. And no offence, I'd prefer it if you were back in 2019. But for the moment, you're stuck here, and we're going to have to get on with it."

"Do you think that Cortina is a time machine? Perhaps there's a way I can go back in that car?"

"Ha, as you pointed out, it hasn't got a Flux-Capacitor. I've no idea why we both ended up in that car. Look, anyway, to get you doing something, I've secured you a job as a stand-in caretaker at the school. Clive, our caretaker, has had to go in for an operation and will be laid up for six months, so you can drop into that position for now."

"A caretaker! Jesus Christ, is that what my life will be? Emptying bins and sweeping the bloody sports hall!"

"No, much more technical than that. You'll be changing light bulbs, and you may even get to wield a screwdriver if you're lucky." I grinned at him as he swivelled around and leaned against the sink.

"Oh, yeah, very funny."

"Well, for the moment it'll give you something to do until we can work out if we can get you back. We need to get you a national insurance number. George has talked me through the process, and it's a lot easier than in our day. We can use this address as your permanent residence. If we struggle, you'll just have to sit on emergency tax. But you'll get paid in cash, so no need to worry about a bank account at the moment."

Martin raised his eyebrows, shook his head and re-joined me at the table.

"You're going to have to get your head around this era, and quickly, I might suggest. You'll get forty-five quid a week, and it's a forty-two-hour working week, not the thirty-five hours you're used to, plus income tax is at thirty-five per-cent."

"Bloody hell, it's like the fricking dark ages. Do they send kids up chimneys as well?" Martin raised his hands and crossed his eyes, giving him the look of Nookie Bear, who was a guest on The Morecambe and Wise Show over Christmas. Jenny found it hilarious, but some comedy just gets stuck in an era. However, I did love the *'Breakfast Scene'* to the *'Stripper'* music. I really enjoyed some of the old TV programmes, occasionally cocking up with comments like, *'Oh, Jen, you've got to see this. I remember it's hilarious.'*

"Martin, please be sensible. My concern with you working at the school is your mum. You can't talk to her. Look, mate, I need you to promise that you'll just keep your head down and avoid all contact."

He looked down to his lap and pursed his lips, I guess contemplating his new job role. When I'd travelled back, apart from Beth, I'd left nothing behind. Martin had left his mother, a plethora of friends, his wife, and probably a gaggle of extramarital relationships – now he had nothing. In his shoes, I would be in the same situation – everything lost.

"Jason, can I have one of your cigarettes?"

"You don't smoke."

"Do occasionally, usually when out on the piss. But I think I need one." I shoved the packet and zippo lighter across to him. He lit up and coughed.

"I think I know why I'm here." He held my stare, coughed again but persevered with his cigarette. Although I'd just stubbed one out, I leant across the table, plucked up the packet and joined him.

"Go on." I nodded, encouraging him to enlighten me whilst my cigarette bounced up and down in my mouth.

"I'm thinking I'm here to prevent my birth in 1988—"

"Why would you be here to do that?" I blurted, confused that he thought his *mission* was to prevent his own future existence. "And if you did, you couldn't go back even if you wanted to because you wouldn't be born!"

"As I said, my father wasn't my real dad, and I didn't know that until after he'd died. When I was about twenty-one, I was helping Mum with clearing out the loft. In one of the boxes that were full of crap which I took up the tip for her, I noticed a folder with some paperwork. It looked like it needed shredding and not just throwing away. So, before I returned it back to Mum, I read through some of it. One of those letters was the official documents from when my father adopted me. So inevitably, the questions came flowing. At first, she wouldn't tell me anything, but my relentless questioning broke her down in the end. Although I regret pushing her on it, now I know the truth."

Martin took another drag on his cigarette, eyes focused on the burning end, which gave him that Nookie Bear look again. Intrigued about where this was going, I kept schtum and waited for him to continue.

"Mum was raped. So basically, my father is the rapist. She never reported the rape because she was worried about her parents' reaction. Apparently, my grandfather was hurt in the '70s when he tried dealing with a sexual assault that my mum suffered while still at school. She said she knew the rapist, so she couldn't risk her father getting hurt if she'd said anything."

He had a look of sincerity about him that I'd never seen before. What he knew about his biological father was a lot to cope with. Thinking about Sarah, it was horrific to know what that girl would go through ten years from now.

"Oh, Martin, I'm so sorry … that's awful. As you well know, I'm crap in these situations so I'm not really sure what to say. I'm so sorry."

"No, Jason, don't worry. It was a lot to take in at the time, but I just got used to living with it over the years. It was hard thinking that my mum must have hated me as the product of the rape, but she never showed it. She loves me ... I know she does."

"And you say that your mum knew her attacker? Did she ever say who it was?"

He shook his head. "No. I asked, but I knew I was just causing her more pain. She admitted once it was a brother of the boy who assaulted her when she was at school. I decided not to push it any further as my mum wanted to forget it, so I thought I should as well. But sitting here for the last few days, it's consumed me. I don't know when she was attacked as a schoolgirl, but she's school-age now, so it could have already happened ... or going to happen."

Martin looked at me and pointed his cigarette in my direction. "I fully intend to find out who assaulted her at school. When I do, I'll know who my father is, as he will be the brother of that bastard. Once I know that I have to stop him, so Mum never gets raped."

Struck dumb, I gawped at him with my cigarette hanging loose in my mouth, causing the end to droop down. I had a pretty good idea who his real father was.

"What's up with you? You look like you've seen a ghost."

"Err ... no ... nothing." I needed to process this information. I couldn't tell him what I knew, not at the moment, as that could lead him off on all sorts of tangents. For now, I needed this bloke controlled and not going off like a hand grenade at any point.

"Look, Martin, that may be why you are here, although we don't know for certain. Of course, I will help you, but I can't risk you going around questioning all the pupils at school and asking your mum if she's been assaulted yet. We have to tread carefully. Do you understand?"

"Yeah, I get it, but this is why I'm here. So, we're going to have to move quickly on this one in case that assault is soon."

"Okay, look, for the moment, let's get you into that job and take it from there. But you're going to have to trust me. Anyone finding out who we are or a sniff that we claim to know the future will end badly for both of us."

"Alright, alright, I get it! You don't have to go on and on." He stubbed out the cigarette on the plate, which afforded the table a look of my old Uni bedsit – unwashed dishes, cigarette butts and empty beer cans liberally scattered amongst them.

I thumbed out some cash from my wallet. "Right mate, you need to get set up with some clothes. I know I dropped off some of mine on Monday, but we need to get you your own. Here's two-hundred quid. Get into town tomorrow and do some shopping, but remember the clothes are different. You're not going to find Nike t-shirts and trainers. Also, you need some shirts and trousers for school on Monday. Can you do that without causing a calamity that ends up putting you on the front page of the Chronicle or getting arrested?"

Martin took the cash, folded it and rammed it into his trouser pockets. "I'll try," he smirked. The normal Martin had returned after the grim conversation regarding his mother.

"I'll keep the denim jacket you gave me. It's kind of retro, but you can have your pants back."

20

22nd January 1977
Ginger Beer

George and I took a trip to Upton Park on Saturday. Although Jenny loved going to the football, she attended less and less now we had the kids. I supplied George with a rundown of the events from Wednesday night and the call I'd made to the Bell Pub. He was shocked but agreed that, although a dreadful event, it would surely nudge Jenny in the right direction to join the group and form a quartet of time travel believers.

Jenny and I had reached a stalemate over my time-travel story, almost avoiding the subject as if it didn't exist. However, I was pleased to be no longer relegated to the sofa. Although the Hammers wouldn't end up on the sofa, the way they were playing, I wondered if they'd be relegated this year.

Jenny was still having that head and heart tug of war going on. As devastating as it was, the bombing had delivered clear evidence I was who I said I was. However, Jesus, asking anyone to believe my past was such a huge stretch, even for Jenny, who I knew loved me unconditionally.

The Hammers lost again, and after watching their woeful performance George and I consoled ourselves in the Three Horse Shoes with a pint each.

"Do they get relegated, lad? If they carry on playing like this, I'm sure they will. Bloody depressing."

"Don't know, George. Remembering all the league positions from the '70s is a bit of a stretch. Liverpool win the league, and Man United win the cup, but I wouldn't have a clue about any other results. Actually, while I think of it, I need you to put a bet on for me. As I said, most bookies in the town groan when I walk in, and it's getting noticed that I seem to have a crystal ball."

"Yes, I'm sure they do. You'll have to be careful," he chuckled. "I can't get into town until next Saturday. Will that be alright?"

I slipped twenty-quid across the table. "Oh, yeah, that's fine. The bet is for Nottingham Forest to win the league next year. The odds should be huge."

George slipped the note into his wallet. "Will do, lad, but I'll be surprised if they don't win the second division this year. Brian Clough has got his team playing well. Although he is such a big mouth, he gets on my ruddy nerves."

"Ha, no, I don't mean the second division. They win the first division next year, straight after being promoted."

George raised his eyebrows, "Good grief, that Cloughy bloke may be excused for the size of his head if that happens!"

"It does."

"Right, well, I'll stick that bet on next week. I think I'll make it forty-quid, and we can split the winnings."

"Good idea, you can't lose. Anyway, enough of that. I need to bring you up to speed with Martin."

"Oh yes, lad. You said there was a significant update on that front. What's happened?"

I filled George in on my conversation with Martin on Thursday evening regarding his real father being the rapist who'd attacked his mother, plus the fact that she never reported the rape for fear of what would happen. I left out the bit about Martin and Lisa, his love of page three, and his disappointment of not being able to enjoy *'Pornhub'* anymore. I didn't think George needed to know about internet porn, and I didn't fancy explaining it.

"So George, you remember back in September when I told you David Colney had assaulted a girl at school? She's the young girl who works part-time in the Maypole Jewellers shop."

"Yes, lad, good job that evil bloke had that accident on the roof of those flats."

If only he knew, I thought. However, I wasn't sure what his reaction would be if he discovered I'd been involved in David's death. Although George knew David was evil, he wouldn't be too thrilled with that news.

"Yes, quite, lucky that. Anyway, that was Sarah Moore, Martin's mother. Martin said her mother told him she was raped by the brother of the boy who assaulted her. So, that means that Sarah was raped in the late '80s by one of David Colney's brothers."

"Good grief!" George shifted forward and leant across the table. We were now talking in hushed voices as the story started to unfold. "Which brother do you think it was?"

"George, I've no idea. David Colney has three brothers. Paul and Patrick are older than him, and I'm confident they are the two who supplied me with my nose realignment last year. Although I don't know his name, there's a younger brother who's about eleven years old."

"Well, it can't be the younger one, can it? He's only a lad, so it must be one of the older brothers."

"Keep up, George. The rape took place in 1987, which is in ten years from now. The younger brother will be twenty-one!"

"Oh, yes, of course, poor girl. Dreadful business. That whole family needs stringing up."

"You two boys look like Julian and Dick from the Famous Five; all huddled up whispering. What's the next adventure, five on a pub crawl?" sniggered Dawn, as she swivelled around on her stool.

George and I both pulled back and looked up at Dawn and Dennis, both of us now sporting a silly grin. It was lovely to see them both, drinks in hand, and I suspected a few more inside them, even at this early hour. We often enjoyed their company, but this evening we needed some privacy.

"Yes, Dawn, something like that," I offered back, although it was more akin to *'Two in a bit of a fix'* rather than the *'Five enjoying lashings of ginger beer.'*

We both leant across the table again, retaking our positions. "When I came around to see Martin the night after he arrived, he was sitting on the bed. He looked a bit rough, and his glasses were on the bedside table. It was uncanny how much he looked like the Colney twins. At the time, I just put it down to the fact I was tired after arguing with Jenny for most of the previous evening. Also, that day I'd seen Patrick and Paul Colney at court, so I just thought it was my mind playing tricks. But it wasn't. One of those three is Martin's real father."

"Right, lad. From what Martin has said, you're certain it has to be one of them?"

"Yes, it must be. Also, the likeness. Martin looks like a Colney. Even Don-Hawkeye-Nears spotted it last Monday when we all sat in the kitchen at number eight."

"Bloody hell, lad, we're back to square one. This is the same situation we had last year with David Colney. This time we don't know which of the three committed the crime. By the sound of things and what some of the chaps at work say, that whole Colney family are a really rough lot."

"Yes, they are. Don knows all about them from his time living on the Broxworth. The question is, what can I do about it?"

"Lad, we won't be lucky this time with all three of them having an unfortunate accident."

"No. Not this time," I huffed.

"Complicated, ain't it, lad? Presumably, if the one who's a rapist had an unfortunate accident, Martin wouldn't be born. I can't quite work out what that would mean. Would he just disappear in a puff of smoke?"

"It will be the same as my situation when Mum and Dad died."

"No, lad. You took the place of that *other* Jason. Martin has just arrived and hasn't taken anyone's place, has he? It's completely different."

"George! That's it, he has! Martin said that his father would've been his age now. They have the same name, just the *other* Martin Trevor Bretton lives in America. My guess is he miraculously disappeared last Sunday when Martin arrived!"

"Gordon-Bennett! You're right, lad. What we going to do?"

"Well, as before, we have plenty of time. This grim event is ten years in the future. My immediate concern is what will Martin do at school when he starts his caretaker role on Monday."

"Lad, you say we have a lot of time, but I don't think we do."

"Oh, come on, George. Ten years is a lot, don't you think? If we can't sort it out by then we want shooting."

"No. Whoever raped that poor girl didn't just do it once, did he? Evil men like that do it many, many times. He could be raping women right now."

"Oh, Jesus, George, you're right. If it's one of the twins, they could be up to it right now. We need DNA evidence that would stop him."

"What's DNA?"

"It's what's called Genetic Fingerprinting. It's really complicated, but it's a science that can identify anyone from the tiniest amount of body fluid or skin. It was probably the primary tool the police had to catch murderers and rapists in my old world."

"That sounds impressive. But the crime would have to be reported in the first place, and I think you said this Sarah lass didn't report it."

"No, because of what happened to her father. As you said, if it's one of the twins, they could be raping women now. Patrick is up for sentencing on Monday. That could rule him out depending on how long he gets because he'll still be inside in ten years."

"I don't think he will be. Even if they throw the book at him, he won't serve the full sentence and could easily be out in less than ten."

"Hmmm, no, you're right. I'm going to have to find a way of working out which one of the three is responsible. But even if I do … what then?"

"No idea, lad. Look, I better get going. Are you still okay to have Stephen tomorrow? Remember, Ivy and I need to visit Eva in Aylesbury?"

"Yes of course, George. He's no trouble, and it's great for Christopher to have a playmate around."

"Must be odd to have your older brother in the house when he's only five years old," he chuckled.

"Ha, yes, it is, but at least now I can tell him off when he's naughty without getting beaten up."

21

Candid Camera

Before returning home, I zipped up to the Bowthorpe estate to check Martin was okay. With the cash I'd given him last Thursday, he now had some independence. However, based on his previous shopping experience at the local newsagent, I was right to be worried he may have caused all sorts of chaos. I'd given him strict instructions on what he could and couldn't do. However, I was concerned about who he'd interacted with, and if he didn't sort his head out quickly, I feared he'd cause all sorts of time-travel cock-ups.

I didn't stop at the house because the Cortina wasn't on the drive. Heading home, I prayed he was behaving himself, wherever he was. Requiring some cigarettes but, more importantly, urgently feeling the need to see what my loose-cannon was up to, I stopped at the Lipton's Supermarket at the edge of the estate as I'd spotted Martin's car parked out front.

I grabbed a wire basket and skulked around the aisle ends, peering around to see if I could spot him. I received a couple of odd stares from other customers who thought my behaviour was strange. Fair enough, I thought, it probably was. One lady wearing a pink headscarf, elevated by the curlers entangled in her hair, asked me if I was from the Candid Camera film crew and was something funny about to happen. I think she had her eye on a tall pyramid stack of Carnation Milk tins which she expected at any moment to tumble. Choosing not to answer and leaving her mesmerised by the stack of condensed milk, I discovered Martin by the small freezer section.

"Martin, you alright?"

Martin swivelled around, holding a small frozen cheese and tomato pizza. "Oh, it's you. Following me now, are you?"

"Err... no, mate. Just nipped in to get some cigarettes and noticed you up the aisle."

"Oh, right. Long way to come for a packet of fags, but if you say so. Look at this shit." He waved the unappetising pizza in the air, then flicked it back into the freezer as if throwing a Frisbee. "I asked one of the shop assistants where the fresh pizza counter was, and she didn't know what I was talking about. I gave up when she didn't know what oven chips were either!"

I rolled my eyes as he carried on.

"Also, what's the half-pence thing? This bottle of Vosene shampoo has a sticky label saying it's twenty-nine and a half pence. Do I have to buy two things that are a halfpenny so it rounds up?"

"Martin, you're making a dick of yourself." I fished out a halfpenny and gave it to him, which he studied as if he'd discovered a first-century Roman coin.

"Martin, this is 1977. I don't know how many times I'm going to have to tell you to get a grip, but it's over forty years in the past. Things were different!"

"That's 'im. That's the strange bloke I was telling you about. He said he was from Candid Camera. I reckon he's lying."

I swivelled around to find the pink-headscarf-curler lady pointing as she stood next to a middle-aged man in a shirt and tie. His badge, printed on Dymo tape, stated Mr Wilkinson, Branch Manager.

"Excuse me, gentlemen, can I ask what you're doing?" he asked very politely in a pompous manner, with his hands behind his back as he rocked up and down on the balls of his feet.

A few other interested shoppers joined the melee, all looking at what the excitement was on a drab late Saturday afternoon. The pink-headscarf-curler lady was joined by her friend, who sported the same outfit of an overcoat, slippers and those curlers poking out from under a headscarf. Also, a shop assistant dressed in a long green smock-over-jacket moved towards us. He stood there holding his pricing gun after expertly thrashing out labels on a tray of canned food at lightning speed, now holding the said gun as if ready to shoot us.

"Sorry, what's the problem? My friend and I were just doing some shopping," I replied.

Pink-scarf lady nudged her friend with her elbow and winked. "Couple of nancy boys, I reckon. Poofters like that Jeremy Thorpe bloke." Her friend shot her hand to her mouth and giggled.

"Mr Wilkinson, he's the odd fellow who wanted to know if we sold meat-free sausages," stated the assistant waving the pricing gun around.

Martin stood with his mouth open, gawping at the scene as if frozen in time by a witch's spell. The Manager rocked up and down on his toes, arching his eyebrows, awaiting an answer.

"Look, I didn't say anything about Candid Camera. Can we just continue our shopping, please?"

"Yes, you did, nancy boy. You were down there hiding behind the end of the aisle, waiting for someone to walk past those tins," confidently stated Pink-scarf-lady, as she turned and pointed to the front of the shop. The pricing-gun-slinger raised his head to follow where she was pointing. Mr Wilkinson didn't move but continued to rock up and down on the balls of his feet.

"Shall I get them to turn out their pockets, Mr Wilkinson? They're probably stealing."

"Yeah, I think I saw that one stick a packet of Spangles in his pocket," announced the Pink-scarf lady pointing at Martin.

"Err ... sorry, but this is ridiculous. We've done nothing of the sort! We were just shopping," I threw back. Martin was still catching flies.

"Two grown men shopping ... nancy boys ... mark my words, that's what they are."

"No, Mr Bennett. There won't be any need for that. Gentlemen, I suggest you leave the store, please," stated Mr Wilkinson, as he raised his head and pursed his lips, still rocking on the balls of his feet.

This was out of control and, although the accusations were outrageous, I knew it was time to go. Martin-the-hand-grenade had pulled the pin and caused mayhem. I grabbed Martin's jacket sleeve, dragged the fly-catcher out of the shop, and marched him towards his car.

"Martin, I can't believe the chaos you're causing! What's the matter with you? I said on Thursday that you're going to have to get your head around this era. Why on Earth were you asking for meat-free sausages?"

"I'm a vegetarian. I like meat-free sausages."

"Well, they didn't exist in this era! For fuck sake, I thought you had some intelligence. You're like a loose cannon ... you're worrying me."

Martin stood with his hands in his pockets, shuffling his feet. Although he was thirty-one, he seemed to have stolen Kevin's brain and attitude from the Harry Enfield shows.

"Those women, did you hear what they said? They called us poofters! You can't say that ... I mean, there're laws against it!"

"Not in this era, mate. I know the words they used are offensive, but that's what people said in these times."

The two headscarf ladies exited the shop as the manager held the door open for them, then he slid the closed sign across the door whilst he kept a watchful eye on us. The ladies nudged each other as they walked past, nodding in our direction. We both watched them walk on as they turned and sniggered again. I was used to this era's language, but it still shocked me when I heard offensive racial or sexual comments.

"Did you go clothes shopping, as I asked? That t-shirt looks new, although you're still attached to my old denim jacket, I see."

"Yep, all done. Went up town yesterday and spent most of the day there. Gotta say the town is pretty crap without the new Mall Shopping Centre. Did you know there's a Wimpy on Elm Hill?"

"Did you behave yourself? No cock-ups, I hope?" After the last half hour's events, I genuinely regretted letting him loose in Fairfield town centre.

"I'm not a total dick you know!"

I shook my head. "Hmmm. Well, mate, you're doing a good impression of one at the moment."

"Thanks!"

I shrugged my shoulders.

"Most of the town was closed off. You couldn't get up St. Stephens Street at all. Anyway, I suppose you want the change from the two hundred you gave me?"

"No, you keep it. You'll have a couple of weeks before you'll get paid. Let me know if you need any more before then. Sorry, but I'm going to have to get going. I suggest you nip in the chip shop and get yourself some fish and chips. I'd bring you back to my place, but Jen and I are trying to work through some stuff at the moment, as I'm sure you can understand."

"How's that going? Is she any closer to believing?"

"Oh, Martin, I don't know. Although the bomb was terrible, I think it has shifted her thinking to maybe believe we are from the future. I tried to think about what I'd do in her shoes. To be honest, I really don't think I'd believe it."

"I still can't, and we're bloody here. Right, do you reckon they sell veggie burgers in that chippy?"

"Oh, Martin, for fuck sake!"

He grinned. "There … got you! Only joking, mate. I know, nothing veggie in this era." He rolled his eyes. "I'm sure they'll do a battered Mars Bar, though."

22

23rd January 1977
Hot Wheels

Sunday was our first opportunity for Jenny and I to properly talk. Stephen and Christopher entertained themselves with a Hot Wheels racing car track that they'd rigged up from Christopher's headboard, which supplied enough gravity to send their cars through two loop the loops. After pleading for my assistance to connect the track, I was surplus to requirement, and the boys enjoyed themselves going by the sounds of their cheerful shouts.

Beth slept soundly in her pram. She looked contented after her feed, and I wondered what she was dreaming about – perhaps a new pair of Jimmy Choo shoes or a Prada handbag – if she was still the same Beth.

The weather had improved, although still a dreary January. All the snow had vanished apart from Christopher's snowman, which had now shrunk, with its head listing to the right. Its carrot nose now lying on the ground and appeared to have been nibbled at by some passing rodent. I stood by the open back door holding a mug of coffee whilst smoking a cigarette. Jenny joined me at the door and lit a cigarette, both of us gazing out into the garden.

"Martin said you were his boss at that steel company, and all of your team hated you. Is that right?" She looked up at me but didn't touch me. Since that bloody doorbell chimed last Sunday, the point at which my perfect life started swirling down the plughole into the sewers, we hadn't enjoyed any physical contact.

I nodded as I blew the smoke out into the garden. It hung in the air for a brief moment before wisping away in the gentle breeze. "I wasn't aware they all hated me. But I do know I was miserable back then, so I guess it's not surprising." I turned and stared at her, scanning those beautiful green eyes, so desperate to know what was happening in her head.

"You said in this kitchen when you were talking to George that Elvis Presley dies this year ... is that true?"

"Yes. Yeah, he does. Heart attack whilst sitting on the loo, if I remember."

"You can't remember when exactly?"

"No. I have absolutely no idea."

"When you were talking to Beth, you said something about dealing with her abuser. What was that about? I'd forgotten it until today, but now it's worrying me."

"You're talking like you've come around to the idea, and you might believe my story that Martin and I have time-travelled. Do you believe me now?" I turned away to gaze back into the garden for fear of seeing the mistrust on her face.

Jenny laid her left hand on my chest and looked up at me. "I want to ... but it's ... it's so hard to believe it."

I leant around her, stubbed out my cigarette in the ashtray then pulled her close to me. She rested her head on my chest. "Beth was abused as a child by a guy called David Colney. David was a sixteen-year-old boy at my school last year, and he's the boy that fell to his death up at the Broxworth Estate last September."

Jenny pulled her head away from my chest and looked up. "And you killed him?"

"No. But I could've saved him, and I chose not to because I knew his future. Not only did he abuse Beth in the '80s ... he also murdered women in the next century."

Jenny rested her head on my chest again. I closed the back door, but we stayed where we were and held each other close.

"I want you to tell me everything. I'm going to try and believe you. But I want you to tell me everything about your previous life, plus everything George said this week."

I babbled on for ages with a run-through of my first forty-two years and then in much more detail about the last five months. I left out two reasonably significant bits of information. Firstly, the Jess bit, and I don't know why. Something in my head told me to avoid that particular part of my ridiculous adventure. Secondly, the belief that one of the Colney Brothers was Martin's father, as I needed to keep the lid down on that one for the moment.

Christopher and Stephen were contented with their toy cars, Beth slept soundly, and Jenny stayed quiet as I talked. Jenny looked up at me a minute after I had fallen silent, with tears filling her eyes.

God, I hated what I was putting her through. Why did Martin have to follow me back to 1977? Everything would have been perfect if he'd just bloody well stayed where he was.

"What d'you think happened to Jason? The one who was here in your life before you? You know the *other* Jason, as you call him."

"Jen, I don't know."

"But, Jason, people just don't disappear."

"People don't time travel either."

"No, they don't. But you believe you have."

"And you don't? Do you still think this is some elaborate story?"

Jen pulled away and grabbed her handbag from the kitchen table. She rummaged through it, tutting to herself as she searched what seemed to me to be a bottomless pit. The bag's contents were now being flung out onto the table, producing a heap of stuff that seemed too large to be able to fit inside in the first place – as if her bag was a Tardis.

I wouldn't have been surprised if she'd performed one of those magic tricks and pulled out a never-ending coloured scarf, probably with Tom Baker attached. Watching Doctor Who on a Saturday evening had become a ritual. Christopher loved it, but Jenny thought some of it was too scary for him to watch, and I thought the special effects were anything but special.

Plucking up a cotton handkerchief, she dabbed the corner of her eyes. I moved towards her, but she held her palm out and shook her head at me. She puffed out her cheeks, returned to where I was standing and took hold of my hands.

"In your racing car notebook, you've written that Carlos Reutemann wins the Grand Prix in Brazil today." Jenny looked up at me. "You've written that he takes the lead from James Hunt halfway through the race with a question mark at the end. Is that what happens?"

"Yes, I think so. I'm right that Reutemann wins, but I'm a little shaky when he takes the lead. As you know, I'm obsessed with motor racing, but there are many races every year and over fifty years, trying to remember the details of all races is nigh on impossible."

"Will it be on TV? Shall we watch it?"

"Yeah, highlights will be on later tonight. But Jen, what about everything I've said? Hasn't it blown your mind?"

"Yes it has. But it's also quite exciting, if I'm honest." Jenny leant up and kissed me. "What I do know is our little boy and baby girl have a wonderful loving father, who I love with all my heart."

Perhaps my life's excursion down that plug hole on its way to the sewers had halted and had now started a reverse journey. I tapped my coffee cup four times to ensure that it would be the outcome – oh, no, I thought, don't start all that again.

Part 2

23

Mister Byrite

Shirley's cold, almost numb fingers ached. She could see her breath despite occasionally restarting the engine and whacking up the heating control. As the sun sunk low in the sky, the temperature started to drop to freezing point. The worn, dark-brown leather seats in her husband's Rover P6 seemed to radiate cold air through her body. Before pulling off her gloves to rub her fingers, she restarted the car engine and slid the heater control to maximum.

It hadn't been too difficult to find their address as she had the contacts. Although she could've instructed anyone to do her snooping, this was personal. This was *her* granddaughter.

Hitchin Road is the main road running east to west through Fairfield. This particular stretch of the tree-lined road has a parade of small shops nestled between large residential properties on one side and the main entrance to Wardown Park opposite.

Parked near the park entrance, Shirley had now sat for over an hour – freezing her butt off. It was a regular occurrence to see cars parked here, either visiting the shops on weekdays or the park as many were today, so she hadn't attracted any attention from any snooping resident.

But Shirley wasn't here to look at the kids playing on the roundabout, swings or climbing frame. Nor was it to look at the teenage girls on their roller-skates giggling as they held onto each other whilst negotiating the icy paths around the park perimeter.

She did glance at two boys pushing model sailing boats in the small boating lake. She studied the older boy as he carefully kept an eye on whom she presumed was his younger brother. He was thick-set, with broad shoulders, and with his shoulder-length hair styled with a centre parting, he reminded her of her precious son.

She swivelled her head to the right and glanced down Homebrook Avenue, a crescent-shaped road with two junctions to Hitchin Road. She'd positioned the car here as it gave a clear view of number twenty-two, the house she was interested in.

As she kept watch on the house, her mind drifted back to last summer when that stupid girl had turned up demanding money and claiming her son was the father of her unborn child. Then she hadn't believed it and quickly dealt with her, as she did with anyone who crossed her path. But now she knew the truth. Last week, that chance meeting as she came out of the changing rooms in BHS had convinced her Carol Hall had been telling the truth.

She'd been shopping in town, mostly in Marks and Sparks because their knickers were better than anyone else's – not that she paid for them. After picking up some t-shirts for her youngest, Andy, in Mister Byrite – and not paying for those either – she popped into BHS. She'd selected six dresses and then waited for the changing-room attendant to become distracted before she nipped into an empty cubical.

Shirley was skilled at this operation, and the dumb assistants were too stupid to notice. She'd undressed, slipped two dresses on, one over the top of the other, and then reapplied her baggy jumper on top. She took great care to fully tuck the hems of the dresses in her knickers, thus ensuring they didn't drop below her skirt hemline. Then, popping her coat back on, she exited the cubical and smiled at the assistant as she handed her the remaining dresses, stating they didn't fit.

It was at that point she spotted that striking redhead, and presumably her mother, as they could almost pass as twins. Shirley recognised the redhead as she was always up the estate, nosing into other people's affairs. Yes, it was her, that interfering cow from the Council. Then Shirley had spotted the boy, the same boy Carol Hall had dragged along with her the day she claimed her son was the father of her baby.

Was it grandmother's intuition? She didn't know, but she was totally sure that when she spotted that cow's mother cooing at the baby girl in her arms, she knew it was her granddaughter without any doubt. Every beautiful feature, the smile, the eyes – yes, that baby was without question her son's daughter.

Shirley hadn't fully decided what she intended to do about it, but she was just gaining information for now. The more she knew, the better placed she'd be to act when the time came. What she did know, with unquestionable certainty, was her granddaughter belonged to her and not them – whatever any adoption court had ruled.

Deciding she'd seen enough for today, Shirley prepared to drive home. The car heater, although on maximum, had monumentally failed to diminish her shivers. As she put the car in gear, she spotted an old red Cortina pull onto the drive of number twenty-two. A couple in their sixties walked up to the house and rang the bell. The redhead answered whilst holding *her* granddaughter wrapped in a blanket.

Shirley flipped the gear stick back into neutral as she watched them enter the house. Perhaps she'd hang on a bit longer and see who these people were, she thought. She didn't have to wait long – they all came out ten minutes later. A little boy climbed into the back seat of the Cortina, and the redhead stood with whom Shirley presumed was her husband as they chatted to the older couple for a few minutes.

Now it was all slotting into place. There he was, that school teacher, with the redhead cow holding *her* granddaughter. Well, that was going to change.

24

24th January 1977

MI6

I picked Martin up at eight. Fortunately, he was ready and waiting, standing outside the house just as he was that day back in August, forty-two years in the future. This time I didn't moan that he hadn't walked to the end of the street, nor did he have his head in his phone, scrolling through Facebook as we made our journey to school.

Cuddled on the sofa, Jenny and I watched the Grand Prix highlights on Sunday evening. My race prediction was correct and, I knew as every tiny event happened that I could predict, it tugged Jenny closer to believing my story. George and Ivy collected Stephen late afternoon and, after the difficult conversation last Tuesday, Jenny took a moment to talk to George and smooth out their relationship. It was a conversation that I could just tell George was so pleased to have. He'd squeezed my arm and smiled as they left, clearly delighted that Jenny and I were moving in the right direction.

"Right, Martin, here we are. I would imagine the school is pretty much as you will remember it. The sixth form block is missing, but the main building is the same."

Martin looked out of the windscreen, glancing left and right at his old school. The school he'd left fifteen years ago, twenty-six years in the future.

"You okay?" I asked, as he'd said nothing for almost half a minute.

"Yeah. There's a lot of kids about."

"Well, it's a school, so no shock there," I chuckled, as I exited the car.

Martin hopped out of the passenger seat and leant across the roof of the car. "Do I have to do this? I just don't fancy it."

"Yes, you do! Until we can work out whether we can get you back to 2019, you're going to have to do something."

Martin huffed and blew out his cheeks as he looked around the central courtyard at the hundreds of pupils chatting before the school opened up. "Okay. But as we said on Thursday, I'm going to find out about Mum and make sure she doesn't have to suffer, even if that means I can't go back."

I'd mulled over this dilemma many times since last week. I knew his mother's attacker – his father – was one of three people. So, do I tell Martin, so we can try and stop it from happening? Or do I keep schtum? Thus, avoiding the inevitable clash with my favourite family – the Colneys.

"I'm free until ten, so I can show you around and get you set up for the day," I said, as we walked towards the stone steps that led up to the entrance.

I noticed Martin had stopped a few feet back as he gawped at a group of senior girls chatting and laughing about thirty feet away. Facing in our direction, laughing at what her friends had said whilst twiddling her long blonde ponytail around in her hand, was Sarah Moore. As I glanced back to Martin, he appeared transfixed by the sight of his sixteen-year-old mother. Worryingly, when I turned around to look at Sarah, she was staring straight at him and smiling.

Oh bollocks.

I bloody knew this was a stupid idea. But as George had said and, let's face it, everything George said was right – I had no bloody choice. I stepped back, grabbed his jacket sleeve and tugged hard, dragging him towards me. Martin continued staring at Sarah and stumbled, causing Sarah to giggle and blush.

"Martin, come on." I continued to drag him until we had vaulted up the steps and into the main entrance.

"That was my mum!"

"Yes, it was. Martin, remember what I said. You can't draw attention to yourself, and you can't talk to her."

"She's beautiful."

I grabbed his arm again and pulled him to the side of the corridor. "Martin, for God's sake! She's your mum, and she's sixteen!" I delivered firmly but in hushed tones as the pupils were filing in through the main entrance like a swarm of rabid locusts.

"You bollocking adults as well as us lot, Mr Apsley? Reckon this Acting Deputy Head stuff has gone to your head," said Steve Warrington, a senior boy, tramping into school with a group of lads and closely followed by the girls Sarah was with. Of course, this caused a burst of laughter.

"No cheek from you, Warrington," I boomed.

"Sorry, sir," Steve threw back over his shoulder. The girls giggled, and Sarah had another good gawp at her thirty-one-year-old son.

I bundled Martin into the school office. The start to this school day was significantly worse than I'd feared. Surely it couldn't get any worse.

"Morning, Miss Colman. Can I introduce you to Martin? He's our stand-in caretaker."

"Oh, good morning, Mr …. err … Mr—"

"Bretton." he grinned, holding out his hand to Miss Colman.

"Mr Bretton, that's lovely. I'm delighted to make your acquaintance."

"You too, Miss Colman. I hope I'll be able to complete all my tasks satisfactorily whilst holding this position. I'm sure the school will miss the caretaker whilst he's off, but I'll work hard at living up to his standards," Martin replied, still shaking Miss Colman's hand, sporting a broad smile. Miss Colman seemed mesmerised by him.

Jesus, this bloke had every woman on the planet, eating out of the palm of his hand.

"Miss Colman. Hello Miss Colman?" I interjected.

She held his gaze, then patted her hair bun, checking it was all in place. An involuntary action which I'd only previously witnessed when she was talking to Clive. Bloody hell, what's the matter with everyone? Yes, Martin was, I presumed, handsome, but he seemed to have a magnetism that made females go all silly.

"Miss Colman, hello."

She slowly turned her head as she appeared to try to continue to gaze at Martin. "Yes, Mr Apsley, how can I help?"

"I'm going to give Martin the grand tour, but firstly is Roy in?" I nodded to his office door.

"Mr Apsley, please address our headmaster as Mr Clark. I'm fed up with telling you we don't use Christian names. Really, you must address the teaching staff correctly. And yes, he is."

My bollocking over, she scowled at me, then turned and smiled at Martin whilst I rolled my eyes.

"Martin, let's introduce you to Mr Clark!" I boomed, somewhat immaturely, at no one in particular.

"Mr Apsley, please don't get silly now," said Miss Colman. She settled down at her desk, peering over the top of her glasses whilst adjusting the paper in her typewriter.

After a whiz around the school, which Martin already knew well, I hunted down my work colleagues to complete the introductions. Finally, I deposited Martin in the boiler room, leaving him to get acquainted with his screwdrivers and the list of jobs Clive had prepared before going in for his operation.

Fortunately, Martin didn't know any of the teachers as they'd all moved on or retired when he'd attended school at the time of the millennium. Based on his gawping performance this morning when he'd spotted his mother, I wasn't sure he'd have coped with seeing his old teachers in a much younger form. I was secretly delighted that Jayne Hart didn't swoon over him. She was polite but immune to his magnetic charms – I could have kissed her.

With time on my hands before my first lesson, I checked out the school library as I was on a mission to hunt down textbooks on police investigations and criminality. Although the school library was extensive, I wasn't sure such a book would exist and feared I might need to visit the main library in town to acquire the answers I needed.

Luckily, I discovered two well-thumbed books, one written in the '30s and a more recent publication from the '50s. The first book yielded nothing, but the second confirmed my fears that fingerprints could be lifted from a porous object years after. My only hope was those envelopes had been thumbed through many times during the sorting and posting process, resulting in my fingerprints becoming smudged beyond all recognition.

The letters were a real problem, although I knew my fingerprints couldn't be on file as I wasn't yet born. As long as I had different fingerprints from *other* Jason, they couldn't pin it to me without organising an extensive fingerprinting operation of all pupils and teachers. I decided it was unlikely the police would take that course of action for some random anonymous letter. I returned the books and was about to nip off to the staff room when Miss Colman poked her head around the door.

"Mr Apsley ... you're a difficult man to find."

"Yes, Miss Colman," I replied, a little stiffly after my bollocking she'd given me earlier.

"Mr Clark has asked if you could pop through to his office."

I strode back through the marbled floored corridors with Miss Colman trotting by my side. I could tell she was itching with excitement and desperate to gossip, so I decided to help her along as we neared the school office.

"Do you know what Mr Clark wants?" I asked, knowing full well she would blurt everything out.

She stopped, grabbed my arm, and beckoned me closer with a furtive nod of her head as she glanced around the empty school foyer. "Those two policemen who were here last week have come back to see Mr Clark. From what I overheard ..." Miss Colman had another scan around the empty foyer and then continued. "They're retaining the typewriter for evidence in their investigations into some serious offences. I must say that's very irregular. How on earth could one of our school typewriters have anything to do with a crime committed in Yorkshire!"

Feeling myself sweating and becoming dizzy, I grabbed hold of the door frame to the school office. This was a disaster, and it seemed my fears had now been realised. The police had confirmed the typewriter was a match for the letter I'd sent; now, they were closing in on me.

"Oh, Mr Apsley, are you quite alright? You look rather pale. I hope you're not coming down with this flu that's going around. We have a lot of the children off at the moment, and I know Mr Waite has been quite unwell."

I composed myself and dragged my hand across my face as I tried to prepare to meet the two police officers. I knew a confident performance was required. I was aware Jon Waite had been off last week with a flu virus and wasn't surprised he'd caught it as the size of his nose could hoover up anything floating around in the air.

"No, Miss Colman, I'm fine, thank you," I delivered in a slightly higher tone than usual.

"Very well, but you must look after yourself. Mr Clark relies heavily on you to keep the school running smoothly. Hot lemon and honey, with a dash of Navy Rum is what you need."

With great trepidation, I padded into Roy's office, then turned and closed the door, leaving Miss Colman standing outside, presumably with her face inches from the heavy oak door as it closed.

"Ah, Jason, good. Thank you for joining us. Gentlemen, you'll remember my Deputy Head?" He seemed to be quite cheerful, which was surprising based on the information Miss Colman had supplied. His introduction this time had promoted me from Acting to actual Deputy Head. Not sure I remember accepting the position.

"Yes, of course," said DI Litchfield. Both officers were seated in front of Roy's desk. They leant forward, and we exchanged handshakes. DI Roberts briefly inspected the palm of his hand after we shook, presumably wondering why I had a sweaty palm as it was still cold and both men hadn't removed their overcoats. DI Litchfield turned and addressed me as I stood to their left with one hand on the wood panelling for support.

"Mr Apsley, we were just informing Mr Clark that we need to retain the typewriter we removed last week and secure it into evidence."

"Oh."

"We don't believe it has any bearing on the case at this stage, but the procedure is to hold it in case it's required at a later time. I know that will be inconvenient, but I'm sure you'll understand."

I glanced at Roy, who seemed to be relaxed; I presumed because the officers indicated there would be no further investigation, thus not affecting the school's reputation.

"Yes, I understand. I must say it's somewhat intriguing. What's the case regarding? It does seem very strange that one of our students has typed a letter about an investigation in … sorry, where did you say it was?" I thought it would be good to give the impression I'd forgotten what force DI Litchfield had come from.

"West Yorkshire, sir. I'm afraid I'm not at liberty to say, but at this stage, we believe the letter to be a hoax and not relevant."

"Right. Have you investigated what the letter said, then?"

DI Litchfield raised his right hand to scratch the end of his nose and afforded me what I can only describe as a Paddington stare before replying. "I'm sorry, sir, as I said, we're not at liberty to say."

"No, of course." I pursed my lips and nodded, now a bit flummoxed on what to say next.

Both officers stood and offered their hand to Roy and me. Although DI Roberts sneered a little before shaking my hand, probably concerned he would again be left with deposits of my sweat.

"Thank you, gentleman," said Roy.

"Yes, thank you very much," I added, slightly louder than necessary. I wanted to give Miss Colman the heads-up the door was about to open, thus saving her from falling flat on the floor. I succeeded as she'd managed to move a few feet away, giving me a smile as a non-verbal thank you for my warning.

Although Miss Colman started most conversations with, *"As you know, I'm not one to gossip",* we both knew she was. That gossiping I'd found invaluable on a number of occasions, so I was pleased to keep my line of intelligence gathering open and secure. I was sure that MI6 had missed a trick in not employing Miss Colman and Mr Nears over the years – if they had, the Cold War might have ended sooner.

I was obviously pleased the investigation into the letter I'd sent had stalled, or as DI Litchfield had said, was a hoax. However, that also meant any inquiry into Peter Sutcliffe wasn't going to happen. As with the investigation in my old timeline, it seemed this investigation was going the same way – nowhere.

25

Annual Appraisal

Martin somehow miraculously made it through the day without causing any calamities following his gawping at his mother episode earlier. He said he'd worked through Clive's list but was amazed no power tools were available, and he had to fix up a coat hook in the staff room with a hand drill. He seemed relieved that I owned a power drill, albeit very archaic, although brand new.

I reminded him that Clive came from the era when those were unavailable. I advised him to ask Miss Colman for twenty quid from petty cash so he could nip into Great-Mills DIY store and purchase one. I then spent the rest of the journey explaining the concept of petty cash and that it wasn't the content of wallets owned by small-minded people. Also, not to expect the choice of drills to be too extensive and not to ask for a cordless one. Once I had explained all that, he then asked what Great Mills was. He was exhausting.

As with most evenings after school, it was a quick nip into the pub for a swift pint with George before going home. A home that since yesterday had started to restore itself back to my sanctuary. Tonight, I took my Martin-shaped hand grenade along to the pub, although he seemed to have reinserted the pin since this morning. I knew the discussion I was planning to have tonight could well pull that pin right out again. But it was the right thing to do as I was determined to stop Sarah from suffering at the hands of a rapist ten years in the future.

Holed up in our usual seats, George informed us he'd completed some research on articles printed over the last year. He'd engaged the support of a young lad in the archive department and was quite excited talking through the microfiche system. George thought it was amazing that so much information could be stored in such a small space. This wasn't the time to explain the memory capacity of a microchip.

He informed us that two rape cases had been reported in the last year. Both attacks took place at the end of the summer near the Broxworth Estate, but there were no recorded reports of arrests and no further articles regarding the attacks. The two young ladies who'd reported the attacks were in their early twenties and lived in the Fairfield area.

I brought Martin up to speed regarding David Colney. I went with the official version of events and not the Don and my version. So, as far as George and Martin were concerned, it was a lucky event that David accidentally fell to his death. Martin was amazed David Colney was the serial killer who was terrorising the London and Home Counties areas back in 2019. He said, at the time, he wouldn't let Caroline go anywhere on her own as she fitted the profile – in her thirties and blonde.

Now, soaking up the news that this same future serial killer had already sexually assaulted his mother and his grandfather had nearly lost his life because of it last year was a bit of a bombshell, to say the least. He could now fully comprehend why his mother had said nothing when she was raped for fear of her father's reaction and his safety. Understandably, Martin was supercharged, gung-ho, and now ready to attack the Colney family. The pin in the Martin-shaped hand grenade was pulled and about to explode.

At this point, George came into his own, as he described the type of family he was up against and their connection to the Gowers. It didn't really matter what decade you came from; if you lived in Fairfield, you knew what the name Gower meant. This had the required effect of calming Martin down.

The conclusion we all came to was a rapist was on the loose at this time, but that didn't necessarily automatically signify it was one of the Colney twins. Also, as no other rapes had been reported since the summer, the rapist could be Patrick or Paul if we assumed that it was one of them for argument's sake.

As for who raped Sarah Moore in 1987, it could still be any one of the three brothers, assuming Sarah had told the truth that the perpetrator was one of David's brothers. We all agreed as far as Sarah's safety was concerned, time was on our side. The next step was to ask John, my father-in-law, without raising suspicion, if he could make some enquiries with his ex-colleagues regarding the rapes a few months ago.

Martin amused himself with the one-arm-bandit, which I could see he'd been itching to have a go on since we arrived in the pub. I took this opportunity to bring George up to speed with my conversation with Jenny and my meeting with Jess last Wednesday.

George was concerned that Jess had arrived on the scene, but we both knew it was likely to happen at some point. He felt I needed to come clean with Jenny sooner rather than later or ensure that Jess stayed away, as this was for sure not going to end well if I did nothing. I feared he was right.

After dragging Martin away from the fruit machine, which he was not happy about due to being convinced that he was close to winning the two-pound jackpot, I dropped him off and whizzed up to the Broxworth to see Jess on my way home.

I parked near the community centre and traversed my way up to her flat. Returning here delivered a cold shudder as I thought I was rid of this place. Leaving the Stag in the middle of the estate also concerned me as it stood out like a sore thumb. Although not bright yellow like the Cortina, it was a car that turned heads, and the sort that lived on this estate didn't just look.

A group of youths stood near the stairwell, smoking and kicking a brown leather football against the wall. They glanced up at me, but I didn't look at them – the best policy in this place was to avoid eye contact. In the two months since my last visit, when I helped empty Don's flat, I'd quickly forgotten how hideous the estate was.

After vaulting up the stairs onto the landing, I zipped around the corner and spotted Paul Colney stepping out of Jess's flat. He appeared to be holding a package wrapped in brown paper. Fortunately, he was facing in the other direction and headed off to the stairs at the far end of the landing. Why had Paul Colney been in her flat? I stepped back a fraction and hovered, allowing Paul to disappear down the far stairwell. As soon as the coast was clear, I nipped along the grim passageway. I held my breath as it always stank of stale urine, and today was no different. With a quick glance at my old flat door, I tapped on the door of number 120.

No answer.

I tapped the obscured glass again, this time a little harder, concerned if I stood there for too long, Paul Colney might come back up those stairs for some reason.

"Who is it?" came the call from inside.

Not wishing to bellow out my name and announce my presence to the whole estate, I bent down and poked in the letterbox flap. I could see legs in a pair of flared jeans which I presumed belonged to Jess. "Jess, it's Jason … your father." I could see the jeans-clad legs move quickly forward and the door opened before I'd even had a chance to stand.

Jess glanced down at my crouched body and smirked, although that masked a sad face. I'm no expert when it comes to analysing women's emotions, but I guessed she'd been crying.

"Hi, come in, Dad."

I bolted past Jess into the depressing flat. The last time I'd been here was the day I first saw Beth after she was born, and today it looked pretty much the same. Although there were a few different pieces of furniture, it appeared the landlord had made little effort to spruce the place up after Carol's body was removed and the flat closed up. That had been the very same day when I dropped David Colney three floors above my head to his death. I glanced up at the ceiling as if I had x-ray eyes and could see the very spot where I stood on that roof.

Jess closed the door and stroked my arm as she quizzically glanced at me. "This is nice. Thanks for coming around … you fancy a cuppa?"

"I'll have coffee if you have it," I replied, as we moved into the kitchen.

A lit cigarette lay in the ashtray on the windowsill, the bluish curling smoke wisped up and entangled with the aerial of the transistor radio.

"Evening listeners, this is Mark Lawrence, here on Radio Caroline. How long has this been going on — ha, well, since four o'clock. Here's Ace, and yes, you guessed it—How long has this been going on."

This song was always a particular favourite. However, the radio's fuzzy reception was horrific as the music came out of the speaker in waves. I leaned against the sink and pushed the aerial in a different direction.

"Push it against the glass. It seems to pick it up better," suggested Jess as she watched me randomly trying to restore the signal before the song ended. I did miss the ability to just pull up a song whenever you wanted. In this era, unless you had the record, your only hope to hear a particular song was to catch it on the radio. Although I thought it made you appreciate it more when you did. As expected, my efforts were to no avail, and alas, the song ended in hisses and crackles. I couldn't remember when digital radio started, but I was aware I had a long wait.

"You okay, Jess?"

She turned and handed me my coffee. I grabbed the mug but kept my eyes on hers, which were red and puffy with fresh tears welling up to replace the previously dried ones. We'd only met once, and although she was my daughter – but not my daughter – I felt the bond that presumably *other* Jason would have if he was standing where I was. I placed my cup on the pot-marked, rusty draining board, pulled her in close and hugged her. The tears flowed as she sobbed.

After a long minute, she pulled away and fished out a scrunched-up piece of toilet paper that she'd stuffed up the sleeve of her heavy-knit white jumper. She wiped her eyes, looked up at me and smiled. "Ha, sorry, I don't know what came over me."

"You wanna talk about it?" I raised my eyebrows as I reached over to retrieve my coffee.

Jess waved the piece of toilet paper in the air. "No, it's just me. I seem to be teary at the moment."

"Can I ask why Paul Colney was here?"

Jess shot a concerned look at me and narrowed her eyes. "How d'you know him?"

"I don't. But I've come across him a couple of times. I hope I'm not talking out of turn, but he's not the sort you want to be associated with."

Jess grabbed the brown, Whitbread-branded metal ashtray from the windowsill. The cigarette had burnt down to the filter, leaving a fragile cigarette-shaped tube of ash precariously balancing on the edge. She placed it on the table next to a packet of Camel cigarettes and eased herself down onto the metal-framed chair; the red leatherette seat cracked and split, causing the hessian filling to poke out of the sides. I remained standing by the sink, sipping my coffee, giving her time to collect her thoughts. Paul Colney could only have been here for two reasons, selling drugs, or Jess and Paul were in a relationship – both scenarios didn't bear thinking about.

Jess lit her cigarette and lobbed the lighter onto the table, which skidded across the chipped Formica top and landed on the lino floor.

"Sorry," she mumbled, as she blew the smoke to the ceiling.

This encounter seemed so reminiscent of the last time I saw Carol when I stood in the exact same spot. At least this time, the sink didn't smell. I bent down, retrieved the lighter and placed it on the table. Jess nodded a thank you.

"Paul Colney, you're not ... you know ... seeing him, are you?"

She shot me a surprised look. "Good God, no!"

Relieved, I let out a long sigh. Although now concerned if she wasn't seeing that thug, was she a customer?

"Do you know Paul Colney has a twin brother?" asked Jess.

"Yes, Patrick."

She nodded and laid her left hand on her tummy. "Patrick is the father of my child. You may not be aware, but earlier today he was sentenced to twelve years for attempted murder." She looked at her cigarette as she gently twisted the end in the ashtray forming a hot glowing pointed end.

"Oh, right." I wasn't sure what else to say. Notwithstanding my relief to hear that she and Paul weren't in a relationship, the news about her and his thug of a twin brother was no better. Patrick and Paul were both evil hoodlums, and one of them I believed to be a vile rapist. If not now, definitely in the future.

"Patrick isn't like Paul. He's a loving man. I know he's no angel, but he does love me, and he'll love our child."

"Jess, he stabbed a man and nearly killed him. Look, I don't know him, but most normal people don't go around stabbing folk."

Jess wiped her eyes with the back of her hand. "I know, I know." She nodded. "But honestly, he really isn't like the rest of his family."

I plucked out my cigarettes from my jacket pocket and joined Jess at the table, snatching up the other chair that appeared to be in a similar condition to the one she slumped in. Based on the pasting I'd received last year from the brothers, I wasn't sure I could agree with Jess about Patrick's character, although I thought it best left unsaid.

"So, Paul was just visiting? Nothing else?"

Jess screwed her face up. "Like what?"

"Look, I'll just say it. I temporarily lived in the flat next door, and I've got a close friend who lived on the other side of this flat." I gestured with my thumb to Don's old flat. "The girl who used to live here was involved with Paul, and I think he had something to do with her death. He's an evil drug dealer. So yes, I'm concerned that he was visiting you."

"You think I'm doing drugs like that druggie girl who lived here?"

"I hope not."

"No." Whilst shaking her head, she shifted in her chair and stubbed out her cigarette before blowing one last plume of smoke towards the sink.

"Okay, sorry." I leaned back and crossed my ankles. Jess avoided eye contact, presumably trying to hide her teary eyes. I thought she appeared beaten down, not the bright girl I'd met last week.

"You mustn't say anything to anyone because he'll kill me. Last Thursday, the estate was crawling with police. I presume it had something to do with the bombing on Wednesday night. Paul must have panicked, thinking it was a drug raid, so he forced his way into my flat to stash some of his gear. I didn't have any choice as he's a violent thug, so I just had to let him. He came back tonight to collect his stash."

"Oh, hell, I see."

"I wish he'd died last year with his pervert brother. I hate him. Patrick knows he's a psycho, but he is his twin brother."

We fell silent for a few seconds whilst Jess wiped her nose with the scrunched-up piece of tissue. I pondered how my life seemed to be intertwined with the Colney family. David, who I'd had a hand in his death, and in another world was the abuser of my best friend, now adopted daughter. Martin, my ex-work colleague, was the son of one of the Colney brothers, and now my newly acquired twenty-year-old daughter was going to have Patrick Colney's baby. Did I really want Jess with her connection to the Colneys in my life?

This Sunday, my life had started to divert back on track after a hell of a week. Considering this new information, I was concerned about letting this girl into my life. Did I want her to know Jenny and the kids?

"Jess, I still haven't told my wife about you yet." She looked up at me. I guess I could see the disappointment in her eyes and probably expected me to now say that she should keep her distance. "There's other stuff going on at home which I need to smooth out first. I will tell her, I promise. But I just need a little space and time at the moment. I hope ... I hope that's okay?"

Jess bowed her head, seemingly assessing the grim Lino, but didn't answer.

"Jess?"

She put her head in her hands and sobbed. Christ, why was everyone crying all the time? If it wasn't me, it was Jenny, and now Jess? I leant forward in my chair, placing my hands on her arms. At least I was getting used to coping when faced with someone blubbering. In my old life, anyone in tears was my instant cue to get the hell out.

On many occasions, Lisa had pointed out that as her husband, one of my responsibilities was to comfort her when she cried. *'To love and to cherish'* was one of the vows she reminded me of, as I would awkwardly hunt for any escape route.

I recalled when I'd completed the annual appraisals of my staff at Waddington Steel. Bridget, a reasonably low-performing sales junior, had sobbed, no, howled, in my office, when I gave her the feedback that she wasn't performing to the required standard. Tracey, a middle-aged lady on my team, who quite frankly scared the shit out of me, had burst into my office and demanded to know what the hell I'd said as Bridget knelt on the floor wailing. I recall my reply was I had to nip out for lunch as I scooted around them and shot out the door.

I inwardly winced as I remembered those events. Recalling my behaviour in my previous life was always painful, but I felt it was necessary to remind myself what a self-centred, uncaring knob I once was.

I now sat here holding Jess as she sobbed, feeling highly embarrassed about my totally shit leadership skills in my previous life. It certainly gave me a metaphorical poke in the chest that I couldn't let this girl down. If she wanted to be part of my life, then I had to make that happen. I had a responsibility.

"Jess, I'm sorry. I'll tell Jenny soon. I promise."

Jess shook her head and looked up at me. Her wild blonde hair hanging at all angles across her face. "I was raped ... I was raped."

My mouth dropped open as I grabbed her hand. "Patrick raped you?"

"No! I was raped last Wednesday night on my way home from meeting you."

"By who?"

"I don't know. I went through the alley from Brooks Road to the estate. It was dark, and he grabbed me from behind." Her breathing came in short bursts as she tried to blurt it all out. "I don't know who it was, but I'm so worried that he hurt the baby."

"Jess, are the police investigating? Have you seen your doctor?"

She shook her head, causing her hair to fly around in front of her red, teary eyes.

I knelt beside her and held her in my arms. Another rape in Fairfield, and it appeared this was unreported.

"Jess, I think you need to report it … you must."

She peered at me whilst scraping clumps of hair away from her face. "No, there's no point. They know who I am and my connection to Patrick. They won't believe me, and even if they did, they wouldn't do anything. Anyway—" she sniffed again and wiped her eyes with the back of her hand. "Anyway … I don't know who it was. In that dark alley, no one would've seen it happen. So it's a waste of time reporting it."

"But Jess—"

"No! There's no point."

"Jess, I'm sure the baby is fine. I take it you haven't bled since then?"

Jess arched her eyebrows, probably surprised that a bloke would say such a thing. "Err … no."

"Okay, good. So, make a doctor's appointment for tomorrow."

She nodded.

"Do you want me to come with you?"

Jess slowly shook her head before glancing at me and offering a tight smile. "No, I'll be fine."

"Jess, I'm going to have to go. Sorry, but Jenny will be wondering where the hell I am. Promise me you'll see the doctor tomorrow morning?" She nodded again. "I'll pop up tomorrow on my way home and see how you are."

I now felt like poo as I left Jess on her own in the flat, but I had to get off home. I'd offered to contact a friend to see if someone could keep her company, but she declined. For sure,

I needed to get back tomorrow and check she was okay. Well, okay-ish under the circumstances.

I fished out my car key and was about to ram it in the lock when I noticed my car aerial was missing. I stepped back to look at the damage, annoyed that I hadn't retracted it and locked it in position. When glancing around as if to identify the perpetrator, I spotted a few silhouettes standing near Dublin House, momentarily giving away their positions as they dragged on their cigarettes. However, I wouldn't be able to identify the culprit. Kids, I suspected, who were long gone.

God, I hated this estate.

26

Orinoco

Paul leant up against the concrete support at the front of the stairwell to Dublin House. From this vantage point, he had a good view of the central square but was reasonably well hidden from view. He'd watched the Apple bloke come from the Belfast block and climb into a Triumph Stag – nice motor, he thought. But he was intrigued to know why he'd been here on the estate. Paul had last seen him at court last Monday. But he had no reason to be here. The Hall girl was dead, which made him smirk, and the old git next door had moved out before Christmas. So why was he visiting Belfast House? He would have to put the word out and find out. However, that wasn't important. He needed to get some information on the driver of a yellow Cortina, although there were probably hundreds of them about.

Paul lit another cigarette, scrunched up the empty packet of Piccadilly and lobbed it at the can of TopDeck shandy perched on the stairwell. Its position almost invited the potshot before checking his watch as he waited for Andy, his little brother.

Now David was gone, he was going to have to get Andy trained and trained fast. David had been a handy errand boy. Although Andy was only eleven, he needed to grow up and grow up quickly; start pulling his weight and pick up some of the slack that David used to. Paul could then focus on growing the family business, like extending their extortion racket, which was just as lucrative and less risky than supplying drugs to the low-life junkies who caused more hassle than they were worth.

"Where the fuck have you been?" Paul hissed, as Andy appeared from the back of the stairwell.

Andy finished his Cadburys Wombles chocolate bar and let the paper and foil wrappers drop to the floor.

Paul watched the wrapper float down.

Andy shrugged. "The Wombles can pick it up."

"The Wombles?"

Andy stared up at his brother as he swirled the chocolate around his mouth and licked his lips. "Yeah, you know ... Orinoco and that lot."

Paul shook his head. "It's not Wimbledon Common, you know. You need to do some growing up, and fast, kiddo."

Although Paul was almost twice his size, Andy wasn't intimidated by him. He knew Ma would kill Paul if he turned violent with him. Now David was gone, Andy knew Ma was his *'ace up his sleeve'* to protect himself from Paul.

Paul reached inside his jacket and had a quick glance around to ensure no prying eyes. He grabbed hold of Andy's hand and slapped the small brick-shaped package into it. "Cal Gower is waiting for it ... you know where to go. Don't fuck it up; otherwise, I'll rip your throat out."

Andy just stared at him but didn't move.

Paul slapped him around the head. "Go on, shit-head, fuck off."

Andy sneered but begrudgingly left to deliver the package as instructed.

Paul flicked his cigarette butt into the air as he made his way over to the community centre. A couple of low-life snoops should be there and, if they wanted to keep their front teeth, they'd better have come up with some information for him.

Although the community centre was a shit hole, he liked the respect he commanded there. If no Gower was in the bar, he, as a Colney, was at the top of the food-chain. The way everyone averted their eyes and stepped a few feet further away when he reached the bar was real power.

Steve, the bar manager, pulled his pint. He was close friends with his old man, so not intimidated by Paul, but he still played it carefully. He knew how to keep his position secure, which was a delicate balance when dealing with Gowers and Colneys. Paul pulled out a handful of change from his jeans pocket, but Steve shook his head, making it clear no payment was required – the power. Paul leant on the bar as two blokes on bar stools discreetly vacated their position and moved to a table at the far end of the room – the power. Sandy, one of the local slappers, made a point of coming up to him, flirting as she seductively licked the straw sticking out the top of her drink.

"Or'right, Paul? You on your own tonight, then?" She continued to suggestively swirl her tongue around the straw whilst gazing up into his eyes.

Paul just looked at her with disdain.

"You fancy a bit of company tonight ... y'know ... comfort you like, after hearing the sad news about Patrick today?"

Paul looked past her as Barry Holland entered the bar and nodded at him. He pushed past Sandy and headed in Barry's direction. "Piss off, Sandy," he muttered.

"Fucking charming," she threw back, but only in a whisper. She knew getting on the wrong side of Paul would be a huge mistake.

Paul grabbed Barry by the arm and led him to a free table near the window overlooking the car park. "What you got?" he hissed, still gripping his arm.

"You gonna get me a drink?" asked Barry, as he looked at Paul's hand, which pinched his elbow. He realised he might be pushing his luck because Paul appeared not to be in the friendliest of moods tonight – not that he often was.

Paul leant towards his face and tightened his grip on his arm, digging his fingers into Barry's skin. Barry winced.

"You can have your face rearranged if you want?"

Barry pulled his head away. "You're hurting my arm."

Paul yanked him back close. "What you got?"

Barry retrieved a folded sheet of paper from the inside pocket of his black leather biker jacket and held it between his middle and index fingers as he offered it to Paul. Paul looked at the paper between his fingers and then back at Barry, arching his eyebrows.

"Couple of the guys have pulled a list together of owners of yellow MK3 Cortina's in and around Fairfield. They've also narrowed it down to male owners between the ages of eighteen and sixty."

Paul took the paper without taking his eyes off Barry and slipped it into his pocket. "Good, that wasn't so hard, was it?" He pulled a 'twenty' out of his wallet and shoved it in the top zip pocket of Barry's jacket. "Get me a pint while you're at it and set them up."

Barry shuffled off towards the bar, stopping only to tell two blokes to leave the pool table, who both gave him a mouthful of abuse. However, when Barry pointed in Paul's direction, they calmly put their pool cues back in the rack and left the table with their game half-finished.

Paul grinned as he watched the two blokes move away from the pool table, then reviewed the piece of paper that detailed the addresses of twenty-eight yellow Cortinas in Fairfield. "For fuck sake," he muttered. Why did it have to be a popular car? This would have to be a scouting job for Andy. He'd have to miss school for a couple of days to scoot around this lot and check them out.

He made his way over to the pool table, feeling buoyed that he was progressing on the hunt for David's killer. If he could pinpoint the bloke who did it, *he* would then become Ma's favourite son.

"Sandy, don't leave until I'm ready ... it's your lucky night, girl," he called out to the table where Sandy was sitting with three other girls. All the girls looked up and giggled.

Paul snatched a cue off the rack and plucked up one of the blue chalks dotted around the edge of the table before carefully chalking the end whilst Barry reset the balls. Sending the cue ball hurtling into the pack, they scattered, resulting in two spots and one stripe dropping into the pockets. The eight-ball bounced off two cushions before slowly rolling towards one of the middle pockets. It teetered on the edge before dropping.

He booted the table, causing it to nudge a few inches. Paul took his frustration out as he smashed the cue into an empty pint glass. Everyone knew making eye contact with Paul at that precise moment would be an unhealthy mistake.

27

Uber

27th January 1977

As the week wore on, it panned out to be a vast improvement on the previous week. Martin had blown my world apart on that Sunday. Now I seemed to have reached the start of the rebuilding stage of my life after clearing away the debris of the fall-out of his arrival. My life appeared to be following a similar sequence of the events of the Bell Pub. The site had been cleared and made safe following the bombing, and now plans were in place to rebuild an even better one.

For most of my life, I'd followed the black-and-white rule, nothing in the middle, no grey areas. As far as I was concerned, everything had to have a slot to fit into, just like the school's office pigeonholes. Jenny had a clearer vision than me. I thought that perhaps she benefited from some sixth sense that John claimed Frances possessed. If she did, something was telling her to believe my stories of time travel.

What I did know – even though Martin had those tattoos along with the bombing knowledge – it still wasn't enough for most right-minded people to believe the unbelievable. I settled on the thought that she did, in fact, have that sixth sense that told her to believe. Anyway, whatever it was, I could have kissed it because my perfect life started to return to me.

The one issue that wasn't improving was the situation with Jess. However, although she wasn't my daughter, I would treat her as if she were and help her as much as possible. So, as promised, I ventured into the Broxworth Estate on Tuesday evening.

A relieved Jess stated the doctor advised her the baby appeared fine but to be more careful and ensure she didn't fall on the stairs again. Clearly, she was sticking to her decision not to tell anyone she'd been raped and had created a fall-on-the-stairs story. Although I wasn't happy that she'd decided not to report the rape, I had to respect her decision. Knowing how the police viewed the Broxworth Estate's residents, I could easily see she wouldn't be taken seriously if she chose to report the attack.

This era's lack of diversity and inclusion initially shocked me when I landed five months ago. Domestic violence appeared to be treated as a domestic incident rather than a criminal act. The 'Rule of Thumb' was very much still relevant in this era. I'd struggled over the past few months with constantly hearing racist, sexist and homophobic comments.

I often challenged my pupils on their unacceptable language. However, I knew it was just a matter of education. I alone couldn't change society, especially when there were programmes like *'Till Death Us Do Part'* with millions of viewers each week, even though Alf was a happy hammer – no, an unhappy hammer. I knew the program makers were not racist, and the program was poking fun at society and its attitudes. However, many in this era agreed with the character's views and found it funny – I didn't.

Every evening after performing the kids-to-bed routine, which now included my recital of the book 'George the Talking Rabbit' to Christopher, Jen and I settled down to our evening of memory capture, as we called it. This involved Jenny capturing my memories in our new *'Year Book'*, a yellow school exercise book, where Jenny recorded all my memories under each year heading. It became quite apparent that my knowledge of world events from the age of twenty-two to thirty-two was poor, and the pages with headings from

2000 to 2010 were somewhat lacking in content. I could only assume that my youthful interest in politics and world events had disappeared, favouring partying and drinking at that time.

There were lots of '*No Way!*' moments from Jen during these sessions, like when I talked about the break-up of the Soviet Union, the fall of the Berlin wall, Chernobyl, the HIV epidemic, Barack Obama, and John Lennon's death. She found the last on this list particularly upsetting, considering her love of The Beatles. She pushed me on the details of his murder. I knew it happened in 1980 in New York. However, as for the actual date and further details, I had no idea. This revelation led us back down the route of Peter Sutcliffe and Tom Pryce. As the meeting with the police at school on Monday proved, bending time to alter events you are not directly involved with was very difficult to do.

Jenny played '*Let It Be*' on our retro turntable to soothe her upset. She was now starting to realise the weight of responsibility and the difficulty that having future knowledge presented. As a die-hard Beatles nut, she started her mourning for John Lennon three years before anyone else.

Martin had settled into the caretaker routine and, from what I could see, was not causing any time-travel disasters. A couple of my colleagues asked how I knew him as they thought he was a little odd and used strange words. Jayne asked why Martin kept saying, *lol*. Although smitten and clearly affected by his male magnetism, Miss Colman didn't understand why, when Martin described things, he prefixed it with the word *Uber*. Apart from that, he seemed to be behaving himself.

On Thursday evening, we took the kids up to see Don. It was becoming a weekly ritual we all looked forward to. Don was their paternal grandfather they didn't have, as both were already dead. Arthur Apsley died in 1968, *other* Jason's father, who I assume was a fine fellow. And Neil Apsley died twice, 1984 and 1976, who was *definitely* a super splendid fellow.

Jenny cooked supper whilst Don and I entertained Christopher. Beth, as usual, slept through the whole affair. Beth rarely woke during the night or had screaming fits. She was a calm, contented little girl. It was difficult to see that baby growing up to be the Beth I knew, who could be brash, wild, loud, and often the centre of attention. Perhaps it was the nature over nurture argument kicking into play. Both of us, especially Jenny, poured vast amounts of love on that girl, something she didn't enjoy in her previous life. Was nurture changing her personality even from this young age?

Don was clearly delighted to see his surrogate family back in a harmonious state. Jenny and I went overboard on delivering this non-verbal impression so he stopped asking awkward questions about you-know-who next door. Although we loved Don and felt guilty leaving him out of the time-travellers-believer-club, we knew that the initiation he'd have to go through to join would be too much for him to believe.

Don said earlier that day that he'd told a couple of young lads to move on as they were loitering outside his house. He'd recognised one of them as the youngest Colney lad and thought that was very strange, especially as the Bowthorpe Estate was on the other side of town from the Broxworth. Uncharacteristically Don seemed concerned about it, but I said he was probably just playing with a friend from school who lived this way.

Jen produced an enormous toad-in-the-hole, Don's favourite. She ensured he got the biggest helping and, as he tucked into his supper, he looked like the cat that got the cream. After we'd cleaned up the kitchen, Jen and Don played cribbage, a game I didn't understand. However, I remember my grandmother playing it with Stephen back in my old life. Don allowed Christopher to move the matchsticks on the Cribbage board, which he found extremely exciting as he carefully counted along the holes.

Leaving them to it, I nipped next door to say hello to Martin. Although we did see each other every day, I was acutely aware of how lonely he must be feeling. He'd gone from having a plethora of friends – and many female ones, I was discovering – to nothing. Now he didn't even have Facebook or Pornhub to amuse himself with.

I let myself in through the unlocked back door and nipped through the hall towards the lounge, where I expected to find Martin watching TV with a barrel of Watney Party Seven which he'd discovered and said was quite drinkable. As I opened the lounge door and poked my head in, the TV wasn't on. There was the aforementioned large tin of Watney's on the table. However, I received my second unpleasant sighting of his hairy arse as it bobbed up and down whilst ploughing his way between two slim female legs tightly wrapped around his back. A complete set of red varnished nails dug into his back as the lady beneath him repeatedly moaned, *"Yes ... yes ... yes ... yes."*

"Oh!" I blurted, as I stood there transfixed, gawping at them in the throes of passion. My intervention appeared to do nothing to halt their rhythm as he grunted and arched his back with pleasure. At that point, I quickly removed myself and headed back to the kitchen.

A few moments later, just before I thought I'd shoot back to Don's house, Martin came scooting through to the kitchen in his underpants, appearing slightly red in the face from his exertions. He was closely followed by a young woman dressed in platform knee-length black boots and a pair of white knickers.

"Oh, Hi, Jason … err, this is, this is umm—"

"Mandy," the young lady offered as she stood there half-naked and lit a cigarette.

I stood there gawping. Martin turned and copied my surprised facial expression, presumably as shocked as I was that Mandy chose to wander around in just boots and knickers. She smirked, blew out some smoke and looked me up and down whilst I continued to catch flies.

"You're not 'alf bad either; maybe a bit old. You wanna threesome?"

Martin looked at me, clearly embarrassed. I shot him a quizzical look whilst Mandy rested her free arm under her chest. She continued to puff at her cigarette with that smirk across her face.

"Both the strong silent type … I'm alright with that." She jolted her arm up and down, which caused her breasts to wobble. "I've got nice tits, don't you think?"

Martin turned, outstretching his arms as if to corral her from the kitchen. "Mandy, you'd better go … I'll see you later in the week."

Mandy stubbed out her cigarette in a mug on the countertop and peered over Martin's shoulder. "Seeya," she chuckled, as they both left the kitchen.

"Christ," I muttered, and there was I thinking he would be lonely and have no friends. Clearly, he'd moved quickly with her and, as I stood there, I wondered where the hell he'd met her. One thing for sure, she was very young. I hovered in the kitchen, waiting for Martin to return so I could interrogate him and ensure he hadn't blabbed his mouth off on the taboo subject. When he returned, he thankfully had thrown some clothes on. I hoped Mandy had too, after I'd heard Martin close the front door.

"What the fuck are you doing here?" he spat aggressively, with his arms outstretched.

"Ha, well mate, I came around as I thought you might be a bit lonely. It appears not!"

Martin grinned. "She's a real goer!"

"Right. Yeah, I got that impression." I arched my eyebrows and shook my head. "Look, mate, it's none of my business, but you were careful?"

"What, you my dad now! Did I use a condom?" he threw back, rocking his head side to side and rolling his eyes.

"No. I mean your tattoos and, well, you know … where you come from."

"Oh yeah! Didn't think about that. Don't think she noticed them, really."

"No, quite. Anyway, where did you meet her? She looked very young."

"We met at school today when she came to collect her younger sister. I was fixing the hinge on one of the school gates, and we just got chatting as you do. We hit it off, and she popped back to school at the end of the day. You know how these things happen?"

"Not sure I do, to be honest." I just didn't get how some men just seemed to suck women to them without any effort.

Although I'd had the average amount of short relationships at Uni, they were always tricky affairs. Most wouldn't have happened if I wasn't part of a group of lads that included Mark, Joe and Sam. There was a pecking order in the group that put Mark at the top and me at the bottom. Whenever we were clubbing, and on 'the pull' as it was called back then, Mark would always be the girl magnet. He was closely followed by Joe and Sam, leaving me missing out altogether. Sometimes I was lucky and managed to cop off with the remaining free girl if she felt sorry for me or had nothing better to do.

Philip, another close friend who was gay, often used to say he was my 'wingman'. I'd never met anyone who had such a natural ability to talk to the opposite sex with no awkwardness. The girls just loved him. He would often introduce me to a group of girls and, almost immediately, the conversation would become awkward, leaving him to give me a bollocking for just standing there with a stupid grin on my face. No, I definitely didn't *'know how these things happen,'* as Martin had put it.

"Okay, Martin, as I said, none of my business. But please make sure you're careful. You need to have a cover story prepared to explain your tattoos."

"Yeah, okay. You don't need to worry," he replied and grinned.

"Hmmm," I replied, not convinced Martin was taking this seriously.

I pulled open the kitchen door and glanced back at him. "How old did you say she was?"

"Who, Mandy? Nineteen, I think she said."

"Jesus, Martin, she's a child! You're twelve years older than her!"

"You're twelve years older than Jenny, so I'd keep your gob shut, mate!"

"But—"

"See you tomorrow, Jason. Oh, and knock before entering next time. You never know who I might have for company," he smirked and shovelled me out of my own rental property, leaving my nose inches from the back door. A position relative to a door which Miss Colman was quite used to, I mused.

28

28th January 1977
Buzz Lightyear

I arrived at school early on Friday morning. My old Cortina was already parked up, so Martin also appeared to have made an early start and hadn't been worn out by his exertions the night before.

Now I'd acquired the Acting Head role I'd taken over running most morning assemblies, a responsibility which Roy was happy to relinquish. I mixed the process up, moving it away from a Christian-focused assembly, thus saving the pain of hearing the students' poor rendition of a hymn. This also avoided having to wince through listening to old Bummer's dreadful performance on the school piano. His recitals often sounded like a sketch from a Les Dawson show, as he randomly banged out the wrong note, although by mistake, and there was nothing remotely amusing about his performance.

I'd encouraged the Sixth Form students to participate. This supported their development in their ability to perform public speaking. Also, I persuaded the various after-school clubs to complete presentations. I'd borrowed my ideas from Mr Elkinson, my Headmaster from ten years in the future, now realising he was quite progressive. However, I could still remember the Deputy Head, Jones, AKA Hermann Göring, occasionally running assembly, which was how I imagined a roll call would have been in a Nazi death camp. I recall praying he wouldn't make eye contact which could lead to being singled out to perform some terrifying act such as reading aloud from the Bible – an act I remember, oh so well, that I was particularly disastrous at.

The students clearly preferred my assemblies to Roy's dreary affairs. I would always round off with a joke, and I'd developed a cult following from the senior year who all held up apples of different varieties as a mark of homage to my new invigorating assemblies.

These morning events were fast becoming one of my favourite parts of the day. I recalled how my disengaged team reacted to me at Waddington Steel when I held sales meetings with them, most of whom stared out the window or scrolled through their phones. Comparing those painful affairs to these informative and engaging assemblies proved to me I'd made a significant change for the better. Moreover, it provided me with a real sense of value, knowing my students enjoyed what I offered.

I was straight in to class this morning with a senior year physics lesson. Although my least favourite subject, I was competent enough to deliver the required syllabus. The class worked through an exercise on the Electromagnetic Spectrum, specifically the properties of electromagnetic waves and their ability to penetrate anything. Based on what I'd witnessed last night, I expected Martin would be exceptionally competent at this subject.

Whilst I prowled around the room, peering over students' shoulders to assess their progress or be ready to offer support, I suffered a shock. I peeked over Sarah Moore's shoulder, fully expecting to see she'd grasped the subject with ease as she was one of my most capable students. However, I didn't see what I expected.

On the cover of her textbook, which she'd covered in a baby blue wallpaper – something that most students seemed to do – she had drawn a perfect heart shape with an arrow threw the middle. Sarah had penned her name underneath the arrow and Martin's name above. The heart had been neatly coloured in red, apart from the top corner, where she'd drawn Martin's face. Sarah was an A-grade student in all subjects, including PE, and she'd represented the school at cross-country running last year. But by far her best subject, where she truly excelled, was Art. Her drawing of the 'handyman' on her book was the closest likeness to Martin I'd ever seen, almost a perfect portrait. It appeared Sarah Moore had a crush on her thirty-one-year-old son.

Oh, bollocks.

Sarah noticed I'd been hovering behind her longer than usual. She nudged another textbook over the picture, thus covering up the heart drawing. Clare Keelan, who sat to Sarah's left, started to giggle, and I noticed that one of her textbooks sported a similar illustration. Clare's artwork wasn't to the same standard as Sarah's, although it was clear to see it was a drawing of Martin with her name in the heart. Oh, bollocks again. I'd introduced a male pin-up to the school in the form of Martin Bretton.

There were another five months before Clive would return to school. I needed his recovery to be swifter because the longer Martin was here, the increased probability of a difficult situation would arise with his mother. Somehow, I needed to make Martin invisible. I thought perhaps I could change his working hours, so he could perform his duties in the evenings and weekends. The less time he was parading himself in front of some young impressionable young ladies, the better.

This new revelation and concerning turn of events required immediate action. Therefore, I felt an urgent need to order an emergency committee meeting of all four members of the time-travellers-believer-club to discuss a strategy for the next few months.

The situation escalated during lunchtime as I enjoyed a coffee and cigarette while sinking into my favourite armchair in the staff room. Jayne was recalling a humorous event from an early morning chemistry lesson that involved a Bunsen burner, an orange rubber hose, and the third-year student Matthew Porter's backside – enough said. I was musing myself listening to her funny tale whilst gazing out of the staff room window. The outlook conveniently provided a clear view of the central courtyard where students would be milling about, playing games or scoffing their packed lunches whilst languishing on the wooden benches.

On warmer days, the courtyard would usually be packed with students and could put to the test the marshalling skills of those unfortunate teachers who had the dubious task of monitoring lunchtime events. Most students stayed in the school dining rooms at this time of year, but there were always a few brave souls who ventured out. Sadly, you would always be able to spot the loners or misfits who sat by themselves regardless of how poor the weather was, just so they could avoid all other students and the teasing or bullying that came with the territory.

In my early years as a pupil here, I could undoubtedly resonate with those students. Even when the weather was shite, I could be found sitting on those benches on my own or sometimes with Beth.

Jayne rattled on with her story and then moved onto a different subject as I drifted off, thinking about Beth and our conversations whilst sitting on those benches, shivering in the cold but determined not to go back into the main hall. I guess I had Beth to thank for my growing confidence in the latter years at school. The toughness she developed from living in that children's home, she managed to instil in me, thus dragging me from the pit of wallow after losing my parents. School break times were a form of natural selection. The strong survived, and the weak shrunk to the dark corners to hide.

"Jason ... Jason, did you hear me?" Jayne asked, as she leaned forward and tapped my knee.

I jumped, which caused a large blob of ash to drop onto my regulation leather-patched-elbow jacket. "Sorry, Jayne, I was miles away. What were you saying?"

She shifted forward in her seat, adjusting her skirt hem over her knees with one hand whilst pointing out the window with the other. She waved her long brown More cigarette, which she expertly held between her fore and index fingers. "I was just saying that you didn't say how you knew Martin. He does seem to attract a lot of female attention." I followed to where her finger was pointing.

"He's an old frie—nd," I slowly replied, as I glanced to where Martin held court with five senior girls who swarmed around him. He appeared to be telling a story with great animation as his hands shot in all directions whilst the girls hung on his every word. They were giggling, playing with their hair and gazing at him as if he was some Greek Adonis. Concerningly, one of the five was his mother.

"Jason ... Jason, are you alright?" Jayne quizzed, as she turned her head to look at me. However, I was transfixed by the view of Martin and his femmes' fatale.

"Yes, sorry, Jayne. I used to work with him some years ago. He's a reliable chap," I replied without taking my eyes off Martin, appearing as captivated as the young girls seemed to be.

"Oh, okay. As I said, he does seem to have the senior girls' undivided attention. And to be quite frank, I find him a little odd. I don't think it's right he attracts the attention of those girls."

"No ... I agree."

"You're sure he's okay and not one of those pervert men?"

"Ha, no. He's no Jimmy Savile."

"Oh, I don't know what you mean. We like Jimmy Savile and always watch *'Jim'll Fix It'* on a Saturday night.

I turned to face her, momentarily taking my eyes off Martin. "Sorry, what did you say?"

"You're away with the fairies today. I said I don't know what you mean about Jimmy Savile."

"Oh ... err ... nothing." Stubbing out my cigarette and keen to distance myself from this conversation about Mr Savile, I sprang out of my chair and headed outside to break up Martin's love-nest.

"Very odd," I heard Jayne reply, but I was already halfway across the staff room.

Whizzing along the corridors, skilfully negotiating the chicanes of students who were milling about, I quickly made it to the foyer and the stone steps which led down to the central courtyard. As I hopped down the steps, the five girls walked back to the main entrance. Glancing up to the bench where Martin had been holding court, he seemed to have disappeared and the girls were excitedly chatting as they passed me.

"Oh, God, he's gorgeous. He looks just like Woody!" cooed Sarah, as she clutched her hands to her chest.

I presumed she meant Woody from the Bay City Rollers, not the cowboy doll from one of the twentieth century's greatest animated films. The girls were oblivious to my existence as I stood on the bottom stone stair, with my mouth gaping open and gormlessly staring at nothing. In fact, if you stuck a cowboy hat on my head, I think I had that shocked appearance which Woody donned when Buzz Lightyear first arrived.

This was a *'Back to the Future'* dilemma. Marty had this very same problem and solved it by ensuring his teenage mother fell for his teenage father at the school dance. Unfortunately, I didn't have the luxury of a Hollywood storyline, and Martin's father was a rapist, so that wasn't going to work. This was a serious problem, and I'd have to sort Martin out as he'd failed to follow my explicit instruction not to talk to his mother.

29

Frenchie

My five mobile-phone-free months had, for the most part, felt like a release of the shackles of that tracking device that was permanently in your pocket. On balance, I definitely didn't miss that all-consuming gadget that informed the world of your whereabouts at every precise moment, nor its magnetic ability to compulsively make you keep looking at it. However, after unsuccessfully searching the whole school and grounds for Martin, I wanted to scream and just pluck out my phone and ring him.

After conducting my first lesson of the afternoon, I had some free time. Although Roy had a pile of jobs for me, I set about on my search for Martin and located him back in the school office, chatting to Miss Colman.

"Oh, Martin, thank you so much. I really do appreciate it because I know you must be so busy." Miss Colman stood holding the small wooden step ladder as Martin expertly wielded his screwdriver, fixing a bracket to the top of the pigeonhole unit.

"No problem, Trish. I'll have this all fixed up for you real soon, lol."

Miss Colman patted her hair bun as she smoothed down any stray hairs which had escaped during her exertions of holding the step ladder whilst gazing up at Magnet-Martin. As Miss Colman turned, she saw me standing there and glanced away, coughed, before staring at the floor. She was clearly highly embarrassed that I'd caught her swooning over Martin with the use of first names flowing freely between them.

"Mr Bretton, when you've finished screwing Miss Colman, I need a word." Martin turned and burst in to laughter. Miss Colman stood open-mouthed, so shocked that she was struck dumb – a rare occurrence.

"Oh bollocks, sorry, you know what I mean … when you've finished putting that screw in Miss Colman … for Miss Colman … or whatever you're doing." I waved my arms about, trying to play down what I'd said and desperately trying not to look embarrassed. Miss Colman was frozen in time as if she'd been turned to stone by Medusa.

Martin grinned, and I could see he was enjoying the spectacle of my embarrassment. He hopped off the ladder and tapped Miss Colman on the arm as if to break the Medusa spell. "Trish, don't worry. Jason can be a bit of a dick sometimes." He turned to face me and grinned again.

I now seemed to have been struck by Medusa, somewhat stunned at what Martin had said. My fear Martin wouldn't fit into the school life of the late '70s was becoming very real. I accept it's not easy fitting into an era forty years in the past, but Martin seemed to make no effort or think about his words or actions.

Roy broke the spell as he opened his office door. His head popped out as he leaned against the door frame. "Mr Apsley, do you have a moment?"

With that stern flustered look across his face, I knew it meant further problems were about to heap upon me.

"Mr Bretton, don't go anywhere. I need to talk to you," I threw over my shoulder as I entered Roy's office. Closing the door, I stood whilst Roy stared out of the window with his hands clasped behind his back.

"Jason, this Martin chap. Did you sell him your Cortina?"

"Err, yes, sort of. Well, yes, that was my old car."

"Yes, I thought so," he replied, without turning around.

"Is there a problem, Roy?"

"Well, I don't know. But there's a chap sitting on the bonnet of Martin's car, and I don't know why he's on school grounds."

I marched over to join Roy at the window.

"He looks familiar, but I can't place him," he added, as I peered out to see who he was looking at.

Half perched on the bright yellow Cortina's offside front wing and facing the opposite direction was a chap wearing a brown leather jacket. We both just stared for a few seconds, neither of us adding to the conversation.

"Do you think he's one of Martin's friends? I think you better have a word with Martin. Remind him that school property is private grounds, and he needs to ensure any acquaintances wait outside the school gates for him." Roy turned to face me, arching his eyebrow that changed what he'd said from a statement to a question.

"Yes, of course, Roy." I was now confused, firmly believing Martin hadn't been in 1977 long enough to form friendships. Well, maybe Mandy, whom I'd the pleasure of meeting last night. But this person sitting astride Martin's car was not female and had clothes on, so it couldn't be her. I was about to turn around when the man sitting on the car wing turned and faced the school entrance as he checked his watch. A cold shiver sprinted down my spine, which seemed to transfix me to the spot. Medusa had got me again.

"Jason?"

"Jason, are you alright, old chap? The colour has drained from your face."

I continued to gawp through the window. Although the windows were only thirty or so feet from Martin's car, the man sitting on it wouldn't be able to see me particularly well due to the window being leaded glass – the original windows when the school was built. However, I could clearly see Paul Colney sitting on Martin's car wing – my old Cortina.

Roy grabbed my arm as he looked at me, breaking the Medusa spell. "Jason, I said, are you alright? You look like you've seen a ghost."

"Roy, leave it with me. I'll sort this out." I turned and exited his office. Miss Colman had reunited herself with her typewriter as she hammered the keys whilst glancing to her left at the notepad on the desk. Martin sat slouched on one of the high-backed wooden chairs near the door. His head leant back, staring at the ceiling, with his legs outstretched and arms folded.

I yanked open the office door and turned to Martin, gesturing with my head. "We need to go."

Martin jumped up and winked at Miss Colman. "He's so bossy!"

Martin followed me out to the main foyer. I grabbed his arm and manhandled him to the stairwell corner.

"Hey, what's up with you?" Martin threw back, as he glared at my hand, which I had tightly gripped around his elbow.

I chose to ignore his inability to fit into this '70s life and the misunderstanding of his position at the school because I needed to focus on our immediate problem.

"Martin, shut up! We have a real problem."

He looked up at me as I kept hold of his arm, pinning him in place.

"After we spoke about the Colneys in the pub on Monday, I said you can't do anything … what have you done?"

Martin frowned. "Nothing. You said to do nothing in your usual bossy way. So, for the moment, I've done nothing."

"You must have! Because Paul Colney is sitting on the bonnet of your bloody car," I hissed and pointed behind me to the main car park.

Martin's eyes bulged. "Jason, I've done nothing. But now he's here, I'm going to deal with him." He shrugged out of my grip and pushed past me.

I spotted Miss Colman's face squashed against the glass panel of the office door as I grabbed Martin's arm again and hauled him back.

"Martin, stop!"

He turned and looked at me.

"Remember what George said about the Colneys? They're violent and have connections. You can't just go out there and confront him."

Miss Colman opened the door a crack and peered through the gap. "Is everything alright, Mr Apsley?"

"Yes, Miss Colman, all under control." I returned a tight smile as I manhandled Martin into the Assembly Hall in an attempt to find some privacy and away from Miss Colman.

I shoved Martin in to one of the wooden chairs in the front row and stared down at him as my mind whirred around, trying to work out our next move. "Martin, you're sure you've done nothing?"

"No, nothing!" he fired back, holding up both palms and shrugging his shoulders. He looked like one of my students who I'd caught misbehaving.

I plonked myself down in the chair beside him. "Well, we have a problem because he's out there perched on your car. It would suggest he's looking for you. But I can't think why."

"Jason, that was *your* car." He turned and looked at me, now calm, as the realisation of the grave situation we were now in had dawned upon him. "I think he's looking for *you*."

"Oh, bollocks, you're right. I've had a few run-ins with him, but I still don't know why he's here." I scrubbed my hands over my face as I leaned forward, trying to work out what to do. I had to act now because I'd told Roy I would deal with it.

"I'll go and tell him to naff off. Although I should kill him as he's likely the one that raped Mum," he babbled, before leaping from his chair.

"Yes, and he could well be your real father."

Martin slowly re-parked his backside in the chair. "Yeah ... wow ... what a thought."

"I think we need to keep you a secret as long as possible. He knows me, so I'll go out there and see what he wants. I don't think he's going to get violent on school grounds." I grabbed Martin's shoulder to get his attention. "Look, can you hang around near the foyer in case things don't turn out too well? But for Christ's sake, keep out of sight."

My two previous encounters with this bloody bloke hadn't gone well. I'd nearly shit myself a week last Monday when he stared me down in the public gallery at Patrick's trial. The other encounter last September was significantly more painful. Lacking confidence but trying to look it, I slithered down the steps and tentatively shuffled towards him. Paul Colney stood up and folded his arms, his menacing eyes boring deep into my head as he watched my progress towards him.

"Apple ... you seem to pop up everywhere!"

"Well, as I work here, and you know that ... I'm not sure what's so surprising, do you?" Good start I thought as I clenched my bum cheeks together. Now half concentrating on my bowel movements and trying not to shit myself.

"Don't get fucking smart with me, or this time I'll tear that bloody nose off your face." He held my stare with his cold evil eyes. I was in no doubt that he was capable of his threat and had probably performed such an operation on many an unfortunate soul in the past.

Taking a deep breath, I pushed on. "This is private property, and you have no reason to be here." Pompously, I stuck my nose in the air and tried to swallow. However, unfortunately, my mouth chose not to comply, now it had dried up, leaving a sandpaper tongue stuck to my Sahara-dry cheeks.

Paul took two steps towards me. Annoyingly, I took two back, an involuntary self-preservation movement. It was the *fight or flight* reaction, and my brain had decided on *flight*.

Paul instantly sensed the upper hand, as I guessed he was well trained in these situations. I fought hard to keep my lower orifices closed – a battle I was only just winning.

'Come on, Jason, what are you – man or mouse?' My brain replied, *'mouse,'* with a squeak.

Paul grinned, enjoying the power he had over me. "Whose car is this?" He nodded to the Cortina that his bum had just alighted. I just stared at him as my tongue struggled to find some saliva in my desert-mouth.

"That Stag is yours. Nice motor for a teacher. So what were you doing up at the Broxworth on Monday then?" He leant forward to close the gap between us. "Apple, I suggest you start talking, or I'll rip that tongue out of your fucking head."

"You need to leave," I managed to fire out. Although in a high-pitched tone which sounded more like one of the first-year girl students than a grown man.

Paul glanced to my right and then back at me as I desperately tried to work out my next move. All the time, my brain was screaming at me to man-up.

"Who the fuck are you?" Paul aggressively shouted over my shoulder. I turned to spot Martin purposefully striding towards us.

'Oh, for fuck sake, why can't Martin do anything he's told?'

"None of your fucking business, you tosser. So I suggest you turn around and fuck off." Martin had closed the gap within inches of Paul's face. Although I feared that the situation was about to escalate out of control, fair play to Martin. There was nothing mouse-like about him. He was confident and in control, but he had no idea who he was dealing with.

I momentarily pondered what part I would play in the impending doom following Martin's verbal assault. I was fully expecting that, at any moment now, Martin and I would be lying on the asphalt in a spasm of our final death throes.

A police panda – new 'R' plated MK2 Escort – gracefully pulled up to a halt just a few feet in front of the steps to the school entrance. A young male officer hopped out of the driver's seat and stared in our direction. It was fairly obvious for anyone to see we weren't having a friendly chat. Then to my utter delight, Frenchie appeared from the passenger seat and marched almost army drill sergeant style towards us as the male officer stood and watched, holding the police car's door.

She muscled herself in between Martin and Paul, which was a tricky operation. Her buxom form – that could support a tray of beer steins at a beer festival – came to a halt as her chest nudged its way in between the opening in Paul's leather jacket. Now millimetres from him, she looked up and glared.

"What ... are ... you ... doing ... here?" she delivered slowly and confidently, which made me grimace thinking about my own wimpy performance thus far.

Paul looked down at her chest. I willed one of her tunic buttons to ping off and garrotte him as he glanced over her head towards me. "We ain't done." He backed up and walked away.

"I don't expect to see you here again," Frenchie shouted after him as Paul hurried to the school gates.

Assuming Miss Colman or Roy had called the police, this would be a difficult situation to explain.

Her partner had now closed the car door and was in the process of locking it. Frenchie turned to address me. "Mr Apsley, whenever I have an encounter which involves the Colney family, you always seem to appear." She barrelled her way over to me whilst Martin just looked on. "Well, Mr Apsley, why was Paul Colney here at the school?" Frenchie stood with her hands on her hips, awaiting my answer. Then in one swift movement, she swung her tray of beer chest in Martin's direction. "Well?"

"I have no idea why he was here. We just asked him that question when you lot turned up. I'm sorry you were called. I think that was an overreaction on the school's part," I replied.

"Sir, nothing is an overreaction where a Colney is involved. I think I've said this to you before, but I suggest you take care with whom you choose to mix with. Paul Colney is not a suitable friend and an extremely unsuitable enemy. Am I clear?"

"Very clear," I responded, *feeling* like I'd just been told off.

"Err, yes," replied Martin, *looking* like he'd just been told off.

"Good. We weren't called to attend. We actually need to speak to you regarding an incident involving some of your pupils at the chip shop on Haverhill Road this lunchtime. Shall we go inside?"

The other officer adjusted his cap and joined us as we walked back into the school foyer whilst Martin trailed behind. Whatever the chip shop incident was, I didn't really care. Martin and I were firmly on Paul Colney's radar and long before I intended us to be. Once again, Frenchie was right. I seemed to be involuntarily involved with the Colney clan.

30

Stifler's Mom

Roy and I listened to Frenchie regarding the chip shop incident. Both of us were not surprised as the culprits had a tendency to cause trouble. Three of our senior boys appeared to have become embroiled in an altercation with a group of lads from the Howlett School. It seemed to be a *'turf'* war over who had the rights to use the chip shop, which was situated an equal distance from both schools. Roy said this had happened before with the troublesome pupils from that rotten school, as he put it. I was fully aware he had a very low opinion of Malcolm McDonough, the Headteacher. The telephone conversation between them was tense, with raised voices, and Roy became red-faced and angry after slamming the phone back in its cradle.

"Idiot! The man's a buffoon! How he's held the position of Head at that ruddy school is beyond any understanding. Jason, can you deal with those three boys? Although I'm certain it'll be that rowdy lot from the Howlett School who caused all the problems. The punishment needs to be severe. I can't tolerate the City School being brought into disrepute."

"Of course, Roy, leave it with me." However, I wouldn't be dishing out the punishment that he expected. Corporal punishment, in my mind, served no purpose, and I certainly wasn't going to spend my afternoon swinging the '*School Slipper*' back and forth at three male arses bent over a desk. As the school day finished, I caught up with Maggie, the school cleaner. She was an unassuming middle-aged lady who diligently performed her cleaning duties in her blue and white house-coat without anyone noticing she existed. Today she'd have three unwilling apprentices.

Maggie found the whole episode somewhat irregular, but I could tell she was pleased as I made her a cup of tea. I raided the biscuit tin that yielded three *Nice* biscuits, although as they'd languished at the bottom of the tin for so long they were now probably anything but nice. I set her up to listen to the radio in the staff room while organising her three apprentices to clean the male toilets.

"Right, Maggie, put your feet up for half an hour and enjoy yourself while those three boys take their punishment."

"Mr Apsley, this is very kind of you. I've never had a teacher make me a cup of tea before. I didn't think I was allowed in the staffroom, well, only to clean. I won't get into trouble, will I?"

"Maggie, you use the staffroom whenever you want. I'm the Deputy Head – *am I?* – so, no, you won't get into trouble. Those three boys have to have their punishment, and I think cleaning toilets is better than the *'Slipper'*. Just sit back and relax whilst I crack the whip on those boys." Maggie smirked and settled into her chair.

As all men know, male toilet facilities are horrific places. It didn't matter whether it was 2019 or 1977 – they were the same. A large proportion of the male population had no concern for what they deposited and where, as long as it was in the vague direction of the toilet pan. I certainly had an affinity to Finch in *'American Pie,'* not that I was desperate to screw *'Stifler's Mom,'* but I tried at all costs to avoid the school toilets when the call came.

My three senior students, Roberts, King and Cooper, all appeared horrified as I provided them with the required cleaning equipment of cloths and brushes to attack the men's toilets. Although, after a full day of four hundred students splattering the facilities, I thought a hose and shovel would be more effective. Maggie should be regarded as a saint for facing this every day.

Roberts turned and looked at me as I leaned against the door frame. "Sir, can I have a hundred lashes with the slipper instead, please?" Cooper and King looked in total agreement as they surveyed the carnage inside each cubical.

I grinned and shook my head. "Gentlemen, that would be letting you off lightly. So no, let's get cleaning."

King approached the first cubicle with his Marigold gloves and a tube of Vim cleaner at the ready. He stepped inside, looked at the carnage he faced and threw up. Maybe I'd gone too far.

31

Timmy

After leaving Roy's office earlier that afternoon, I'd called George at work and Jen at home. Jen would drop the kids off at her parents, and we all agreed to meet at the pub for a crisis meeting at six.

I was genuinely concerned that Paul Colney might be lurking around after school, as he'd made it clear earlier in the day that our conversation wasn't finished. I chose the pub for the meeting as I didn't want him to know where I or Martin, and for that matter, Don, lived. Maybe I was overreacting, but I was fully aware of what he was capable of.

Martin and I arrived early, as I needed to deal with his fraternisation with his mother earlier in the day. After the three boys had completed their punishment and left, looking rather green around the gills, I was confident they would not be getting into another fracas outside the chip shop. Maggie had enjoyed her break and said she would be more than happy if any other students were in trouble, they could have the same punishment.

As we'd arrived early, we grabbed the window seat after a quick chat with Dawn and Dennis. Dawn said Martin was a very handsome chap and wanted to know if he had a young lady. I avoided saying he had too many, and I expected many more on the horizon as it seemed a fair few females he encountered were charmed by him – including his mother.

"Right mate, before the others get here, I suggest you tell me what was all that goings-on when you were chatting up those senior girls at lunchtime, including your mother?"

Martin nearly spat his beer back out as he slammed his mug on the table. "What the fuck! You're joking right? I was *not* chatting up those girls and certainly *wasn't* chatting up my mother!"

"Keep your bloody voice down!" I glanced up to see Dawn, Dennis and Brian the landlord, break from their conversation at hearing Martin's outburst.

"You sick fuck! You think I would chat my own mother up?"

"I can't tell you again. Keep your bloody voice down."

Martin huffed and sat back in his seat. "I was just having a friendly chat with some students. Yes, okay, one happened to be my mum, but hell, we were just chatting."

"I said you need to avoid talking to her. It just isn't right. We don't know the time-travel effects of you engaging with her eleven years before she gives birth to you."

Raising the palms of his hands, he nodded, "Yeah, I know. It's just so weird seeing her as a teenager, and I just wanted to talk to her."

"Well, apart from your potential rapist-father turning up at school today, we have another problem." I flipped open my cigarettes, plucked one out and lit up.

"Oh, what's that? And do you have to smoke? I'm going to die of lung cancer before I'm forty, living in this era. When do they ban smoking in pubs? I can't remember, but I hope it's soon."

"1st July 2007," I replied. I remember we had a smoking party at the local pub on the night of 30th June and a lock-in until one in the morning so we could all defy the law for one hour. The landlord had slapped a sign up on the pub door stating only smokers were allowed in that night, which caused some arguments. What he meant as a joke turned out to be a disaster, resulting in the police attending to deal with a stand-off between rival punters.

"Oh yeah, I remember it happening when I was at Uni. Pity they didn't bring it in earlier. Then you'd have to stand outside and stop polluting my air."

"That's a bit rich. You had a cigarette the other day!"

"Yeah, but I don't normally smoke."

"Well, Mr High-And-Mighty, as I was saying, we have another problem. Your mother has a serious crush on you!"

Martin frowned and shook his head. "Oh, I don't think so. You're taking it too far now."

"I wish I was, mate. But she's drawn a heart on her exercise book with yours and her name on it. Also, when she was walking back into school after lunch and following your little chat, she was cooing over you and giggling with the other girls about how gorgeous you are."

"Oh." Martin closed his eyes and sunk down in his chair. "You'd better give me one of your cigarettes."

I shoved the packet in his direction. "So, mate, we have got to put a stop to this, and fast!"

When Jenny arrived, I left Martin pondering our new dilemma and jumped up to purchase her a drink. Now Jenny had joined the troop, she would probably have a different perspective on what we could do about this situation. Although George was a great sounding board, he rarely came up with solutions. I needed to bring Don into the group, but as Jenny and I'd agreed, that was a step too far for now. I gave Jenny a kiss and ordered her drink whilst she chatted to Dawn, who wanted the full lowdown on how the kids were getting on.

George arrived a moment later and joined Martin. After prising Jenny away from Dawn, we all convened in a tight huddle in the window seat. After Dawn's reference to the *famous five* on Saturday, all we needed now was Timmy the Border Collie, and we could have neatly fitted into one of Enid Blyton's books. Although, I guess we were a little old for that, and I didn't believe her books included a storyline regarding a serial rapist.

I brought George and Jenny fully up to speed on the day's events. George shot Martin a worried look, and Jenny moved her chair a few inches away from him as I described the events with his sixteen-year-old mother. Perhaps I painted a picture that made Martin appear like a pervert. Martin stayed quiet as he smoked another one of my cigarettes whilst performing his Nookie Bear impression, which was quite off-putting.

"Lad, the only reason I can assume that Paul Colney wants to know who owns that car is because he's interested in the driver. The good news is, as he asked you who it was, he clearly doesn't know at this point."

"Exactly. I had that car when living up at the Broxworth. But it's a common car even in bright yellow, so I don't think he ever connected it to me. The bit I don't understand is where he's seen the car, which has made him want to know who the driver is."

"Yeah, and I'm the driver of it now! So, what does that mean for me? I now have my rapist father, who is a complete psycho, hunting me down!" Martin stubbed out his cigarette. I swiped my packet off the table before he started chain-smoking, which rendered his earlier rant somewhat ridiculous.

"We don't know he's your father. It's possible and likely, but we don't know for sure."

"Darling, the twin is in jail, so I think we should assume it's him. That awful family have so much to answer for up at that estate. We know all about them at work, and Dad could write a book on that family's exploits from his time in the Force."

"Lad, Jenny is right about the family. I think you need to get rid of the car, and as soon as possible."

"Why don't we just put it in our garage, darling? At least it will be hidden."

"Yes, we could do that. I still want to know why he's looking for it, though."

"Lad, the lass is right. Let's just get it under wraps for the moment."

Martin shifted forward, "Oh, that's just fricking great! I get teleported to the dark ages, get stuck in a shit job, lose all my friends and my bloody wife, and now I don't even have a car!"

We all turned and looked at him as he slumped back into his seat, gulping down his beer.

"Jen, sweetheart, will you let me buy that Hillman Hunter from Coreys Mill Motors? Martin could then have your old Viva?"

Jenny sighed, "Well, yes, we could do, but I love my Viva."

"I know, but you need a car with rear seatbelts."

"You fuss too much, darling. Chris likes standing on the seat and looking out the back window."

A cold shudder ran through me as I pictured him standing there, Jenny breaking hard, and he suddenly being catapulted through the front windscreen. I know my old world had gone health and safety crazy, where kids weren't even allowed to play conkers for fear of a potential eye injury. Still, I was right about seat belts, the evidence was there, and even that sicko Savile had been doing his clunk-click TV campaign for years. Jimmy Savile, there's another one I needed to alert the world about, but as I knew from my Ripper letter experience, it was pointless.

"Jen, it will be the law soon that you have to wear seat belts. I can't remember when, but it will be the law for rear seat belts as well."

"When I was a kid, my mum and dad always made me wear a seat belt in the back of our car. Dad had a brand-new Honda Accord; it was really posh at the time."

"Honda, that's one of those Jap-crap cars? Can't believe that we have to import cars from that bloody place, not after what that lot did in the war!"

I huffed as this was going off track. "George, I know that's raw for you, and you had brothers who suffered in the Far East. But in our old world, Japan is probably one of our closest allies. As for cars, well in the future, they produce some of the most reliable vehicles and electronics in the world. I know that's tough, but we have to draw the line somewhere and move on. Otherwise, we'll have to talk about the British Empire's atrocities which were on the same level."

George nodded, "Alright, lad." He plucked up his beer and fell back in his chair. This was going nowhere. Martin and George now had the hump, and Jenny was pining for her Viva, that she didn't want to let go of.

"Look, everyone, can we get back to what we are talking about? We have to hide the Cortina ... agreed?" I looked at them in turn, they all nodded.

"Jenny, the Hillman Hunter, for the kid's sake?"

She nodded and smiled. "Yes, darling, alright." That smile melted me. I'd been so consumed with the events of the last two weeks I'd almost forgotten what a lucky bloke I was. Although Martin was stuck in a world he didn't want to be in, I, on the other hand, was in heaven – Jenny was truly an angel.

'*Your job is to keep that lovely girl of yours happy, my boy'.* Don's voice rolled around my head.

I took hold of her hand across the table and squeezed it tightly. "Thank you, sweetheart."

"Give us a ciggy, Jason. If you two can separate for a moment."

Jenny beamed her smile, then broke the handhold and delved into her handbag. She plucked out a pack of ten Embassy No1, a box of Bryant and May matches and handed them to Martin.

Martin lit up again and performed his stupid Nookie Bear face as he studied the burning end. After a further moment of silence, he leant forward. "Right, what are we going to do about Mum?"

George thumped his beer down. "Well, lad, you're going to have to avoid her. It's just not right your mother swooning over her son … it's … it's immoral!"

"It's not my fault!" Martin blurted back.

"I knew placing him in that job at school was going to be a disaster." I gestured my thumb towards Martin.

"Wha … What? I didn't ask for this, did I?"

Jenny shot me a look. Those eyes were telling me to calm the whole situation before our raised voices alerted the entire pub to our rather strange conversation.

"Alright, hang on. What is done is done." I tapped the palm of my hand on the table, which seemed to have the required effect of calming George and Martin.

"It feels like I'm in the film *Back to the Future*," said Martin.

"Precisely the thought I had earlier."

"Is that the lightning film you were both talking about last week?" asked Jenny.

"Yeah," both Martin and I replied.

"What's that, lad?" George enquired, as he leant forward, folding his arms on the table.

"That film I said about with the Flux-Capacitor and the time-travelling car."

"Darling, when does that film come out? I'd like to see it as it sounds really good."

"It is!" we both replied.

"The mid-eighties, if I remember correctly," I added, before we all fell silent again.

"Martin, did your mum ever mention any boyfriends she had at school? I was just thinking if she did, we could engineer that they hook up sooner rather than later."

Martin blew out his cheeks as he tried to think before raising his finger. "Hang on. Mum was really friendly with this couple. He was the editor of the Fairfield Chronicle, and Mum knew him from school." He clicked his fingers, trying to pull the name from his memory. George sat even further forward at the mention of the Chronicle. "Dad played golf with him a couple of times, and there was always this suggestion that Mum and he were close in their school days. Christ, what was his name? I should be able to remember him as I only saw him a few months ago when visiting Mum."

"Come on, Martin, think. This is important."

He clenched his fist and thumped the table. "Got it … Carlton King. That's his name, Carlton King."

George turned to me. "You know him, lad?"

"Err ... yes, I know him. Got to say I'm amazed he becomes the editor of the Chronicle. He's not the sharpest chisel in the toolbox and always getting into bother one way or another." I thought of him only a few hours ago when entering the toilet cubical and donning a fetching pair of pink Marigold gloves, brush in hand, then pebble dashing the toilet seat.

"You'd be amazed at what idiots they appoint as an editor at that place. The current one, Braithwaite, is a complete idiot. Can't spell to save his life, I can tell you. As for punctuation, the man's obsessed with using a comma ... total idiot!"

"So darling, is that the plan? Somehow you get Carlton and Martin's mum together so she forgets about Martin?"

"I think so. Martin, you're really going to have to keep a low profile. I don't know how I'll do it, but somehow, I have to get your mother to stop looking at you and develop a crush on Carlton King."

"Blimey. What if they really get it together and then end up, you know, doing, you know what?"

"What?" we all said together.

Martin nodded his head and grinned. "You know, my mum and this Carlton boy, get it on. She falls for him, has a baby, never meets my dad ... Martin, that is, not the rapist. Then maybe that changes history, and Mum never gets raped."

Jenny placed her hand on Martin's arm and looked at him. "And you never get born."

We all sat back for a moment, contemplating what Jenny had said. She was right. If I interfered too much, then I could change history. Although we'd already decided we had to stop Sarah from being raped. Martin wanted to go back to 2019, but in reality, that was never going to happen. Also, both Martins couldn't exist when we got to 1988.

The other problem I faced, and I'd had this rolling around my head for weeks, was that everything I did or said was changing history because I wasn't even born the first time around. Every day that ripple effect sent further far-reaching circles of change out into the world which altered history. There surely would come a point when those ripples would travel far enough to change events in the future which I could remember happening and knew would take place.

Perhaps those sporting and world events would change. Maybe my planned financial investments would not prove as lucrative as I thought. I needed to ramp up my short-term betting and continue to build my portfolio of assets before the world I knew changed forever. Surely those ripples hadn't already gone as far to nullify my bet that Nottingham Forest would win the league next year or that Niki Lauda would be world champion later this year – or had they?

We finished our drinks with little achieved, apart from my challenge to encourage Sarah to look at Carlton. George said he needed to be off, Jenny and I planned to spend the evening with her parents, and Martin said he had a hot date with one of the young mums he'd met at the school gates earlier today – the man was an insatiable screwing machine.

Martin drove out of the car park ahead of Jenny and me. I had to brake hard as a white Ford Capri, sporting a coat-hanger aerial, sharply pulled off from the opposite side of the road behind Martin's Cortina.

32

The Damned

John and Frances always made a huge fuss of the kids. They'd turned a spare bedroom into a playroom-come-sleepover den for Christopher. John had set up a large Scalextric and a Hornby railway set which I imagined had cost a fortune. Frances maintained that the train set was John's and not really Christopher's, as John was obsessed with expanding his portfolio of rolling-stock at every opportunity. Although Frances was on rocky ground when highlighting the number of boys' toys that had been amassed, as she had gone slightly crazy with dolls houses, Tiny Tears and Cindy dolls.

Frances spoilt both Christopher and Beth as they had far too many toys that he could find the time to play with or Beth could appreciate; my two adopted children were spoilt. Tonight, Chris had his Chitty Chitty Bang Bang car, which rarely left his pocket, while having a tug of war with John. His Stretch Armstrong toy had his arms and legs pulled as if stuck on the torture rack in the dungeons of the Tower of London.

Before tea, I had to intervene in an argument raging between John, Jenny, and her younger brother, Alan. The disagreement was regarding Alan's attire, which John and Jenny thought was horrific. He'd attached chains to his black jeans, had a padlock securing a chain around his neck and had modelled his hair in spikes with the content of a whole can of Frances's Harmony Hairspray. There was no question of *'Is she or isn't she'* or, in this case, *'he'* as in those dreadful cheesy adverts on TV. However, hair spray aside, the real fury was regarding Alan's decision earlier that day to have his ear pierced.

Apparently, a mate made the hole in his ear using the pin of his The Damned badge whilst his girlfriend held an ice cube to the back of his ear to numb the pain. I tried to convince John and Frances it was a phase and he would probably grow out of it. Jenny was furious with Alan for his lack of respect, and how could anyone like that dreadful music. Although only just born at the birth of the Punk movement, I grew up to love that genre and was secretly jealous of all the bands Alan would have the opportunity to see.

Frances said that Alan's girlfriend was a shocking girl who constantly chewed gum and wore fishnet tights with only the skimpiest black leather skirt which, in her opinion, didn't sufficiently cover her modesty. Frances also thought her dreadful thick black makeup was utterly horrible, *"What kind of girl would wear black lipstick?"* she'd exclaimed over tea.

After we'd dealt with the dishes and, at last, the conversation had moved on from Alan and his girlfriend's dress sense, John and I enjoyed a cigar in the conservatory. Frances and Jenny attended to the kids getting them ready for bed. Christopher wanted to stay the night, and John agreed to perform the bedtime story routine after we'd finished our *Man-Chat,* as he put it.

Frances had said not to let Jonny push me into joining his secret club, where they got up to all sorts of sordid things, as Jenny was enough woman for any man. She delivered one of Jenny's super smiles, slapped my bum and left us to puff away. Although Frances was joking, the subliminal message was clear, reminding me what a wonderful wife I had – not that I needed a reminder.

Back in my old world, Lisa's mother had suggested to her husband during mine and Lisa's troubled marriage that he could enrol me into his secret organisation, which involved funny handshakes and rolled-up trouser legs. *"It might straighten him out a bit,"* she'd said at the time, desperate to do anything to improve my lacklustre performance as a husband and son-in-law. However, Lisa's father had nearly choked at the idea, stating the club was only for like-minded businessmen. He feared he would be blackballed if he attempted to introduce a new member who was an incompetent idiot like myself.

All of this conversation took place as I sat in their lounge as if I didn't exist. Lisa didn't defend me from her father's rather unpleasant description of my personality. At that point in my relationship with my in-laws, I'd lost interest and didn't care one jot what they thought of me. I recall helping myself to another glass of wine whilst Lisa's mum questioned Lisa if I had an alcohol dependency problem.

It had become common to sit and listen to a conversation between the three of them about my apparent incompetence as a husband and son-in-law. The last such discussion I'd suffered was her mother questioning whether I was a 'Jaffa', as she put it. Her reference to the seedless orange was questioning if I possessed a low seed count as we hadn't managed to procreate any children.

Her father had said to thank our lucky stars we hadn't, as the idea of more idiots like me being born was not a pleasant thought. At that point, I did man-up and tell her parents to piss off and advised Lisa if she wanted to agree with her bigoted, fuck-stupid, self-centred, offensive wanker parents, then she could piss off as well. I left the house, leaving them all shocked at my outburst. I had berated myself for not being a man and saying those exact words years before as I should've done. I never revisited their house – a real blessing.

As I stubbed out my cigar, Frances popped her head in the room whilst bouncing Beth in her arms. "Jason, your lovely friend, Don, is on the phone. He's been trying to ring you at home and now rang here. He says he needs to talk to you urgently."

Jumping up, I scooted into the hall to get to the phone. Don would have only rung around urgently trying to track me down if there was an emergency. As he'd phoned, I presumed he was okay, so that was a relief as I plucked up the receiver. My guess was it was something to do with Martin.

I was correct; it was Martin.

33

TCP

After relaying our conversation to Jen, we agreed she would get Beth home, and I would zip up to Don's house. As the police hadn't been called, we decided we'd leave it that way until I'd caught up with Don. I could see Jenny was worried and asked me to be careful, grabbing me before I went and hugging me tightly.

Don stood hunched with his thick Crombie coat on in the driveway as I pulled up and abandoned the car on the slew, jumping out of the car before the engine had even had time to cut itself off.

Don shouted across to me, "Son, don't panic; we're all okay."

"What's happened? You're okay, aren't you?"

"Yes, son, I'm alright. Come on, you better come in."

I followed Don as he shuffled into number eight. Closing the front door, I noticed the Yale lock hanging loose on the inside with splinters of wood sticking at right angles to the frame. Don stood in the kitchen doorway and blocked my view. However, as I shimmied around him, I could see Martin sitting at the kitchen table, his head back and staring at the ceiling as he held a scrunched-up blooded tea towel to his nose. A young woman I'd never seen before, I guess in her early thirties, stood beside him, dabbing various cuts to his face with a dishcloth.

"Martin, you okay?"

"Fricking hell, dick-head, do I look it?" he nasally replied, as if auditioning for a flu remedy advert. "You should see the other guy!"

The young woman tipped her head sideways and looped her dark hair around her right ear as she continued to dab away at Martin's battered face, which now resembled a splat pizza. She glanced in my direction and smiled.

I returned a tight smile. "Hi, I'm Jason," unsure what else to say.

"Yes, I know who you are. My eldest, Craig, is a first-year student at the school. He thinks you're great!"

"Oh, thanks. That's nice to hear."

"Yes, he's really enjoying school at the moment. He thinks you're hilarious at assemblies." She stopped dabbing and looked up at me. "I'm Nicole, by the way."

"Hello." I smiled again. "Well, I'm not supposed to be hilarious, so I may have to change tack on that one."

Nicole moved over to the sink to wash out the cloth in a bowl of water that contained copious amounts of TCP, judging by the pungent smell engulfing the kitchen. Fair play to Martin, though, as I would be yelping every time that liquid touched me.

"No, no, sorry. I meant that he really enjoys them. He says he learns a lot, and it's good fun," Nicole replied, as she prepared to attack Martin's face again with a fresh cloth.

Martin tipped his head forward, gingerly taking the cloth from his face. "When you two have stopped talking about the Jason Apsley fricking fan club, perhaps we might discuss how I ended up looking like this!"

"Easy, son. Tip your head back again. It's running out of your nose," stated Don, as he pulled at a chair opposite

Martin and eased himself in. Nicole bent Martin's head back and pinched the top of his nose.

"You seem to know what you're doing?" I questioned her, as she stood there, pinching his nose and holding Martin's wrist, presumably feeling his pulse. However, he was very much alive based on the continued liberally thrown obscenities pouring out of his mouth.

"I should do as I'm a nurse at Fairfield General. Ha, and there was I thinking we were going to have some fun this evening, not continue to carry on my duties from today."

Martin grinned as she removed her fingers from his nose and placed a damp cloth on his forehead.

"Met Nicole this afternoon; always been a sucker for a girl in uniform."

Nicole gave him a wink and a seductive grin. Christ, he even had that magnetic pull when he was beaten up.

"Yeah, okay, whatever. Now can we run through what's happened?"

"Gents, I'm going to clean up in the bathroom. Martin, keep the pressure tight at the top of your nose," instructed Nicole, as she dried her hands, tossed the towel on the draining board and left the kitchen.

"Can you bring my glasses down? They're on the bathroom window sill," Martin shouted after her.

He tipped his head back and kept the cloth to his nose. "So, I got back after the pub and waved to Don as I got out of the car. It all seemed pretty normal, but I did spot an old Ford Capri park up outside Don's but thought nothing of it. I was going to have a wash and change before Nicole came around when some tosser started hammering on the door. I knew it wasn't Nicole, as it was like someone was trying to break it down." He rechecked the cloth for signs of fresh blood. "Fuck, he's broken my nose."

"Yes, son, I saw him pull up a few seconds after Martin. I was standing having a cuppa, just looking about out of the window. Knew exactly who it was as soon as he got out of the car."

"Paul Colney?"

"Indeed. He marched straight up to the door and started hammering on it. Wasn't sure what to do at that point."

Martin looked up, satisfied his nose had stopped bleeding. "Yeah, and before I could even get down the stairs, he'd kicked the fricking lock in."

"What happened then?"

"I just froze on the spot for a second ... I couldn't believe what he'd done. Then I think I told him to get the fuck out. That's when he leapt up, grabbed me and dragged me down to the hallway. I think he punched me in the face at that point and pinned me against the wall. He started shouting at me that I'd been on the flats' roof the day his brother died."

I shot Don a look. He nodded. Both of us, I was sure, were thinking the same thing.

Martin threw the blooded towel on the table. "Give us one of your cigarettes."

I fished them out of my pocket and tossed them on the table.

"It was at that point I thought I'd better come around and see what was going on. I saw him boot and then shoulder the door in," Don added, as Martin lit his cigarette, his hand still shaking as he tried to line up the end with the lighter flame.

"I'm surprised he didn't wallop you as well. He didn't take it?"

"No, son. By the time I'd found my coat and shuffled over, he was coming out of the front door."

Martin eventually managed to light the cigarette, blew out smoke to the ceiling and carried on. "The bastard kept ranting that he knew the driver of my car was at the flats that day, and I better start talking. The fucker then headbutted me. That's when he broke my nose, I think. I told him I'd only had the car a couple of weeks, but he didn't believe me, so he laid into me again. I managed to get a few swings at him that connected with his head, so the bastard didn't come off scot-free."

"So, did he just leave then?"

"No … after I had landed a few punches to his face, he got the upper hand. He's a big bloke, you know."

I touched my nose and nodded. "Yes, I know. I've a broken nose by his hand as well."

"Yeah, I'm sure you have. Typical, you always have to go one better, don't you? I can't even have a broken nose on my own. For fuck sake mate, I'm the one who's been beaten up because of what you did! It's always the same with you, Apsley. Whatever carnage you cause, some other fucker has got to clear up the bloody mess!"

I held my hand up and shot Don a quick glance which he knew was my suggestion to be quiet as I could see he was about to tear a strip off Martin. But to be fair, Don only knew me in this life and not Jason Twat Apsley from my previous existence. Don performed his fish mouth routine, then shut up as he clocked my glance.

"Okay, sorry, mate. What happened then?"

"Well, as I said, he had the upper hand and pinned me to the floor. He wanted to know who I was and who I'd got the car from. He said if I lied, I was as good as dead. The bastard wasn't joking!"

"Jesus! What did you tell him?"

"I told him I got it from the car-lot down the road. That's where you sold it to, ain't it?"

I nodded. "It is."

"Sorry, Jason. I know that's put you in the shit. I can hold my ground, and I don't lose fights very often. But this bastard was going to kill me."

I scrubbed my hands over my face. "Martin, don't worry. We'll figure something out."

"What we going to do, son?" Don looked concerned, and rightly so.

"I don't know. Somehow, he's connected me to the flats on the day David died. We thought no one saw us, but someone must have. But if they did, why didn't they say something at the time or call the police?"

"You're forgetting the type of person who lives up there. No one on the Broxworth talks to the Old-Bill. And if the Colney boys are involved, they all keep schtum."

"Yeah, and to think that nutter could be my father!"

Don and I both shot Martin a look. Mine was eyes bulging, urging him to correct his time travel balls-up. Don's was utter confusion about what he'd just said.

Martin waved his hands in the air. "What?"

"Son, what are you talking about? Paul Colney, your father ... you're older than him."

"Martin, I think you're concussed, mate." I nodded and raised my eyebrows, willing him to realise what he'd said.

Martin frowned as his eyes shifted back and forth between Don and me.

"Son, you okay?"

He shook his head, blinked and looked down at the table. "Yeah, sorry, I must have got confused for a moment. Maybe I *am* concussed."

Nicole opened the kitchen door and stepped up to Martin. "I don't think you've got concussion. Let me look at you again." She turned his head in her hands and stared into his eyes. "Is your vision blurred? Do you feel dizzy?"

"No. No, I'm okay."

"Okay. I think perhaps up to bed for a while is what is needed."

"Now you're talking, girl," he grinned and grabbed her jean-clad bottom.

"There's nothing wrong with him," I chuckled.

34

Black Queen

Nicole said she could stay, as her kids were at her mother's for the evening. I guessed Martin's planned night of frolicking with his newly acquired nurse friend wasn't going to pan out as he'd hoped.

Don and I decamped back to his house to leave Martin and Nicole to do whatever. And to think, only yesterday, he was enjoying the delights that Randy-Mandy had to offer – he really was quite unbelievable. I wondered what Nicole would make of his tattoos if she were given the opportunity to see them. As I was starting to get to know Martin better, I was in no doubt he would make every effort to ensure she did.

Don produced two glasses of whisky. I ensured mine was a small one after the pint in the pub. All I needed now was to get breathalysed, and the day would just be perfect.

"What we going to do, Don? Colney ain't going to stop until he finds me." I performed an involuntary shudder at the thought.

"Not sure at the moment. One thing for certain, he'll want to deal with it his way and won't be reporting it."

"I don't think that makes me feel any better."

"No, agreed."

"He'll be up at Coreys Mill Motors next. I don't think Mr Thacker is the sort to tell him anything. But as we have just seen, Paul Colney can be quite persuasive."

Don took a large gulp of his drink, grimaced and topped up his glass. I thought he looked older tonight. He was eighty, and the thought of what Paul Colney would have done to him if he'd shuffled across to Martin's a minute earlier sent another shiver through me.

"If he causes a scene at Coreys Mill Motors tomorrow, and the police get called, then the circumstances of David's death will all come to light. I've only just stopped looking over my bloody shoulder, expecting to be arrested. Now it's all starting again."

"Son, calm down. Come on, take a seat," he gestured to the chairs around the kitchen table, then pulled out the nearest chair and gingerly sat whilst still wearing his thick overcoat. "Right, as I see it, someone has mouthed off to Paul that they've seen a man get into that Cortina after David fell from the roof. So that means he doesn't know who. Also, I suggest he doesn't know the driver was responsible for David's death."

With my head in my hands, I racked my brain to work out our next move. I felt we were nearly facing checkmate. Paul Colney was the Black Queen systematically scything through my defences, and now we'd reached the point of Check. I had nowhere to go and was only a hand full of moves away from Checkmate.

"That may be. But in the next couple of days he's going to get the information he wants, and then he'll know it was me." I blew out my cheeks and huffed. Whatever I did, I had to keep him away from Jenny and the kids.

I leaned back in the chair and took a sip of my whisky. "Did he see you today? I'm just thinking he knows the connection we have. He may then start joining all the dots without the need to turn Mr Thacker upside down."

"No, son, I don't think he did. As I was crossing the driveway, he came barrelling out of the house. He didn't turn and look at me, and by the time he got to the car, I'd probably made it inside."

"Don, there's another development that I need to make you aware of."

"Oh."

"Yes, oh! I have a daughter from a relationship a long time ago. She surfaced for the first time last week. To cut a long story short, we met a week last Wednesday. And you won't believe this, but she's now living in Carol's old flat."

"Good grief! You two kept that one well under wraps. I take it she's not a child, then? And living on the Broxworth ... oh dear."

"She's twenty. What did you mean you two kept it under wraps?"

"You and Jenny."

I rubbed the back of my head and looked away from Don, embarrassed at what I was about to say. "Err, well ... Jenny doesn't know ... yet."

"Son—"

I didn't look at him.

"Son?" I slowly turned my head. As always, my close friend was there for me. Not judgemental, but there as support. I could see it in his eyes, and I knew I needed to explain.

"I'm just getting used to the idea that I have a daughter. I keep wanting to tell Jenny about her ... but ... it's been difficult with the situation with you-know-who." I nodded in the direction of Martin's house.

"Okay, son. And what is that situation with him next door? Are you ready to tell me?"

I shook my head. I hated not being able to tell him the truth – but the truth just wasn't possible. As always, Don respected my non-disclosure without judgement or disappointment that I couldn't confide in him.

"Alright, son, that's okay. As I said before, when you're ready. But you said you are only just getting used to the idea of your daughter. Are you saying you didn't know you had a daughter until last week?"

"No, no. I knew but never met her before."

"And she's definitely yours?"

"Oh yes, she's mine." But she wasn't, and only George and I knew that. Jesus, why was everything so bloody complicated.

"Not sure what that's got to do with our current situation?" Don peered over the top of his glasses. He knew there was more to this, so he waited for me to continue the story.

"Right, well, listen to this, because, unbelievably, it gets worse. Jess, that's her name, had a spot of bother with Paul Colney. Last week after the bombing, he stashed some drugs in her flat for fear of police raids."

"Oh, bloody hell. She's your daughter and in league with him!"

"It gets even worse … far, far worse. She's pregnant … and … the father is Patrick Colney."

Don held his whisky glass just short of his mouth, shaking his head. "Stone-the-crows! What a mess!"

Don offered me the bottle of whisky. I shook my head, and he knew not to push it.

"Hang on, son, let me get this straight. Paul Colney doesn't know you're her father?"

"No. Well, I don't think so. I get the impression Jess absolutely detests him."

"Right. And does Paul know this daughter of yours is pregnant?"

"No, not that either. She's not showing, and I'm reasonably sure she's only told her mother and me."

"And Patrick, I would presume?"

"Possibly."

"So, have you seen her mother recently, then?" I shook my head. "Son, if you have and not told Jenny, that ain't good. Mark my words, my boy, it'll all end in tears."

"Don, no. I've had no contact with her for over twenty years." The truth is we'd never had contact. Pretty impressive to produce a child in that scenario – the immaculate conception. Shove that up your arse, Lisa's mum. "I'll give you Jaffa, huh!"

"Sorry, son? Don looked at me with that same confused look that he'd shot Martin with his outburst about Paul Colney being his father.

"Oh, Nothing, Don. I was mumbling out loud."

"Did you want a Jaffa cake? I have some in the tin."

"Oh, no. Ignore me." Christ, Don must think I've concussion along with my sex-mad tenant next door. And as for Jaffa cakes, well, I know most of the planet love them, but for me, they were one rung up from Wagon Wheels and not much better than *Nice* biscuits.

"Right, okay, this is becoming complicated. And bloody odd what the boy said about Paul Colney being his father." Don pondered that thought and rubbed his chin. "We've said all along they do look very similar. Ha, silly idea. He must have really banged his head in that fight."

"I'm sure he's okay. Right Don. So, we have to worry about Paul going to Coreys Mill Motors and possibly coming back to see Martin. I think I'd better get down to see Mr Thacker first thing in the morning and give him the heads up of what is coming over the horizon. Then we can take it from there."

"Yes, son. I think you're right. But make sure Paul doesn't see you there. Otherwise, he is going to start to join the dots, so to speak."

"I better get going … it's been one hell of a day. You going to be okay?"

"Me, son? Sure, you know me. Not much gets under my skin. Just be careful in the morning, and let me know how you get on."

I laid my hand on his shoulder as I extracted myself from the chair. I was so lucky to have Don. He really was my father figure.

"Son, it will all work out right in the end. And as they say, if it doesn't, then it's not the end."

35

29th January 1977
New Dawn

Jenny slept soundly beside me as I awoke early. I guess the thoughts whirring around my mind had forced their way to some spot in my brain and banged on the wake-up door. I gently eased my way out of bed and laid the covers back so as not to disturb her. Her bright red hair was a mass of tangles sticking out in every direction. A wisp lay across her eyelids as she slept – she's beautiful, I thought. "I love you, Jenny Apsley," I whispered, as I grabbed my dressing gown from the hook on the back of the door and sneaked out of the bedroom. I poked my head in on Christopher and Beth, who, like Jenny, were sound asleep. Dawn had just started to break, but the closed curtains kept the house cloaked in darkness.

I stood in the back garden with a cup of coffee and cigarette in hand, thinking about the last two week's events and what was to come. Up until two weeks ago, my life had become very simplistic, easy to manage and happy. Okay, the lying was an issue. But as I was the only time-traveller, that was a necessary evil which I had to accept. Now it had become complicated again, with different strands of events that each precious person in my life knew to be the truth, but only I knew the whole story.

Sure, it had to be a step forward that Jenny now knew where I'd come from, so I had her and George in that camp. My next move would be to tell her about Jess. I couldn't work out why I hadn't come clean about her earlier. Perhaps fear of her reaction, but that was unfair on Jenny as she'd proved her love for me. I felt sure Don was right, and the news of Jess's existence wouldn't change the way Jenny felt.

Don not knowing the truth about Martin and me was a problem. With Martin encamped next door, it would only be a matter of time until something happened. I'd then have to explain, and would the four of us be enough for Don to believe the unbelievable?

The biggest issue now was someone else's knowledge of David's death. Only me and Don knew that information. Jenny had an inkling, Martin knew some details, and George had no idea. But yesterday had landed my worst fear since last September because someone else had seen what happened and that someone had informed Paul Colney. Unless I could conjure up some amazing plan, this could only end badly.

To add to this entangled mess – what was I going to do about Jess? Okay, not technically my responsibility. But I'd made that decision to help her, and I had to stick by it. As far as Don was concerned, Jess *was* my daughter – not *other* Jason's daughter – and quite rightly, he'd expect me to help her.

"You bloody well should. You have a responsibility," I muttered. Yes, I will get Jess out of the Broxworth and far away from Paul Colney.

Of course, what about the rapist? From the old newspaper reports and what happened to Jess, there *was* a rapist on the loose. Is that Paul Colney? Well, yes, he's certainly evil enough. If he's Martin's father, which he probably was, then he committed rape in 1987. So, is he raping women now and on at least a ten-year campaign of terror and rape? Is this even possible? Surely, he would've been caught at some point in those years?

Martin. What was I going to do about him? He was a loose cannon, and as much as I could manage my existence, I couldn't handle him as well. The other problem was he had no back story, so issues about his presence in this world would bubble up to the surface sooner rather than later. When that happened, it could erupt like a volcano, throwing not only my life in the air but also Jenny's, Christopher's, and Beth's. Had he taken the place of his father? Was his father now missing in America, and Martin should be there doing his job at BP? What a mess – again.

Today, I had to get up to Coreys Mill Motors and warn Mr Thacker about Paul Colney. What the hell I'll tell him, and what he'll then do, I had no idea. More to the point, what will Paul Colney do? Any police involvement was an absolute no-no because that would accelerate the unravelling. If Paul did cause problems with Mr Thacker, he'd call the police. There was no way I could stop that from happening.

Then the police would be knocking on my door. I just had to hope Don was right and whoever saw me on that roof that day would never talk to the authorities.

The day had arrived, literally, as the grey skies pushed the dark night around the curvature of the earth. Also, metaphorically, as I had a feeling today would be a watershed moment in my life.

Part 3

36

12th August 1976
Guillotine

"Come on, Chris, stop your dawdling." Carol grabbed the back of his t-shirt and hauled him up the last few steps to the top landing of Dublin House, his black plimsols scraping up the last step. She paused and held onto the metal railing, presumably in place to stop you from leaning too far over the edge of the balcony.

"Shit!" Carol pulled her hand away as the steel rail was burning hot. Today was a scorcher as it had been every day for weeks. In this heat, she was panting and out of breath. Carol leaned against the wall and took a moment to collect herself. Chris stood with his arms loose by his side, staring down at the concrete landing.

Carol knew she was a shit mother and had let Chris down. She also knew she'd be a crap mother to her new baby. Carol rubbed her tummy through her blouse, stretched to the limit, buttons ready to ping off at any moment. She couldn't afford any maternity clothes, so the ones she had would have to do.

"I want to go home," mumbled Christopher.

"Oh, shut the fuck up. You're always whining."

Christopher wiped his eyes with the back of his hand, sniffed and snivelled as he continued to gaze at the concrete floor. Carol took another deep breath to calm her breathing and her nerves. She knew this wasn't going to be an easy chat. However, she was skint, and someone had to help. The landing smelt of stale urine, and now Carol felt sick again as she gulped in piss-ridden air as she prepared to walk along to the most frightening door on the estate.

Carol banged on the door and took an involuntary step backwards, perhaps knowing what was on the other side and the danger it represented. She looked down at Christopher as he sat with his back against the wall, his arms tightly wrapped around his knees and his head buried between them. He looked like a hedgehog curling up to avoid danger.

"Don't you fucking cause a scene. I want none of your fucking antics today. You just keep your mouth shut, d'you 'ear?"

Christopher didn't reply. He just gave a slight flinch as he probably expected a smack was coming, which it often did.

The door flung open, and there she stood. Up close, she looked younger than Carol thought she was, or it could've been the heavy make-up disguising the monster which lay beneath. Carol gulped and froze. Now she was here, she didn't know what to say.

Shirley folded her arms and inspected the piece of trash who'd knocked on her door. She looked it up and down from the greasy unkept mouse-coloured hair down to her dirty blouse which stretched over her protruding belly. Shirley noticed a little boy scrunched up by the wall who peaked at her, then quickly buried his head in his knees.

"Well?" Shirley asked the trash.

Carol couldn't look Shirley Colney in the eye. This was a mistake and a dangerous one. She started to feel light-headed again, caused by a combination of heat, being pregnant, the smell of piss on the landing and pure fear. "Can I talk to you?"

"Can't hear you, girl. You're mumbling. What d'you want?"

Carol blew out her cheeks and looked up into Shirley's eyes. Now terrified, she could feel herself starting to shake.

Shirley grabbed the door frame preparing to slam the door. "I'll ask you one more time. What d'you want?"

"I wanted to talk to you, *please*," she delivered slightly louder this time, with a tone that suggested almost begging.

Shirley refolded her arms and arched her eyebrows as an indication for her to continue. Shirley presumed the girl was terrified, and she should be. No one in their right mind knocked on the Colney's door without an invitation.

Carol rubbed her tummy. "Your son ... your son is ... is the father." She looked away, down the corridor. There she'd done it. Although now shitting herself about what would happen next.

Shirley laughed, or more of a cackle akin to a Tricoteuse, knitting and cackling as the guillotine severed the head of another poor soul. "Patrick or Paul wouldn't go near disgusting trash like you!" Shirley curled up her lip at the hideous sight in front of her. "Now, piss off before I make your life hell." She grabbed the door and flung it shut.

"Not Patrick or Paul," Carol blurted, before the door slammed.

Shirley grabbed the door to stop its flight into the frame and yanked it back open. "Well, it's not the other two, you stupid cow; they're just boys!"

Carol steeled herself. Now she'd got this far, she had to carry on. "David ... David is the father."

Shirley stepped forward as Carol retreated. This continued until Carol's back hit the wall on the other side of the landing. "You've got a fucking cheek, coming up here and talking shit like that." She raised her hand to slap the trash girl across the face.

Carol looked at the hand hovering in the air, then closed her eyes. Shirley smacked her hard, causing Carol's cheek to burn red, leaving three white finger-striped marks on her cheek.

Carol opened her eyes. To her left, she could see Christopher looking up. He was probably confused that his mother had been slapped, as he was the one who got beaten, not her. Shirley had closed to within inches of her face, fury and hate radiating from her.

"David ... David is the father." Carol closed her eyes again, expecting another slap.

"You stupid cow, he's only sixteen. He's a boy! He wouldn't go sniffing around the likes of you ... you're just scum!"

She'd come this far, so she might as well carry on. However, it wouldn't surprise her if Shirley lifted her up and tipped her over the railing. Then it would be a flight of five storeys down to her death.

"I owed Paul. I owed him and couldn't pay ... I couldn't pay. He ... he said if I made a man of David, that would pay off the debt."

Shirley narrowed her eyes and pointed at Carol. "You're taking a risk, you slag. If you're lying, you know what will happen."

Carol nodded. "Yes ... but I'm not."

Shirley placed her arms on either side of Carol, leaning her hands against the balcony wall and pinning her in place. "Anyway, slags like you put it about. I bet that bastard in there could belong to any number of men."

Carol shook as shivers terrorised her body. "It's David's." She looked down and patted the bump. "This is your grandchild."

37

29th January 1977
All Mod Cons

"Mr Apsley, good to see you. I presume you've come about the Hunter. Knew you'd be back. It's a great car, and I've had a fair bit of interest in it." Mr Thacker stood in his double-breasted pin-striped suit, puffing on his cigar, grinning now he could smell the chance of a sale. He again looked and sounded like 'Boycie' as he delivered that familiar machine-gun laugh.

I'd parked up a few minutes before the sales lot opened and scanned around out of the windows, looking to see if I could spot Paul Colney. It was reminiscent of that day last September when I'd parked up on the Broxworth – the day David died. And here I was again in a very similar situation, repeating the same actions caused by the events that day. I hadn't seen Paul Colney and prayed he wasn't a morning person.

"Morning, Charles. Good to see you again." We shook hands enthusiastically. Although yesterday evening's events had negated the need to hide the Cortina, as *'the cat was already out of the bag,'* I still wanted to replace Jenny's Viva.

"Malcolm, grab the keys for the Hunter, please," Charles called over to the young salesman I'd seen two weeks ago. "Let me show you around. It's got some great features on this model."

"Okay, Charles, but I'm short of time. I'm sure it's all very self-explanatory." Cars built in the '70s weren't complicated machines. I thought even a chimpanzee could understand the finer points of the car without a detailed run through.

Charles took the keys from Malcolm, unlocked the door and offered for me to take a seat. I obliged in order to get through this charade quickly and move on to the more difficult conversation regarding Paul Colney.

Charles bent forward to position his head at the same height as mine. "So, some fantastic features on this model. It has the 1725cc engine with a four-speed transmission and overdrive. All of that will get you from nought to sixty in less than fifteen seconds! Careful motoring, and you'll get over twenty-five miles to the gallon ... pretty impressive, wouldn't you say? Also, you'll see that it has many new electrical features for modern driving, such as an electrically operated screen washer, and a heated rear windscreen."

"Yes, Charles, all very impressive." Although it wasn't. Also, notwithstanding his enthusiasm regarding the car's technical specifications, I couldn't care less if it took two hundred seconds to get to sixty miles per hour – those rear seatbelts were the only feature I was interested in.

"And this car is for your wife, I believe?"

"Yes, that's right. An upgrade on her old Viva."

"Well, that's perfect, as it has the Servo Brake System; that's one for the ladies."

I shot him a look, confused at his odd comment. "Oh," I replied.

"Servo Vacuum brakes means you don't have to push on the pedal so hard. Just right for a nice shapely leg in a court shoe. Ladies need all these new features to help them to be able to drive cars properly," he replied with a smile.

I know Charles meant nothing derogatory or sexist by his comment. Of course, it was, but it wasn't for the era I was living in. If I wasn't shitting myself that Paul Colney was about to show his face, so a need to quickly conclude the deal, I would have burst out laughing. I momentarily thought of what Beth would have said or done to Mr Thacker if he'd offered that comment in 2019 – I think she'd have flattened him.

I'd enjoyed the trawl around the opulent car showrooms with Beth when she bought her new sports car. I'd marvelled at the amazing machines and loved being able to sit in those brand-new supercars. Unfortunately, whilst I jumped in and out of the cars and feeling somewhat jealous, Beth had cause to verbally maul one of the salesmen. I remember the poor chap almost shaking when she'd put him straight on a few points.

He was a lad in his late twenties with flawlessly trimmed designer stubble, a fake sun tan and perfectly barbered hair. He wore a designer suit over what looked like a spray-on shirt. Extra slim fit, or muscle fit, I think they call the cut. His winkle-picker patent-black boots must have extended about six inches past the end of his toes, and I was sure they would pierce steel with one quick kick.

Beth had delivered the verbal mauling when he continued to only offer her flirtatious comments and focussed on me to explain the flashy car's features on offer. Unfortunately, he'd made the grave mistake of assuming the car was for me, not Beth. As always in these situations, Beth employed her sharp tongue to rip him apart – similar to a Great White shredding a wayward swimmer. Once the verbal mauling was over, what was left of him shrunk about six inches. He'd met his match, as most men did when confronted with a disgruntled Beth – the flirting instantly stopped. I wondered if Beth would be the same second time around, or would her new life showered with love from Jenny and me soften her edges.

"Yes, Charles, I'd like to buy the car."

"Good man – you know it makes sense." A statement that sounded as if delivered by Del Boy. I wondered if I was now the *plonker* for buying the Hillman Hunter and half expected Charles to rub his hands together and utter *'Lovely Jubbly'*. The last time I was here, the other salesman stated the car had only one lady owner – a statement they probably said about all their motors.

"Come inside, and we can talk business." Charles held out his arm, inviting me into the Portakabin sales office.

"Take a seat, Mr Apsley."

"Jason."

"Good. Can I offer you a cigar?" Charles opened an ornate wooden box full of large cigars, which sat on his desk amongst paperwork and car brochures.

"No thanks."

"So, the Hillman Hunter," he muttered while sifting through a pile of buff-coloured files heaped on a steel filing cabinet next to his desk. "As I said, Jason, great car, with all the mod-cons."

Presumably, he wasn't referring to the album by The Jam. That particular LP would be released a year from now and was on my list of records to buy. I had a notepad with all the albums I wanted and the year of release – some even had the actual month.

'All Mod Cons,' by The Jam, was one such record detailed on that notepad as they were one of my favourite bands. Jenny had perused the list but didn't see any bands that interested her. She'd asked when the Bee Gees released a new album, but I had no idea. However, she sounded excited

about the film *'Saturday Night Fever'* and pestered me to remember the year. I'd said it was very soon but couldn't be sure if it was this year or next. I'd also said she would probably really enjoy the film *'Grease'*. When I'd described that it was about two high school kids falling in love in the '50s, she said it didn't sound very good and was surprised a storyline like that would be a success. I guess my description was lost in translation.

"Ah, actually, before we strike that deal, how did you get on investigating what happened with that Cortina? I must say I forgot all about it. But now you're back, it's reminded me. Bloody strange affair that was!"

"Well, yes, Charles, that's the other reason for popping in today." From where I was sitting, I had a clear view of the sales lot. I scanned the view again to see if Paul Colney had shown up. Charles followed my sightline, presumably wondering what I was looking at as my gaze had been longer than a casual glance.

"Everything alright, Jason?"

"Err … yes, fine. Sorry. Ummm … the Cortina story is a bit complicated. There's a bloke trying to track me down, as he's explicitly looking for the previous owner of that Cortina. So, it's, as I say, a bit complicated."

"Oh?"

"Charles, I think this chap will turn up here at some point and ask questions about who you purchased the Cortina from. I'd appreciate it if you didn't say."

A deep frown formed across his face as he puffed on the unsupported cigar in his mouth. He leant forward, removing the cigar. "I would never give out that information. This does sound very strange, though. I do hope you're not in some kind of trouble, as I wouldn't want to be involved in anything dodgy."

"No, Charles. It's just difficult to say. But this chap isn't the nicest. His name is Paul Colney."

"Never heard of him," he replied, as he waved his cigar and reclined back in his chair.

"He has close links to the Gowers. Have you heard of them?"

His complexion instantly changed. I watched as the blood drained out of his face as if a plug had been pulled in his neck, causing the blood to gurgle out somewhere below. I half expected to see seven pints of the red-stuff pool under his chair. Pale and giving the appearance he was about to faint, he gripped the arms of his swivel chair.

"I'm sorry, but I think we'd better end this conversation. Also, I've just remembered I've already agreed to a sale on that Hunter, so it's no longer for sale. I'm sorry, Jason, but I think you'd better leave."

"Look, I am sorry to put you in this situation. But rest assured, this has nothing to do with the Gowers. Paul Colney is just a lowlife who thinks the driver of that Cortina had something to do with an accident involving a member of his family."

"Mr Apsley, that may well be. But I run a respectable business, and I don't want anything to do with anyone connected to them. I have my reputation and good name with the authorities to consider."

"I understand, and I'm so sorry to have put you in this position."

"So am I!"

"Look, Charles. I'm just a schoolteacher. I'm not from the underworld, and I have no connection to the authorities. Could you just tell this bloke if he asks that you bought it for cash and not through the books?"

Charles stood and shoved his cigar back in his mouth. Although it had burnt out ages ago, I think it was just a habit to have one on the go. He shimmied around his desk and sat on the edge leaning towards me. "You're not from the Inland Revenue? You're a schoolteacher, you say?" he quizzed, the cigar now skilfully shoved to the side of his mouth.

His slightly greying hair gave him the Jonah Jameson look. I now half expected him to scream at me to get a picture of Spiderman. I could certainly do with the support of a Marvel character at the moment – that would sort out a certain Mr Colney.

"Yes, Charles. And to show my appreciation, let's say I take that Hunter off your hands for eight hundred... cash. That's two hundred over the asking price."

Charles leant back and fished about in his suit pockets. Catching a box of matches, he plucked them out, shook them and then lit one. He puffed heavily at the stub of his cigar, at the same time alternating his glances from the lit match and my face. I guessed he was weighing up his options.

I knew Charles was money motivated, and I hoped the offer of an extra two-hundred quid would be enough for no more questions and for him to create a suitable back story for the Cortina. Satisfied the cigar end was burning after a few puffs and blowing on the lit end, he looked back at me through the blue haze that now engulfed the Portakabin.

"Eight-hundred. And you say cash?"

"Yes, Charles. I can bring cash next weekend. In the meantime, any questions about the Cortina, you say it was a cash deal and off the books. Do we have a deal?"

Charles eased himself off the desk and stood. I followed suit.

"Deal, Jason."

We shook hands after I'd left him fifty quid as a deposit. I didn't hang around as I was keen to get out of there in case Paul turned up. Unfortunately, my desire for a classic sports car had left me in a position where, once again, my motor stood out like a sore thumb.

Pulling onto the main road, I headed up to see Don and check on Martin. However, I would knock this time, as I was sure he and Nursey Nicole would be enjoying their Saturday morning. If they were playing doctors and nurses, adult style, I didn't want to see them in action.

I waited for the lights to change after getting caught at the red traffic lights a hundred yards from Coreys Mill Motors. As I glanced in the rear-view mirror, I spotted a white Ford Capri with a coat hanger aerial swing into the car sales lot.

38

Spit The Dog

Thankfully the rest of the day was uneventful. Martin and I had a long chat about our situation, his mother and Paul Colney. By the time I arrived at his house, Nicole had gone. I found him lying on the sofa in the lounge laughing at Tiswas.

Both of us were too young to remember the show the first time around; in fact, Martin wasn't even born. The slapstick comedy wasn't my thing. Even though it was aimed at children, I wouldn't have enjoyed it even if I was the right age to see it when first released. Judging by Martin's reactions as we sat and chatted, he would have, as he continually laughed at the clown-like antics. I'll admit I did enjoy watching Bob Carolgees and Spit the Dog, and both of us couldn't stop laughing as the dog spat at all the show's guests. It was good to laugh at something after the tough week we'd endured.

Martin's face appeared better than I expected, although his right eye was severely swollen. He said his nose hurt like hell and, between that and the attentions of Nicole, he'd achieved very little sleep.

I decided I'd been way too tough on him. Let's face it, time travelling back forty years and knowing you're never going back is tough to take. I was conscious all I'd done for two weeks was berate him daily. He was still a loose cannon, but I needed to cut him some slack.

Don and I discussed the events at Coreys Mill Motors, and both felt it had gone as well as could be expected. After seeing that white Capri on Friday and today, we knew it was a stroke of luck I'd just missed Paul earlier that morning.

Don pushed me regarding the need to have a conversation with Jenny about Jess and, as always, both George and Don were right. Their wise counsel was invaluable, and I promised Don that I would come clean with Jenny over the weekend. *"It's for the best, son,"* he'd said as I left to go home.

Passing Coreys Mill Motors on the way home, I was relieved to see it still standing. As no police cars were in attendance, I hoped the last couple of hours had been uneventful. It appeared that Paul Colney had left without killing anyone and hopefully not managed to extract any information about me. However, I knew this wouldn't be the end of the matter. Oh no, he would continue to pursue the owner of that Cortina, but maybe today had bought me some time.

Don was right; well, of course he was. Jenny was disappointed that I'd not told her about Jess earlier, but she was supportive and understood my desire to help Jess. However, it did add further complication to an already difficult situation. I guess the conversation was more straightforward than Don suggested it might be, as he thought Jess *was* my daughter. But of course, Jenny knew differently, as Jess was the daughter of *other* Jason.

Jenny thought once we'd moved past the Paul Colney issue – easily said, I reminded her – and perhaps when Martin had started to settle, he could find his own place, and we could slot Jess into the house next to Don. A perfect solution for the next ten years – until Patrick was released – then there might need to be a rethink.

The news events were very repetitive, with nothing reported that stood out as an event that I could remember and then predict what would happen from there. Although Jenny firmly believed who I was, an event that I could predict was going to happen imminently would just help cement that belief.

The national newscasts focussed on the continued grumblings from various trade unions regarding pay, or lack of, and the link to inflation. But as it had topped out at twenty-four per cent, it was clear the government would not be able to sanction any public-sector pay rise anywhere near that. Otherwise, inflation would get to the levels of post WW1 Germany. The comparison between West Germany's solid economy and the UK's, which was in freefall, was often a conversation in the staffroom. Many of my colleagues were unhappy with the lack of pay increase since the agreed pay deal in 1975 of twenty-seven per cent. I would have loved to tell them in 2019 a full half a per cent was the average public-sector pay deal – but I guess these were different times.

Unemployment was another heavily discussed subject when us teachers fell into our moaning sessions. Even though I benefited from hindsight, it was tough to see how the government could *square that circle* of inflation, pay demands, and unemployment. I knew they didn't and was also aware of the economic doom that the next few years would bring.

Jenny and I watched the Saturday lunchtime news, which was as depressing as usual. Jenny had said, *"It can't get any worse, can it?"* Unfortunately, I wasn't able to alleviate her concerns as I described the up-and-coming '*Winter of Discontent,*' which would spiral the UK economy to even lower depths of depression over the next two years. Jenny thought it sounded horrific as I described the strikes that led to dead bodies stacked up as the gravediggers' pay dispute was unresolved.

The picture I painted of rubbish piled up on the streets when the council collection operatives refused to resume their weekly collections was equally grim to hear. However, Jenny did laugh at my description of 'dustmen', as she put it. I remember George in my previous life recounting these times, and now the poor bugger had it all to come again. Well, no, it seemed like again, but it was the first time ... again.

The local news continued to report about the bombing in Fairfield, with a different angle on the story each day. It had slipped off the national news as it was now ten days old. Although, on Saturday evening, the Fairfield bombing made it back to the national news as a reference point to the events unfolding in Oxford Street. The IRA had accepted responsibility for seven bombs, one of which caused Selfridges to be set alight.

Jenny was pleased to hear that the Good Friday Agreement would bring lasting peace. However, the news that it would take another twenty years to get to that point was not so good, especially as I advised her that there would be many more bombings on the mainland in those preceding years.

Sunday was a quiet, uneventful day, which was a bloody miracle in itself after the last week. After we'd finished our Sunday tea, which consisted of sandwiches and cakes, we settled into early evening television. Christopher loved the lemon-curd sandwiches but had spat out the Heinz Sandwich Spread ones, saying it was yucky. So after I dished out his telling off for saying horrible things about Jenny's sandwiches, I banished him to the naughty step – the bottom step of the stairs in the cold hallway.

In my view, he was totally correct in his assessment of the sandwich filling. Not in his earshot – I agreed with him. After suffering a decade of the stuff in my school packed lunches in the '80s and definitely not daring to criticise the sandwich filling choice with my grandmother, Jenny agreed not to purchase the product again – what a relief.

After Christopher had served his ten-minute sentence on the naughty step, we allowed him to watch some TV with us before bedtime. He was super excited watching the biplanes on the TV show *'Wings'*. The basic plot was about a blacksmith's son becoming a pilot in the First World War. I was sure the storyline was sugar-coated, and I expected Don would be berating the TV as he sat and watched it. The show appeared dated, with over-exaggerated accents and shockingly poor cinematography.

To me it was tame and boring, but this was all we had in this era, and I had a long wait for the digital age and hundreds of channels to choose from. Although I used to moan about that at the time, *"Thousands of channels and piss-all worth watching,"* I could hear myself ranting at the TV.

Jenny thought the show was too scary for Christopher, which did make me laugh as I thought back to my youth when I'd watched the film *'An American Werewolf in London'* at the age of ten and the *'Evil Dead'* only a couple of years later. Children's innocence eroded at a lightning pace over those forty years from the '70s through the millennium.

After Christopher was soundly tucked up in bed and Beth had her last feed for the evening, the doorbell rang.

"I'll get it." I sprang off the sofa, surprised with my enthusiasm, although it was probably to avoid any more pain of the utterly dreary TV on offer. That said, I was looking forward to *'The Rise and Fall of Reginald Perrin'*, which was showing later – now some comedies were timeless.

Standing a few feet back from the doorway was a forty-something woman wearing heavy makeup, which appeared to have been applied with a trowel. She stood with her arms folded in what gave off an aggressive aura.

"Hello," I greeted her and smiled, now slightly concerned who this woman was standing on my doorstep on a cold Sunday evening.

She stepped forward with her arms still tightly crossed. My smile wasn't reciprocated, just the offer of a cold stare.

"Err ... can I help you?"

"You know who I am?" she coldly delivered, and there appeared to be little chance of a smile coming. Presumably, her concrete makeup had set her face to a scowl. I had now developed a growing unease about where this conversation was heading.

"Sorry, no. Can I help you?"

Jenny joined me at the front door and nuzzled up to my side, her head resting on my arm as I waited for the woman to answer.

The scary woman took a further step forward, closing the gap between us to less than a yard.

"Shirley Colney. We've never met. But you've 'eard of me, I'm sure of that." With her bleached hair, dark roots and evil voice, it appeared Cruella de Vil had left *'Hell Hall'* and arrived on our doorstep.

As with Mr Thacker, yesterday morning, when it appeared that a plug had been pulled out of his neck, the very same effect seemed to be syphoning out the blood from my veins.

"What do you want?" I heard myself say, although I didn't remember my brain deciding to instruct my vocal cords to speak. I could now feel Jenny gripping my arm.

"That baby is my granddaughter."

Her words took an age to register in my brain, and they seemed to hang in the air before deciding on their final destination. It then took a while for me to compute those five simple words and the meaning they delivered. Jenny's grip on my upper arm tightened even further as if feeling the pressure of the pump on a blood pressure machine reaching its optimum peak point.

"We've unfinished business, you and me ... you'll see. Your time is nearly up, and when that happens ... that little girl will be mine."

39

31st January 1977
Bunsen Burner

Sunday night was a return to those nights of a week ago, as in achieving very little sleep. After getting rid of the monster disguised as Shirley Colney from our doorstep, Jenny and I felt the cracks widening in our perfect life. That bloody Colney family, which I seemed unwittingly to be totally entwined with, had just rammed another wedge in the cracks.

Shirley was clear that Beth was her granddaughter, and her evil child-abusing, future serial killer son, David, was Beth's father. I'd pulled myself together after the shock of her visit and banished her away from our home. However, I had no idea what she meant by that statement, *'Your time is nearly up'*.

I stayed strong for Jenny, who was terrified of what would now happen as I was, although I didn't show it. Keeping a level head and a lid on my emotions was critical to convincing Jenny that it would all turn out okay. I was putting on a good show. However, Jenny was right to be worried.

Shirley Colney had stated that Carol Hall had told her last year that she and David had got it together when he was fifteen. A coming-of-age present from her son, Paul, as she put it. Shirley claimed the product of David and Carol's liaison was apparently Beth. She added that she'd dismissed the slag at the time, as she described her, but now knew the truth that Amy Elizabeth was her granddaughter. She made it quite clear she would be part of Beth's life as she was a

Colney and, if we knew what was good for us, we would comply with her demands.

Jenny planned to call her boss, Barry, and set up a meeting to discuss what support we could expect from the Child Protection team. Although Jenny knew the guidelines for these sorts of situations, her head was in a mess and needed Barry's calm manner to get it all in perspective. We agreed to talk to her parents on Monday evening, and we could then formulate a plan from there.

I had my own separate challenges to deal with today, which involved turning Sarah Moore's lustful gazes from her thirty-one-year-old son onto the Fairfield Chronicle's future editor, Carlton King. Although Carlton was a bit of a dickhead at school, he managed to aspire to a decent job in the future. Maybe Sarah could do worse, I thought.

"Good Morning, Miss Colman," I announced, much brighter than I was feeling, as I slugged my way into the school office to prepare for another week.

"Oh, good morning to you too, Mr Apsley. And what a lovely morning it is!" she replied enthusiastically. She seemed to have developed a glow about her.

"How was your weekend? Did you get up to anything exciting?"

I thought for a moment before replying. The events from Friday to yesterday evening could not be described as exciting, but definitely eventful. "No, nothing really," I replied.

"I had a wonderful weekend. Truly wonderful!"

"Oh, pray tell," I asked over my shoulder as I hauled out the usual Monday morning heap of paperwork from my pigeonhole, which now hung straight again after Martin had skilfully wielded his screwdriver last week.

Miss Colman didn't answer. I turned and glanced in her direction, now wondering what was going on. She was grinning from ear to ear, glowing like an angel from heaven, and almost hovering a few millimetres above her seat. Knowing she was the biggest gossip who'd ever graced the planet, I was surprised and intrigued by her silence.

"Miss Colman?"

I'd have been disappointed if she hadn't performed her next moves, as it was who she was. She beckoned me closer with her middle finger, reeling me in. Then conducted the furtive glance left and right, before excitedly blurting it out.

"Mr Trosh proposed to me on Saturday morning!"

"Whaaaa, what! Fantastic! I can't believe it. What happened ... how? Tell me everything. This is exciting!"

Miss Colman almost hopped up and down on her seat. Seeing someone so happy just lifts your spirits and, although my weekend had been a large pile of doo-doo, I was starting to feel better. The glow radiating from this lovely middle-aged lady, who was probably more excited than she'd ever been, caused my clouds of doom to begin to evaporate.

"Mr Apsley, it's because of you. It's because of what you said last week."

Sporting a furrowed brow, I was now confused at what she was on about. Although I was delighted for her, I couldn't imagine what I had to do with Mr Trosh's proposal of marriage.

"Don't you remember? You said I should go and see Mr Trosh in hospital, so I jolly well did. When I visited on Saturday morning, he said he'd been thinking about his life, and the operation had spurred him into making some important decisions. He said he'd wasted so much of his life and wasn't going to waste any more time."

With all the events of the last two weeks, I'd forgotten about pushing Miss Colman to visit Clive. So, I'd been right all along, and that little nudge was enough to get these two lovely characters together.

"So, he proposed?"

"Yes! He called for the nurses, and they helped him out of bed and to get down on one knee. Then in his pyjamas, he asked me to marry him!" She clasped her hands together as if praying. "Mr Apsley, it was the most romantic moment of my life."

"Oh, that's wonderful news. I'm so pleased. Have you got a ring?"

A slight dent formed in her smile. "No, not yet. Mr Trosh isn't very wealthy, but he said he'll save up for one as soon as he gets back on his feet. But that doesn't matter. I'm so happy."

"No, you're right ... it doesn't matter."

I wondered if Mr Trosh had proposed to Miss Colman the first time around. Perhaps that tiny butterfly effect of my existence and the nudge I'd given Miss Colman had changed their futures. I decided it had, and that was a good thing. I felt a need to nip up to my safety deposit box, and another trip to see Mr Maypole was required. Jenny and I had more than enough wealth for our lifetime, and I thought one diamond less in that box and sitting on Trish's finger felt right. I would get up and see Clive this week and float my idea to him.

"Well, Trish, I better get on. Just think you will be Trish Trosh when you're married!"

"Oh, yes, I will! Trish Trosh. Trish Trosh. Trish Trosh," she repeated to herself in different tones and accents as if deciding which sound she liked best. It was the first time I'd used her Christian name without her pulling me up and putting me straight on the need for formal address during school hours. Trish had other things to think about, and so did I. My matchmaking skills needed to be put to the test once more when I planned to align Sarah Moore and Carlton King's planets over a Bunsen Burner in this morning's chemistry lesson.

"Right, all settle down, please. Quiet!" I boomed. My first request had no effect. However, the second shorter, one-word demand had the desired effect as the class all turned, looked in my direction, and closed their mouths.

"Mr Roberts, you can remove the rubber tubing sticking out of your trouser zip unless you would prefer it inserted up your backside," I bellowed.

Stephen Roberts pulled out the tube and adjusted his trousers. Carlton King smirked, and a few of the girls giggled but soon returned to silence as I delivered one of my now-perfected Paddington stares.

"Okay, this morning, we're going to be conducting experiments in pairs. But rather than working with the person next to you, I'm going to mix it up a bit. The purpose of this is to encourage you to work with others and, ultimately, collaboratively deliver the conclusions to the experiments."

The class groaned and started to look about the room, I guess scanning the faces of those they prayed would not be their allotted partner. The murmuring stopped as a few clocked my stare. Yes, I had a lot to thank the cardboard-cut-out cartoon character of Paddington Bear. The crowd or rabble control tool I'd copied from that Peruvian brown furry orphan was invaluable in maintaining class order; over the past few months, my students had grown wise to my stare and consistently obeyed.

Once I'd set them into their new partnerships, I instructed them on the gripping task of identifying cations with metal salts through the use of the flame test and left them to crack on.

Sarah Moore and Carlton King seemed nonplus with their pairing, but I guess I was optimistic to expect Sarah to gush over this immature lad as he held a wooden spatula to the burner flame. However, I needed Mr King to recognise the lovely, intelligent girl he was paired with and take the initiative to ask her on a date. The main problem I faced was Carlton's lack of maturity. Although sixteen-year-old girls were maturing and, if this lot were anything to go by, their male counterparts were not. In Sarah's eyes, Martin probably appeared sophisticated and exciting. Whereas Carlton, I imagined, looked like a dork.

The lesson ended with only a few pairings delivering a full set of correct answers from their experiments. Sarah and Carlton were one such pairing, and they appeared pleased with their collaborative achievements; also, they looked okay about the fact that the pairing would stay the same for the next lesson. I was fully aware their partnership had produced successful academic results because Sarah was a grade-A student. What frustrated me was in the future, she didn't aspire to a great career which I knew she was capable of. Carlton-Dork-King, who really was a bit of a pillock, became editor of a newspaper. I was sure Sarah would've performed far better in that position based on her academic capabilities.

My matchmaking skills didn't seem to progress any further than the Bunsen Burner. As break-time arrived, Sarah quickly migrated back to her friends whilst Carlton looked about for his delinquent mates – Roberts and Cooper.

"Mr King, a word, please," I boomed out over the melee of chatter as the whole class attempted to squeeze out of the door simultaneously.

"Sir?" he replied, as he sauntered back to the front of the lab, I guess fully expecting to be reprimanded for something. His head sagged, awaiting the bollocking or worse, probably expecting a pair of Marigolds and a toilet brush to be thrust into his hand.

"Well done with today's lesson. That was some of your best work this year."

His head shot up in surprise. "Oh, fanks, sir." He performed an odd chicken-style movement as his head repeatedly enacted small nodding actions whilst he contemplated the compliment he'd just received.

"Was working with Sarah helpful?"

"Yeah, she's really cleva. 'elped a lot."

"Right, that's good. So, working as a pair in the future should help you?"

He continued his chicken-style nodding. "Yep," he over pronounced the 'p', leaving his bottom lip slack. It wasn't a good look.

"Great! Maybe you should catch up with Sarah and thank her for her help."

My plan to help the relationship along just got another nudge. Martin was unsure when his mother dated Carlton. However, it was in her school years and, as this was her final year, it had to be soon. I felt Carlton had some serious shaping up to do if Sarah was to fall for his charms unless she had a thing about nodding chickens.

"Yeah, I will, sir. Cheers. Be good to have another gawp at her great tits as well." With that, he sloped out of the lab and fell into the swim of students cruising down the corridors.

"Okay. Surely he'll grow up soon?" I mumbled, and shook my head in disbelief at his comment regarding Sarah's anatomy. I did remind myself that I'd said a similar comment to my prospective ex-mother-in-law about Lisa's chest at the age of twenty-six. Based on the fact Carlton was ten years younger than I was then – there was no hope.

The plan Martin and I'd conjured up involved him keeping away from any students during breaks. So, he'd stay in the boiler house with his tools and only exit his hideout when classes were in full flow. We felt sure this would prevent him from having any further contact with his mother. In addition, I suggested he wasn't to complete any jobs near the school gates as the students were piling out at the end of the day – fully aware this severely reduced his chances of courting any more yummy mummies. Martin recognised the seriousness of the situation and accepted he would have to satisfy himself with Randy Mandy and Nursey Nicole for the time being – a real hardship, but I thought he could cope.

40

Twiggy

"It's gonna get really tough for you. Don't think, just because Patrick is the father, that I won't deal with you." She leant in closer to her face. "Don't underestimate me, girl; you should know better."

Jess knew she was right. She was under no illusion that Patrick's mother would make her life hell or worse if she chose to. Leaning away from Shirley with her back to the sink, she glanced between the evil woman and Paul.

"Well? I'm waiting," Shirley stabbed out, as she folded her arms across her tartan-checked coat, with a cigarette poking out the side of her mouth. Paul moved closer, sliding his backside along the edge of the kitchen worktop. Although he had those evil eyes, it was clear to Jess who was in charge as Shirley unfolded her arms and slowly raised her right index finger. She continued to stare at Jess, but the raised finger was enough to stop Paul's advance towards her.

"I told 'im, all I know," Jess replied. Relieved the evil bastard hadn't encroached any nearer. Jess knew if Shirley wanted to, she could click her fingers, and her well-trained pit-bull-son would rip her guts out.

"Hmmm. Well, tell me."

"I was walking down the lane at the back. Y'know, Thetford Lane that goes around the field up by those trees." Jess thumbed over her shoulder, indicating through the kitchen window behind her.

Shirley removed her cigarette from her mouth and flicked the ash to the kitchen floor. "Go on."

"I heard some shouting and, when I looked around, I could see some bloke hanging over the edge of the flats' roof. I didn't know then it was David. Some other bloke was hanging over the edge holding him. Another man was standing on the roof ... he was ... just standing there. Then the bloke hanging over the edge seemed to just let go, and I watched David fall to his death. As I said, I didn't know it was David ... well, not until I met up with Patrick later."

"You said you saw this geezer throw him off the roof. You changing your story?" Paul barked, as he stepped closer but halted when Shirley shot him a look.

"Why didn't you say anything?" Shirley held her stare and again dashed the ash to the floor.

"This bitch needs sortin' out!"

"Shut up!" she barked at her son without looking at him. Paul shrank back and moved a few steps away from Jess.

Jess knew why she'd said nothing. She remembered thinking at the time it was good riddance to that little perv. Knowing that David was Shirley's favourite, she couldn't say that without dire consequences. Nothing came to mind about what to say, so she shrugged her shoulders.

"And this bloke, you saw him later?"

Jess nodded. "I was walking back from the shops about an hour or so later. I recognised the denim jacket he was wearing, and he looked about the same size as the man on the roof. He then jumped into a yellow Cortina and drove out of the estate."

Shirley nodded and dropped the cigarette to the lino floor, crushing it under the sole of her black knee-length boots. Jess glanced at Shirley's foot but said nothing. The burn hole would just mix in with all the other burn marks accumulated over the years across the orange-coloured lino.

"Well, girl. You're carrying my grandchild. Patrick will want you looked after while he's away, so you don't need to concern yourself with anything. You're carrying a Colney; that alone will protect you. But let me be clear." She stepped towards Jess, closing the gap which caused Jess to lean back against the sink. "You talk to me now. You tell me everything, not 'im … just me." She thumbed over her shoulder in Paul's direction.

"Ma?"

Shirley turned to her son. The height difference between them was over a foot. Paul, like Patrick, was built like a brick shit house. Shirley had a frame more like a short Twiggy, but it was clear to see Paul was terrified of her.

Shirley sneered at him. "Shut up." She held his stare for a few more seconds before turning back to Jess.

"Patrick will be out in less than ten. You're going to be a little angel in those years."

Jess nodded.

"You'll go every week to visit him. You won't get involved with anyone else … you're his woman, and you'll stick by him … you clear?"

Jess nodded.

"You and I will bring up this child, and Patrick will come out with a faithful woman waiting for him."

Jess nodded and swallowed hard, unable to avert her eyes from Shirley as they pierced into her skull.

"We understand each other? Woman to woman."

"Yes." Jess knew this was her opportunity to rid herself of Paul. She mustered up some courage from somewhere. "I love Patrick. I'll do everything you say, but keep him away from me." She pointed at Paul.

Shirley didn't move for a few seconds, then leant back. After already being told to shut up twice, Paul presumably had decided to keep schtum in fear of another verbal mauling by his mother. He edged closer, his fists balled and appeared ready to smash his fist through Jess's teeth.

Shirley nodded, then glanced at her son. "You 'eard her. You keep your distance."

"Why would I wanna touch that?" He curled the corner of his mouth and looked at Jess as if she were something he'd scraped off his shoe. As Shirley turned back to look at Jess, he suggestively stuck out his tongue.

"You sick git. I wouldn't touch you if you were the last man alive."

"Too late, girlie. I've already fucked ya."

"No you haven't. No you haven't!" Jess shot back at him, concerned that Shirley would believe his lies. She was going to comply with her demands and always be faithful to Patrick.

"The alley a couple of weeks ago. As I said, I've already been there!" he grinned.

Jess froze and felt her knees weaken – grabbing the edge of the sink to support herself as she became nauseous. "You? You … you … raped me? You raped me!" she shrieked.

Shirley swivelled around and glared at Paul, a steel-cold stare. Paul now appeared uncomfortable as he retreated from his mother. He winced and stepped back further, clearly concerned about what was about to happen.

Shirley didn't need to ask the question. She had four boys who she ruled with a rod of iron. She knew when they were lying and when they fucked-up. She never needed to ask. Shirley swung her arm with such force that the slap knocked Paul off his feet, causing him to crack his head on the countertop as he crumpled to the floor. "You disgusting piece of shit. Get out. Get out!"

Whilst Shirley physically threw her son out of the flat, Jess slid down to the lino floor. Tears flowed, and she tried to control her breathing and was now hyperventilating.

Shirley strode back into the kitchen, leant down and slapped her across the face. "Get up!"

The shock of the slap instantly brought her breathing back under control. Jess crawled to a kitchen chair, hauling herself onto it before staring down at the table and wiping her eyes with the back of her hand.

"Who've you told?"

Jess didn't look up.

Shirley stepped forward, forcibly grabbing her chin and yanking it up. "Talk, girl. Who've you told?"

Jess suppressed her tears as she shook her head. "No ... no one."

"No one?"

Jess shook her head again. Thinking of her father and how much she needed him here now.

Shirley leant forward, her nose now inches from Jess. "That's how it stays. You tell no one. Patrick must never know ... you understand?"

Jess nodded as the tears escaped again and poured down her cheeks.

"I'll deal with him. He'll never come near you again. But ... you utter a word about this, and your life will be over ... over!"

Jess nodded again. Shirley released her chin from her tight grip, then gently stroked Jess's hair. She pulled out two cigarettes and lit them, then offered one to Jess and sat in the chair opposite.

"Smoke that, then go and have a wash. You're a mess."

41

The Long Kiss Goodnight

"Hold the line, caller."

I waited, holding the curly telephone cord. Well, that's what the lady said at the other end of the phone to do – so I did.

"Jenny Lawrence speaking, how can I help you?"

"As far as I'm aware, you married me five weeks ago. So, unless you're leaving me, I believe your name is Jenny Apsley," I chuckled.

"Oh, darling, I keep forgetting!"

"Forgetting your name, or we got married? As I said, it was only five weeks ago. Has your memory gone? Oh, hang on, don't tell me your real name is Samantha Caine from the *'Long Kiss Goodnight'*?"

"Who, darling?"

"Oh, yeah. Don't worry. That's another great movie we'll have to plan to watch. Although we've about twenty years to wait for that one."

"Oh, okay, darling. We can add it to the list," she chuckled.

"How did you get on with Barry?"

"Yes, he's been very helpful. As I thought, Shirley doesn't have a leg to stand on, well, legally. As Beth is our adopted daughter, she has no rights."

"I thought so. That's good news."

"Yes, it is. After talking to Barry, I feel so much better. But of course, that's only legally, and I'm not sure that woman operates within the law."

"No, you're right."

"Let's talk to Daddy tonight and see what he thinks we should do."

"What time did we say to be at your mum and dad's?"

"Have *you* lost your memory now?" she chuckled again. "I will go there straight after work, as Mum will be whacked out after having Beth all day and doing the school run to get Christopher. Will you be late?"

"I might be. I've had a distress call from Jess this afternoon. She said she urgently needs to speak to me about Paul Colney. I think I need to go and find out what it's all about."

"Oh no, not him again?"

"Yes, exactly. That bloody family."

"You're not going up the estate, are you?"

"No, I said I'd meet her at six in the Bramingham Arms. I'll quickly see what she's got to say and be over about seven. Is that okay?"

"Yes, darling. But please be careful, won't you?"

"I will, Mrs Apsley."

"Good to hear, Mr Apsley!"

~

The Bramingham Arms Pub, situated on Eaton Road, often played host to the school teachers after a particularly difficult day and always after parents' evenings, which were torrid affairs. It always seemed to be the *'posh'* fathers who were not happy with their little *'Jonny's'* school report that caused the problems. Their views were that it must be the teachers' incompetence and not their spoilt little brats who were the cause of the poor feedback received. So far, I'd only had the pleasure of one parents' evening and according to my peers, it lived up to its typical hellish experience.

I had to intervene to calm down a particularly obnoxious tosser who told Jayne Hart she was incompetent and should be at home doing a real woman's job – which, in his view, was looking after her husband instead of ruining his child's education. Then I had no choice but to get involved with another posh pillock. This particular prat stated that his son was destined to be Prime Minister and Colin Pool's assessment of his son's *slow* performance was totally inaccurate.

Graham Holborn struggled with most lessons, and I knew it was due to his dyslexia. Although a recognised condition, I discovered that schools in this era rarely accommodated and supported pupils with this affliction. No, the way we dealt with it was to call them *slow* and drop them to the lower bands. Graham was exceptionally skilled at practical science experiments, verbally competent and had above-average intelligence. However, his written English and numerical skills were horrific.

After trying to explain to a red-faced Mr Holborn that his son had dyslexia and we would like to support him with extra lessons, the conversation turned heated.

Mr Holborn sprung up from his chair and warned me if I ever repeated the accusation his son had a *'condition'*, he'd see to it that I never taught again. He had connections, and members of his club would ensure I regretted what I'd said. Roy, a member of the same club, expertly smoothed things over in his office after I'd called Mr Holborn a dick-head. After this incident, Roy quite rightly reprimanded me regarding my choice of words but did agree with my assessment of Mr Holborn. During the whole unfortunate encounter, Mrs Holborn picked her fingernails and made no eye contact; I suspected she agreed with my assessment of her husband.

After this eventful evening, we all hit the pub. Whilst swigging our pints, G&Ts and glasses of wine, we collectively discussed Mr Holborn's claim that his son was destined to be Prime Minister. We all agreed as most Prime Ministers managed to competently perform like dick-heads, and if Graham followed his father's lead, it was highly likely.

Over the five months of teaching, I'd gained the respect of my peers. That respect flew up several notches as they all recounted the evening's events and specifically when I'd delivered my assessment of Mr Holborn for most of the assembly hall to hear.

~

I arrived before Jess, so I grabbed a barstool and chatted with Derek, the landlord. He knew most of the teachers by name and many of the sixth-form students as well. But hey, it was his licence to worry about, not mine.

After putting the world to rights with Derek, which involved slaughtering Jim Callaghan and Dennis Healy's economic policies, Jess arrived before the conversation moved to religion. Thank God – no pun intended – as Derek was very opinionated and would've got on well with me in my previous life. Although an okay guy to chat to, Derek was a miserable bugger that reminded me of someone I wished to forget. Jess's arrival saved me from regressing and becoming one of those wretched souls at the end of the bar, nursing a pint and feeling how unfair the world was.

I ordered an orange juice for her, and a Coke to replace my half-drunk pint. Jess appeared quiet, and the radiance I'd seen from the last time we'd spoken had evaporated. As she had asked to meet, and the subject matter was all to do with Paul Colney, then no surprise. To get her away from that evil man, I thought Jenny's suggestion about getting her into number eight when Martin moved on seemed like the best idea.

Jess ran through the news that Paul Colney had admitted raping her – a shocking account. I held her hand as she relived the hideous events of that night after our first meeting. Although she was not my daughter, it hurt me to see her pain as if she was my own. This news undoubtedly gave great sway to suggest Paul Colney was the rapist of the two women last year, which were in the news reports George had unearthed from the Chronicle archives. Presumably, it also confirmed he must be Martin's father, suggesting his reign of terror continued for many years.

I tried to think of any news stories from when I was a teenager or young adult of a serial rapist caught in Fairfield, but I couldn't. Therefore, I could only conclude that he went on raping indiscriminately for decades or ran out of steam at some point. On his current run-rate, he could progress to rape over a hundred women. Paul Colney was turning out to be potentially as bad as his younger brother, David, would have been if I hadn't dropped him off that roof last year.

"Jess, you didn't say why Patrick's mum and Paul came around to your flat. Was it just to check up on you? You know, the baby situation."

Jess shook her head. She continued to hold my hand but used her Afghan coat's other sleeve to wipe her eyes. "The day Paul hid his stash of drugs, I was angry with him … I wanted him to get out of the flat. Little did I know then the evil bastard had raped me the night before. He got physical with me, and there was a lot of shouting between us." Jess blew out her cheeks and looked up to the ceiling; it appeared, willing herself not to cry again. "I yelled out that I wished the blokes who killed David had killed him as well."

I was concerned about where this conversation was going. "What blokes?" I asked too harshly, but Jess didn't notice my change of tone and carried on.

"That's what he said. I was across the fields at the back of Belfast House the day David died ... I saw it all happen. I wasn't ever going to say anything as I was pleased that the little pervert was dead. But I blurted it out after he tried to choke me to death. I thought of my baby ... Patrick's baby. So, I just told him what I saw so he'd stop strangling me."

"Paul told Shirley, and Shirley came around to get more information. Is that correct?"

Jess nodded. "I thought whoever killed him were low-life, same as Paul, so what did it matter?" She released our handhold to fish around in her pockets for her cigarettes. Jess sat as she had in the Beehive with her elbow balanced on her knee as it jiggled up and down, causing her cigarette in her hand to bounce. Nerves, I presumed. "I don't know what you must think of me." She looked up as she dragged on her cigarette. "Are you disappointed?"

Leaning across the table, I rested my hand on her arm. "Oh, Jess, no. Don't you ever say that. You hear?"

She nodded and continued to jiggle her knee whilst looking down to inspect her white boots.

"You didn't get a good look at these blokes on the roof when David died, then?"

"No." She shrugged her shoulders. "The guy who sort of threw him off had a denim jacket on. I could see that much, and then I saw him, I dunno … 'bout an hour or so later leave the estate in a yellow Cortina."

It was my turn to fumble for my cigarettes. Sitting back, I afforded myself a moment to think. This was crazy how our lives were intertwined. Here she sat, my daughter, but not my daughter, but she thought I was her father. She witnessed me kill the brother of her unborn child's father – the father of my best friend. Who *is* now my daughter. Well, alright, adopted daughter. And then this daughter, but really *his* daughter, sitting in front of me, didn't know it was me, her father, but not her father, but yes, her father, as far as she is concerned, kill her future brother-in-law. The very person, who in another life becomes a serial killer, and his older brother, who raped my daughter, is the father of Martin, my fellow time-traveller. Beth and Martin were cousins. To top it off, I now had the scary mad mother of these evil boys claiming to be the grandmother of my best friend, who is now my adopted daughter. "Jeeeesus!"

Jess smiled. Well, more of a smirk. "You okay, Dad?"

"Yup." I leant forward. "I'm worried about you living up at the Broxworth. I have some ideas of how to get you into a house in a better part of town. In the meantime, I could rent a flat somewhere else so you're not near that monster."

"Shirley will protect me. She said she'll deal with Paul, whatever that means."

"Yep, I've no doubt she will. But will you consider my offer?"

Jess nodded and blew smoke to the ceiling as a smile brightened her face.

"And you're adamant you won't report him?"

She shook her head as she dragged hard and then stubbed out her cigarette. "Not worth it. Shirley would have me killed."

"Yep. I have no doubt she would."

42

Honey Monster

I grabbed some more drinks, temporarily halting Derek from depressing another punter who slumped at the bar. When I returned to our seats, Jess had started to pull apart a beer mat and now formed a small heap of the damp card in the centre of the table.

"I need Shirley to protect me now. Not only from Paul, but from whoever killed David."

"Why d'you say that?" I certainly knew she had nothing to fear from me; quite the opposite.

"Shirley told me today Paul was certain he'd identified who killed David. He and Shirley are just now biding their time to deal with whoever it was. It could lead to warfare as they'll deal with whoever in the Colney way, if you know what I mean?"

"Yeah, I think I do."

"If David's killers find out I saw them, which led to Paul finding them, it could put me in further danger."

I leant across and took hold of her hand. "Jess, 'cos of the baby, you said Shirley will protect you? Why do you think you'd be in danger from these other men?"

"Because they've murdered before … they might come after me now. Patrick and his father can't help me. Paul is a psychopathic rapist with a short fuse. And Shirley, although terrifying, is only one woman. I don't know who these men are, but sure as hell, they'll be dangerous."

I could feel her trembling as I held onto her hand. It might be a mistake, but I had to stop this girl from worrying herself to death.

"Jess, I want you to listen to me." I took a deep breath as one side of my brain screamed at the other not to do this. The internal cranial war carried on as Jess stared at me, waiting for me to continue.

"What?"

"Oh, God. Look, these other men aren't going to harm you. I guarantee it."

Jess shook her head, frowning at me and clearly confused at what I was saying. "You don't know that. The Colney family operate in a different world from the rest of us. I begged Patrick so many times to leave that life behind. But they're just, well ... just ... hmmm." She dropped her head, staring down at the table. "Dad, they deal with people their way. That's what got Patrick into trouble by protecting his perverted brother. And these other men will be just like them. I know you must wonder why the hell I'm with Patrick." She looked up at me, her eyes watering again. "Patrick is different. He has a gentle and loving side to him that others don't see. You can't help who you fall in love with, can you?"

"No, Jess, you can't. But I can promise you that you're in no danger because I was the bloke who dropped David to his death."

Jess shook her head and released her hand from mine. "What? You killed him!" she blurted.

"Jess, keep your voice down. It was me. But hell, I need to be able to trust you. You can never tell anyone. Only one other person knows, and if this gets out, I could go to jail or worse," I whispered as I leaned forward.

'Brilliant, Apsley, you and your big mouth!'

I shrugged at my mind talk.

"It can't be you. And why?" Jess blurted.

"Shush!" I scanned around the pub. It was early, and fortunately there were very few punters. Of the few that were at the bar, none of them looked around following Jess's outburst.

"Look, Jess. I was up at the flats seeing a friend that day. David was defacing Carol Hall's front door."

"Which is now my front door?"

"Yes. I had dealings with David at school, and that day was the final straw. You're right when you said he was a pervert and he just needed stopping."

Jess narrowed her eyes. I could see she was now wondering what type of man her father was. "So, you just decided to kill him?"

"Oh, Jess, no. It was an accident. I chased him off, and he ran up to the roof. I was going to make him clean off the graffiti from Carol's front door when he stumbled and fell. I tried to save him, but I just couldn't hang on. It was an accident."

'No, it wasn't! Don told you to let go, so you did. Stop kidding yourself, Apsley. You purposefully dropped him to his death!'

This time I nodded to my mind talk, accepting it was the correct account of that day's events.

"Oh shit. Dad, we have a big problem, and it's all my fault."

"What d'you mean, your fault?"

"I said I saw the man and, if that's you, I have unwittingly told that monster who you are."

"No you haven't. Paul doesn't know it's me. Okay, he tracked down my old Cortina, but I sold it on to a second-hand car place. There's no way he can find out it was me. Stop worrying."

"Dad, I think he does know. Shirley said that Paul had squeezed the information out of a car dealer on the other side of town. He tracked the car down last week, but the bloke who owns it had only just bought it. Paul apparently applied pressure on the car dealer this bloke got it from, and you can imagine what that was like?"

'Told you, Apsley. You're fucked, mate!'

My mouth instantly dried. I gulped the last of my Coke as I tried to gather my thoughts. "Jess, he's bluffing. The car dealer wouldn't say who sold it to him. Paul can't know, and I'm sure he wouldn't risk getting caught by the police for assault."

"Dad! Understand who Paul Colney is. He doesn't give a shit about the police, and he's out of control. He'll do anything to find out who killed David. I don't think he really gives a shit about who killed him. But if he can find out, it will put him back in the good books with Shirley and his dad."

"His father is in jail … he can't do anything."

Jess shook her head. "Paul Colney Senior can do what he likes, even from a prison cell."

Sitting back in my chair, I closed my eyes and scrubbed my hands over my face.

'What you going to do now, you knob? You're in the shit again!'

I nodded at that annoying voice in my head.

Jess attacked her second beer mat, tearing small pieces off and making a pile in a ring stain on the wooden table, carefully nudging the card pieces to stay inside the circle.

"What else did Shirley say?"

"Something about it was all coming together. When she and Paul had decided what to do, she'd get her granddaughter back."

"What?"

Jess shook her head. "I dunno … it didn't make any sense. I didn't ask as Shirley Colney is not someone you challenge or ask questions of."

I thought of that last line Shirley had calmly thrown at me last night. I didn't understand it at the time, but now it was clear. *"We have unfinished business – you and me – you'll see. Your time is nearly up, and when that happens, that little girl will be mine."*

She knew last night that I'd killed her son. Mr Thacker must have spilt the beans when under pressure from Paul. I didn't feel angry that he'd blabbed. No, anyone would have when faced with that monster who was about to kill you.

"Dad, what we gonna do?"

"Oh, bollocks, I don't know. I guess I'm going to have to scare him off."

'What, you're 'aving a laugh, boy. Scare Paul Colney, a powder puff like you!'

I winced as my mind delivered its accurate assessment of the situation.

Jess shot me a confused look as she moved to rip apart her third beer mat. I imagined that was what Paul Colney would do to me – I shivered at the thought.

"Dad, you're not going to scare Paul Colney. He's a monster and not the cuddly Honey Monster type."

A picture formed of little Christopher jumping around in front of the TV as the Honey Monster adverts played. Christ, I had to think of a way out of this mess. Otherwise, that little boy's life was going to turn upside down again. Paul Colney will finish Jenny and me off in some accident. Shirley would have her revenge for David and then convince the authorities Beth was her grandchild. My best friend would return to the Broxworth, just as it was the first time, but not with her mother.

No, this time, it would be with her grandmother – even worse.

43

3rd February 1977
Wacky-Backy

After I arrived at Jenny's parents' on Monday evening, we didn't stay long. Jenny could tell my mind was somewhere else and knew I desperately wanted to talk to her about my meeting with Jess.

John was very supportive and told us not to worry. Shirley Colney was all-mouth, as he put it, and he'd have a word with a few of the boys at the station who could put the squeeze on the Colneys. Of course, he didn't know what I now knew, and he had no idea of the added complication that I'd killed David Colney.

Even if I could avoid the potential prison sentence if I came clean about David's demise, it would surely be enough to suggest Jenny and I were not fit parents for Christopher and Beth. Keeping under wraps the events of that day last September was crucial, which meant I couldn't get any official support to hold off the impending doom of what Shirley and Paul had planned.

I concluded Shirley Colney was intelligent and calculating. That skill I don't believe she passed to any of her four boys, as I knew David hadn't shown those attributes, and Paul certainly didn't. Whatever hellish dick-dastardly plans they had in store for my family and me, Paul Colney would be itching to get on with it.

Jenny and I agreed to stay with Don for a couple of days. We could get away without telling anyone, and it would give us a little bit of time to think about our next move. Don, as always, was so supportive. Apart from the time-travel situation, we were able to talk freely with him about our dilemma without the terrifying thought of Paul or Shirley knocking on the door. Christopher loved the adventure, and Beth didn't know any different.

The three of us concluded that Shirley intended to get Beth by legal means. This meant we didn't see any danger to either Christopher, Beth or Jenny's parents, so we relaxed about the days when John and Frances had the kids – they would all be safe.

For Shirley to achieve her goal by the legal route, she'd have to ensure that Jenny and I were removed from the picture. We debated this for hours, going around and around in circles. Jenny's view was very much in the camp that although the Colneys were evil, they wouldn't risk killing us both to get Beth. This idea was too fanciful and stuff of crime thrillers, she'd said.

Don was at the other end of the spectrum, stating he knew what the family was capable of and firmly believed they would be prepared to *do us in*, as he put it. I sat somewhere in the middle. I was sure Shirley was calculating and ultimately didn't really give a toss about what happened to Paul. If she was as switched on as I thought she was, she knew Paul would eventually come to a sticky end. Either dead by another's hand or a stretch in prison. She probably expected he'd be caught for peddling drugs, dishing out beatings, or, as she'd just discovered, his other passion in life – rape.

On Thursday evening, we sat around the kitchen table. This time, Martin joined us as we repeatedly mulled over our plans to get out of this mess. The kids were tucked up in bed, although Christopher played up a bit as he'd pleaded for his grandpa to read at least two stories. Don, his honorary grandpa, of course relented. I knew Don loved every minute of reading stories infinitely more than Christopher enjoyed listening to them.

With a near-empty bottle of Whyte & Mackay and a new bottle of Johnnie Walker Black Label in the middle of the table, we all held our glasses and stared at the ceiling. It was as if we were trying to grasp divine inspiration or having a séance. Martin was becoming impatient, saying we had to deal with the bastard, and quickly.

"He raped my mother, for Christ's sake! We can't just sit around any longer doing feck all … let's just go deal with the fucker!"

"What you on about, son? Who's your mother?" Don questioned, as he peered over his glasses.

"Ow! Bollocks, that fricking hurt!" Martin scraped his chair back and grabbed his shin. "You've drawn blood, I expect." He scowled at Jenny, who appeared to have rammed the heel of her stiletto down his shin as a warning to shut up after his outburst.

"Oh, I'm sorry, Martin, I didn't realise your leg was there." She glared at him, willing him to realise what he'd said.

"Don't worry about your leg, son. Jenny didn't mean it. I've seen blokes have legs blown off in the trenches make less fuss. Now, what you on about Paul Colney raped your mother? Who is she?"

Martin continued to rub his leg, but I could tell by his expression he'd realised the cock-up he'd made.

"Oh, nothing. Nothing. I don't know what I was talking about."

"It's that funny tobacco you smoke, son. I can smell it over the garden fence. It'll send your brain skew-whiffy."

I looked at Martin and arched my eyebrows.

"Mandy gave it to me. Haven't had a spliff for years. It's good stuff."

I rolled my eyes. "Randy Mandy?"

"Yeah."

"What happened to Nursey Nicole then?"

"Nothing. Alternate days, you know ... variety is the spice of life, and all that." He grinned, clearly proud of the little harem he'd forged for himself.

"Well, I don't think that's very nice at all!" Jenny scrunched her nose up and looked at Martin with disdain. I suspected she was considering ramming her stiletto down the other shin.

"I'm sure neither lady would be very pleased if they knew what was going on," she added.

"Anyway, mate, you need to be careful putting it about. AIDS is just around the corner, and you never know who's been with who."

"What?" Jenny and Don blurted in unison.

Martin burst out laughing and looked pleased it was my turn to throw out a time-travel cock-up. Although I'd told Jenny about HIV, I hadn't referred to it as AIDS. Don was now looking confused ... again.

"What's funny?" Jenny asked, still looking at Martin. Her nose turned up again as if he had a bad smell fuzzing around him.

"Nothing!" He held his hands up whilst grinning at me.

"Well, son?"

I turned to look at Don, then back to Jenny. "Nothing. I think the smell of his wacky-backy is getting to my head."

"Son, you're not smoking that stuff as well?"

"No, Don. Absolutely not. I've done it in my youth, but not for many years. Look, let's get back to what we were talking about. We can't keep hiding out here. We'll have to go home soon, but we haven't got anywhere with all our yacking this week, so what we gonna do?"

"Darling, I've just thought. D'you think we could pay him off? We can afford it, can't we?"

I clicked my fingers, rocked back on my chair and turned to Don, "What d'you think? It's the best we've come up with all week."

Don grasped his glass and downed the amber liquid, wincing as it slipped down his throat. "Pour me another, son. Lass, you might have something there. You're not only beautiful but clever as well."

"How much will it take to get them off our back, d'you think?" Jenny asked, as she gently lifted a strand of her hair behind her ear, a reaction I knew she always performed when complimented.

"That lot are all about power and money. The offer of cash will play to their thirst for money, but I fear they'll have power over you. If you gave them a few grand it might work, but what's to stop them just coming back for more?"

"Shit, you're right." I downed my whisky. Now feeling deflated Don had popped a hole in that idea.

"Son, it's not all lost. A few grand might get them off your back and buy some time. It's not ideal … but as you said, you have to get your life back on track. A little bit of extra time might be all we need to work out a better plan."

Jenny leant across and grabbed my hand. "Don's right. How much can we afford?"

"Yes, a few grand is easily acquired and won't dent our finances too much. I think that's all we can do for the moment."

"What about the fact he's a rapist? He may well go on to rape many women. Paying him off ain't going to solve that, is it?" Martin added and nodded at me, conveying the concern for his mother.

Clearly, he'd thought this time and not blurted it out, which would have sent the conversation spiralling back out of control and left Don wondering what the hell we were talking about.

"No, Martin, you're right. But I don't know what to do about that at this point."

"Son, can't you persuade that girl of yours to come forward? If she did and they convicted him, that would solve everything. Wacky-backy-boy here has a good point." Don pointed at Martin as he gripped his whisky glass.

"Thanks!" Martin clearly wasn't overly enamoured with his new nickname.

"Darling, let's bring Jess here tomorrow. I can meet her, and perhaps I can talk to her woman to woman like. If we pay Shirley off handsomely, she might not care if Jess then reports him." She turned to Don and grabbed his hand. "Would that be alright, Don?"

Don put down his glass and took her hand in his. "Of course, my girl, anything for you."

I remembered his comment last year when advising me it would be a good idea to '*step out*' with Jenny—

'If I were a few years younger, I'd be chasing that girl myself.'

Bless him, I thought.

44

4th February 1977
Friends Reunited

The plan was set. What I wanted to be able to do, was send a simple text to Jess to say I would pick her up, and we would spend the evening together. However, although I thought my life was infinitely better without a mobile phone, now I needed one. As Jess didn't have a landline, the only option was to go to the Broxworth and ask her face to face. The other options to contact her in these dark ages were to write a letter – take too long. Send a carrier pigeon – didn't have one. Send a telegram – didn't know how to. This left the one option – go back to that bloody estate and knock on her door.

With Shirley's threats and her out-of-control son, this strategy was perilously risky, but hey, we had no bloody choice and time was seriously against us. If we could persuade Jess to report the rape and get that bastard arrested, I felt sure I could pay Shirley off. What the long-term solution to this dilemma was, at this point in time, we had no idea. So, what we'd come up with last night was the best we could conjure up, although we all agreed it was risky and potentially stupid.

I decided to leave my car at Don's, so Martin and I could car-share to school on Friday. This meant we could ride up to the estate together after school. It was a toss-up whether to take the Stag or the Cortina, but based on the fact we now believed the Colney clan were out to get me, the Cortina seemed to be the lesser of two evils.

The not so cunning plan we'd decided upon would only work as long as I could nip through the Broxworth labyrinth, grab Jess and get to Coldhams Lane without being noticed. Martin would park up at the top of Coldhams Lane, near the Beehive pub, and keep the engine running like a well-trained get-away-driver. I felt sure Jess would come with me on the pretence of meeting my family over a free meal. Unfortunately, Martin appeared far too excited by the challenge, and I think he fancied himself as a bit of a Steve McQueen type character.

After lunch, the first lesson was Chemistry and very aptly named considering my new pairings in place. Surprisingly, young Carlton seemed to have made significant progress. I assumed he'd revised his plan to thank Sarah for her help in Monday's lesson from his original idea of an offer of gratitude whilst gawping at her *great tits,* as he put it. I'm no expert, but I felt Sarah wouldn't have been overly enamoured and seen Carlton as potential boyfriend material if he'd taken that route.

I observed a shift in their relationship from working partners to a point where they could have been the only pupils in the room as far as they were concerned. There was definitely chemistry between them. Carlton seemed uncharacteristically to be totally focused on the school work, and I spotted him constantly saying to Sarah how clever she was. At no point was he distracted by his mates, Roberts and Cooper, who, as usual, were taking every opportunity to act the prat – a skill both boys had mastered over their final school year.

When I asked Sarah and Carlton to talk through their results from the experiments, the whole class fell about laughing as they both hadn't heard me due to being engrossed in gazing into each other's eyes. Although they both were highly embarrassed, I was delighted my matchmaking skills had resulted in Sarah hopefully no longer being obsessed with the school caretaker.

I caught up with Martin as we relaxed in a couple of shabby armchairs in the boiler room. We sipped coffee made in the kitchenette Clive had constructed, which involved a hot plate dubiously rigged into the boiler electrics. I was confident both the seating area and kitchenette Clive had set up near the main boiler wouldn't have been allowed in my day. No, there would be some weekly checklist or task sheet required to be completed and emailed to the local authority to state all areas had had their full health and safety assessment. Presumably, the inspection would have to be carried out whilst wearing a hi-vis vest, goggles, steel toe-capped boots and a hard hat. Combustible tatty sofas and dodgy electrics, I assumed, wouldn't have passed said inspection in 2019.

Martin appeared relieved that Sarah seemed to have shifted her thoughts from him to Carlton, although I guess watching your mother coo over a spotty dork was difficult to be too chuffed about.

"It does feel bloody odd though. I mean, I can't believe Carlton turns out to be the bloke I remember as he looks such a pillock!"

"Ha, yes. He can be a bit of a knob. Certainly got the brains, but just a bit childish and immature. But, then, thinking about it, he is a child ... they're both only sixteen, remember."

Martin traced the scar on the side of his face, a habit I'd noticed him form over the last couple of weeks.

"I've accepted I'm never going back. And like you, I think I died after that crash. Well, I can only presume I was in a coma for a while before I died. It's occurred to me Caroline may have had to make the decision to turn my life support off ... that's a hell of a thing for anyone to have to do."

I pointed at his scar as he continued to rub it. "Probably suffered a brain injury, and they opened you up to try and relieve the swelling."

Martin nodded as he placed his coffee cup on some part of the boiler machinery that whirred and clanged. "Yup, I reckon something like that. I actually think I like the scar. Nicole says it gives me a manly rugged appearance ... would you believe?"

"I'm sorry." I dropped my eyes and looked at the coffee, which I tried to balance in my lap. "If I'd been concentrating and not doing my usual of analysing everything, moaning about everyone – which we both know I used to do all the time – I wouldn't have hit that van. You wouldn't have died, and you could be happy living your life in good-old 2019."

"Don't worry. Jason ... Jason?"

I looked up at him.

"Look, mate, I don't know if it's Jenny or your job, but you're a different person in this life. Don't get too excited, but I might even stretch to say I quite like you." Martin grinned, presumably waiting for a reaction, but I didn't comply.

He continued. "You've made a life which certainly agrees with you. I think my time was up in 2019 and, now being alive again in 1977, I have a second chance. Apart from you ... who else gets this fantastic opportunity?"

I chuckled and pointed my coffee cup at him. "Remember saying the very same thing a few months ago."

"The important thing is to get that bastard arrested, so he can't rape Mum. That's what's important now. Mum had some sad points in her life, and I'd like her to be happy. I know she loved my dad, but their time together was so short. If we can rewrite history so she doesn't get raped, she might meet someone else. Mum could then have children that she actually plans to have and perhaps a marriage that lasts longer than ten years."

"Got to give it to you, mate; you have a brilliant attitude to this."

"She's my mum, and I want her to be happy. I know I won't now be born, and I'm struggling to get my head around the fact she isn't now my mum ... well, y'know what I mean."

I nodded. "Bloody confusing, this time-travel malarky, ain't it?"

"You're not wrong. Anyway, when we've dealt with Paul Colney, I thought I might go travelling ... see the world. Caroline and I married quite young and, if I'm honest, I always regretted not going travelling. There's a big world out there."

"Good idea ... God knows how we get you a passport, though."

"We'll work it out. No offence, but I don't miss working for you at Waddington Steel, and this place ain't my idea of paradise."

"No offence taken. To be honest, I don't miss working with me at Waddington Steel either!"

Martin stood up and took the empty coffee cup which I'd handed to him. "Yes, I'm sure you're right," he chuckled. "Well, I have a door hinge in classroom eighteen to fix, and I expect you have a class of juvenile delinquents to teach, so best we get on."

This had been a crazy two weeks since Martin landed. Today's short conversation surprised me as he seemed to have moved on and developed a maturity that I hadn't witnessed before. Time travel appeared to have improved us both.

Nipping along to my next class, I thought of quite a few old acquaintances who could also benefit from the character development that time travel appeared to provide. Still, I very much doubted they would have the opportunity. Or would they? Hell, I had no idea. The world, for all I knew, could be full of people like us.

I perused the idea of starting a time-travellers group on Facebook but would have to wait a good twenty-five years or so for that. Perhaps Friends Reunited; that was a bit earlier? No, the only option was a newspaper advertisement. However, I thought it would attract all sorts of nutters, and I had no desire to complicate my life any further. I certainly didn't want to receive a million letters from God knows how many weirdos out there who thought they were time travellers – unlike me and Martin, who were the real deal.

45

Blind Date

"Right mate, I won't be long." I hopped out of my old Cortina and flung the door closed. The super poor part of our plan was my walk into the Broxworth, but there was no other way to get to Jess. With my previously used disguise, which had served me well last year, I wrapped the scarf around my face and stuck on my trilby hat. Head down, I trudged my way into the estate whilst keeping an eye out for who was about and praying to some higher being that I could get in and out without incident. If Jess was out, then the whole plan had turned to shit and, it would be back to square one – but time was now running out.

The estate appeared quiet, probably a combination of it being around tea time and the biting wind which ripped through the concrete alleyways. Trotting up to flat 120, I gave the door a quick tap and pushed the letterbox flap.

"Jess … Jess, it's your dad. Are you there?" I could see the kitchen light on and hear the radio – first hurdle accomplished – she was at home.

Still crouching and peering through the letterbox, I spotted her come out of the kitchen. Jess faced the front door whilst she appeared to wipe her hands down her jeans.

"Jess, it's Dad." She rushed to open the door. I sprung through the opening like an Olympic sprinter pushing out of the blocks, keen to get inside without being spotted.

"Dad, what the hell are you doing here?"

"Thought I'd come up and see if you'd like to come over to ours for tea. Y'know, meet Jenny and the kids."

"D'you realise how dangerous it is coming up here? I said on Monday, Paul must now know it was you who killed David."

"Yes, I know. But I had no other way of contacting you."

"But it's so risky! Hell, what will he do to me if he knows you're my father?"

"Alright. Yes, yes, I know. I'm sorry. So, shall we go?" Now unsure what else to say, so I just grinned.

Jess frowned, and I could almost see the questions running through her mind. "Okay, yes, that'll be nice."

"Great! Err ... shall we go?"

Jess grabbed her coat from the hook in the hall. "Give me a minute, and I'll be ready," she threw over her shoulder, as she disappeared back into the kitchen.

"Okay."

"Not that we know each other very well, but there's something you're not telling me," Jess shouted from the kitchen as she silenced the radio. "Dad?" Jess now stood in the hall, pulling her coat on and flicking her hair over her collar.

"No, not at all. Just thought it would be nice for you to meet Jenny and the kids. We ... err ... we're eating at a friend's house as we are living with him at the moment. He's nice, though ... you'll like him."

Jess stopped adjusting her hair and narrowed her eyes. "Dad, this isn't a blind date you're setting me up with, is it?"

"Ha, Christ, no! Don is in his eighties, so unless you're in to old boys, it's not a blind date." Although I thought of Martin and, sure enough, my newly acquired daughter was right up his street.

"Phew, you had me worried then."

"I have a friend waiting in his car to take us up to Don's. He's a nice bloke."

Jess was ready and stood looking up at me, her eyes narrowed. "So, *he's* the blind date then?"

"No, no. He's just a mate giving us a lift. I thought it would be sensible not to bring my car up here as you-know-who knows what I drive. Last thing I need is Paul spotting my car."

"No, definitely not. I don't think you're welcome around here."

I'd heard that before only a few months ago, standing in this very same flat. What was it with this bloody estate?

"Right, come on then. If we turn left at the bottom of the stairs, we can nip through the alley and on to Coldhams Lane. Martin is parked near the Beehive, so we can hopefully get there without being seen."

As we ran across Coldhams Lane, I relaxed and stopped clenching my bum cheeks tightly together, now relieved that somehow we'd made it through without incident. Although by no means in the clear, at least we were out of the estate. What Jess didn't know was the whole evening was a ruse to get her to report Paul Colney. If we could get her to do that, she'd be sleeping in the spare room at Martin's tonight. I was sure Martin would be well up for that, although I'd made it clear to him – Jess was off-limits.

"Right, we're here."

Martin had already started the engine, preparing himself to perform his Steve McQueen impression. He revved the engine a few times just for extra drama, I suspected.

"Bloody hell, it's that ruddy Cortina! Not exactly inconspicuous, is it?"

"Agreed, but Paul's not looking for this car now. As I said, better than bringing the Stag up here."

Opening up the back door for Jess, I followed her in as Martin was ready to fly. Like the getaway driver he aspired to be, he pumped the accelerator, so not exactly keeping our presence low-key. Oh well, we'd made it now, so no drama here, I thought.

"Jess, this is Martin."

Still revving the engine, he turned and smiled. "Hi, Jess."

Jess didn't reply or smile back. Her complexion had changed, and her mouth dropped open as if in shock or surprise. Although there was the likeness between Martin and Paul, I was surprised she could see the resemblance in the dim light. Martin and I were looking at Jess, but I realised Jess wasn't looking at Martin. I turned my head and followed her gaze to the front passenger door, which at that point had opened. I hadn't heard it happen as Martin, throughout this whole encounter, was pumping the accelerator.

The slow-motion feeling I'd had when I ploughed the Beemer into that white van forty-two years in the future returned. I had just enough time to swivel my head to watch Paul Colney slide into the passenger seat next to Martin and ram a sawn-off shotgun in his face. The barrels of the gun pushed his cheek inwards, distorting his appearance. The sound of the engine returned to a low idle as Martin's foot slipped off the accelerator. Those few moments now seemed as if the four of us were in some alternative remake of *The Matrix*.

"My three favourite people all together ... how nice!"

None of us replied. Martin swivelled his eyes, I guess to confirm what was the cause of his cheek indentation. Paul lowered the gun and pointed it at Martin's lap.

"Drive, dick-head, or I'll blow your dick off."

Jess grabbed my hand as she turned to look at me with pure horror etched across her face. I thought we'd made it out of the estate unseen, but what an idiot I'd been. Now I, Jess and Martin were in significant danger. In this short space of time living in the '70s, I'd learned that the Colney family were pure evil. However, although evil and doing the Gowers family bidding – Paul Colney was mentally deranged. He was a psychotic rapist nutter who'd act without thought of consequence. The chance of any of us surviving this encounter was extremely low.

"I said drive, dick-head," Paul spat at Martin, who for a few seconds hadn't moved as he stared at Paul in shock. The trajectory of the gun barrels, now pointing at his crown jewels, jolted him out of his trance. We shot out into Coldhams Lane, causing Jess and I to be flung back into our seats.

"Where … err … where to?" Martin croaked.

Jess and I just sat holding hands. Paul was in front of Jess. With no headrests blocking my reach, I considered leaping forward. I could quickly wrap my arm around his neck and he wouldn't be able to do anything about it. As I mustered up the courage to move, I released my hand from Jess's, ready to strike. Paul turned slightly, adjusting his body so he could have half an eye on me.

"Just keep driving … we're going to meet some acquaintances of mine who make me look like Mother Teresa." He grinned. "Don't do anything stupid, Apple … otherwise, this tosser loses his dick."

Glancing at the shotgun with both barrels inches from Martin's groin, I quickly dismissed my heroic plan as Martin would acquire a large hole between his legs if I moved a muscle. I sat back as Jess took hold of my hand and squeezed. I could feel the relief radiating through her that I'd changed my mind. Although obeying this psycho would avoid the shotgun being emptied in Martin's lap, thus rendering his overused tackle useless, this journey's final destination would certainly deliver worse consequences. Not that Martin would see it that way, but then it wasn't my dick with a sawn-off nuzzled against it.

'For fuck sake, Jason. Think. Think man. You've got to come up with a plan, or we're all dead!'

I considered that my mind talk made a valid point.

46

Mrs Blunders

Whether it was fear, adrenalin, or he'd formulated a plan that involved high-speed driving, Martin pulled through the gears at a pace and dexterity that Ayrton Senna would've been proud of. However, that didn't end well for him in the San Marino Grand Prix in 1994. For a brief moment of distraction, I made a mental note that I had to somehow stop him from racing that day. He was my hero and, if I survived the night, I made a promise to Ayrton that I'd do whatever I could to change his future.

I can only presume I spotted the bikes a good few seconds before Martin because his reactions appeared slow. Three young lads on bikes careered out of the cut-through lane, which leads down to the City School. Unfortunately, they didn't check their surroundings as they bumped down the kerb and swerved out onto the road.

Paul didn't see them as he faced Martin whilst gripping the shotgun, and Jess's view was blocked by Paul. Martin reacted at the last possible moment and avoided ploughing through the lads, who all sported surprised expressions as the Cortina headed straight for them. Ripping the steering wheel to his left, Martin steered the car away from the frozen-in-time cyclists. The car's speed resulted in us careering across the road in a nanosecond and successfully demolishing a bus stop shelter leaving crumpled metal and shattered glass in our wake as the front of the Cortina met with a large oak tree.

The tree, which had presumably resided in that position way before the Broxworth estate was built or even planned, had probably been planted during Queen Victoria's reign and didn't waver in this new event in its long life. The Cortina crumpled and now shortened to the length where the wheelbase would be more fitting for a Ford Anglia.

It appeared I hadn't moved as I remained in the rear seat, holding Jess's hand. However, my nose which had previously been broken by the monster sitting in the passenger seat throbbed, and I could taste the blood that now flowed down it. I can only assume I'd been flung forward, smashing my nose on Martin's seat and then catapulted back as the large oak halted our path. Jess and I looked at each other; her face was almost identical as the blood flowed from her nose.

Martin and Paul were not sitting. Instead, their bodies were positioned through the car windscreen, stopped in mid-flight as if diving into a swimming pool. Paul's body was slightly further through the 'dive' as Martin's progress towards the oak had been halted by the steering wheel, which appeared to be embedded in his chest. Without a word, Jess and I opened the rear doors. Jess's opened as expected, mine I had to put my shoulder to as the crash had reshaped the door frame.

Martin's head was turned towards me as I approached the front of the car. He stared directly at me, but I knew his eyes could see nothing. At the age of forty-two, I'd never seen a dead body close up until now. Although I had no medical training, I knew my work colleague and fellow time-traveller was dead ... again.

"Fucking hell, man, that's awesome!"

I turned to see the three lads who'd quickly recovered from their near-death experience with the front of the Cortina, standing with their bike frames between their legs and gawping at the front of the car.

"That one's got a windscreen wiper stuck through his neck! Fucking gruesome!" exclaimed another one of the lads as they took in the horror in front of them.

I glanced from Martin to Paul. He did, in fact, have a windscreen wiper protruding out the back of his neck and was fully impaled on it with what appeared to be gallons of blood pumping from him which poured across the now crumpled car bonnet. Jess stood on the other side of the car, transfixed by the sight of Paul Colney in front of her. Ignoring the sight-seeing cyclists and leaving them to take in the scene, I slowly made my way around to Jess. Grabbing her hand, I squeezed it to bring her out of her trance.

It was only a week ago when Jenny and I had argued about my wish to replace her car with one that had rear seatbelts, plus my annoyance that she never wore her seatbelt when driving. We'd watched the *'Blunders-family adverts'* on TV, which showed the nightmare-driving family causing havoc. That particular advert showed a man, not dissimilar in appearance to Martin, travelling through his yellow MK3 Cortina windscreen after encountering *Mrs Blunders'* woeful driving.

I stood with Jess staring at our own real-life road-safety TV advert as two cars stopped, and two men and a woman rushed over to the scene.

"Bloody hell! What's happened here?" called out the first guy who'd run over from where he'd abandoned his car a few yards away. Within less than a minute, the road was blocked as half a dozen vehicles had slowed or stopped. Many drivers jumped out of their cars to see if they could assist, whilst others stayed in theirs and gawped at the scene.

I tugged Jess's hand and stepped back, pulling again to get her to react. Fortunately, this non-verbal communication worked and, as the crowd of onlookers closed in on the gruesome scene, we moved behind them.

"Come on … quickly." I held her hand and tugged Jess across the road, stepping into the cut-through lane so we were out of sight of any onlookers.

"Jess, you okay?"

She nodded, although I could see she was starting to violently shake as she fumbled for a tissue in her coat pocket and then applied it to her nose. I took a moment to deal with my face with the corner of my coat. I could feel my neck stiffening, and I suspected we both would suffer severe whiplash.

"We need to get out of here. Paul was holding that shotgun and, when the police arrive, there will be a bundle of questions I don't fancy answering." She nodded as I took her hand, and we nipped down the lane to the school playing fields.

The first phone box we came across, a hundred yards down from the school on Eaton Road, I phoned George. Within half an hour, we sat in Don's kitchen, whisky in hand, as George and Jenny attempted first aid to our noses.

47

5th February 1977

Hamleys

Jess was okay about sleeping at Martin's, as there was no more room in Don's. I, as predicted, had a very stiff neck in the morning. When we reconvened for breakfast at Don's on that Saturday morning, Jess seemed to be physically in much better shape than I was. However, mentally the events of the previous evening had taken their toll on her. She appeared very quiet and withdrawn as we all sat around the table mid-morning when George arrived who'd brought Stephen with him to keep Christopher amused.

Christopher had become quite grumpy as the adventure of the last five days at Don's had lost its appeal, and he now missed the plethora of toys that filled his bedroom at home. In a few short weeks, by being spoilt by Jenny, me, her parents, Don, George and Ivy, he'd amassed a toy collection that put the boys' section of Hamleys to shame. He'd quickly forgotten Lexton House children's home, with its stark grey walls and the small communal toy box that contained donated outdated and sometimes broken toys.

Jenny persuaded Jess to go up to the hospital with her to get checked out. The story would be she'd tripped and fallen, so a quick check to see if the baby was okay was the sensible thing to do.

George, Don and I discussed the previous evening's events. Once again, I had to 'manage the room' as I had my two closest friends together. Don, knowing my misdemeanours over the last five months, and George had the knowledge of my time-travelling skills.

As we all were, Don was delighted that a twist of fate had removed another Colney from the planet. This one we all were convinced was the 'Fairfield rapist' as we'd named him. George and I believed we'd stopped his future career as a serial rapist as he must have carried on right into the late '80s when he presumably raped Sarah Moore – Martin's mother – a discussion we had out of Don's earshot.

I was beside myself that I'd caused Martin's death. Although it was a complicated conversation because George knew it was the second time I'd been in a car with Martin when he'd lost his life, whereas Don believed it was the first time. Either way, both fully understood my distress and were insistent it wasn't directly my fault.

Jenny and I planned to decamp back home on Saturday afternoon, safe in the knowledge that Paul Colney no longer posed a threat. Shirley Colney, for the moment, would be consumed by the death of another son to cause us any immediate issues.

Jenny and Jess returned before lunch. As Jess was pregnant, she'd jumped the queue at A&E and had been quickly assessed. The baby was fine, and I thought that baby was a tough little bugger after the last two week's events. He or she, probably taking after their father – another bloody Colney.

I considered perhaps the Beth I knew from my previous life had acquired her toughness from her father, David, and not the Lexton House experience. Only time would tell when she grew up for the second time. I hoped that steel-like persona was a product of her time in the children's home and not inherited from her future murderous now-dead father. I had many years to find that out, so I chose to dump that thought back in a 'keep-closed-pandora's-style-box' in a dark recess of my brain.

Don had taken an instant shine to Jess and insisted on helping her settle into what was Martin's temporary home. George said he knew a couple of chaps from work he trusted to return to her flat on Sunday and collect her personal belongings. Jenny said she would ask one of her female colleagues to go with them, as she didn't feel it was appropriate for George's friends to rummage through Jess's knicker drawer. Jess had sobbed with relief in Jenny's arms when she realised that with the help of a few people, she was never going back to the Broxworth.

Leaving Don to fuss over Jess, George and I chatted as we ferried our belongings out of Don's house and packed the cars up to go home.

"It's crossed my mind, lad ... about the car you had the crash in."

I glanced at George as he handed me one of the bags I was about to lob in the fairly uselessly sized boot of the Stag. "You thinking what I'm thinking?"

George raised his eyebrows. "Yes ... maybe. Although it's a bit silly, really. Both of you ended up here in that car ... and now ... well, you know."

I gently closed the boot, propped my bum up on its edge, and considered what he was suggesting. "So, Martin and Paul could have been teleported to another life because they were in that bloody car?" I shook my head. "It can't be ... can it?"

"I don't know, lad. But you both time-travelled back forty-odd years and woke up in that car. May suggest it has some strange cosmic power."

"George, can you hear yourself!"

"Ha, yes, lad. I know. I can't believe I'm saying it ... but you did, didn't you!"

"Yeah, we did. The thought of Paul Colney now waking up in some other year to carry on where he left off from, though, doesn't bear thinking about."

"I'm sure he hasn't. Anyway, that's the car you arrived in, not departed in. It's not the same, is it?"

I gingerly lifted my bum off the boot lid, unable to turn my neck without suffering severe pain. "No, George, it's not. They're both dead ... I'm sure of that."

"Yes, you're probably right. Anyway, that Cortina didn't have a flux thingy, type thing Martin said about."

"Flux-Capacitor?"

"Yes, that's it. What does that do anyway?"

"George, I have no idea."

48

6th February 1977
Time-Bend

Sunday morning, I stayed in bed. Jenny told me, no, instructed me to rest. She was quite insistent that if my neck hadn't improved by the time I got up, we were going to the hospital to get me checked out. Not relishing an afternoon sitting on those uncomfortable straight-backed wooden chairs up at Fairfield General, I complied with her directive. Although my neck was painful, I managed to sleep without worrying about the next day and what drama would evolve. I achieved some proper sleep for the first time since that Sunday when Martin had arrived on our doorstep three weeks ago.

Last Friday, Martin had talked through his plans for his new life with such excitement. He really had embraced his time-travel leap with real enthusiasm after a predictably tricky start. I shed a tear for my fellow time-traveller and prayed he was now at peace.

I'd always wrestled with my ability to bend time and how it always seemed to pull back to the laid-down path it already had set in motion. However, David's death last year had proven I could bend time. Now for sure, I'd achieved it once again. I knew for certain Paul Colney had raped Jess, as he'd admitted it. Which would also suggest he raped those two women last summer. So, assuming that Martin's mother had told the truth, and why wouldn't she, it had to be Paul Colney who raped her in ten years' time.

Convinced I'd successfully achieved another time-bend, I balanced off the sadness of Martin's death against the knowledge that young Sarah Moore's future life had indeed changed for the better. Martin would be happy with that knowledge, as it was his primary target to achieve. I would watch Sarah's progress through life and now hoped she'd go on to achieve what she wanted, and when she wanted. However, I did laugh at the thought of that dork Carlton King and her together.

Although it hadn't, I convinced Jenny my neck had improved as I had no intention of spending my Sunday afternoon in A&E.

The local radio station's lunchtime news item reported the car accident on Friday evening. The newscaster stated there were two fatalities with no other vehicles involved. There were unconfirmed reports that two passengers had fled the scene, and the police were appealing for witnesses. One of the deceased was confirmed as Paul Colney, a twenty-three-year-old man from the Broxworth Estate. The other deceased had not yet been identified. The incident was reported as gang-related, as firearms had been recovered.

Although the police were appealing for witnesses, I wasn't unduly concerned about Jess and my descriptions being circulated. Those first on the scene that evening hadn't looked at either of us. They were all consumed with the crash scene and the two dead bodies on the bonnet of my old Cortina. I certainly had no concern about the three lads on their bikes, as I believed they were from the Broxworth – you can just tell, can't you? We were safe in that knowledge, as no one from the Broxworth talks to the police. I'm led to believe it's an unwritten requirement of living on the estate.

No surprise Martin had not been identified, as he didn't exist. Nowhere on the planet was there any record of Martin Bretton, aged thirty-one living in the United Kingdom. That would be a mystery the police would never resolve.

Eventually, resources would dry up, and it would end up in a case file on a dusty shelf of unresolved cases – I was confident of that.

Pondering the Colney family and their evil ways dragged my mind to the Yorkshire Ripper. Over a year had passed since any reported murders which fitted his modus-operandi. I'd often tried to pull out of my memory the dates he murdered those women. That book Lisa had bought me, and I'd read that Christmas Day, had unfortunately not held in my memory. Apart from a few odd details like being repeatedly arrested and a lorry driver, nothing else stuck. However, over a year had elapsed since his last murder, so I deduced that time had bent again. Somehow, this time, Peter Sutcliffe had stopped his murderous campaign. Had perhaps my anonymous letter worked? Maybe the police interviewed him last year when following up on the letter, and he was sufficiently spooked to stop.

That Sunday evening, it seemed as if time cruelly dealt its fate when I'd reached a point of believing I'd once again successfully moved its planned direction. Only a few hours earlier that day, I'd relayed my thoughts to Jenny about the Yorkshire Ripper, and we agreed that a prolific serial killer wouldn't rest up for over a year. No, we both firmly believed he wouldn't have taken a serial-killer vacation but would regularly continue his murderous campaign until caught. Which is what my limited memory believed to be the case.

The early evening national news reported a young female's body had been discovered that morning by a man walking his dog in a park in a suburb of Leeds. The brutal attack was dubbed the work of *'The New Jack the Ripper'*. The police had instantly linked this attack with the murders in January 1976 and October 1975.

Time was a force of nature that wouldn't bend at will. It was official – a serial killer was on the loose in the north of England, and there was bugger all I could do about it.

49

Some weeks later

'Murrayisms'

There were no more reports regarding our crash in February. It was treated as just another road traffic accident, as I thought it would be. The fact that Martin couldn't be identified was presumably incidental. The case was probably just filed away, awaiting a missing person's report to link it with – and that would never happen.

The Deputy Head position at school had to be resolved. I and another applicant, who, until the day of the interviews, I didn't know, were put through the process in late February. Roy was frustrated and stated that he wanted his man, as he put it, and thought I should be appointed.

I was super relaxed about the whole interview and assessment process, probably as I really didn't give a toss whether I got the position or not. My laid-back attitude must have helped as I subsequently was successful and appointed to the role. Roy was delighted, far more than I was.

I met the other candidate on the day of the interviews when we shook hands before going in to my assessment. I'd met him before in my previous life, and the memory flooded back of him marching Beth and me into the Headmaster's office when we were both sixteen in the early nineties. Keith Jones still appeared to have the grace and humility of Hermann Göring. Although, on our brief meeting this time, he didn't seem to be the sort of chap that might have your fingernails pulled out with a pair of pliers.

Now Martin had vacated, Jess moved into the house next to Don. I now had both houses rented out and received meagre rent. But that didn't matter as it felt bloody fantastic to be able to help these two people who'd entered my life. Jess was very much Don's surrogate grandchild, and he doted on her.

Don, as always, had his ear to the ground, and a few old acquaintances liked to keep him up to date on the events up at the Broxworth. Shirley Colney, as expected, was devastated that she'd lost a second son within the space of six months. She'd apparently skedaddled and was living it up in the Costa Del Sol, so no longer the controlling factor in Fairfield she once was.

The Gower family had apparently become frustrated with the Colneys and their lack of control, now considering them to be a liability. You didn't need to move in those low-life circles to know if the Gowers were no longer supporting the Colneys – they were finished.

Shirley had dumped Andy, her youngest son, on her sister. Both Don and I agreed he'd probably grow up to be a low-life as well. Unlike his older brothers, Andy Colney wouldn't have the backing of the all-controlling and powerful Gower clan.

Clive Trosh left the hospital and was recovering well. I had one hell of a battle on my hands persuading him to take one of my diamonds. In the end, I introduced him to Don, who worked his magic, resulting in Clive accepting my offer. So, I took another one of my diamonds from my safety deposit box and visited Maypole Jewellers. Terry Maypole was disappointed I didn't need the ring made in an hour, as he said it was one of his best pieces of work when he'd made Jenny's ring. Mr Maypole got to work on producing another masterpiece which I couldn't wait to give to Clive.

The ever-efficient Miss Colman, although still efficient, seemed to have taken on an air-head persona. I think she'd copied the stance of Mr Humphries, as she continuously held her left hand slightly raised in the air to ensure everyone could see the engagement ring.

Roy was disappointed that Martin had urgently returned to South Africa as he had received a job offer that he couldn't refuse. It was the best story I could come up with to cover up his disappearance. We agreed that we would just get by until Clive returned, so decided not to look for another temporary replacement.

Following that promise I made in the Cortina that I would somehow stop Ayrton Senna from dying in 1994, Jenny and I thought we should firstly try and save Tom Pryce and the marshal, who would die in a few weeks.

We constructed two letters this time. Using an ancient typewriter once owned by Frances, we were super careful to ensure we left no fingerprints on either paper or envelope. The first letter we sent to The British Racing Drivers Club informing them that Tom Pryce would die on March 5th. The second was an airmail letter sent to the Midrand race track in South Africa, stating that track safety could be significantly improved if marshals were placed on both sides of the track. This added measure would improve track safety and, if an incident occurred, there would be no requirement for a marshal to cross the track mid-race.

I took a trip out to London one Saturday morning and, with a gloved hand, slotted the two letters in an unremarkable red post box near Marble Arch.

I was living in that era when motor racing was not the hyped-up sport it was in my day. The lack of TV channels was a big part of that reason, so limited air time resulted in limited programmes. I knew I was only a few years away from enjoying live races on the BBC, with the one and only Murray Walker commentating. However, I did enjoy the highlights he presented at this time with his comical blunders or 'Murrayisms' as they were later called. I always looked forward to the highlights and now realised in 2019, I hadn't appreciated the fantastic coverage on offer.

Sunday, 6th March, I didn't watch the BBC2 highlights. Instead, I stood in the back garden, smoking a cigarette as Jenny tried to console me. My tears weren't for Tom Pryce specifically, who had died as he had the first time. Nor were they for the marshal, a teenager called Jansen Van Vuuren, although before the news reports today, I hadn't known his name. No, my tears were for the fact that I couldn't stop these events. I knew women were going to die over the next few years at the hands of Peter Sutcliffe. I also knew more motor racing drivers would die doing what they loved. I had future knowledge of world events that would cost thousands of lives, but I was fully aware I was powerless to change that history.

I felt utterly helpless.

As Jenny said, I'd changed some history for the better. Beth and Christopher now had a real chance of a better life. I'd stopped two evil men from carrying out their future rapes and murders, and I should be proud of what I'd achieved. She was right, but my frustration was unless these events were intrinsically linked to my life, I could do bugger all about it.

I would now spend the next forty years knowing the disasters and hideous crimes were about to happen and, once again, I was powerless to change it.

50

15th August 1987

Ferris Bueller's Day Off

"Jenny, are you ready yet? We're going to be late!" I bellowed up the stairs.

"I won't be long, darling. Just give me a minute," she shouted back. Although, for some reason, when Jenny shouted, it was gentle. On the other hand, I sounded more like a market street trader offering a pound of brussels for twenty pence.

"Dad, you got a tenner I can have?"

"What about your own money you get from your Saturday job? Don't Sainsbury's pay you for stacking their shelves?"

"Yeah … yeah, but there's … this girl I want to impress. A few extra quid will help." Christopher grinned. He knew how to extract money from my wallet without moving a muscle.

"Oh, I see! Well, why didn't you say so … err, you are being careful, aren't you?" I whispered, leaning towards him. I no longer needed to look down as he was already my height, fully past the bum-fluff stage and now had to shave every morning. His natural father, whoever he was, must have been a giant gorilla – King Kong, maybe?

"Don't know what you mean, Dad," delivered with a deadpan face.

I handed him a tenner. "That enough?"

"Yeah, cool, Dad. And it's a bit late for the birds-and-the-bees chat, if you know what I mean." He winked before allowing his aviator shades to slip back down onto his nose.

I wasn't sure if he saw himself as James 'Sonny' Crockett from Miami Vice or Lt. Pete 'Maverick' Mitchell from Top Gun. Either way, my son had a coolness about him that regularly sucked in girls to his manly charms. It seemed only yesterday that I used to call him 'Benny,' named after the cute little cat in Top Cat.

It seemed overnight he had morphed from Top Cat to Top Gun, and most girls at school could see it as well. That all said, Jenny and I couldn't be prouder of him. He worked diligently at his Saturday job and grabbed copious amounts of overtime on Sundays when the shop was closed to help restock. The manageress, a Miss Osborne, had made a point of telling me so last weekend when I picked him up after his shift.

But what we were really over the moon with was his schoolwork. It was difficult having his father as the Deputy Head at the school he attended, but Chris took it in his stride. Top of the class in all subjects, football and cricket team captain and all earned through his own hard work and determination. Maybe his father was a hybrid of Gary Lineker, Ian Botham, King Kong and Einstein ... an interesting fellow, I might suggest.

Christopher Apsley was definitely our version of The Jam's Davie Watts.

"Oh, Chris ... Chris?"

"Whaaat?" came the reply from the kitchen.

"You know you're going back with Stephen to George and Ivy's tonight as your mum and I are out late?"

"Yeah, no worries. Didn't know you had it in you to see it past midnight."

"Cheeky git," I threw back at him.

"What film you seeing?" I called into the kitchen.

"Jen, we're going to be late," I called up the stairs. I needed an intercom system in the house, as you had to shout to be heard. We'd moved into number eleven Winchmore Drive in the Summer of '77. Ten years on, we both believed we were so lucky to have such a large luxury house.

"I'm coming, darling ... stop worrying," Jenny gently shouted back down the stairs.

"Ferris Bueller's Day Off," Chris replied.

"Oh, really!"

"Oh really, what, darling?"

"Wow, you look gorgeous! Not that you're not always gorgeous, of course ... you always are ... you will be the belle of the ball."

"You need a shovel, Dad?" Christopher offered, as he joined me in the hall.

"Thank you, darling." Jenny stopped on the second from last step of the stairs, making her about an inch taller than I was as she leaned in and kissed me.

"What do I need a shovel for?" I asked Chris, breaking the kiss from my gorgeous wife.

"For the hole you're digging yourself in with Mum! Gotta say, Mum, you look pretty cool. Anyway, what's wrong with that film I'm going to see? You said, 'Oh really' as if it's rubbish? It's supposed to be really cool."

"Chris, it is really cool ... probably one of the greatest cult films ever made."

"Mum, why does Dad always make out he knows things he can't possibly know? Like this film, for example. He's so odd ... he always talks about things as if he knows about them, but he's never seen them!" Chris turned to me with a questioning look.

Jenny laid her head on the bannister, smirking. "Get out of this one, Mr Apsley!" she chuckled.

Time-travel cock-ups were an everyday event. My usual escape when this happened with either Chris or Beth was resorting to bribery. "Here's another tenner. Enjoy yourself, and make sure you're back at Stephen's by ten. Otherwise, Ivy will have your guts for garters!"

"Cheers, Dad ... works every time," he replied under a cheeky grin.

"Is that daughter of ours ready yet?"

"Beth, honey, are you ready? I said we'd get you to Melanie's house by seven," Jenny called up to her bedroom.

The door flung open, and out stepped a perfectly formed tornado capable of wreaking havoc that could destroy a medium-sized mid-state American town in seconds.

"I'm here," she announced at the top of the stairs. Ten years old going on twenty-one.

"Good. Now make sure you're polite to Melanie's parents, and when they say it's time for bed ... it's time for bed," Jenny Instructed.

"Yes, I don't want to hear tales of destruction on the breakfast news in the morning that a category one tornado has devastated a large detached house in Fairfield," I added.

"Dad, do you mind! I'm a perfect proper lady."

"Beth, sweetheart, you're perfect. Proper ... I'm struggling with ... Madonna could learn a few things from you!"

376

"Cool. Give her a call, and we can hook up!"

I turned to Jenny— "She's ten! What's she going to be like when she's sixteen, for Christ's sake!" I exclaimed.

"Darling, you should know!"

I looked at my truly wonderful daughter as she stood smiling down at us. "That's what worries me!"

Back when I was in the throes of killing David Colney and worrying if I would have to wait years to discover if baby Beth was actually Beth, my best friend from back in 2019, I, of course, at that point, had no definitive way of knowing. She had the same mother, the same birthday and the same name – but I could never be certain.

Looking up at my ten-year-old daughter, I was certain. She looked exactly how I remember Beth looking on that first day of school when old Bummer had forced me to sit next to her. Well, not exactly the same because this version of Beth was confident, fun, loving and didn't harbour a hint of anger. Nurture had won over nature. Jenny and I had a wonderful daughter that, all too quickly, I was fully aware, some boy would ask to take her away from me. But she would be happy – I just knew it.

Roy was promoted in 1984 to an offensively sizeable comprehensive school in London. The education authority urged me to progress and thought I could take the City School in a new, modern direction. As I loved my job, I declined as I had no desire to take up the role which Roy had held for all those years. The stress had taken its toll on Roy and, although we were the same age, he looked at least fifteen years closer to a date with the grim reaper than I did. Mr Elkinson was appointed as Head, as he was in my day as a student there. He was still a quiet and unassuming man and very much left the school's running to me, which I enjoyed without the pressure of the ultimate responsibility.

Don still lived at number ten. Although in his ninetieth year, he was very spritely and had a caring neighbour called Jess, who always looked out for him. Jess didn't wait for Patrick and, as the years slipped by, her unconditional love for the twin of Paul Colney faded.

Patrick was involved in a prison riot in 1979, resulting in two other inmates being shanked with a sharpened toothbrush. One of them died. Patrick was arrested for murder and convicted for a further twenty-two years to run consecutively to his sentence for attempting to murder Sarah Moore's father. He would be in his fifties before he saw the outside world again.

Jess married in 1980. She met Colin at a party at our house that previous summer and, although he was twelve years older, they fell instantly in love. A whirlwind romance ensued, which I could easily empathise with. I met her mother, *other* Jason's former lover only once, on Jess and Colin's wedding day. It was an awkward encounter to say the least, so we didn't converse much, and I didn't have to pretend to be who she thought I was.

Jess's daughter, Faith, and our Beth were bridesmaids at the wedding. Both little girls were beautiful in their tiny versions of Jess's long flowing hippy-style wedding dress. Faith, as far as the whole world was concerned, was my granddaughter. Jenny, George and I knew differently, and I often silently thanked *other* Jason for this gift.

Colin adopted Faith, and the new Mr and Mrs Poole settled into their new married life. There had been nothing I thought would be an appropriate wedding present when reviewing the gift wish list. So, assuming someone else would buy the Teasmade, Jenny and I presented them the keys to number eight on the Bowthorpe Estate.

51

Dad Dancing

Tonight's event was the Fairfield District Council Summer Ball. Jenny said it was more of a party in a tent than a ball in a marquee, and there was no requirement to wear a black tie. Jenny was now head of Child Services, so tonight was a big deal as she and two other department heads would give a speech and conduct the prize giving.

The applause continued for over a minute, ending with a few cheeky wolf-whistles as Jenny finished her speech and left the stage. The disco restarted, causing hordes of now-pissed party revellers to stampede and swamp the dance floor as *'Never Gonna Give You Up.'* pulsed out. A new song that had rocketed into the charts last week by a clean-cut young lad called Rick Astley.

I never danced. Although I'd perfected that demented baboon-style dancing in my previous life, even that skill had now left my repertoire of bad moves. I was now only endowed with poorly choreographed dad-dancing abilities, and I thought the world was better off not witnessing them.

When the slow dances started, I would take my wife to the dance floor. Not that I was any good, but I could just about manage it without realigning Jenny's toes. More to the point, I wasn't allowing any other bugger to take her hand and whisk her around the makeshift wooden dance floor.

I gave Jenny a hug and kiss as she fell into my arms, relieved she'd delivered her speech and that particular nightmare was over.

"You were brilliant, sweetheart."

"Thank you, darling. Thank God that's over with!"

"Shall we get another drink?"

"Yes, darling. I need an ice-bucket full of G&T … I'm still shaking."

I grabbed her hand, and we weaved our way through the crowd to the bar. Before we made it there, we both stopped near one of the back tables and observed an argument which appeared to be getting out of hand. Wearing a short black dress, a young slim blonde lady with her back to us was berating a bloke who was giving as good as he was getting. As we drew near, voices became raised above the music.

"Piss off, Paula." The blonde pointed at a woman a few feet behind the bloke she was previously directing a torrent of abuse at.

"Sarah, for Christ's sake, you're overreacting!" the bloke responded.

Not wishing for Jenny's special evening to be remembered for some catfight between two women brawling over a man, I thought I'd just step in and calm the waters.

"Sorry to interrupt. But this is a works' event, and you're representing your workplace. I think it's best you take your argument elsewhere so everyone else can continue to enjoy the party," I calmly delivered to both of them.

The bloke looked for a second like he might punch me. But I guessed I appeared to be the respectable fifty-two-year-old that I was, so he changed his mind. Both he and the woman calmed down as my schoolteacher persona appeared to have worked, but more so because they both recognised me.

The bloke turned, huffed and walked off. The young blonde looked at me, and I instantly recognised her. I hadn't seen her for a few years now, but I would never forget her as she had been a significant part of my new life.

"Sarah ... Sarah Moore?"

"Oh, sorry, Mr Apsley. It's my boyfriend ... he's acting like a right tosser."

"Don't think you need to call me that anymore. My name is Jason."

"Oh, Mr Apsley, I'm a bit embarrassed now."

"Jason ... I'm not your teacher now."

"Yes, I know. But I have to call you Mr Apsley ... I just do."

"Okay," I chuckled. "Are you alright?"

Sarah scraped back her hair and huffed. "Yes, I'm fine, thank you. I think it's time Scott and I went home. But thanks again."

I touched her arm. "Alright. Well, you take care, won't you?"

~

It had been a long time since I'd thought about Martin, but seeing his mother tonight brought those memories back. Jenny was fast asleep, but I was restless, so, not wishing to wake her, I plucked up my book and decamped to my office. I made myself comfortable in my brown-leather studded chair and read for a while, hoping diving into my latest time-travel adventure book would calm my brain.

As I sat there in the early hours of Sunday 16th August, I thought about Martin and Sarah. I wondered what would've happened if Martin hadn't died in that Cortina back in 1977. Assuming back then we had rid the town of the Fairfield rapist when Paul Colney had died, I thought Sarah was now safe. The few years after that event, there were no reports of a serial rapist on the loose, so I deduced we'd solved that problem. Martin was born in May 1988 – the product of the attack Sarah suffered – the event that should have happened or was about to happen. Feeling safe in the knowledge that Sarah's life wasn't now going to take that route in this timeline, I settled into reading my book.

I regularly read time-travel books because I enjoyed seeing what mere mortals wrote about a subject they couldn't possibly know anything about. Often, I found myself tutting and muttering – *"Ridiculous, that wouldn't happen!"*

52

Gold Dust

Detective Constable Kevin Reeves pulled out his cigarettes from inside his jacket, lifting his bum from the driver's seat to retrieve his lighter from his trouser pocket.

"Not while I'm in the car," came the response from the passenger seat.

"Ma'am?" Kevin questioned, as he held the cigarettes and looked at the Guv, hoping she would relent.

DI Heather French just raised her eyebrows, and that was enough for the young detective constable to replace the packet back in his pocket.

Heather had been promoted to DI last year, and this new position now gave her the power and the resources to start cleaning up this town. She knew DC Reeves thought tonight's stake-out operation was a waste of time, as the vast majority of her team had since they started these covert operations some weeks ago. Heather suspected Kevin would probably rather be in town getting pissed with his mates. But she was the DI, so he just had to do as he was told.

Since joining the force in the early '70s, Heather had endured years of mickey-taking from her male counterparts. There were constant referrals to the size of her chest and what they'd like to do to it. All of them, including senior officers, would publicly offer lude remarks and suggestions. This barrage of sexist taunts, along with having her arse pinched and chest fondled, hadn't changed even when she'd joined CID. That said, Heather started to gain some respect when she passed her sergeant exams, but now as DI, things were very different.

Along with many of her colleagues, Heather had a thirst to bring down the Colney and Gower families. The Gowers would prove a tougher nut to crack, but in time she would. The Colneys were as good as wiped out, with two of the brothers dead and one serving a long stretch. That just left one still on the loose. But she knew it would only be a matter of time before she'd arrest him for some misdemeanour.

Ten years ago, when still a PC in uniform, a series of rapes went undetected. At the time, Heather had raised with her sergeant that she didn't believe enough resources were being assigned to catch the evil bastard. However, after being ignored and balled out by the DI at the time, she was encouraged to stop voicing her concerns.

The rapes in the late '70s, which were all committed near the Broxworth Estate, ceased almost as quickly as they'd begun. She believed it was no coincidence that this happened at the exact same time when Paul Colney had ended up skewered on a windscreen wiper. Also, there had been several retracted sexual assault allegations against Paul at the time. Women had come forward and then changed their stories, presumably once they'd received pressure from the Colneys.

Ten years later and, almost coinciding with her promotion to DI, a series of rapes had started again, and all of them in and around the Broxworth Estate. Heather harboured a theory that she knew her team were not entirely on board with. However, that didn't matter because she was the DI and called the shots.

The four rapes which had been committed and reported over the last three months had provided DNA evidence. Gold dust, as far as Heather was concerned. She would have been happy to set up a mass testing site and have every male in the whole town tested. Although a ball-ache to organise, they could pinpoint their man. Last week she'd had a stand-up slagging match with the Divisional Superintendent regarding such an idea. As he was her boss and refused, she was forced to back down. The crown-epauletted dinosaur had instructed Heather to use her bloody detective skills and catch the rapist the old-fashioned way by employing tried and tested police work. Although the Super was an ancient reptile, Heather was convinced his response would've been different if he'd been born a woman.

One of the reasons she'd been promoted to DI was her success rate in catching and sticking behind bars the low-life scum that roamed Fairfield, most of whom originated from the Broxworth Estate. Much of that success was down to her hunches which, more often than not, proved to be correct.

One such hunch was why she and one of her DCs were sitting in their unmarked car parked along Coldhams Lane. She knew all she needed was a reason to arrest, and then a DNA sample could be taken, and this new amazing science would do the rest.

Sod all had happened the whole time they'd sat there and, as midnight approached, Kevin appeared fidgety. She had pointed out to her dopey DC, who now sulked because she wouldn't allow him to smoke, that a dodgy character had hovered at the entrance lane that cut through to the City School.

"What's he up to?"

"Probably just cutting through the school playing fields on his way home, Ma'am," Reeves emphasised the 'Ma' presumably showing his frustration of being a DC and now having to perform a beat-bobby job on a Saturday night.

"No I don't think so. I've got a hunch on this one," DI French replied.

DC Reeves rolled his eyes but ensured the DI didn't see him do it.

Both of them stayed in the car for a few more minutes when they witnessed what appeared to be a lover's tiff, resulting in a young lady being left standing on the pavement. The car she'd alighted screeched up the road, to then only a few minutes later return to repeat the rubber-burning exercise. After the car had screeched past them, the young lady in a short dress, clasping her shoes in her hand, disappeared down the lane to the City School.

"Driving without due care and attention, Ma'am?" Kevin asked, as he watched the prat in the Beemer wheel spin his way up the road for the second time.

Heather didn't even bother to reply as she grabbed the door handle. "Come on. I've got a bad feeling about this."

53

A few minutes after midnight ... 16th August 1987

Sweet Jesus

What a wanker! Apologise to him! No way, she thought. Scott had shown his true self tonight with all that business with Paula. Sarah was seething as she stood looking into the dark cut-through lane that led down to the City School. Sarah took a moment to decide whether to take the long way home or make a dash for it across the school playing fields. Sweet Jesus, she thought, if she stood there much longer, it would take all night to get home. "Come on, Sarah, get on with it," she muttered, huffed, and stepped into the lane picking her way down on tiptoes. Although the lane was paved, all she needed now was dog poo between her toes, which would slap the icing on the cake of a really shite evening.

Releasing his breath when she was twenty feet ahead, Andy Colney pushed away the laurel hedge branches, taking care to place them back, thus ensuring he created no sound. The Sarah bird was hot, and he was ready. He would have his way tonight and go home satisfied. The adrenalin shot around his body; the anticipation was always better than the act.

He made his move. He licked his lips.

"Police. Stop where you are."

Andy swivelled around. Ten feet behind him stood two figures, a dumpy woman and a younger male. He glanced back down the lane, but the fit bird had disappeared through the gate onto the school fields. When he turned around, the young male was on him; he had no time to move.

Handcuffed and pinned to the hedge by the young officer, the dumpy woman approached.

"Andrew Colney. Well, this is a nice surprise," she chuckled, as she looked up at him.

"What you doing? You can't fucking arrest me for walking down a lane."

"Problem is, Mr Colney, you're not walking, are you? You've been hiding in the bushes for nearly ten minutes. So yes, I can arrest you. Andrew Colney, I'm arresting you on suspicion of the intention to cause harm to others. You do not have to say anything, but it may harm your defence if you do not mention when questioned something you later rely on in court. Anything you do say may be given in evidence."

"Fuck off!"

DI French looked up at him and smiled, "Noted."

54

Ahead of his time

As I arrived back home after collecting Beth from her sleepover, a woman approached the front door. I'd seen her get out of her car as she parked along the street as I pulled onto the drive. She looked familiar, but I just couldn't place her.

Beth bounced inside the house, still bubbling with the excitement from her night at Melanie's. I was relieved my perfectly formed tornado-shaped daughter hadn't wrecked her friend's house and appeared to have behaved herself. *"She's a perfect angel,"* Melanie's mother had stated. I did have to chuckle when thinking of Beth from my old life, as that Beth could never be described as angelic.

I waited on the doorstep as the woman approached.

"Mr Apsley?"

"Yes."

"DI French." She held out her hand.

"Frenchie! Yes, I thought I recognised you."

"It's DI French, sir. Not Frenchie."

With me firmly put in my place, we shook hands.

"Well, err … how can I help?" I asked, as Jenny joined me on the doorstep.

Frenchie held out a brass Zippo lighter with the initial J engraved on the front. "Sir, I believe this belongs to you?"

"Oh, darling, that's the one I bought you, and you lost years ago."

"Good grief, so it is! But why on earth would you, a Detective Inspector, be returning lost property?"

Frenchie smiled. "I guessed it was yours, and my hunch was correct."

I wasn't sure I was particularly comfortable with where this conversation was now heading. With all the events of ten years ago, and now a DI returning a lost cigarette lighter suggested something was up.

"Sir, we've been closing down some old cases and archiving evidence. This lighter was in the evidence box from a car crash ten years ago." Frenchie offered me a skull-splitting glare; I could feel a hot flush rising up my cheeks.

"Oh?"

"We discovered the lighter, along with a sawn-off shotgun, at the scene of that car crash that killed Paul Colney, but you'd know that because you were in the car that day." She raised her eyebrows whilst shifting her sizable chest in my direction. It was a question, not a statement.

Not wishing to incriminate myself any further, I held my newly returned lighter and kept schtum.

"Yes, well, we both know I'm right. Anyway, I thought I'd let you know we've arrested Andrew Colney on four counts of rape."

I shot Jenny a surprised look and then turned back to Frenchie. "Andrew Colney?"

"Yes, sir. Brothers alike, wouldn't you say?"

I nodded and pursed my lips. As I'd always known, Frenchie knew that Paul Colney was a rapist. But this new revelation suggested that Martin's real father was Andrew, not Paul, as I'd always thought. Thank God I'd seen Sarah Moore last night because apart from a bust-up with her boyfriend, she didn't appear to be a recent victim of rape.

"Well, sir, that's all from me. Just thought you'd like to know."

"Oh, why?" I asked Frenchie, as she turned to go.

"Mr Apsley, I know you were there the day David Colney died, and something tells me you and Mr Nears always knew more than you were telling."

Frenchie raised her eyebrows again, moving her statement to a question, but again I kept schtum. Jenny's grip on my arm tightened.

Frenchie continued. "I also know you had an interest in Patrick Colney as you were in court that day he was convicted of attempted murder ... and I know you were in that car when Paul Colney died." She looked down at the Zippo lighter that lay in my hand.

All three of us stayed silent for a moment as Frenchie's ideas hung in the air. This was a blink-first game which I wasn't prepared to lose.

"So, Mr Apsley, you and I know what evil that family represents. I thought you would like to know I've dealt with the last one of those evil brothers. I think you were instrumental in the three others' demise, and I also think you were ahead of your time. Our lot, the police, have just caught up."

"Right," I replied and nodded.

"Don't suppose you're ever going to tell me who was driving that car the day Paul died?"

I returned a tight smile and gave the slightest shake of my head.

Frenchie smiled. "Thought not. As I said, Mr Apsley, I think you were ahead of your time."

Jenny's grip on my arm relaxed as the tension fell. Frenchie hovered for a brief second, offered the slightest nod of her head before turning around and walking back down the drive.

"DI French," Jenny called out.

Frenchie turned and glanced back.

"You're correct in what you say. My husband *is* ahead of this time."

~

So, what next?

Jason returns in his third adventure, *Force of Time*. It's 1987, and as Frenchie backs away from his door after returning his Zippo lighter, life takes a dramatic turn for the worse – will Jason, once again, prevail, or will the demons from his new past destroy his future?

Thank you for reading this book, and of course, Jason Apsley's Second Chance. As an independent author, I don't benefit from the support of a large publishing house to promote my work. So, may I ask a small favour? If you enjoyed this book, could I invite you to leave a review on Amazon? Just a few lines will help other readers discover my books – I'll hugely appreciate it.

For more information about Adrian and to sign-up for updates on new releases, please drop on to my website. You can also find my page on Facebook.

www.adriancousins.co.uk

facebook.com/adriancousinsauthor

Other titles by Adrian Cousins: -

<u>The Jason Apsley Series</u>

Jason Apsley's Second Chance

Ahead of his Time

Force of Time

Standalone Novels

Eye of Time

Deana – Demon or Diva series

It's Payback Time

Death Becomes Them (Due for release February 2023)

Acknowledgements …

Thank you to my beta readers, Adele, Brenda, Lisa, Ricky, and Andy. And, of course, to Jacky for your suggestions.

Also, a huge thank you to Sian Phillips, who makes everything come together – I'm so grateful.

Finally – thank you for reading.

Printed in Great Britain
by Amazon